Random Attachment
By
Gertrude T Kitty

CHAPTER 1 HANDCUFFED

"This is total crap!"

"Shut it."

"I want to lodge a complaint; victimisation of the victim."

"I said, shut, your, mouth," DS Raymond spat in the girl's ear; his hand hard on her tender back, shunting her toward the duty desk.

"She's yours," he said dismissively.

The custody sergeant shook his head. Surely it hadn't been necessary to cuff this kid.

Mia felt a level of confusion only accessible if you were in deep shit. She'd been here before; twice, maybe three times? Crap thinking hurt; the pain in her head was intense and branched upwards and backwards. Why did everything look bluer: the floor, the doors, the long custody desk? The area felt smaller too, no, narrower. Had the wall, with its helpline posters and safety info, always been this near the counter? The room was more of a hallway than a processing area, despite two rows of chairs. Maybe the tattooed mugger with a police officer either side reduced the area somehow?

As if feeling Mia's eyes, the mugger turned his head. His neck was tree-trunk thick.

"Name?" asked Sergeant McKinley.

The offender smirked at her, pursed his lips and blew an air kiss.

"Name!" Sergeant McKinley repeated firmly.

Mia looked away from Prison Break and up at the sergeant. Her tongue felt thick in her mouth, sticking to its roof.

"Mia Dent," she whispered.

"Speak up."

Mia tried to clear her throat, but it was dry and rough.

"Mia," she swallowed. "Dent."

"Date of birth."

"30 August 2001."

Immediately an image loaded; a female teen, mouth straight, eyes startled.

"Already on our system," commented the sergeant. "Still living at 175 Whitstable?"

A wave of nausea flooded Mia as zapping images of the estate carpark crashed into footage of her abduction.

"Address!" demanded the sergeant slowly losing patience.

Mia's mouth gaped open. How could she concentrate if her headspace was jammed by a criminal multi-collision? She swallowed hard before giving her Hayes address.

"Are you carrying on your person anything that may harm yourself or others?"

Mia looked down at her torn blouse and bare feet.

"No," she answered.

"Do you have any belongings on your person?"

"No."

"Are you allergic to anything?"

"No."

"Injured?"

"Yes."

"I'll flag it with the duty doctor. Until then you will be detained in holding cell three."

"A cell? I...I don't understand. I'm the victim."

"Constable Boyle will bag your clothes for forensic examination and provide you with something to wear."

"Fine, but why was I cuffed? Why am I being held? This doesn't make sense."

"Let's take the cuffs off, shall we?"

Mia nodded. The pain of having her arms restrained had been replaced by pins and needles followed by numbness. Right now, she felt like an armless torso.

"Am I being arrested?"

"No. Detained."

"This is mental! What am I supposed to have done? Is it my mum? It looked bad; her leg twisted like that."

No information was forthcoming.

"Do you want to call someone?"

"Yes! Please."

"Go ahead. Use this phone."

Mia hesitated. For so long she'd had Flynn's number memorised, but right now brain fog and pain cruelly camouflaged it.

"0721...no....0712...shit...07721?"

"Problem?" asked Sergeant McKinley.

Mia felt close to tears.

"No...I just need a sec."

"You can't take all day," said the sergeant.

"But I know it," said Mia shaking her head frustratedly, noticing how her hand shook. "I've got it!" she said ferociously, her fingers barely able to target the buttons.

It rang one chime.

"Flynn Mason."

Mia felt sick with relief on hearing Flynn's voice.

"Flynn," she said thickly, trying to withhold a breakdown.

"Mia?"

"It's me Flynn."

"Fuck!"

The relief in his voice was so deep and solid, Mia cradled the phone like it was a remote piece of Flynn.

"Jesus Mia...where are you?"

"Paddington Police station...Flynn...I think I'm in trouble."

"Fuck! Listen Mia, say nothing, absolutely fucking nothing. Got it?"

"Yes."

"I'm coming...with back up; hang in there, ok?"

"Ok."

Flynn disconnected. Mia dived from euphoric to desolate in seconds.

"This way."

A constable led her to the holding cell; ten by thirteen feet of cold concrete.

"Remove and place your clothes including underwear in this bag."

Deja vu tore at the seams of Mia's composure; her skin crawled at the memory of what he'd made her do. *Raise your arms. Turn around.*

"I need to talk to someone, anyone but Raymond, there's girls in danger."

"You need to calm down luv. If you want to help, start with removing your clothes."

"This is bullshit," Mia shouted, fighting the urge to cry.

Undressing was a slow process. Her jeans were stiff. There was barely a button remaining on her blouse. Trembling she pulled up the paper knickers; sick that her underwear was gonna be examined. She stepped into starchy tracksuit bottoms before pulling on a sweatshirt equally as rough. Maybe the more reasonable she was the quicker she'd see a detective.

The door clanging shut made Mia's teeth rattle. She sat, folding inward; only her feet, knees and hair visible. Her hot breath, heavy with dread, filled the chasm between her legs and chest. She thought she heard him breathing…and on the edge of that his laugh but it was her, puffing out air so quickly her face dampened.

She raised her head which pulsated like it was repeatedly swelling then shrinking. Maybe she had an aneurism; would that be such a bad thing? Jesus, lives depended on her! But she felt so fucking ill she wanted to lie on the floor and die…Except it was cold and looked filthy.

What would Flynn think? This twisted drama she was central to. Would it be the last straw? She lifted her hand to where her head ached; pulling it away she saw blood.

"Crap!"

She might have concussion, but for Mia life couldn't be clearer.

"I'm fucked."

Mia had no idea how long she'd sat, hunched up in the cold, picking at her nails, badly needing to wee. Her eyes stared first at the metal toilet bolted to the floor then at the camera in the corner of the room. She crossed her legs tightly.

Time was uncooperative; minutes seemed like hours. Eventually keys clanked in the lock. By then Mia could muster only the slightest effort. She raised her head; her eyes peering between her knees and hair.

A tall, muscular man, early thirties entered with the policewoman. Mia sat up.

"I know where Gabby and the other girls are," Mia gushed before

4

registering the inaccuracy of her words. "That's wrong…I was with them, but I don't know where…"

"I'm not the police. I'm a forensic scientist, I'm here to collect samples from you."

Mia slumped, hit by a fresh wave of helplessness.

Newman pulled on latex gloves. Mia shrunk further back not wanting to be touched.

"I need a DNA sample."

"What if I don't want to give one?"

"Mia we have the legal right to take one."

Newman took out a long cotton bud and labelled a test tube. Mia hesitated as the latex gloves approached her mouth.

"It doesn't hurt Mia. It's a tickle on the inside of your cheek…perfect," said Newman depositing the sample into the test tube. "A quick pull," he continued depositing a strand of hair, follicle attached, into a sample bag. "Now a sample from under your nails…think another manicure might be in order," he smiled.

Mia couldn't smile; maybe she would never smile again.

Newman was in no doubt that being touched was distressing for this girl.

As Mia shifted position, the sleeve of the sweater moved up revealing restraint marks. Newman pulled the sleeves up to her elbows.

"How did you get these Mia?"

"He…he…" Mia's voice cracked; she felt sickly hot. She pulled at the collar of the sweatshirt; it was loose, yet her throat felt constricted. If she could just focus but everything was blurry.

"Mia?"

She swallowed hard. She had to fucking pull herself together.

"He used electrical ties. They bite right into your skin."

"I'll need to photograph your wrists."

Mia nodded.

"FLASH."

Mia recoiled from the light. *She heard him in the dark hissing her name.*

"How bout you close your eyes and I say 'when' as I'm about to snap. Ok? Mia? Can you keep still if we do that?"

5

Mia nodded.

Newman took a succession of photographs.

"Are you hurt elsewhere Mia?"

"My head…do you have any painkillers?"

"Sorry. Constable," Newman addressed the stony-faced policewoman. "Once I'm done get Mia a sweet tea, a sandwich, water and a blanket."

Newman outstared the officer until she nodded. Using saline, he separated Mia's hair strands. It was a nasty blow requiring stitches though it had presently stopped bleeding.

"Mia look down at the ground."

"I feel sick."

"Tea and food will help. Any further injuries?"

"My toes and feet."

He photographed restraint marks at ankles, ripped toenails and cut soles.

"Anymore?"

The Wolf had dragged her over rough ground. Her blouse had risen, bunching up under her armpits; the skin on her back grazed badly. Currently Mia was braless and couldn't bear being naked and gawped at again. *His breathing was deep, a long pause between the inhale and exhale, she imagined his chest rising and falling.*

"No."

"Ok. I'll flag your injuries with Sargent Raymond and ask him to chase up a medical doctor asap."

"He hates me…he won't do it…ask Constable Hall; please."

Newman nodded.

"Thank you," said Mia desperate for a reprieve from her mental headache. "Ok Mia…all done. Thanks for cooperating. Try to eat and drink plenty of fluids."

She nodded.

"Can you tell Constable Hall I've been with Gabby; it's important."

Newman nodded.

As the heavy door clunked closed Mia was again alone with the snapshots of her ordeal. They cut across the pain, momentarily piercing her brain and interrupting the equilibrium she was trying to retain. She drank the tea, grateful to have something to warm her. The sandwich tasted ok. She took small bites and chewed slowly; it was an activity to pass the time. But the time refused to pass so she curled up on the hard bench, pulling the rough blanket over her, unable to fight off exhaustion.

He rubbed the ointment generously into his knee before strapping it up and pulling a knee support over it. His forehead was badly bruised. His shoulder was fucked.

Reclining on the sofa he swallowed a cocktail of painkillers and muscle relaxants along with a glass of wine.

He considered the situation. She could not identify him. She had no idea where she'd been held. He could walk right up to her, look her straight in the eye and she'd not know he was The Wolf.

He smiled. She was a surprise; feistier than expected, a real risk taker. He'd underestimated her.

He looked at the photos beside him on the couch. Her face turned away from the camera. Her bare body, stiff with cold and fear. His smile widened. He wanted her back.

CHAPTER 3   THE GRILLING

"I need a break," said Mia.

DI Webber studied the young woman opposite. Dirt smudged her small face; in places it was interrupted by long streak marks from tears. She sat rigidly; it looked…painful. Nothing about her was at ease. Webber wondered if her trembling was nerves, drug use or her ordeal – if it was true. He noted the thick dirt embedded beneath her fingernails and her wild hair…the seventeen-year-old had been in some sort of altercation.

"I'd rather we continued a little longer," replied DI Webber.

"May I have paracetamol please?"

"Could you be more specific about where you were taken?" asked Webber gently.

"I'm trying," she breathed out, brushing her fringe to one side and dislodging dirt particles that had hardened and made clumps in her hair.

"How long were you in the van for?" pressed Sergeant Raymond, the younger, less senior but much pushier detective.

"I told you; I was unconscious for a time."

"Was the house terraced or detached?" Raymond asked.

"I've no idea. I was underground. He didn't bring me through a house."

"Describe it again," demanded Raymond.

"Describe what?" Mia almost screamed! "Jesus this is crazy. There's a beast, slapping girls around, making them do horrible, horrible things while you waste time. You're obnoxious, rude, your nose doesn't fit your face, your hair's naff and…"

"Mia," interrupted DI Webber, his voice even. "You're right, time's important, think."

Mia felt her heart pumping pure frustration.

"It was a building with a basement."

"You think or you know?" demanded Raymond.

"I…I think. It was dark, airless and it smelt of wet dog."

Mia shivered. She almost felt the heavy dampness with its musty smell, heard the creak of the dungeon door with its rusting hinges. *He's coming.*

"There were stairs," she said so timidly she wasn't sure they heard.

"And?" said Raymond sarcastically.

"And, I've told you countless times already!"

"Come on, how often have you ended up in this nick with a cock and bull story," Sergeant Raymond goaded.

"Ok! Yes! I've had drama in my life, but I've never lied. Jesus! He's got them like scared rabbits in traps."

"Did you see them?" asked Raymond.

"We spoke."

"Really?" derided the sergeant.

Mia blew out an exasperated breath.

"Yes! Really!"

"Did they identify themselves?" the sergeant pushed.

"I haven't names but it's..."

"Did you try to free them?" Raymond interrupted spitefully.

DI Webber observed Mia's eyes darting away.

"No."

"No?" questioned the sergeant.

Run. Don't stop.

"It happened too quickly." Mia's voice was low and shaky. "I'd barely a split second to react. I felt sick leaving them." Mia lifted her head, her eyes pleading for sympathy.

"But you did," said the sergeant accusingly.

Fresh tears sprung from Mia's eyes; she wiped them away with the back of her hand. Mia knew what it was like for the Salem witches. Sitting on a ducking stool, breathing air, clinging to life then dunked beneath rushing water; lungs filling.

"I should have done more. I'm sorry. I panicked."

She wasn't justifying her actions, thought Webber, she was accepting blame; a rare occurrence in teenagers, in his experience. He watched her pulling at her crumpled, disintegrating tissue.

"Constable go grab a box of tissues. For the benefit of the tape Constable Hall is leaving the room."

"What else can you tell us about where you were Mia? Think about noises and smells," encouraged DI Webber.

Mia took a minute. Her lids flickering down as she attempted to visualise the place. She did not see the sergeant raise his eyes to the roof.

Flynn saw, and Flynn's lips thinned. He shifted agitatedly on his chair in the corner of the room. It was hard to be still when Mia was being grilled like a career criminal.

"It was dark. No windows, just a large, wooden door. The air tasted damp and earthy and thick…it felt hard to breathe like I was in a grave."

"Been in many graves have you?" asked Raymond flippantly.

Mia wanted to bite back but didn't.

"I heard water dripping; it was louder than when your tap leaks, it dripped into another liquid because it was more of a plop than a drip."

"Very helpful! We'll have the case solved in no time at all," said the sergeant sarcasm slipping off his tongue like he was bi-lingual.

Mia's eyes sprung open; their anger brightly piercing through.

"I never said it would help. You asked me a bloody question and I'm answering it."

"It's alright Mia," reassured Jim Pascoe, Flynn's solicitor friend. "DI Webber. If your sergeant can't come up with a constructive way to interview then I would rather he leave?"

Any response regarding his new sergeant was avoided by the door opening.

"For the purpose of the tape Detective Constable Hall has re-entered."

"Thank you Emma," smiled Mia weakly, drained by her emotional outburst.

"Sir, did you hear that?" asked Raymond. "She's been in this nick so often she's on first name terms with the staff."

DI Webber was not drawn in.

Mia swallowed. Taking a fresh tissue Mia blew her nose; a sharp sting sizzled in her head. Mia's grimace didn't go unnoticed by Webber. His gut told him Mia needed medical attention but her history with the police resoundingly supported Mia may be guilty of a serious assault.

"I hate blowing my nose with an audience."

"What did you hear when you escaped?" prompted Webber wanting Mia to focus.

"The wind…it was strong, my hair was whipping my face and

obscuring my vision."

"Traffic?" asked the Inspector.

"No…Oh! I did see a horse," she blurted out.

"Was there a rider?"

"I don't know...not on its back but maybe having a wee or..."

"Having a wee?" The sergeant started laughing.

Mia jumped up.

"Don't you dare laugh. Horrible, unmentionable things are happening to those girls. You know what's funny? You! You're the Mr Bean of Paddington Green. You couldn't catch The Wolf in a hundred years. "

The solicitor placed a hand on Mia's arm; the pressure encouraging her to sit.

"And you're an attention seeking liar," responded Raymond.

"DI Webber! Your sergeant is sabotaging this interview," Joe Pascoe claimed.

"Excuse me, um excuse me," called Mia quietly.

Three heads turned toward Mia who was experiencing a heavy nosebleed. Only Constable Hall was on it.

"Pinch here Mia, where my fingers are. Good. Tilt your head back."

Raymond was seething. Looking at the dried droplets of blood on the table he wondered if a nosebleed could be self-induced. For fucks sake, she had a history with the police as long as his arm. He wanted this girl locked up. He was sick to the teeth of her.

"Mia…focus on the horse…can you do that?" asked Webber.

Mia nodded. She appeared to be deteriorating by the minute. Blood had dried around her nostrils and her features looked pinched.

"Yes...there was a white, wooden fence around it. Oh, and there was a burnt-out car, semi concealed by long grass. How had I not remembered?" she asked confused.

"Umm. How?" said Raymond snidely.

Mia ignored the blatant dig.

"I looked around; there were no landmarks, no obvious direction to run in. I wasn't thinking; I was too scared; my heart was pumping painfully, and my lungs were burning from breathing in the harsh wind.

Despite the pain I ran for my life."

He's behind you.

"How long did you run for?" asked Webber.

He's coming.

"Mia?"

On the verge of answering, Sergeant Raymond piped up again.

"Did you run for five minutes, ten minutes, what?"

"Umm...I...I don't know...fear distorted everything." She took a breath and continued. "My brain was slow. I needed to find a road, find a house with lights on. What if I stopped a car? What if 'he' was the driver? What if I found a house? What if 'he' was in it? Every horror movie I'd seen careered into my memory."

Mia swallowed hard.

"I ran toward the woods, but fear weighed me down, it made my legs heavy. I'd never been in so deep, in a wood, not ever. The trees were dense, the foliage thick, it was like the threads in my sewing box, all confusingly intertwined. I'm a Londoner...to me the countryside is alien...I went on a school trip once to Wales, God it was boring."

"Stick to the facts pertaining to this case," ordered Sergeant Raymond.

Mia's eyelids partially lowered as she cast an evil look at Raymond.

"I remember the landscape creaking and rustling and branches scratching my bare skin. I wanted to drop to the ground, but my legs were compelled to run because I'd hurt him, and he was going to make me pay. My chest burned, my body felt like it would split and all I smelt was the vomit I'd puked up but still I ran."

Mia sat back. She tried to run her fingers through her hair again but they got stuck.

"I've seen that in a movie, a victim being sliced vertically."

Mia looked at DI Webber.

"Do you know what it's like to be terrified? Because I do."

Webber felt uncomfortable. The truth had a certain ring to it and Mia's words were chiming loud and clear. Mia continued.

"I threw up again."

"I thought you didn't stop," challenged Raymond.

13

"Why are you picking holes in everything I say? Smell my hair. Smell it! It reeks."

"Ok," said Webber trying to diffuse the tension. "That will help the tracker dogs."

Did he believe her? No. Yes. He must if he were considering stretching his already overspent budget on a search party.

"I need a break. I've told you everything. My head is pounding. The couple that found me said I must have run into a branch."

"They were two geriatrics who fell for your story."

Mia looked at Raymond; her eyes narrowing and her lips thinning into an accusing look only teenagers can achieve.

"They were not geriatrics," responded Mia through gritted teeth.

Webber shot Raymond a quizzical look. Head injury?

"Emma, hurry up the doc. For the purpose of the tape DC Hall is seeking medical assistance for Mia Dent."

"Let me tell you what I know," continued Raymond. "This abduction is fictitious. You were jealous of the attention Gabby Preston's getting, Flynn Mason wouldn't participate in your crazy lovesick obsession and your mum was on a bender again."

Mia's hand came to her forehead; her elbow resting on the table propping up her head.

"Playing the victim again?" taunted Raymond.

"Please. I need a break. I don't feel good."

"My client has requested a break Detective Inspector."

"Interview paused at fourteen ten for a comfort break."

DS Raymond stopped the tape begrudgingly. Its click echoed around the small, characterless room. DC Hall returned.

"Dr Kirby said Mia's next on the list."

"Can I go to the toilet?" Mia's voice was unsteady, each word wavered.

"Yes, of course," agreed Webber. "Constable Hall will accompany you."

Mia pulled out her chair; it scrapped loudly across the floor.

About to walk, everything around Mia shifted, her eyes blurred, and she grasped the chair to steady herself. As Constable Hall held the door open Mia felt a warm hand find hers. Flynn. He was paler than usual;

still his skin was a luscious cream. She couldn't believe he'd come; not after what happened. She wanted to sink onto his lap and be wrapped in his arms. Instead she followed Emma to the toilet.

"I'll arrange coffee," DI Webber informed the solicitor and Flynn.

"Inspector, I want Mia's initial forensic and medical assessments by Denham Police Station. I find it worrying she wasn't suited down there."

"I'll look into it. Excuse us," replied the DI; his tone more even than he felt.

Webber and Raymond slipped next door to the control room.

"She could be telling the truth?" offered Webber.

"Jesus boss it's fucking farfetched and each recount is different."

"Yes, but not with inconsistencies; she's remembering the incident more vividly.

"Remembering or inventing boss?"

The DI shrugged. He hated to make snap judgements, but Steve Raymond had a problem with women. His questioning of female suspects lacked finesse but with Mia he seemed particularly harsh.

Constable Hall thought so too. Raymond had been off with Mia from the outset.

"Mia? Are you managing in there?" DC Hall asked genuinely concerned.

"Not really, it's hard to wee when someone's waiting."

Coming out of the loo Mia stood in front of the mirror.

"Jesus...my hair?"

"Definitely a bad hair day," replied Emma.

Splashing water over her face Mia wiped the dirt away with paper towels.

"Why did I have to get Raymond?" asked Mia her voice high and wobbly.

"Luck," Emma replied "Here," she said offering Mia a mint.

In the control room DI Webber also questioned his luck.

"Head wound Steve?"

"It's a scratch."

"Let's hope the doc agrees. We need to stay open minded Steve."

"It's simple sir. One victim, one perpetrator. Boss, I know this girl. She's damaged."

15

On CCTV they watched Mia re-enter Interview Room 2. Flynn Mason was on his feet; his hands gently on Mia's upper arms, his head bent in a sympathetic, listening position.

"Mason had a restraining order against Dent. Interesting. What's the set up between them now?" asked Webber referring to the twenty-year-old son of financier Gareth Mason.

"Complicated boss."

Mia swayed, and Flynn Mason steadied her. The DI wondered was she always uncoordinated or was the pressure getting to her?

"Steve, get onto the lab, we need her tox results."

"Sure boss," the sergeant replied too quickly to instil confidence.

Webber flicked through Mia's file.

"Steve."

Raymond turned his attention to Webber who was a walking advert for corduroy and cosy jumpers. Unlike most of Raymond's colleagues, Webber's face did not tell the story of long days and sleepless nights. He looked late fifties but not years beyond his age.

"Denham nick's medical report is not in her file," stated Webber.

DS Raymond shrugged.

"You need to slow down Steve. Not ensuring the medical report's in the transfer documents is poor. Go back and double check your paperwork. If you haven't got it ring Denham nick. I want it faxed and on my desk, asap. While you're onto Denham locate the statement made by the couple who found her. That too is not in her file. Jesus Steve…this is a farce. I want their statement and I want them to show one of our csi's where Mia was found. Treat it as a crime scene; the full works."

Webber noted colour raising up Raymond's face.

"I'm not disputing she's a liar, potentially a dangerous one, but we follow procedure therefore treat this case as an abduction. Am I clear?"

Sergeant Raymond nodded uncommittedly. Webber could tell his new sergeant hated chasing down paperwork. He hadn't yet grasped the answers were always in the detail. Steve needed to up his game and reduce his alcohol intake; Raymond smelt whiskey on his breath.

"Let's get back in there Steve. She's dead beat and confused. If she's going to trip herself up it'll be now."

As her inquisitors returned Mia sat down unsteadily, all her energy drained.

"24 August 2018 resuming interview at 2.35 pm. Present in the room myself DI Webber, DS Raymond, DC Hall, Mia Dent, solicitor James Pascoe and Flynn Mason."

Pause. Webber continued.

"Mia, your account of events leading up to today is patchy. We need..."

"What colour was the van?" Raymond interjected.

"I was unconscious."

"Was it red, white, blue, what?" Raymond grilled.

"Um..."

"Toyota, BMW, Vauxhall, what?

"You're not listening."

"You don't know do you!" shouted Raymond.

"Exactly," said Mia frustratedly her voice shrill. "I don't know. Are you thick?"

Mia dropped her head in her hands. Worn out and totally baff'd she was nanoseconds from crumbling. No wonder innocent people confessed.

"Mia, it's okay. Tell us at your own pace," DI Webber said gently, prompting Mia to remove her hands and sit up. Sergeant Raymond continued to throw grenades. He pulled a sheet from the folder marked with her name.

"In 2017, 19 December you came into this station, is that right?"

"You know it is you've got my file."

"What did you claim?"

Mia breathed out frustratedly but answered.

"I wanted to kill my mother."

"You have a history of wanting to hurt your mother," Raymond gleefully accused.

"Yes," confirmed Mia knowing the truth softened the punch of his accusation.

"You know your mum's in hospital," said DI Webber kindly.

"We found her unconscious, at the foot of the stairs in your home, where you'd left her," stated Raymond

Mia turned a paler shade of pale, her skin almost translucent.

"175 Whitstable Close isn't my home."

"But you have a key, right?" stated Raymond.

"No…I put it through her letter box soon after I was chucked out. I wanted her to know she'd burnt her bridges…that I was never coming back."

"Did anybody see you put the key through the door?" demanded Raymond

"No."

"On the day of your mum's attack how did you enter the flat?" asked Webber.

Mia stiffened. She took a shaky breath. She almost smelt the chloroform.

"The door was slightly open." Mia could see it now. Her heart was pumping. "Like she hadn't pushed hard enough to shut it," answered Mia quietly…adding… "I did not leave her there. I was ambushed."

"Your mum is difficult…isn't she Mia?" Raymond asked knowingly.

"Yes."

"Were you lonely?" Webber interrupted Raymond. There was something so still about her, like she knew how to blend into the backdrop or into the shadows. She was…the girl at the party who people didn't remember being there, decided Webber.

"Yes…overwhelmingly lonely."

Webber noted the Mason boy shifting slightly.

"The morning I first saw Flynn I was very fragile. I wanted to cry a tsunami, scream an avalanche. I know that seems dramatic but when the Circle Line pulled in, the urge to make my life go away was strong. Two stops later Flynn sauntered onto the train and I wanted to live…with him…in a cottage with chickens and three rescue dogs. Flynn was shiny; almost polished. He radiated self-assurance. I mean he literally glowed with it. I wanted to touch him, to slip my arms around his waist and rest my cheek against his chest. I'd never wanted to physically connect with someone so much."

"How did your attachment to Flynn affect your relationship with your mum?" asked Webber.

"I was less tolerant of her but more positive about myself; I felt optimistic. When she found out about Flynn, she became more unhinged, more vindictive. It's hard to explain – she's mentally sick."

"Thanks to you she's now physically sick," accused the sergeant.

"How do you feel about your mum's attack?" asked Webber.

"Not as joyful as I thought I'd be. In the cell I was thinking about Christmas; they were so crappy. Now we may never share another one. We'll never be able to fix it."

"I'd like to understand your relationship with your mother."

The detective watched Mia consider his interest.

"It's incomprehensible, I've tried."

"But you, were on the inside…I'm, on the outside," stated Webber calmly. If this girl's account was to be believed Webber's gut told him that Mia's mum's attack must be linked to the abduction – how was it not; coincidences were rare.

"Then I'll need to tell you about Flynn," said Mia.

"It's not a lover's stroll down memory lane. You need..."

The sergeant was interrupted by his superior.

"Yes, start there," agreed Webber.

"It was nearly **a year ago. September sixth, 2017** to be precise…I was on the train…"

YEAR 13

12 MONTHS EARLIER

CHAPTER 4 JAY HIDDLESTON

Mia stood on a train, packed full of passengers, silently cursing herself for taking up the guitar. Bodies pressed hard against her and a stranger's sharp elbow poked in between her ribs. The perspiration, resulting from the clammy heat of the train, rolled down her back. Sweating made Mia feel fatter than usual. She imagined her body heatedly swelling; one roll of fat pressing against another. Mia shifted her weight. She was conscious that strands of hair had matted to her damp forehead and hot cheeks. She knew with certainty her face was rash red and she itched to scratch it. Mia took a minute to hate herself, but self-loathing was rudely interrupted by a man who kicked her guitar; he was an arty, full of himself twat. She didn't say it only thought it. She must be the only one on her estate who didn't fucking swear about every fucking thing every fucking second of the day.

Flynn boarded at High Street Kensington. His confident air caught Mia's attention and his looks held it...until Flynn's eyes randomly shot in Mia's direction and she quickly looked away her face flushing even more.

Her head down she noticed her sweaty palms leaving damp handprints on her guitar cover. She looked at her fingers with their ugly bitten nails. Then at the hands of the woman who sat neatly in one of the seats, her fingers slim and her nails painted red. Mia wondered if her hands would ever look beautiful. If she lost weight would her fingers lose weight too?

Flynn's mind was not on the schoolgirl sweating near the doors. It was on Steph, the receptionist at his dad's firm. Christ, he couldn't believe he'd got off with her again. She was vain and vacuous, but he was lazy and easy when it came to women. He'd avoided relationships because of the state of his parents' marriage. Roll on October, Exeter Uni and the one, seven, four miles between him and his father.

Mia snuck another peep at Posh Boy. He looked cool and relaxed...not hot and bothered...just hot! Turning his head, Mia redirected her eyes to the headline of The Metro, held between the fingers of numerous passengers.

"Petra's Body discovered in West London Canal."

An image swept into Mia's mind of a teenage girl floating fatally in dark water, her lips blue, her eyes blank. Mia's gut twisted. The Wolf's third abductee; his first murder? Did that mean Becca and Ashley were dead too? Their bodies undiscovered. Their families in limbo. It gave Mia perspective; so her life wasn't perfect; boohoo, get over it!

The train doors opened and a woman squeezed into a space that didn't exist. Flynn saw right down her blouse. Flynn breathed in. The woman took this unconscious bodily function as an invitation. She smiled and sardined him a little more. Flynn looked away; he wanted a woman who didn't rub up against a stranger on a train. One who knew the square root of four but wasn't a bank balance groupie.

Mia shifted her weight again and considered the day. It was Wednesday, first week back of the autumn term. A very important year yet Mia's homework was barely legible, and she was already late. She felt rattled which increased her breathing. Could passengers hear, she wondered? The more she tried to suppress her exhaling the more her chest rose and fell. She thought of her breakfast: a large bowl of sugary cereal followed by a thickly buttered hot cross bun and a chocolate milkshake. Why was she still hungry? Maybe she'd pop to Wenzels; she was already late – what were an extra few minutes? She considered their torpedo rolls. Should she go with egg mayonnaise or chicken and sweetcorn? A Belgium bun or a donut? Coke or orange juice? Her indecision continued until the train pulled in at Sloane Square, juddering to a halt.

It was excruciatingly hard to get off a packed train with a guitar. The arty man used this excuse to throw shade on Mia who promptly kicked him in the shin.

"I'm sorry, it's the guitar."

As arty man left the train, he gave Mia a look that conveyed she wasn't worth a verbal response. She didn't care…but she did a bit…weighty people got way more dirty looks.

Mia stepped forward as did Posh Boy. Automatically Mia hesitated, giving him room to pass. Posh Boy had the looks and obviously the money to brush off people like dust on a book. Mia was surprised when he spoke.

"After you."

His voice, light and smooth, had enough depth to prevent it being dragged into the bustle of rush hour passengers disembarking. Posh Boy surprised her; it wasn't often strangers were considerate of the fat girl. Mia's gaze met his and warm brown eyes met startled, shy blues.

"I like my shins."

A smile played on his lips and a huge grin broke out on Mia's face as she stepped off the train. Flynn thought how real and spontaneous her smile was. Mia wondered was he watching her. Did she walk like a fat person? Maybe she waddled. She certainly felt her thighs rubbing uncomfortably together but she couldn't worry about that now...not when all she wanted was to look over her shoulder at Posh Boy.

On the escalator, she stood whilst Flynn passed her running upwards. Outside Mia looked around. He was nowhere in sight. It was James Blunt syndrome; a beautiful stranger, there one minute, gone the next.

Mia's shoulders slumped; her intention to walk tall and maintain good posture disappeared as quickly as chocolate spread on toast. Heading for Wenzels she slipped a Minstrel from her pocket to her mouth.

By the time Mia reached school the bell had rung and only stragglers hung outside form. Mia rushed to the music room; her guitar banging repeatedly against her back. She put it with the other guitars then scrambled from Block M to Block B. No one looked up as she entered form not even Mr Coombe.

"Sir, can you mark me in, I dropped my guitar off, I wasn't late."

"What's your name?"

"Mia Dent."

It irritated Mia that three days into term her tutor couldn't remember her. She saw his eyes stray to Gabby Preston. She was pulling off her jumper, which wasn't easy with double 'D' boobs. Mia bet he knew her name.

"Gabby, settle down please."

****

Outside a tall, glass building Flynn put his earphones in, pressing play before entering Mason Asset Management.

"Hey Flynn."

23

Barely five hours ago he'd been naked with a girl he couldn't bear to say hello to. What kind of man did that make him he wondered?

"Steph, I thought you were gonna make Flynn take you to dinner."

"I know but he's sexually charged, and he needs me Jaz. It's spontaneous between us. We're on fire."

"Like consumption?"

"Yeah, exactly, consumption. Shh here's Mason senior."

A tall, distinguished businessman, with flecks of grey hair and an aloof air crossed reception in the direction of the lifts.

Flynn waited for the lift doors to close. Bloody holiday work. Why wasn't his father in the music or film industry? Because he's a boring tit decided Flynn. Talk of the devil. Their eyes met as Mr Mason entered the lift. Neither smiled. Thinking about it Flynn couldn't remember his father ever smiling - miserable git.

****

Mia lined up for Spanish.

"Hola, how's it hanging?" said Ben, his tone bored, as Mia took her seat beside him.

"Muy bien. ?igualmente?" replied Mia.

"Yo shit."

"Si...que es esto?" asked Mia

"What?   Oh this, it's some crap libro?"

And so the hour went on, it was eternity but longer.

Break followed. Mia shuffled over to an empty spot on a bench and parked herself. She pulled out Atonement and became so engrossed she was oblivious to the bell.

"You!" Miss Benjamin roared.

Startled Mia jumped; her book sliding off her lap into a puddle. Other than a very fierce deputy head, the playground was empty. Mia grabbed the sodden material and legged it to Music.

No one welcomed her. She wasn't disliked. She simply didn't fit a particular group; she wasn't gifted or talented, popular or bullied, nerdy or sporty nor was she delinquent. She wasn't even particularly musical. Mia was a spare. Like a tyre; only appreciated in a predicament.

"Have you practiced much?" asked Isabel.

"Not as much as I should."

24

"Me neither. I know the notes but I get nervous performing."

"I'm not sure if I know it backwards or I play it backwards," laughed Mia, but Isabel was turning away, uninterested, her attention captured elsewhere.

"Hey Anna," called Isabel to her best friend. "Come listen to this, Stormzy's latest."

Anna popped an earpiece in and, shoulder to shoulder, they listened whilst Mia stood on the outskirts of friendship.

"Tickets go on sale today for a Brixton concert," said Anna excitedly.

"Don't know if my mum will let me go to Brixton," replied Isabel.

"YOLO," said Anna. "You can get around her Iz."

Mia hated 'YOLO'. What if everything about you was dying: your will power, your self-esteem, your relationship with your mother? Mia was trying to live but her body was a tomb, encased in fatty tissue, trussed with criticism. Mia immediately felt guilty. Petra had only lived once…one short life.

Double Art followed, and English was the last lesson of the day. Queuing outside the locked class Mia thought about Posh Boy. Which celebrity did he most resemble? He had Jay McGuiness's hair. He was super confident and mega gorgeous like Tom Hiddleston. It would be cool if he danced. Mia named him Jay Hiddleston. It was hard to picture Jay because she'd only caught a fleeting look. His hair was golden brown, long and wavy. He'd worn a pale pink slim fit shirt and tie with navy skinny trousers. A gallery; she saw him working somewhere arty but plush. She settled on age twenty-one. He wanted to travel, and he loved romantic comedies. He wasn't a slave to the gym, and he wasn't into himself and…

"Oi! We're going in," prodded Jamie.

"Settle down year thirteen. Texts out please; silent reading."

Mia smiled, delighted her teacher was sick. Sitting in a single seat by the window, Mia pulled out a book. She never turned a page, but she regularly popped a chocolate peanut in her mouth as she constructed scenarios with her beautiful stranger. It was the most creative she'd been in weeks.

The bell, signifying the end of school, rang sharp and clear. Mia didn't jump up like the others, she slowly packed away and was last to leave the classroom. The only evidence of other kids were dust particles floating in the corridor. Mia decided if reincarnation was real then this was her least happy life.

Casually she walked toward the station taking in Chelsea life. Here, the harsh reality of the estate and alcoholic parents couldn't touch her. Instead, shoulders: cashmere, wool, silk, pure cotton brushed against her and aromas; sweet and spicy drifted around.

"Hey!" said Ben catching up.

Ben was fit, strong featured and cheeky enough to work an angle.

"Mia, please do my Spanish homework. It's footy training. I will owe you big time."

Mia was a 'pleaser'. She didn't mind what chocolate she had from the box, she'd hang back when girls rushed to claim netball positions and on field trips she'd sit in whatever coach seat was empty.

"Sure," replied Mia, at a loss what to say next. She found conversation difficult; hers was hesitant…stilted. Her mother's skill of turning Mia's words against her had Mia rethinking every response. There was no spontaneity in her conversation, it was sadly careful – nothing like a teen.

"Mia, I owe you. Shit my bus. Thannnnnkkkkks Miiiiiia," floated in the air.

Mia didn't mind; it was nice to share a moment with someone.

Travelling home Mia struggled with her guitar. First on the Circle Line to Paddington, then down a set of stairs leading to the Bakerloo escalator. Mia was at its top when air pressure breezed upwards indicating the arrival of her train. She didn't fling herself downwards like most passengers. Stepping onto the platform the train doors closed and a slow conveyor belt of faces quickly converted to a stream of strangers far more eager to reach their destination than Mia. For Mia home wasn't home; it was an address, but Mia would board the next train as she had no alternative place to be.

At Warwick Avenue Mia flashed her Oyster and walked towards the canal, left would take her to Little Venice and right took her to the estate. Walking alongside the water she stared hard at each narrow boat.

"Someday I'm going to board one, steer downstream and never

return. I'll make a new family. I'll tell them I've amnesia. No, too complicated. I'll be an orphan."

Mia surveyed the low-rise estate on the water's edge. These canal facing flats were the more desirable. Mia walked along a path separating one block from another, then across the central area of the estate with its grassed verges and mini playgrounds, to identical flats facing Shirland Road. Mia looked up at her block; at the balconies with their washing lines. For every ten of them was a balcony with a broken fridge, a discarded settee; some kind of junk. Then there were the boarded-up flats; what had happened behind those windows Mia didn't want to know.

Walking into the building Mia noted the lift was broken again. Mia wasn't bothered. It creeped her out. The way the ugly corrugated steel door stuttered to a close and how she imagined cables unravelling and her plummeting to the ground.

She trudged up the stairs breathlessly.

"I told that dirty skank I'd fuck her."

"Crap," whispered Mia immediately tensing.

"Do her Cerise, bitch's asking for it. She fuck your man, you fuck her."

Mia froze. Fuck. Bitch. Fuck. Bitch. The words scared her. The hate behind them scared her more. Mia hastily retreated to the second floor to hide in the rubbish shoot alcove. She waited ten long, anxious minutes while the stink of cheap wine and rotting food clung to her. The dilemma to move or not move crowded her head.

"Oh God," she whispered taking the few steps to the stairwell. Scared, she scurried upstairs, along the poorly lit corridor to flat 175, the number of doom.

The maisonette was unusual. The entrance was on the top level as were the bedrooms - the kitchen and lounge were downstairs. The flat was deserted but a mess – the usual - a full ashtray, an empty bottle of wine, one make-up bag and a collection of cotton pads smelling of acetone. Relieved to be inside, alone, with no homework, Mia pulled her Justin Bieber nighty on. His eyes had faded, and his face stretched wide across Mia's stomach, the tension distorting it. In the kitchen she pulled the last two waffles from the packet putting them in the toaster. She buttered two thick slices of bread that weren't the freshest but had no mould. Fried an

27

egg. Topped it with ketchup. And assembled.

"Ummm," murmured Mia taking a large mouthful of sandwich before throwing herself onto the settee, immediately getting up again in search of remotes. For a couple of hours she binge-watched Love Island only to feel like shit because the girls were reed thin, with amazing thong bottoms and great boobs…and she was…none of the above.

Passing a mirror Mia caught the reflection of a girl with fit to burst chipmunk cheeks, breadcrumbs in her hair and tomato sauce running down her chin. She was ashamed.

"I don't want to be you anymore," she said. "I can change."

Change is never easy; Mia didn't know how to stop that agitating expectancy of what to consume next. She'd gorged for so long; she didn't know what hunger was. Usually she'd eat too quickly. The moment her plate was clean a wrangling anxiousness kicked in and the guilt of eating too much would wrestle with the need to eat more.

That night Mia slept badly. On the edge of reform, her body was already retaliating. She dreamed chocolate became a banned substance and she'd had sex with some pervert for a Freddo.

****

Mia woke up tired, breakfast the first thought of the day. Sitting on the edge of her bed she studied her knees; they had no definition; no bone was visible. Looking in the mirror, wearing her grey, low achiever underwear she confronted the inches of fat around her waist. Why was there no fat absorbing cream? It could have magnetic fat extraction…called Fat-netic or Mag-fat-ic. It was 2017. Where was this cream!

She looked at her uniform hanging on the back of the door and wanted to burn it. Instead she shuffled her largeness into its spaces, breathing in where necessary. Rummaging in her drawer she slipped her hands through pairs of tights looking for ones without ladders.

"Bugger!"

In the bathroom Mia pulled the light cord even though the bulb had blown weeks ago. There was no shower, only a scummy, old bath. The laundry basket overflowed. Worse was the sink, covered in five-millimetre, coarse hair that some bloke had shaved, most likely with Mia's razor.

In the hallway her mum's discarded high heels lay three feet apart and her handbag was upturned on the carpet. She'd obviously come in hammered again.

Before leaving Mia opened Joslyn's bedroom door.

"Crap!"

The smell made her cringe. Her mum had wet the bed again!

"Mum."

Shaking her mum roughly only acid burps escaped Joslyn's loose lips.

"Mum, wake up, you'll be late."

"What?" murmured Joslyn. "Late? What's time is it?"

"7.30."

"For feks sake Mia why can't you get up on time? Put the carmen rollers on and make a brew."

Mia didn't care that her mum blamed her for everything that wasn't her dad's fault because today she might see HIM; Posh Boy.

She headed to Warwick Avenue with a skip in her step. At High Street Ken, loitering around the stairs, it was twenty minutes before a lithe, fresh Jay appeared.

"Oh my God," whispered Mia deciding Jay was more beautiful than she remembered. Cutting in between him and another passenger Mia boarded the train and lent into Jay. It was ecstasy; his spicy cologne and the heat from his body. While Mia rested her head against his chest Flynn wondered…was this schoolgirl resting her head against his chest? Mia had a thought! It was a bit sick. She could follow him. That would be totally weird. No; not that weird; it was a little Amelie; it wasn't like she was stalking the boy.

At Sloane Square Mia hopped off and recklessly ran at the escalator.

Jesus thought Flynn; her body's doing a reverse Mexican wave.

Despite her giddy start Mia scrambled up the escalator, threw herself into the photo booth; sweeping the curtain across before peeking between the gap. There! Mia followed; up the Kings Road he walked, past the Saatchi Gallery and through rotating doors into a world Mia couldn't enter. For a moment Mia stood outside the plush office entrance, her feet itching to follow. Till through the glass window she saw a wall clock above reception; five past nine.

"Shit!"

She bolted to school, glad it was Art first period, it was the only lesson she knew what she was doing.

In her free, Mia googled Mason Asset Management. He worked in financial services.

"Crap, he's probably boring."

Mia decided he was a fraud undercover operative.

In Spanish Mia got her head down. She had this romantic idea of going to Spain and opening a pastry shop/café...or a small gallery with a studio. She knew that education was her way out...she also knew she wasn't clever clever but she was good at three things; art, baking and languages. But A' levels were so much harder and needed so much attention and her mum was so needy that everything was spiralling out of control. But that was yesterday, not today Mia decided. Thinking about Jay led to thinking about herself. She didn't want to be a lazy, demotivated loser; she was better than that. So she sat up, focused and engaged.

Needing to avoid home, and her mum's abstract concept of parenting, Mia hung around the art room working on a project whilst the TA tidied up. She found it scary how quickly a sharing bag of Starburst disappeared when you actually shared.

When the caretaker rattled his keys Mia packed up and headed to the station. Behind her strolled Flynn enjoying the spectacle of the girl's portfolio bouncing off pedestrians.

Mia could kick herself; somehow she got stuck in the ticket barrier;
If it.
Pull.
Wasn't.
Pull.
The portfolio.
Pull.
It was.
Pull.
The guitar.
"Arhhh!"

"Shit," whispered Flynn as the barriers sprung open and the girl toppled backwards impacting with an old dear laden with shopping. Flynn

30

looked between his feet where a satsuma rolled.

Mia was flustered. Jay had seen her make an idiot of herself. It didn't bare thinking about. She sat on the platform bench her head all over the place. Jay sat beside her. Oh my God thought Mia quickly lifting her feet to tiptoe to avoid spreading thighs.

Together they watched the circle line pull into the station. The train carrying Mia from the rich and affluent to the poor and hopeless.

"Excuse me."

Mia stopped breathing. Jay was talking…to her. TO. HER!

"Your portfolio."

She looked only at his mouth whilst adoring his tone with its clipped Britishness.

Passing Mia the forgotten portfolio; their hands lightly brushed. On the train there were no seats; they stood opposite. There was an agony about it. Although Jay was less than two metres from Mia there was an ocean between them, a council estate and a stone of flab.

Flynn stepped off at High Street Ken; with Mia on his tail despite the portfolio, despite her heart pumping bruisingly hard. She'd never been impulsive, but loneliness compelled her. Mia was done with her passive, agreeable, wallpaper self.

She followed him past the high street shops toward South Ken station. At Exhibition Road Flynn took a right onto Hamilton Road, then halfway down Flynn turned into the entrance of a large town house - number twenty-seven.

Opposite, Mia's eyes leapt to a flicker of light two stories up. This was Jay's house! Suddenly she felt ridiculous.

"I'm fucking sad," she said disheartened, turning away, with no intention of ever returning. On the train the pressure of school manifested into a vice like headache. She had a brilliant English essay to write. If she couldn't go to uni she'd be forever in her mother's clutches and on an episode of How to Get a Council House.

Walking away from the sunlit front gardens of Warwick Avenue Mia turned into Shirland Road; the houses along it darker and crowded. Mia's eyes glanced at their windows, some dirty, some stuck with children's stickers and others covered with metal grills. If there was a fire how would children get out? That's the sort of thing Mia worried about.

31

She passed the Chinese very conscious of the sweet aroma of chicken and pineapple. She crossed the road, into the shadow cast by the estate's grey concrete walls. She turned into her close.

"Princess, owz you been?"

There were five of them. Posing and gesturing to the soundtrack of rap. Not the commercial, top forty variety but the scary stuff.

"We'll call de lift for you."

Mia swallowed hard. The tall, scarred one who Mia named Scar Tissue pressed the call button. It was the longest two minutes in the history of time.

"Why nervous princess? Or isn't we good enough?"

The lift thudded to a stop; its door inch by inch opening.

Streaking colours distorted Mia's vision.

"Bitch, you ignoring me?"

The more she blinked the quicker shapes formed and faded. She stepped inside; feeling hot like a fever, followed by one, two, three of them. Mia was in the smallest space; avoiding eye contact was impossible.

"You starin' bitch. You like me?"

There was no good answer. Mia looked at her feet, scared of the eyes dismantling her violently. Her heart pumped painfully in her chest. Scar Tissue spat on the elevator floor before leaning in. Up close his white skin was pasty in contrast with his two black friends. His rough finger ran down her cheek; it smelt of weed.

"I see something I like."

His tone was mocking. Mia swore she heard saliva moving around his mouth as his lips threatened.

"Fear," smiled the shorter black boy.

"Better than that," said Scar Tissue, his dry, crusty lips brushing Mia's ear. "Virgin."

The lift rattled open. Mia flung herself out; cruel laughter followed. Her key was barely in the keyhole when she fell through the door. Panting, dropping her bag, she inhaled the cloying aroma of perfume.

"Shit."

"Down here Mia."

In her head Mia was screaming.

Joslyn sat on her throne at the kitchen table, carmen rollers in, plucking her eyebrows. Noting the empty bottle Mia tensed, her mum had stolen Jesus' miracle and turned rent money into wine again. Mia's anger tasted all the more bitter because she had to swallow it. How do you tell your mum you love her but you hate her more?

Mia kissed Joslyn's cheek; from habit rather than affection.

"Mum, I've had the most awful."

"I've been rushed off my feet," Joslyn interrupted. "Twenty-one for lunch today. Mr Powers took me aside and said Joslyn, you're a treasure. Such a trooper and so professional. We'd never manage without you. You're genuine, honest and hardworking."

She's not interested in me thought Mia, not in the slightest.

"That's nice, mum."

"Then I had to get provisions on the way home. Mia unpack the bags. Be careful with the wine! And don't squash my fags. Pass them love." Joslyn lit one and inhaled lung cancer. "New samples arrived today but they had no plus sizes."

Mia squeezed the pound of butter in her hand, that's what Mia was, fat and lardy. Negative thoughts crammed Mia's brain all triggered by the word 'plus'. Her mum was an assassin, with an arsenal of vocabulary – letters placed together to cause maximum damage.

"Mia did you hear? There were no samples for generously sized girls."

Mia was bleeding…her fragile confidence trickling from a wound, unable to heal, because her mum kept picking at it.

"Mia!" her mum said sharply.

"Thanks for looking."

Mia was sweating; her polyester school shirt stuck to her back fat.

"There's a lovely piece of ox tongue; I know how you love it Mia."

"Actually Mum I…"

Joslyn cut Mia off.

"And there's a selection of leftover cheese and pate from the directors' lunch."

"I'll save them for you mum; they're a bit smelly for me."

"Mia you are fekking ungrateful. Honestly, it's not easy Mia with your giant appetite. You're looking very chunky love. Boys prefer girls who look after themselves."

Tears sprung to Mia's eyes.

"You're not upset are you Mia?"

Mia shook her head not trusting herself to speak.

"I want the best for you Mia, you know that don't you?"

"Yes mum," she replied staring at the cigarettes. 'WARNING: Smoking Kills'. Not fast enough thought Mia.

Mia worked hard at not seeing Joslyn refilling her glass. Not watching her drawing in the nicotine that promised to kill but didn't. Mia preferred her alternate reality with a mum who loved her, woke her for school, listened, helped her not to be so fucking fat. It's not easy for a child when they become disillusioned with their parent. It's a blow; bigger than finding out there is no Tooth Fairy and no Father Christmas.

"Where you off to tonight?"

"The Rising Sun."

"Lovely."

In her mum's company Mia's language quickly settled into passive, sympathetic phrases: oh dear, poor you, that's horrible.

"Hugh's picking me up at six."

"That's great."

Joslyn's on off relationship with a widower from Dublin was doing Mia's head in. Joslyn dragged Mia through every word and gesture of every fight…repeatedly. Until Joslyn's diatribe slurred into the bottom of her whisky glass.

"Mum do you know where my swimming costume is?"

"Mia don't you think you should wait till the summer?"

"Mum that's a year away! Swimming's an all year round sport; there are hair dryers, I won't be walking around with wet hair."

"I meant, you know?"

A wave of doubt crashed against Mia's fragile confidence.

"Your weight love. I've got to be honest, I don't want people staring, judging, laughing at you."

Mia's hate flared up. Inadequacy extinguished it. It was like being stoned to death.

"I've homework."

In her box room, in front of her mirror, Mia stared at her dimpled skin with its fatty speed bumps. Not only did she consume cake she resembled one, a rocky road.

"I'm off Mia," called Joslyn, quickly out the door. Mia joined her hands in prayer looking upward.

"Please don't let her come back."

Pulling her school books from her rucksack Mia settled down for a long night. No more slacking; ridiculously Jay motivated Mia to work. She was imagining a future with a random boy on a train. A future where she was a stone lighter and a successful artist. It had more credibility than her Justin Bieber fantasy.

She practiced guitar, read the homework chapters of The Importance of Being Ernest and opened her hardback A3 Art book. On the inside cover she artistically wrote Joslyn's put downs in black and words associated with her feelings for Jay in pink. Enjoying herself Mia went on to produce a brainstorm and a collage all the while not thinking about food.

It was gone eleven when temptation to grab a cookie rushed her. It was so overwhelming Mia threw herself into bed determined to sleep hunger away. She'd just lulled into a cosy sleep when she heard the click of the front door.

"Nooooh," she moaned into her pillow squeezing it mercilessly.

"Meeeyahhh, come here."

It was the pathetic slur in Joslyn's tone that instantly wound Mia up. The pleading, pitiful enunciation of simple words telling Mia her mum was totalled.

"Meeeyahhhhhhhh."

Downstairs Mia homed in on the kettle. She couldn't look at her mum.

"Tea Mum?"

"Oh Mia."

Joslyn repeatedly shook her head, mumbled and hunched further over the table.

Mia was about to spoon sugar into her mug. She stilled. She thought. She said no. "It's over Love."

"Oh dear," Mia's automated response.

"Meeya love; it's over."

"You'll be ok Mum."

The instinct to comfort her mum had diluted slowly over the years.

Joslyn's crocodile tears no longer elicited Mia's pity. But Mia wasn't a monster; she pulled off some kitchen roll, placed it in her mum's hands and squeezed Joslyn's shoulder. She wanted her mum to be happy but Mia resoundingly knew her mum was incapable of that. She also had an incurable disorder – allaboutme-itis

"You need to know the truth Mia."

The truth was a language Joslyn didn't speak.

"Are you hungry Mum?"

"How can I possibly eat?"

Mia thought. Well...you fork food off a plate and...

"Love, it's over. He hit me love. He was a mad man."

Not this record on repeat again.

"Where Mum?"

"He struck me Mia."

"Where?"

"Here," she cried pointing at her face.

"I can't see anything mum?"

"I don't bruise."

"No you booze," swallowed Mia so the words were incoherent.

Mia's eyes narrowed as her mum took a drag on her cigarette swallowing the nicotine with a mouthful of wine. Mia wondered would her mum get repetitive strain injury. Was the continual motion of fag to mouth, alcohol to lips damaging? Mia hoped so. She hoped Joslyn's accounts of being beaten up were true. Potentially a third party might kill her.

The kettle clicked off.

"He hit me Mia; he was a devil. Your dad never struck me."

"Then you shouldn't have treated him like shit," said Mia under her breath, moving toward the stairs with tea in hand.

"Miawhereyougoing," Joslyn mumbled.

"Upstairs Mum. It's late."

Like Alien Joslyn unfolded to an upright position. Mia thought wine and vodka incubated inside her, forming a character so cold, so selfish she'd rejected her daughter's birth. Thirtieth of August; did that mean nothing to her mum?

"Hehitmelove. Pleaselove."

Mia had no intention of comforting a mother so entrenched in self-pity and bitterness that, last week, her only child's birthday went unmarked.

****

Early Saturday a burst of energy, triggered by a renewed determination to change, had Mia rummaging under her bed for her swimming costume. She'd swung chaotically between going, not going, going, not going but now she was going. She was. Going.

"An emery board towel, eyeball burning shampoo, bodywash that irritates your vag and a swimsuit."

On the bus Mia's buzz was less buzzy. She didn't sit. Her finger hovered over the bell whilst she craned her neck around people to see further ahead.

Getting off the bus she felt a little wobbly. Walking toward the large grey building Mia felt totally unprepared. The automatic doors swung inwards and people jostled around her, scanning membership cards on fast-track ticket machines. The leisure centre had changed, and Mia lacked confidence in new environments. She joined the queue at reception.

"This was a stupid, stupid, treble stupid idea," muttered Mia.

"Sorry, did you say something?"

"A swim please."

"Student?"

"Erm, I go to secondary school?"

Mia's qualms increased…second…by…second.

"That'll be one pound."

"Do I need change for the locker."

"A pound coin. I can change up notes if needed."

"Erm, no, I'm good thanks."

At the turnstile Mia froze but kids bounced into her propelling her through. The noise and the disregard of personal space made Mia choke. Lockers banged, children hollered, hairdryers noisily hummed. She threw herself into a cubicle collapsing. This was not the place for her. This was a nightmare – people took their clothes off here! How had she not remembered! Her every physical flaw would be on display until she hit the water.

Mia sat engaged in a war with herself until she began undressing.

37

She looked down at her legs. Crap they were hairy. She hadn't thought this through. She needed to shave, she needed a new costume, she needed to not be such a fucking tit. Out of nowhere tears sprung. Whilst kids danced around in excitement or moaned about not staying long enough no one heard the girl bawling a metre from them. About to admit defeat, about to pull her costume off, the memory of Jay's hand brushing hers led Mia to make the longest walk of her life.

"Shit!"

In the pool Mia clung to the rail in the deep end. The water was freezing. She looked over her shoulder; the shallow end was a bloody long way off. She let go...of fat Mia and swam toward slim Mia. Six lengths later, about to cardiac arrest, she hung about the ladder waiting for the area to clear. She didn't want an audience, not with her bikini line and mammoth backside. Hands on the railings, arms exhausted, the pool scene from Shallow Hal energised her exit. Walking gingerly back to the changing area Mia passed a mirror. She ignored it, like the dark hairs on her legs, like her gross costume with its lost elasticity and worn patch right by her nipple.

"Her legs," giggled a tall, slim girl to her friend.

"I know, she's a Gruffalo."

Mia ignored the bitchy teens she recognised from the year below. She felt under scrutiny; that slimmer, fitter people were judging her for being weak and greedy. Sod them, the fat, the hair and the costume thought Mia. She opened the steam room door, brushing past people to squeeze into an area far too small for her bottom. She was oblivious to the odd stare and raised eyebrow. She sweated for fifteen minutes thinking about Jay. She knew where he worked, where he lived. Jesus that sounded wrong yet in the shower she thought more about him. It didn't matter that her supermarket brand products didn't lather, she felt sparklingly clean and for the first time since forever she felt hope.

Dressed and feeling a stone lighter Mia strolled toward the bus stop breaking into a run when she saw the number six approaching. Breathless she flashed her oyster. It was a relief to sit...until she felt her chair being kicked. Trying to look like she wasn't bothered she picked up the discarded newspaper.

Petra, a young life violently taken.

38

The met still chasing their tails as the Wolf alludes them.

Blunt force trauma, restraint marks, sexual activity. Mia felt sick to the pit of her stomach. The nausea magnified as her chair was repeatedly booted.

"Faiser, your mum, she watch that supersize superskinny shit."

"So?"

"Is this bitch supersize or what?"

Chuckling ensued.

"Yo fat girl."

Mia tensed.

"You ever heard of a diet?"

Passengers shifted their bodies away, as if she'd brought this on herself.

"Maybe she not talking coz she hungry," one sniggered to the other.

"She look like she always hungry...You ever banged a fat bitch?"

"Shit no! You?"

"I ain't gonna lie to you bruv, I'd fuck her."

Mia's cheeks burned with humiliation. She struggled breathing; like a torturer was placing pavement slab after slab on her chest, crushing her lungs. She rang the bell even though it wasn't her stop and stumbled off. She had the newspaper in her hand. She rammed it into the bin because it was hateful...like the boys on the bus...like The Wolf.

Anger propelled her toward the Westway. Beneath the long, elevated dual carriageway, in the cold and shadow of its bridge, Mia's anger cooled. Walking her eyes checked out the businesses operating from lock-ups. Cars revved, music blared, vans were loaded. A sign; *Stan's* with two boxing gloves caught Mia's eye. It was above a door, at the top of old, wooden stairs. It looked the sort of place porn was made yet her feet carried her up the brittle staircase.

Inside, seeing the serious boxing equipment and ring, Mia realised she'd made a mistake. About to turn...

"What you want love?"

Whoever he was, he was unexpected.

"Well?"

She felt uncomfortable. One because he was short, very short, a dwarf in fact. Two because this was a man's club, a violent man's club, probably a killer's club. But wasn't she dealing with potential killers?

"Cat got your tongue?"

"What does that mean? Practically how does a cat get a human tongue?"

She was rude, it wasn't her intention, but it riled her that yet another person had her under pressure. She straightened up, sticking her chin out.

"I want to learn to box."

He was silent. He wore soft gym bottoms and a sleeveless tee showcasing multiple tattoos. His face was defined by a strong jaw, a broad nose and a number two crew cut. His skin was rough, with at least two day stubble and peaky like it never saw the sun. His eyes were clear and piercing; Mia knew they were eyes that saw everything.

"Go to the leisure centre, there's boxercise, karate. More your cuppa."

He was about to turn.

"Are you saying I can't join this club."

"Love I'm saying this club is not for you; the blokes here aren't used to being around girls. No disrespect but you don't look like you can afford to waste money."

"What nights are you open?"

"Love we're always open. You come, you do the circuit, you match up with whoever's around."

"Do you need your own gloves?"

"Are you serious or you pullin' my fuckin' leg?"

"I'm deadly serious. I don't want self-defence, that I can google. I want to learn to fight, like if a man came at me I want to be in with a chance. That's fair isn't it?"

He stared her out. She looked away but remained.

"The blokes here aren't pta daddies, they're ex-offenders, they'll give you grief but if you insist so be it…all welcome."

Mia approached him putting her hand out.

"I'm Mia."

He ignored her hand.

"Stan."

Mia left with no intention of returning but life has a way of overturning decisions.

Entering the estate Mia felt semi-chilled; it was too early for violent crime. Inside the flat she pulled off her pongy trainers; inspecting her burning heels. Sizeable, hot, squashy bubbles had risen beneath the skin. Mia pressed them gently.

Hungry, she went in search of lunch. In the fridge was...nothing.

"Urh, it's germ city."

Mia decided to clean the fridge because she intended to use it; this led to clearing out the cupboards. On a roll, no longer hungry, she scrubbed the toilet, the sink, the bath and sorted the overflowing laundry basket. Her stuff she bunged in a laundry bag. Her mother's she tossed down the estate's rubbish shoot.

After sweating some calories away homework loomed. Instead of working in her cramped room she set up at the kitchen table. Autumn light streamed in and Mia enjoyed the warmth on her face as she drafted an English essay. Hours passed as she regularly picked up her text searching for quotes to back up her argument. Her rumbling tummy eventually had her packing up for the night. She smiled; a sound essay and she'd had the strength not to stuff her face. If she could do it today, she could do it fullstop!

In her nighty, wrapped in her quilt, laying on the settee, she wasn't so sure. All she thought about were her favourite sweets and chocolates. Her craving was so strong it was hard to enjoy the crap movie she was half way through. She was too tired to start anything else, so tired that as her eyelids began to flutter she snuggled down further on the settee. In her head reality mingled with fantasy creating Fifty Shades of Jay.

Waking up with the tv on was disorientating. It evoked an inkling of not being alone; like there was someone inside, watching. Mia brushed the thought aside as an image of pancakes with poached pear and liquid chocolate filled the screen. Why did the day start with cooking programmes?

Mia checked the time; 7.35. She had a lot to do. She grabbed her laundry. Opening the flat door she glanced left and right along the low lit, narrow corridor.

"All clear."

She walked skittishly across the estate and out onto the walkway alongside the canal. It was well lit, like a stage. The open space quelled her anxiousness. No alleys or recesses for baddies to hide. There could be head on danger, but she wasn't going to think about that now.

The launderette was in darkness. Mia dropped her weighty bag down against the locked door and sunk onto it. She resembled someone sleeping rough. This was the alternative to living with her mother. The streets.

A gust of wind caught up a disused newspaper, separating its pages. The front page blew into Mia, wrapping around her leg like paper mache. Pulling it off she couldn't ignore the headline; *Abduction now Murder*.

"Arhhhhh!" she screamed, her body jerking

The abrupt rattling of keys had her heart vaulting to her brain. A twenty-something, Eastern European bloke with hawk eyes wanted access. He was handsome in an unhappy way. Mia decided he was a Syrian refugee. He carried unimaginable pain in his heart. Filling the drum of the large machine with uniform, bedding and underwear, she named this quiet hero Boris. The launderette was a cover for his real job as a hit man. He needed a lot of money quickly to save his family. Leaving, Mia wanted to run after him and beg to be his assistant. He'd show her how to dismantle a semi-automatic hand gun. They'd kill baddies…and her mum AKA Cersei.

Sitting in front of the washing machine, her trainers bouncing loudly off the drum Mia noticed the sign 'Do not put footwear in the washing machine'. What Boris didn't know wouldn't hurt him.

Mia read her set text – Much Ado About Nothing only lifting her head when the vicious spin cycle distracted her. Staring at the round door Mia worried there would only be a large collection of threads on opening; no uniform, no bedding but her wash survived. Carrying it to the drier she couldn't remember a wash smelling so clean and fresh. Maybe because she'd added conditioner…unlike her mum who didn't buy liquid she couldn't drink.

****

CHAPTER 5   THE WOLF

He'd been a lonely child, a shy teen, an awkward adult; someone girls were never interested in. He had a predilection for teenage girls. For years he'd merely observed; a dreamer...until Sammy Quigley. Sweet Sammy.

His parents' house backed onto the Quigley's. After work he'd eaten dinner with them. They were in bed when he'd climbed over the shared garden wall. It was the Quigley's son's eighteenth. Although uninvited he'd wanted to catch a glimpse of Sammy.

Drifting into the crowd he picked up a glass of whisky, knocked it back and slipped the whisky bottle under his sweater. Looking around he couldn't see her. He wandered down to Quigley's shed, he'd been in it once, it was a good place to get pissed and hole up for an hour...fifteen-year-old Sammy might make a late entrance.

Sneaking his head around the shed door, his heart almost stopped. He entered, hurriedly stacking beer crates against the shed door. Looking out the window, above the workbench, the nearest people were thirty meters away, still, he pulled the dusty, old curtain across the glass window; total privacy.

He took an electrical tie from Mr Quigley's odds and ends box. He tied her floppy hands in front; she was totally out of it. Standing back his eyes ran the length of her. He decided then to order electrical ties. That's how calm he felt, excited yes, but in control.

Sammy laid on a discarded sofa; a bin beside her with sick in it. She'd regretted swallowing the MDMA straight away. Masie had brought them. Everyone else was fine but Sammy felt dizzy and sick. I'll stay here she said, don't want my mum seeing me like this. So her friends, on a high, left Sammy safe, at the bottom of the garden while she came down.

His hand stroked the warm skin on Sammy's cheek. He ran his rough finger across her lips then kissed her hard. Again and again until her lips swelled and split.

Sammy dreamt; it was a nightmare but she couldn't shake herself awake. A phantom untied her halter neck.

Staring at her breasts he came. It soaked through his boxers and into his jeans. It didn't prevent him from groping her and filming it...filming her.

He hitched her skirt around her hips. His long fingers crept under her knickers, touching places he'd seen only in lad's mags and on websites.

In the darkness Sammy felt hands roughly touching intimate places but her own arms wouldn't move. She knew her knickers were being pulled down. Her legs arranged.

He took photos. He'd upload enough to prove she wasn't a princess. When the school audience googled Sammy Quigley they were in for a treat. Phone away he pulled a dirty, dusty picnic blanket over her face in case she came to.

The nightmare felt real because he was heavy on top, then inside her; it hurt so much but she couldn't move and her scream was muffled.

****

Mia sprung out of bed as if she'd been reprogrammed. She was clear headed, seeing everything for what it was. A mother was a noun it didn't naturally convert into a verb.

Downstairs Joslyn applied makeup. Descending, Mia thought maybe now was a good time?

"Hey mum," she smiled pouring herself Special K. "There's a Spanish exchange…"

"Oh Mia that's awkward."

"Why?" asked Mia confused.

"You'd be flying Mia. You're a big girl, you'd probably need two seats."

Mia was harpooned. She was a whale beached on an unreachable shore. She couldn't look at her mother. It wasn't true, she wouldn't need two seats. Yeah she was fat but not obese. Why was her mum such a bitch! Why did she continually derail her opportunities?

Mia took her cereal upstairs. She pulled a leaflet from her blazer pocket. It was carefully folded. Mia opened it and read.

Hola! Spanish Exchange 2018,
Have fun, experience Spanish culture within a safe and happy family environment

So far Mia had spent her life a spectator desperate to compete. This seemed unlikely to change. Mia scrunched the leaflet up. Another dream binned. Hatred for her mother multiplied like mould on stale bread. Mia was big. She knew that. She also knew she wasn't THAT fat! Mia pulled her v neck jumper over her face and sobbed into it.

Crying made Mia late. Rushing to Warwick Avenue Mia thought of slow, painful ways to kill her mother. This thick spread of hatred began to thin as Mia changed at Paddington. Her heavy plod became sprightly as she climbed the escalator. She pranced up the next set of stairs and onto the circle line experiencing a level of excited anticipation that was hard to control. The mere thought of catching a glimpse of Jay made her head spin.

"There!"

Startled commuters watched as Mia squeezed her way between

passengers and along the carriage until Jay was in arm's reach. Off the train, walking toward the Mason building, Mia breathed in deeply like the Chelsea air was oxygen with a hint of Jay. A few feet behind, Mia synchronised her pace with his until Jay rotated into the Mason building. Mia felt a twinge of anxiety. This wasn't normal behaviour, Mia knew this, but if her head was filled only with her mum, then what was the point?

Legging it to school she rolled into English red and puffing. Art followed; as usual it was therapeutic. With oil crayons she pushed hard, using their gaudiness to depict the redness of thread veins beneath dark eyes. Every curve and line was harsh and unrelenting. In the emotion of her piece Mia drove her bad mojo away; she didn't sense Mrs Mullaly behind her.

"Mia I seriously hope you intend to study art at university; your work is powerful. This piece for instance; the vulgar tones, the cutting lines; it's truly frightening. Who is this menacing character?"

Mia smiled at the likeness.

"My mother."

The bell rang and Mia, for a change, rapidly threw everything in her rucksack before heading to Ealing; to The Admiral. Walking through the pub doors her spirits lifted. The music, the buzz of customers, they were a welcome diversion from the perils of a council estate and an empty shell of a mother who sedated her with food; namely animal organs.

"Mia!"

Embraced in a bear hug Mia felt a surge of love. Her dad smelt of Old Spice and something else…something unfamiliar…a coppery smell.

"Hey Dad. I phoned but you were obviously busy."

"Down the cellar love, cleaning the pipes, you know the drill."

"Yeah," Mia smiled.

"What's your poison?"

"Diet pepsi please dad. I've got us chicken sandwiches."

"That's my Mia, always resourceful. Salt and vinegar?"

"Nope, no crisps for me thanks."

"Rob," called Reggie. "Taking fifteen, Mia's here."

"Take as long as you need mate, me and Sharon can manage."

Reggie sat opposite Mia welcoming a break. Mia looked bright and energetic, he hoped he didn't look as bad as he felt. The last thing he wanted was to be a burden to Mia…not when she had Joslyn to contend with.

"How's your mum?"

"Currently MIA."

They took a bite of sandwich. Mia looked around the bar; it gleamed. Her dad was house proud. If only his energies went into her home. She chided herself for being petty. Things were hard for her dad, she could tell by the lines on his face. He looked much older than fifty four.

Reggie ate his sandwich in between swallows of Grolsch. His ulcerated leg was on fire. The strong beer hardly anesthetising the pain.

Mia sensed a hundred questions about Joslyn on the tip of his tongue. He'd never get over her; Mia knew that. She felt gutted by it.

"Has your mum got any new man on the scene?"

"She dabbles, you know mum."

"Are you ok at the flat Mia?"

In his eyes she saw the answer he needed.

"Course Dad, don't be silly," she said giving him a nudge with her foot. "How cool was getting these sandwiches for eighty pence?"

"Cool," Reggie laughed. "How's school?"

"Hard but I'm trying."

"Good girl. What you up to this afternoon."

"Homework and tv."

"Is your mum out tonight?"

Mia shrugged; she bloody hoped so.

"I had a bit of luck on the geegee's love."

Reggie pulled a few notes from his pocket.

"Dad I don't need money, I'm fine," Mia protested; her last few quid blown on Special K and sweetener.

"Win the lottery did you? Put my cheque in the post love," he smiled pushing notes into Mia's hand. Mia felt emotional…sad emotional. Why did she feel guilty when he was the adult and she was the child? He'd stopped being her rock. Roles had reversed; she needed to protect him from the reality of her dire life and how little her mum thought of him.

"Love I'd better get to it but don't be a stranger hon," said Reggie.

Mia smiled. She wasn't smiling inside, she'd caught the grimace on her dad's face as he stood. He was covering up his pain. Hugging him she wanted to hang onto him for dear life because she loved him so much.

On the bus Mia unscrunched the cash – forty pounds. She wondered was it winnings or was there another court hearing on the horizon. She prayed her dad wasn't dipping his fingers in the till again or seriously gambling. Mia didn't blame her mum entirely for her dad's demise but it was the old chicken and egg question, what came first? Her mum's desperation to be the centre of every man's world or her dad's drinking? Mia thought she knew the answer.

Jumping off the bus, walking over the estate bridge, muttering to herself, Mia didn't hear the footsteps behind her.

"Jesus he has nothing; no home, no partner, no friends," she said as a tap on the shoulder had her turning. She recognised the boy as one of the gang's gofers. Before she could react he brazenly grabbed her breasts; roughly squeezing them. Mia heard herself screaming…a high pitched howl that rang in her ears.

"That's assault you fucking piece of shit. I'm phoning the police."

"Fuck off fat bitch!"

She looked beyond him to the street where others were hollering…but she lost focus as her eyes filled with tears. She turned away. The landscape appeared cloudy, it was tilting sideways, it no longer felt solid beneath Mia's feet. She moved slowly and heavily like her body was dead weight. Once in the flat she couldn't remember coming up in the lift or opening the door. Panicked she looked around. Running to the front door, her keys were in the keyhole, there for anyone to take. Snatching at the keys she slammed the door, her body weight tight against it, rigid, cold, expectant; maybe they'd followed. Waiting with bated breath for trouble; totally keyed up, Mia knew this was bad. They'd crossed that line…between verbal abuse and fucking assault. It would worsen; she was just meat to them. She let out a low guttural cry before pushing herself away from the door. She was exhausted. She lumbered down the hallway her movement uncoordinated. Throwing herself on her bed she sobbed; intermittently her limbs jerked and flinched until sleep claimed her.

"Five minutes," Mia mumbled as her alarm activated KISS FM. Usually breakfast got Mia out of bed but she couldn't get excited about a fruit pot. Instead her unsettled mind, crowded with dark matter, had her pushing back the quilt determined to fight back.

"Fucking shit heads!"

Downstairs she poured milk over oats putting the bowl in the microwave.

"Wankers!"

"Berdinggggg."

Mia added currents, chocolate drops and chia seeds to her porridge.

"Umm lovely," said Mia talking to herself. "I want Jay to hold me. To close the gap so tightly our bodies lock together. Words unnecessary."

Passing the hallway mirror Mia saw her nemesis; a weak, sagging, misshapen thing.

"Yeah you're a mess but no fucking way is anyone ever going to assault you again."

Mia maintained her level of hate until High Street Ken.

"Oh my God," she said her voice quivering with delight as Jay, in a quarter length cashmere coat, boarded her carriage. Mia couldn't help thinking that 'chance' was on her side, that destiny was leading her into Jay's life. Mia checked her watch, she had time to walk with, well behind, Jay to work.

In LFL, pumped up by her sighting of Jay, Mia thought about his starched shirt. Its stiffness, its whiteness. Who knew a shirt could be such a turn on. Her shirts? They were a clear statement. They said your mother doesn't love you. She doesn't care if the pointing and comments made by girls in P.E. humiliates you.

Mia looked at her cuffs, folded four times at her wrists because they needed cufflinks because it was a man's shirt…one of her mum's freebies. The long sleeves either hung down or bunched uncomfortably under Mia's jumper because they were double her arm length. Kids called her the abominable snowman.

Feeling eyes on her Mia looked up…toward Gabby…catching the edge of a turn. Gabby hadn't joined in with the cattiness but she'd said nothing…did nothing.

49

Flynn decided he was a knob for agreeing to spend the last weeks of his holidays at Masons; the work was bloody, mind numbingly boring. He had to stop trying to please his dad. The man was unimpressible.

"Flynn, these figures need adjusting up by thirteen percent then faxed to Lloyds. Have you got the figures for the Davis account yet?"

"Right here."

"And five cups of coffee are needed in meeting room two, then get to Marks and buy an assortment of sandwiches and soft drinks."

Thank God this was not his future. A decision that wholly irritated his father. All his life his parents had worked at moulding him into a mini Gareth but Flynn didn't give a dick about the Davis account. He cared about images, scenes, photography, editing film and storytelling. 'Crap' his father called it. It frustrated his father that he couldn't use money as a carrot because Flynn was financially independent thanks to his forward-thinking grandma.

Flynn left the Mason building, breathing in air like he'd been starved of it. He felt like a man on death row each time he entered his dad's very corporate office. Plotting down on a bench on Sloane Square he looked around as he consumed a pizza slice. Flynn's eyes settled on a girl; sixteenish, walking his way. Hair blew across her face and hands attempted to push it back when a flurry swept a sheet from her grasp. Trying to reclaim it the wind cruelly and repeatedly blew it out of reach. A mum with a pram joined in, her toddler amused by this funny game. The girl finally nabbed it; thanking the mum before crouching down to the toddler to shake her tiny hand. Flynn felt himself grinning. It was her.

Mia's eyes widened; a sense of alarming excitement had her turn away. People passing in ear shot glanced at the school girl frozen to the spot, talking to herself.

"Oh. My. God! What to do, what to do," she whispered in close succession; her heart thudding so fast it hurt.

****

Totally bizarre thought Flynn about the girl who'd squeezed in between him and another man.

****

50

Mia curled her fingers into her hands vowing never to bite anything not covered in chocolate. Her school skirt rose a little but there was no room for adjustments. Mia stared at her thighs, how their flesh spread so they touched each other and Jay's. She knew they'd never have a gap. It was disappointing to be young and know your limitations. She was glad she'd worn black tights. She looked down at her scuffed, trampy shoes wishing for polished brogues with fresh innersoles. She checked her posture, lifting her ribcage to separate the fat under her breasts from the ring of fat around her waist. She wished…she wished this moment would last forever. But it didn't. From the corner of her eye she watched Jay stand and brush himself down. Sadly, she watched him walk away but so many times their paths had crossed. It was fate. Mia was certain of it.

Buzzing all day from her lunch time encounter Mia looked up and down the platform checking out her fellow travellers…no sign of Jay.

Flynn heard his train pulling in so legged it down the stairs managing to slip between the closing doors.

Mia silently freaked out. Jay! In the flesh!

Flynn loosened his tie, releasing his top button. Mia found it totally erotic. She didn't want him to stop. She smiled all the way to his home, thinking of his shirt coming off until her smile totally died.

Flynn's car. Its panels bursting with bedding, kitchenware, clothes and whatnot. Mia knew what it meant but she had to stay to the bitter end.

Showered, in his Gym Sharks, dinner eaten, Flynn made his goodbyes. He threw the house keys in the glove compartment, patted his pocket for his wallet, sat in the driver's seat and turned his attention to the satnav.

"Turn left…at the end of the road turn left."

As the key in the ignition fired up the engine, tunes streamed from Spotify.

Mirror. Signal. Manoeuvre.

Jay. Was. Gone. To uni most likely. Funnily enough in her bag was a guide on how to apply to uni's through UCAS. Suddenly it felt real; the possibility of escaping her mum and the estate. She wanted it so much she trembled. All the way home her head was jammed with competing dramas – Jay gone and estate life…possibly death. Turning the corner of the block Mia lost the ability to think; fear muted her.

51

"He knew I needed that shit! He like, yo bitch I ain't got no time to go to Cerese's."

Mia couldn't reverse. They were on her. Four of them. Leaning against a wall looking for entertainment in between selling drugs.

"What the fuck, if it ain't princess."

Mia didn't respond. Goosebumps the size of grapes raised in alarm all over her. Scar Tissue stepped into Mia's path. The fear was debilitating...until a shove from Forty Pence had her stumbling forward...but her tongue was frozen

"Yo, fat bitch, I'm talking to you."

Another shove in the back.

"Think you're fucking better than us."

"Chez we gotta go."

Chez aka Scar Tissue pressed his face into Mia's. He spat out pure hate.

"Your tits was foreplay Bitch!"

****

The others had lived in houses. He'd watch when their curtains weren't drawn; admiring their curves, their bone structure. They wore so little. Strappy vests, skimpy bras, strings; his zoom lens left little to the imagination, especially when they fake tanned. It's like he was in the room with them. Sometimes he was. Seeing, listening, occasionally touching.

She, lived on a trashy estate. The logistics of this one were a challenge. He'd observed as she'd walked toward her block. She got as far as the estate play area. They'd been draped across the equipment like a photo shoot for Coffee and Gangs.

He'd felt her tension; she was wound tightly like a coiled spring. And her fear tasted delicious. He'd hardened in seconds. Had he wanted the others this much? He thought not.

****

Joslyn sat at the kitchen table, shaking her head woefully. Mia wanted to scream at her mum that she was scared, that they needed to move, that she was in terrible danger but her mum had again succumbed to bills and booze. Mia found herself drowning in the murky waters of her mum's financial crisis instead of getting on with homework.

"Love, what does DR mean?"

"It means you owe money."

"DR £264. What does that mean Mia?"

"Mum," Mia breathed out in frustration whilst Joslyn cried unrestrainedly. Jesus, did she have special reserves; her crying was The Never Ending Story. Maybe a cocktail of wine, scotch and ratatouille increased tear fluid? It might be a scientific discovery.

"Mia! If it weren't for you I'd get a live in job like your dad."

Great Mia thought. She wants to reverse me up her fallopian tubes!

"Mia love what does it mean?"

"It means you didn't pay the fucking rent."

"What did you say?"

"I said it's mean dad doesn't pay a cent."

A swallow of Jameson, a lighting of a cigarette.

"Court Mia court!"

Mia used caution. A wrong word and her mother flipped from victim to prosecutor.

"Make a payment no matter how small…And stop spending the rent money on fucking alcohol." Mia whispered under her breath.

"What's that love?"

"Nothing mum." Die you evil creature. Die!

Joslyn emptied the purse so coins rolled around and off the table. She'd choreographed this routine for optimum irritation. First the pennies, then the twos, followed by fives; towers of self pity. Minutes became an hour.

"Darling check this for me," was on a loop.

"Mum!" Mia was losing the will to live. "It's correct. Give me the payment card."

Mia hovered agitatedly as the whisky bottle emptied.

"Mum, I've got work to do."

"No Mia!

Gulp.

It's your dad's mess, you need to work it out.

Gulp.

Fourteen I was when my parents put me on the boat to England.

Gulp."

53

Mia had heard this so often she wanted to superglue her mum's lips together.

"I was treated like a slave. By my own aunt. You've got it easy."

"I know Mum."

"You know what Mia?" Joslyn's sharp tone could pierce a brick.

Silence. Mia's mind was buffering, what words diffused anger?

"I'm waiting Mia. What do you know?"

"Nothing mum."

"It's hard being a single parent, raising a child alone."

Anger simmered in Mia's belly; its bitterness rising and burning her throat. Her mother wasn't raising her; Mia was a pop-up-tent.

"Look Mia my hands are shaking from worry."

No mum they're shaking because you're an alcoholic Mia screamed silently. And what was she Mia wondered…an earthworm…spineless…waiting for her mum to prise her from the ground.

With just the two of them, no background noise from a radio, Mia heard sounds she'd come to detest. The untwisting of the whisky cap, the glucking as the liquid poured heavily into the tumbler and the long swallow her mother took. It was that sound effect that made Mia's stomach churn with loathing - the gulp. Then the refill. Another slamming of her dad. More drink. More Mia bashing.

Upstairs Mia powered through homework like her life depended on it because actually her life depended on it! Crashed out at midnight Mia crawled under her duvet, pulling it over her head. Being poor was exhausting but being poor and Joslyn's daughter? That was a torture that had Mia staring at her wrists. It was never one thing that had Mia thinking the unthinkable it was a series of daily battles building up like plaque: how hard A levels were, how people only saw her weight, how she wore shoes a half size too big because they were cheap, how the gang on the estate singled her out. The list was endless; Mia fell asleep on number twenty-seven - reasons to top yourself. She sunk lower, into a dark well of night terrors. The ones that had you waking suddenly, rigidly, reaching for the light switch.

Mia woke with the taste of hopelessness on her tongue but she didn't wallow in it. She threw trackies and trainers in a bag. On route to school Mia thought about boxing. She hadn't wanted to set foot in that gym again; it was scary but maybe she needed scary?

As the train pulled in to High Street Ken her eyes automatically searched out Jay but Jay was gone. Negativity slowly drained her spirit, she dreaded boxing but the memory of being grabbed clung to her. Instead of soaking in knowledge, school embedded, all the more deeply, her sense of isolation. She had no friends, no one to turn to. She had to cope with being violated and powerless alone. In the school loos she changed into trackies. For once she was glad her clothes were washed out; anything better would reinforce her unsuitability to the club. Mia felt conscious of how badly dressed she was. What manner of parent let you dress like a vagrant in material that kept stretching no matter how much you ate. The government should ban materials with stretch. It was as dangerous as sugar. If people's trousers got tight it was a sign not to eat.

Annoyingly one train connection came shortly after another so Mia found herself at the stairs leading to Stan's Boxing all too soon.

Inside it appeared causal, no structured lessons but it was busy, there was a body at every station and that body was swole, sweaty and intimidating. Through a Perspex window she saw Stan? She should pay him.

Hovering in the office doorway she felt like an intruder. Another man, his back to her, was sat of the edge of Stan's desk, on Stan's side. Their heads were almost touching. Behind a desk Stan looked standard height but his glare toward her was anything but standard, it was up there in menacing scowls as he abruptly ended his conversation. The other man turned. He was a rock face; unyielding and expressionless.

"You wanted something?" asked Stan sternly.

Mia approached the table.

"It's all there, £5," said Mia happily putting her mother's towers of self-pity to use.

"Tombstone meet our newest member."

"Hi," Mia replied her eyes straying to the tattoo on the dorsal side of his hand. It was like an x-ray; penned on him were the twenty-seven bones within the wrist and hand.

Tombstone was unresponsive. He strode past her. Alone with Stan she asked,

"Why is he called Tombstone?"

"Why do you think," said Stan grimly.

Was Stan for real? If Tombstone was that dangerous he'd be in prison?

As a black, shiny, six foot skin head came off the running machine Mia bolted to it, cutting across Tombstone. Mia smiled – his features remained set in concrete.

"Someone's not good at sharing," she whispered under her breath.

Mia's exuberance to workout died as she looked at the buttons on the keypad.

"Umm?"

She glanced over her shoulder. Tombstone was still there. He thought himself menacing but he wasn't her mum. Confident she pressed start.

"Ahhhh!"

****

"Mr Coombe."

He looked up.

"Yes?"

"I'm Mia."

"I know that Mia."

"I need help."

"What sort?"

Interesting; she has a voice.

"Money."

"What's your financial situation?"

"Dire."

"See me after school next Monday, I'll talk to admin see how we can help."

Mia smiled to herself. Inside a ripple of possibility turned her tummy.

For the remainder of the day she got her head down because everything she wanted for herself meant hard work and self-discipline; two traits her character as a rule lacked. A little surprise that kept her mood buoyant throughout the day was that her skirt shifted around her waist as she walked; proof of her weight loss. Because she wanted to survive long enough to live the dream, after school Mia changed in the loos and headed to Stan's.

She hoped Stan and Tombstone had gotten over her little accident. Was three days sufficient cooling off period?

"Hi Stan. Look a whole five pound note this time."

"You're banned from the running machine."

"It was a freak accident. It's not like I hurt him," said Mia turning and seeking Tombstone out. "Look, he's fine. Anyway aren't boxers meant to have quick reflexes?"

"You hit him at speed."

"True. Perhaps if you show me how to use it."

"You're banned."

"Fine," Mia said crossing her arms across her chest. "What can I do?"

"What do you want to do?" he asked.

Mia looked around, to the punch bag.

"I want to hit that."

"Go for it."

****

Flynn was hammered. He'd spilt his last pint over himself. He was flagging but laughing at how the fridge door in his uni hall's flat had come off in his hands. His flat mates cracked up. Chuckling away Flynn slid down the wall, onto the floor, his back against the uni bar wall. He closed his eyes. Bad idea. He opened them…he saw a girl, same position as him, opposite wall. He caught glimpses of her in between the legs of dancing students. She looked familiar. Yeah, she looked like that jinxed girl from Sloane Square. He spluttered out beer as he remembered the satsuma. Then he remembered standing opposite her on the train. How sad her eyes were.

"Sad, sad, sad. Too sad. Much too sad. Enormously sad. Beautifully sad. Fuck I'm wasted."

Flynn awkwardly stood. Another bad idea. He spewed.

****

Mia's hands were so sore and bruised it was hard to focus. It hurt to think Stanley had stood by knowing hours later she'd be in pain.

"Que the fuck have you done to tus manos?"

"I stupidly, repeatedly hit a punch bag without gloves."

"Mia, do you even know how to punch the bag?"

"No! I don't know anything because the old git in the gym won't show me."

"Ok. I'll show you."

"When?"

"Next week when your fists have healed. You'll need gloves and wraps."

Ben gently picked up one of Mia's hands, he placed her palm against his.

"My girlfriend's hands are about your size, she'll have an old pair."

"Thanks Ben."

"De nada."

****

58

Mr Coombe was as good as his word he sat with her filling out applications for the school bursary and free school meals. He didn't delve into her background which was good because Mia was bored with the whole drama that was her mother.

"The other details you'll find on your mum's payslip and a bank statement."

"Thanks sir, you've been so helpful."

Mia folded the forms putting them between the pages of Atonement.

"So much for an Indian summer," said Mr. Coombe looking out the window. Mia watched a blanket of grey cloud billow and darken.

"Looks like a storm's coming," said Mia. "Night sir."

"Goodnight Mia."

Leaving the class Mia walked along the short, narrow corridor. The florescent light above buzzed then shorted. The sizzling was unnerving. The dullness of the day and the greyness of the hallway created a premature darkness. It was always creepy in the tower. Hers was the one remaining form using the nearly condemned structure. Older kids always scared the new year sevens with the ghost story of the suicide pact that happened twenty years ago. Looking down the concrete spiral staircase...Mia shivered at the thought of being pushed.

"Ahh!" Mia yelped, jumping in her skin, startled by a door banging in the wind. She'd felt jittery ever since the sexual assault. Looking behind her crisp packets and flattened water bottles were the only evidence of the day's activity. The tower came alive at this time; like an abandoned house, all creaking and rustling. Mia descended three flights. The only exit was closed, darkening the small, square, windowless ground floor. Mia imagined them not opening but a firm push on the bar led Mia into the fresh air. Walking across the playground she had the eerie sensation of being watched. She stopped, turned and looked up to Mr Coombe's form room; the lights were off...but movement, at the adjacent classroom window, had Mia peering into its space. She made out a shape. She blinked. She expected it to disappear, but it remained. The biting wind spun around her; cold, she turned away, a little on edge...but unsure why.

Mia headed to the leisure centre. She powered down to the pool floor swimming under water until her lungs ached. Emerging with a smile she breathed in and front crawled to the end of the lane. She'd lost five pounds. It didn't look obvious but her bra no longer left red track marks around her body and her skirt was very loose around her waist but what gave her most confidence was the full leg and bikini wax she'd blown her dad's money on. She couldn't remember the last time she felt in control.

Nurturing and maintaining that level of confidence around her mum was challenging. "Mia is that you love," Joslyn sing-songed up the stairs.

"Yeah, it's me," replied Mia through gritted teeth, dropping her bag and descending. Turning into the kitchen a man who was not her dad sat at the table. A man who was making himself comfortable in a home that wasn't his! He was tall, red headed and unwelcome. But could he be the golden goose – the poor chump who'd take her mum on permanently?

"Mia darling," said Joslyn embracing a stiff daughter. "This is Kevin."

Mia noted he was youngish for her mum and bulky. He had a mole on his cheek, his hair was dowdy red; wiry and his nylon trousers pulled inappropriately around the crotch. Standing he embraced her. Mia froze; she hated blokes touching her and her breasts being grabbed was still a brutal memory.

"Nice to meet you Mia. Your mum's told me lots about you."

It was weird because they all knew he was lying.

"Same here," Mia returned the lie pulling away discomforted that he was cold stone sober whilst her mum was tanked.

"Are you alright Mia," asked Kevin. "You seem jumpy."

Mia instantly disliked him. Who was he to ask her that?

"Mia love," said Joslyn nearly cutting her tongue with her sharp tone.

Say love again and I'm going to slap your face thought Mia who despised the pretence, the false proclamations of love, the fake caring.

"Mia, don't frown, it's not a good look for you Love."

Stop fucking saying love begged Mia itching to strike out. She wanted her mum not to drink…not to hook up with strange men. Why was Mia never enough? They could be close…do so much together.

"Mia, did you hear Kevin?"

"You're late home from school," he repeated.

"Yes," interjected Joslyn leaning against the worktop, a bottle of wine in her hand. "She's very worried about her weight, aren't you Mia."

Bitch, thought Mia, unpacking her 'Count on us' meals.

Joslyn reached over and squeezed Mia's bum.

"Mum! Don't do that."

"Puppy fat we called it in my day," said Kevin.

For her weight to be opened up like a dissected frog was totally humiliating.

"Mia wasn't always huge. Reggie's rejection was traumatic but we're very close. Like sisters."

"Joslyn, you said it, sisters, that's what I thought."

The microwave ber-dinged. Mia pulled out her three hundred and twenty four calorie meal, hating herself, hating them.

"I don't know why you waste money. There's lovely pate and cheese in the fridge. It's the chocolates making you plump. Kevin, she's always munching. I tell her a minute on the lips, a lifetime on the hips."

Joslyn grabbed a handful of fat from Mia's waist and Mia jerked away, water spilling from her glass into her plastic meal container.

"Mia! You're so clumsy."

Mia's hating grew with each embarrassing prod, poke and squeeze; for some reason her mum became sickly tactile with Mia around men.

"Look!" shrieked Joslyn waving a bill in front of Mia's nose. "The telephone bill. Over a hundred pounds Mia and you're spending money like it's water."

It's your fucking inability to prioritise bills over booze, it's your fucking need to drink yourself stupid every time you have a fucking emotional melt.

"I don't use the phone Mum."

Joslyn's lips trembled. Jesus, she's spectacular at this, thought Mia as Kevin rose reaching to comfort Joslyn.

"Now Mia…blaming your mum isn't the way forward," said Kevin. Mia glared at Kevin, hate oozing and encompassing the pair of them.

Upstairs Mia continued to boil. How dare her mum bring strange men into the flat. How dare he speak to her like he had the right. Lying in

61

bed Mia hated that two doors down a bloke her mum randomly picked up was snoring.

****

Mr Coombe noted Mia's downcast expression.

"Mia, sit a minute."

"Sir I submitted the school meals on line and my mum signed the bursary form."

Mia wondered how illegal it was to forge a signature.

"Good," said Mr Coombe. Mia was a bad liar.

"I didn't tell you earlier Mia but I handed in your letter re your circumstances."

Mia's mind drew a blank?

"The board have issued you a cheque for three hundred from the hardship fund."

Three fucking hundred? Mia was aghast!

"It will keep you afloat till your bursary," Mr Coombe added handing Mia a cheque.

Mia stared at it, incredulous.

"They've also agreed to meet the cost of the Spanish exchange in March."

"Sir, I can't go…I mean, I can't have someone staying over…my mum's difficult."

"It won't be a problem Mia…and you must go…have you a passport?"

"No."

"Get a form from the post office and I'll countersign it."

"I'm confused sir, I didn't write a letter, I…"

Mr Coombe's head swung from side to side.

"You…You..."

Mr Coombe raised an eye in warning.

"School meals start today. Call in at the IT department, there's a laptop for you."

Mia nodded. She felt choked with gratitude.

"Off you go now, I have high expectations of you."

Mia concentrated hard; by the end of the day her eyeballs nearly hung from their sockets, yet she read her English texts on the trains back to

Warwick Avenue. Smiling, she ran up the escalator, feeling totally empowered.

"Tttttthut." That tsking viper sound Forty used before speaking – each letter stretched out – had her break into a sweat. They congregated at street level, at the top of the station stairs.

"You want some fun, innit bitch?" Forty sneered.

Those words, signalling her out, made Mia uncoordinated; she tripped up the steps.

"Ya on yer knees too early bitch," he goaded rubbing his crotch. "Come nearer this and kneel," he laughed.

Mia reached for her fallen pencil case but three inch ruby talons wrapped around it. Unzipped and upturned it. Stationery spilled down the stairs. Mia's head was buzzing as she scrambled to the street only to be encircled. Pushed and pulled she stumbled toward the estate her chest tightening like a fitted corset. They couldn't do anything in plain sight, right?

"Don't rush. Come see what I got between my legs. You know you want to."

Mia couldn't breathe, she was drowning on land, her lungs filling with fear.

"You puttin out like your trashy mum? Make a sandwich do yer?"

The chip shop! Mia barged through the circle, legging it.

"I don't want none of you kids in here!" shouted the chippy rudely.

"Let me out the back," demanded Mia looking over her shoulder.

They stood in line, their faces pressed to the glass chippy window, their features squashed and distorted.

"Please! I was your best fucking customer." Mia croaked.

"Go on," he said lifting the counter door up.

Mia bolted through the kitchen, knocking over a five litre oil drum, and down the alley, scratching her legs on crates. Regardless of cars braking, her ramming pedestrians, she didn't stop. Flying up the stairwell she jettisoned through her front door. Realising she was alone Mia sunk to the floor sobbing.

She cried on and off all evening until she fell asleep. She didn't hear her mum rolling in with Kevin at two am. She didn't want to hear anything. She wanted to sleep forever.

The radio roused Mia; Imagine Dragons. Mia didn't have to imagine. Although light penetrated her unlined curtains Mia didn't want to get up. Or swim. Or school. Or gym. She wanted to flatline.

In the hallway Mia stalled. The loo door was wide open. The blast from a stream of urine hitting toilet water was unmistakeable. Kevin was pissing with the toilet door ajar – sicko! About to reverse – Kevin came out pushing his dick in his boxers.

"Awright love," he said in passing.

Oh my God, thought Mia, Kevin wasn't even going to wash his hands! As her mum's door closed the noises coming from the bedroom made Mia want to puke. It was annoying they never stayed over at his. Why was that? Married like the others?

Mia's first lesson wasn't until ten twenty; she had time to fit in a swim. She saw no reason to hang around because the smaller her waist got the more scornful Joslyn became.

"Hey mum. I'll be late this evening, a trainee is cutting my hair at Toni and Guy."

"What are you having done?"

"Probably a bob."

"Oh Mia love, bobs are unforgiving. Your face is too full and your nose too large. Also you've a slightly jutting out chin. Keep it as it is. It's lovely. Don't waste money. Mia love...if you've got a few bob could I borrow it?"

Mia gritted her teeth; the words fuck and off trying to slip through the gaps where Mia flossed. She'd done it again; shared info with the enemy leaving herself vulnerable to attack.

"Sorry mum...I was going to ask you for money."

Mia saw the heat of anger bleeding through Joslyn's foundation. How had a woman this bitter been fertile?

Throughout the day, at school, Joslyn's disparaging observations effectively undid Mia's confidence. She did walk toward Toni and Guy after school but instead of turning into the salon she walked passed and kept walking until, looking around, she'd lost her bearings.

"'Scuse love."

Mia realised she was blocking the entrance to a pub; The White Bear.

"Sorry," she apologised standing aside to let patrons in. Unsure of what to do, about to head to the station, a sign in the window caught Mia's attention:

'KITCHEN STAFF REQUIRED ASK INSIDE'

Money. Work experience. Having grown up in pubs, Mia was confident she could do this job well. She didn't think twice, walking across the threshold of opportunity.

The bar was left of the entrance with a collection of tables set in front, facing the windows. To the right was a split-level space. It was light and spacious with more tables, parquet flooring and ceiling lights. Dusky Grey's One Night was playing. Mia liked the pub's vibe instantly. She approached the bar. She didn't feel nervous: the row of optics, the tall fridges, the shelves filled with mixers; they were familiar to her.

"Can I help you?"

"Yes, I'd like to apply for the kitchen job."

"I'll get Alex, he's the bar supervisor."

The young man ducked his head into the office.

"Alex, another applicant."

Alex was a string bean, maybe thinner. With jet black hair; skin faded, a sharp jaw line and dressed in black, he looked attractively menacing.

"Hi, I'm Alex, take a seat."

His voice was deep like a canyon; Mia warmed to it at once. She relaxed.

"Thank you, I'm Mia."

Mia sat; her hands neatly in her lap. She glanced at her thighs; their spread capacity had reduced.

Alex liked her smile. It was wide and reached her eyes. She didn't appear nervous which was positive because in the pub game you had to be calm, reasonable and firm.

"How old are you?"

"Seventeen."

"Tell me about your work experience."

Alex's questions were curt but his grey eyes shone like polished granite making it easy to maintain eye contact.

"I've never been employed but my parents were publicans and I

65

helped in the kitchen with food orders, glass washing, cleaning toilets; all behind the scene jobs. I know how busy a bar gets and how a good assistant finds things to do instead of waiting to be told."

"Good answer."

Mia had never seen such clear, creamy skin on a boy. For someone so dark she would have expected black stubble.

Alex was smitten. Not only did she look sweet, her voice was bright and sincere.

Mia beamed her smile; it was her favourite physical characteristic.

"Are you local?"

She could live in Dubai. The job was hers decided Alex.

"Not exactly. My school is and I'm always on time for school and never ill."

"What's your availability?"

"I'm free evenings and weekends."

A loner thought Alex. Maybe that was a status he could change.

"Perfect. Can you start tomorrow at ten am?"

Mia nodded.

"Great. Bring your birth certificate, evidence of your address, your bank details and your national insurance number."

Alex stood.

"We provide aprons but you need to wear all black. It's company policy."

Mia offered her hand and Alex shook it firmly. He held on to it a little longer before releasing it.

"Thank you Alex. See you in the morning."

He was already looking forward to it.

Mia was barely out the door when she rushed toward the station and Primark Hammersmith. Thank goodness for school bursaries! Mia bought black trousers. Also three fitted black t-shirts and black canvas shoes, like Vans, but not Vans, like Converse but not Converse. Mia named them Cans. In Marks she bought a plain black cardy and black bra and knickers. Queuing to pay she touched the items in her basket; she loved the feel of new. She couldn't wait to put them on and start work.

"£44.99 please," asked the cashier.

Mia tapped in her pin; she'd changed it to the day she met Flynn.

Putting her bank card away safely Mia walked through the automatic doors.

"Hi Mia."

Mia stopped dead in her tracks; shoppers nearly toppling into her. "Gabby."

As pedestrians flowed around them an uncomfortable silence followed.

"I'm sorry for what happened to you at my house."

"It's fine Mia it was a long time ago."

"My mum's a dangerous, jealous woman. It was all staged. She got insanely drunk after you left. I checked her bag...and there it was. I'm sorry Gabby."

"Mia it's ok. It's fine now. I still like you. It's...well...you know."

"Yeah...I do."

"You look great by the way...it's brilliant how you've turned things around. I know you were unhappy Mia and I made things worse."

"It's fine Gabby. Honestly. My life was shit way before you...you."

"Say it Mia...I told the class about how weird your mum is."

"Well...it's true. She's almost savage."

"It was cruel; I shouldn't have."

"Quits then?"

Gabby nodded.

"Have a good life Gabby Preston."

"You too Mia Dent. Won't see you Monday."

Mia laughed.

"Won't see you back."

"So you're saying you and Gabby Preston were friends?" asked Webber wanting confirmation.

"Yes, best friends, for nearly a year."

"When?" asked Raymond his tone mocking.

"Year 8. Chloe was my Year 7 friend. After Gabby I realised I wasn't suited to relationships. I couldn't bring friends home; their emotional wellbeing was at risk around my mum and she made it difficult for me to go out. I was always making up excuses for why I couldn't hang out or go to parties…then kids stopped asking."

"Did she restrain you?" asked Raymond sarcastically

"Yes! She did restrain me! Not physically, you can restrain someone emotionally. She guilted me into staying at home. She made me feel disloyal when I hung with friends. I let a lot of girls down making promises I broke because I had to prioritise my mum. I didn't understand her then. I didn't know what an attention seeking, selfish witch she was. She kept making me chose between her and my friends. I was young then, I loved her, I wanted to make her happy, I kept thinking I'd do things her way this time and next time I'd put myself first. She had me needing her approval, she would get so sad, or so angry or so drunk that I always conceded. I know now it was abuse, but when it was happening I couldn't see that she was alienating me from life. I don't know what else to say; she's a fucking nutter!"

"That's easy to say when she's not here to defend herself," said Raymond.

"I don't know what to say to convince you," said Mia in frustration. "When is this doctor thing happening because I seriously need pain relief."

"Soon," said Webber. "Drink some water, being dehydrated won't help."

Mia took a large swallow of stale, warm water.

"Tell me what happened to end your friendship."

"Ok but only because I think Gabby was abducted because of me."

CHAPTER 9 FLASHBACK

"Mia, I can't wait for school to end; we are gonna have so much fun. I've got popcorn, a one kg bar of chocolate, face packs, nail polish, scary film to stream."

"Only two lessons to go Gabs. Your dad picking us up is cool. I can't remember the last time I was in a car."

"Mia you're adorable," said Gabby giving Mia a squeeze.

In Maths, watching the clock, listening for the bell, Mrs Raffety, the school secretary, stuck her head in the door.

"Mia, a minute please."

In the corridor Mrs Raffety produced her fake concerned expression.

"Your mum's work colleague phoned. Your mum's unwell Mia; she needs you at home. She thinks your mum might need help getting to A&E."

Mia nodded; her lips tightly compressed muzzling the words liar, snake, pagan! Not Mrs Raffety, her mum! She wasn't fucking ill!

Mia stormed out of school her head fit to explode? Not thinking clearly. Rushing. Not looking left. Mia stepped out into the road.

"SCREECH!"

Hard metal skidded to a stop; barely an inch from Mia.

"Jesus. You kids, never fucking looking," shouted the driver from the car window.

Mia stood...transfixed by the bonnet...how much would it hurt if it hit her?

"Are you ok?" shouted the driver roughly.

How fast did a car have to be travelling to kill you instantly?

"Jesus, you stepped out of nowhere. What the fuck's the matter with you?"

"Everything," said Mia desperate to escape before she sunk onto the road and attempted to dig underground to the earth's core. "It's my fault," she said. "It always is."

On the train Mia subsided on to a seat, weak, drained by her mum's plotting. On the second train Mia's disappointment turned to hope. Maybe her liver stopped cleaning spirits.   "Mum," she cried flying through the door desperate to find her in cardiac arrest.

"Down here love."

Her mum was fused with the kitchen table. Carmen rollers on full heat. Foundation dotting her cheeks, chin and forehead. Slowly she covered her crevices. A cigarette was lit, balancing on an ashtray. A glass of wine had a lipstick mouth imprinted on it.

"Mum, I...I don't understand," Mia panted.

"Oh Mia a migraine struck at work. It was crippling. Mr George, the chairman, said 'Joslyn, we're sending you home. You've worked too hard. You're so dedicated. There's no one like you'."

That's fucking true. Mia's chest tightened. A dizziness, a loss of focus; confusion that her world was rotating too quickly culminated in Mia wanting to strike, to kick out, to scream till her lungs burst. Instead, she sucked the anger in but internalising her hate was poisoning her...making her think dark thoughts.

"Mia, don't worry Love. I'm fine. Hugh's picking me up shortly."

"But I was going to Gabby's and then..."

"Then what Mia? Gabby this, Gabby that, I'm sick of her. Oh Mia, you really let me down. I'm seriously ill and you're thinking about yourself and some girl you hardly know."

Her mum's bitter words, her abrasive tone, warned Mia to tread carefully.

"I didn't expect you to be going out, that's all, not after being terminally ill."

"How. Dare. You! I'm up every morning, working my fingers to the bone, worrying about food, electricity, rent. No wonder I'm ill. But I don't make a drama of it. I carry on. I won't let Hugh down. If I make an arrangement, I honour it. It's not good to be selfish Mia."

After Joslyn left, Mia wandered aimlessly around. She wouldn't phone Gabs until certain she wouldn't break down. Sitting on her mum's bed she stared hard at a notepad. A page had been half ripped off. An indentation was visible. With a pencil Mia shaded across a series of numbers. She turned to S in the phone book. It was the school's number. Her mum had phoned the fucking school. Not a colleague. Her mum!

Mia no longer referred to Gabby in her mum's presence. Mia kept secret the four times she'd slept over at Gabby's. The comparison of family life was unsettling. Gab's family were relaxed, teasing, helpful and loving. Her and her mum weren't normal.

When her mum went to Dublin on a long weekend Mia invited Gabby over. They'd watched scary movies late into the night, stuffed themselves silly with sweets and it was fun because Gabs had never been home alone. For breakfast Mia grilled bacon, scrambled eggs, and toasted waffles. Gabs was dead impressed. The girls were chomping away, the radio on loud, nattering, when Mia heard.

Metal twisting in metal; the front door opening.

Mia's head, like a deflating balloon, whizzed erratically as panic escaped at speed.

The stairs; the click of nails against the wooden stair rail.

Gabby's lips moving.

Another step; the thud magnified. Mia's ear drums swelled, trapping the noises of Joslyn's descent.

"Mia?" said Gabby nervously.

Joslyn appeared out of focus. Her lips massive; forming friend-breaking words. With that chilled, acidic voice of hers.

"I'll pack my stuff Mia; nice to meet you Mrs Dent," Gabby smiled weakly.

"No! Stay!"

Two sharp words, so cold they stuck together like icepops.

"Where's my jewellery?"

Mia knew what was coming. Joslyn had played this trick with Hugh's daughter.

"I left the bracelet your dad gave me for my twenty-first in this bowl."

"You can't have mum, otherwise it would be there."

"It was there when I left on Friday."

"Then it would still be there."

"Are you calling me a liar?"

"No Mum...Mum, please," Mia begged. "Don't."

"Don't what Mia?"

Tears were on tipping point.

"Please Mum I won't ask anyone over again...I promise."

Tears rolled over the rims of Mia's eyes. She retreated, huddling

71

in the corner of the kitchen wanting to disappear, to be the grout between the kitchen tiles, to be the water dripping from the tap escaping down the plug hole.

Gabby, pale and shocked was horrified by the sight of a desperately crying Mia. Joslyn's words were like her alcohol: sharp, bitter and hard for a teen to swallow.

"You have my bracelet."

"No, Mrs Dent."

"Liar!"

Gabby turned to a distraught Mia.

"Mia! What's she talking about?"

"It's my fault. I'm so sorry Gabs."

"Yes Mia, it is your fault, for befriending a little tart who's a thief."

Gabby crying, raced upstairs with Mia not far behind.

"Gabby, I'm sorry...please talk to me. Tell me what to do and I'll do it." Mia crying, tried to hug Gabby but Gabby shook her off and phoned her dad.

"Gabby, are you still my best friend? Please Gabby, say we are friends."

Gabby never spoke to Mia again. At school their estrangement was hot gossip. Mia knew Gabby had revealed all because of the way kids looked at her; like she was to be pitied.

****

"Your recollection of events gives you a motive to harm your mother," Webber pointed out.

"I've never denied wanting to hurt her."

"You spent a great deal of time considering how to bump your mum off...did that concern you?" asked Webber.

"I reported myself to the police, so I guess it worried me at one point. Retrospectively, I think the time spent was proportionate to my mum's character."

"But things changed?" asked Webber.

"Yes, not overnight, but over a period of time."

"And where was Flynn in all this?"

"I dipped in and out of my fantasy with Flynn, mainly I thought about him at night, romanticising. Sometimes I spotted him on the train, sometimes, when I felt down, I'd seek him out on the platform. Flynn was an innocent teenage crush at this point."

"Ok, take us back. What happened after your reconciliation with Gabby?"

"I started working at the White Bear. I remember weighing myself that first morning, in my new black underwear. I'd lost nine pounds, the swimming was firming me up, I was beginning to like the way I looked...I felt happy.

****

CHAPTER 11   BAUBLES AND BREAKUPS

Alex cast an eye over his new employee. She was doing well; competent and not a slacker. She seemed a genuinely nice, straightforward girl, if a little shy, but pub work brought people out of their shell. He'd sat with her at break; they'd had a full English. Alex liked how unselfconscious she was eating. The twenty minutes left little time for chatting, just movie talk between mouthfuls, but as first impressions went, Mia was a ten.

****

School was ok. Even the arduous journey from the flat to Sloane Square was less bothersome. It was the reverse journey that disturbed her. Leaving Chelsea for West London was bordering on cruel. As Mia walked toward Peter Jones, with its large lit windows filled with beautiful Christmas displays, a dull pain would settle like sediment in her chest. It wasn't merely the beautiful things in the shop windows, things she couldn't afford, it was the town houses. They elicited an unsettled response from her. Their lights glowed from dusk till dawn regardless of fuel costs. Mia would look beyond the gleaming black painted railings, through the large, ornate windows graced with fairy lights. She saw the mantels of elaborate fireplaces with shiny photo frames but it was the evergreen fir stretching up to the high ceiling that made her gut contract. The desire to walk through a glossy painted door burned painfully inside her. She wanted to hang her blazer on their stair post, sit beneath their Christmas tree. She hated her estate with its dark corners and creepy lowlifes. She hated the lift some screw-up pissed in every day. She hated the stairwells that were a collage of everything wrong with the world. She hated the airless, colourless corridors with their artificial light. But what Mia hated most was the relationship she had with the woman beyond the door. How it festered in a prison with no decorative iron front gate, no geraniums in large terracotta pots, no street facing windows. No hope.

One thing Mia remembered from GCSE Biology was osmosis; she worried her mum's cells had moved into hers during pregnancy. Determined not to be a self-centred, joy sucking parasite Mia wore her happy face and swung through the doors of the White Bear.

"Hi guys," she sung taking comfort from new friendships.

"Hi Mia," said Kelly. "Bad news; there's puke in the toilet again."

"Hi Mia," welcomed Alex.

"Hi Alex. No worries, I'm on it."

"At least it's not a stuck sanitary towel blocking the bowl."

"Kel, too much information alert," chastised Alex watching Mia pick up a cork and pocket it. He smiled; it seemed he was attracted to a pretty magpie.

****

First term at uni over; Flynn's guts felt poisoned from alcohol and his throat was raw from cheap corner-shop spirits. Driving home was a mistake. He should have caught the train. Instead here he was…what a wanker! Shaking his head, Flynn's eyelids wearily fluttered; his vision was losing focus; he wasn't used to driving long distances and Exeter to London was a bloody long distance. He glanced at the speedometer; sixty miles per hour; he reduced his speed to fifty. The rain didn't help; it merged the landscape; grey sky, grey trees, grey road.

"Swindon. Services five miles ahead, thank fuck."

Flynn parked near the complex, in a space among other vehicles. Locking his car he felt a vulnerability that went hand in hand with unfamiliar, isolated carparks. He speedily strode inside the building with its lights, warmth and people. In the coffee bar, with a latte, pain au raisin and The Evening Standard, he sat near the window to keep an eye on his car. The Wolf headlined. Flynn wished he could turn the page and ignore the freak preying on young women, but his eyes ran left to right and down a line until he turned to page sixteen where the article continued. The Wolf's first victim, sixteen year old Becca Smith went missing four years ago. She'd left a friend's house at ten pm to walk the short distance home. Somewhere in between she vanished. Becca's family life was unstable, she'd runaway before so the police deemed nothing suspicious about her disappearance. Ashley Tate was the second victim. Eighteen. She'd done time in juvey. She was couch surfing. Leaving a pub, she'd never made it to her friend's settee. The police decided she was a runaway.

Flynn sat back. He looked out the window for a minute. The darkness embedded a mounting sense of dread. Eight fucking girls in four years; all under twenty, all from West London. It wasn't until Tilly Andrews disappearance that the police started asking questions. Tilly, the third victim, A* student, the daughter of MP Clare Andrews.

Flynn suddenly felt under scrutiny. In the window, he saw the reflection of a bloke's gaze; locked on him. Maybe he wasn't staring at Flynn? Maybe he too was looking out the window. Slowly Flynn turned around catching the man's eye. He looked rough and muscled up. Shit, thought Flynn, he's standing up.   He's walking toward…

"Mate, you finished with the paper?"

"The paper?" asked Flynn cautiously.

"Football mate, quick catch up before I head off."

Flynn wondered, if he was scared of a bloke in a coffee shop, how fearful had Petra been, when hands tightened around her throat? Had she gasped frantically, hanging onto her last breath, terrified, knowing no one was coming for her, that this was it.

****

Everyone was talking about the school disco, what they'd wear, arranging shopping outings, chatting about music and slow dances. Mia bought a ticket. It was red with a sprig of holly in each corner and *Christmas Disco, 7pm-10pm, School Hall,* written in italics. Mia felt a quiver of excitement. Music and dancing…it had the potential to be so much fun if she found something to wear. She'd left it to the actual night giving herself optimum time for weight loss. Bad idea!

Traipsing from one store to another she concluded she was too fat for fashion. Skinny jeans needed skinny legs. Sleeveless garments needed toned arms. The changing room mirrors famous for making girls look slimmer were faulty. Dresses highlighted her rounded stomach or strained unpleasantly across her chest. Tops fitted in one place then gaped in another.   She thought everything looked ugly on her fleshy body but she was wrong. She judged herself through her mother's eyes which were skewed. She decided not to go to the disco, but walking into the flat of impending doom Mia was told otherwise.

"Mia, did you get something for the disco?"

Her mum's voice, rich with excitement, immediately put Mia on edge.

"No. I'll give the disco a miss I have a tummy ache."

"Mia, you're going." No discussion. No conferring. Do as you're told language. Her mum was fluent. Each word that followed struck Mia.

"I've." SLAP.

"Got." SLAP.

"You." SLAP.

"The." SLAP.

"Perfect." SLAP.

"Outfit." SLAP.

Mia stared at the yale lock, considering escape, before zombie-like descending to the kitchen. She didn't speak. Whatever she said would be wrong unless it was: I. Love. It. But she didn't. The cerise, ruched, silky, trouser two-piece was hateful, tacky and gaudy. Mia stretched her eyeballs, painfully trapping the tears.

"Mia, why so quiet."

Joslyn's sharp tone tore at Mia's confidence.

"Tummy bug; I can't go. You should take it back."

"Don't tell me what to do."

The walls closed in on Mia.

"Look at me when I'm speaking."

Mia raised her eyes. Joslyn noted their brightness.

"It's lovely isn't it?" Joslyn asked smiling, her lips thin, her eyes hawk-like.

"It's different," said Mia carefully.

"Mia, why the sour face?"

"It's not what kids wear to discos."

"Don't be stupid Mia, it's exactly that. Where else would you wear it?"

No fucking where! She'd never live it down. They'd remember it at school reunions years down the line.

"I work bloody hard. For a selfish daughter with a figure that's hard to conceal."

"TWIST."

That noise, the turning, the breaking of the wine seal. Mia's head pounded.

"BLUB, BLUB, BLUB."

The liquid pouring into the tumbler. Mia couldn't breathe.

"GULP."

The sound of the swallow. I can't do this anymore, Mia screamed in her head.

"Bleddy hell Mia! You've lost a little weight but you're not a standard size."

"It's too fussy for me. Kids wear jeans to school discos."

"Mia you're too big for jeans. How many times have I told you?"

Mia felt dizzy...she wanted to go to the knife draw and slit her wrists.

"I tried it on myself, I looked fabulous."

Mia wanted to scream, LIAR! Nobody could make that polyugly wearable.

"Get ready."

"Mum, please, I." Mia was cut off.

"I'm phoning Faye and Iris; they'll be shocked at how ungrateful you are."

 Mia's aunts. The Macbeth witches. Gathered around a bottle of Jameson's they saw things. Blurred things. Crazy things. Dangerous things.

"Mum it's got nothing to do with them."

"I'm honest Mia; don't put lies on me. You explain to them right now!"

"I'll wear it."

"I should think so. You'll be the death of me."

Die then, Mia wanted to scream until her throat was raw.

Upstairs, in front of her mum's long mirror Mia roughly pulled the monstrosity on.

"The award for most fugly freak goes to...yes...Mia Dent. Well folks Mia's won this award three years running, let's give her a round of applause."

Mia raised her hand to her head, her thumb and forefinger pointed like a gun.

"Bang!"

"Mia come down," Joslyn shouted excitedly. "Mia you look lovely. The rouching covers your width beautifully."

Kelis' I Hate You So Much Right Now, played repeatedly in Mia's brain; only that line. Real mothers didn't strap their daughters to a rack and pull them apart for the world to see.

Constable Emma Hall hated working the Friday night shift – dawn of the walking wankers. Drunks falling over, getting up, drinking, falling again.

Crossing reception, Emma noticed the teen sitting beside a chavalanche of drunk girls with running mascara. Emma took the lift to the canteen. As the doors opened, buzzing conversation and the smell of coffee reminded Emma she'd not had a break in five hours.

"Hey Emma," shouted Dave from a table filled with laughing officers. "Hear you're moving in with those tossers upstairs?"

"Got the confirmation yesterday," replied Emma, joining the food queue, still on a high over her sergeant's recommendation to the Major Incident Team.

"Hey Carol…cappuccino and rhubarb pastry please."

"Three days in a row constable," smiled Carol from behind the counter.

"Need my sugar rush Carol."

Emma clocked DS Raymond at a table. Her dealings with him were limited but he had a habit of cutting her off mid sentence and dismissing her feedback. He was the only member of the team she disliked.

"Two twenty love," said the cashier.

Rooting around her pocket, Emma dug out the right change. Coffee in hand, she headed back to reception only to witness a man staggering in with blood pouring down his face. Emma glanced toward the teenager; she looked ready to keel over.

"Excuse me, why are you waiting?" asked Emma putting her body between the teenager and the bloodied man.

"I want to turn myself in."

"Have you committed a crime?"

"Nearly," admitted Mia; half-scared, half-desperate to say it aloud. "I'm worried I might harm my mother."

"Where is your mother now?" asked Constable Hall.

"The Prince of Wales or The Bull or The Case Is Altered."

"Is she safe there?"

"I hope not."

Constable Hall assessed the teenager. Wide-open eyes, never

79

shifting, no nervous tick, no self- hugging, no tapping of fingers or feet.

"Mia. We are busy people. I appreciate you dislike your mother but wishing a parent dead is not unusual. You've no police record, no history of violence or mental illness so there's not much we can do."

"But thinking about committing a crime must be illegal?"

"Have you purchased a weapon to commit murder?"

"No. I'd probably use something handy at the time."

"Have you asked anyone to support you in committing a murder?"

"No. It's a personal matter."

"Relationships with parents can have more lows than highs."

"It's more than that," Mia interrupted. "My head is bursting with hate. I'm frightened I'll lash out. I do want her dead but I don't want to go to prison or have to tell my children I murdered Granny."

"Mia, you being here tells me you're a good kid struggling with the emotion of hating. You're not a killer."

"I get urges, I could snap. I'm an active volcano; one more slurp of alcohol or puff of a cigarette and they'll be lava everywhere."

"Mia, could you sleep over at friends now and again?"

"I don't have friends."

"What? Come on you must have mates."

Mia shook her head convincingly.

"You have no friends whatsoever?" asked Constable Hall.

"Correct."

"Why?"

"My mum is dangerous. People around her get hurt. Like Chloe."

"Who's Chloe?"

"My best friend before Gabby."

"What happened?"

"Chloe and I travelled on the Circle Line to school. We met in the end carriage. We laughed about nothing and everything. Together we made thin air hilarious." Mia paused, remembering. "I miss those days," she sighed. "I haven't laughed; I mean belly laughed since Chloe left. Anyways, I asked my mum could Chloe sleep over. I didn't understand my mother back then. How racist and jealous she was. I hadn't thought about Chloe being black – why would I? She was just Chloe. All the while my mum teetered on the edge, gulping wine, unnerving me, giving me evils, pinching me, whispering horrid things about black people in my ear. I was sick scared: what if Chloe heard, what if she thought I was racist. I never asked Chloe back. Then she moved to Northampton. We were pen pals for ages until she stopped writing. I wrote asking had I upset her, but she never replied. I was gutted. I questioned myself. Had I said something bitchy…did I come across like a loser? Then randomly I was searching through the suitcase under mum's bed where her paperwork is; I needed my vaccination date for the school records."

Mia gulped. Although the crime was years ago, the pain still lingered.

"I found pink and blue envelopes with an s.w.a.h."

"What did that signify," asked Constable Hall.

"Sealed with a hug...Are you getting the picture?"

"Yes," said Emma sympathetically.

Mia stood up. It had to be done. She shrugged off her coat.

Emma's eyes all but popped out of her head.

"Now that is a motive."

****

He watched her exit the police station. She stood for what seemed an age; the loneliest girl in the world. She had shades of his second, Ashley Tate. Taking her had been a mistake. She'd been a small, brittle girl; her skin nearly transparent. She looked much younger than eighteen and that's what attracted him. The first girl had been completely random. He came across her arguing with a boy. He appreciated how impulsive and reactive teenage girls were. She'd freaked out at the boy; fuck this, fuck that. The boy strutted away; the girl stormed off. He'd: followed, watched, taken. Now? He'd go to his office, stare at a spreadsheet whilst delicious images of him restraining a girl played out in his head. He was sick, he knew that, but he was also without conscience…a requisite if you wanted to abduct schoolgirls to use for your pleasure.

****

On autopilot her legs took her to Jay's; a boy she was attracted to, who she didn't know, who'd barely spoken to her. She knew it was odd. Weird. Obsessive. Yet she sat on the garden wall of the house opposite, her eyes fixed on the third floor. Her body was shivering from wearing thin polyugly, but her head was filled with so much possibility she felt woozy. His car was parked outside. Jay was back.

****

Alex had one eye on his job, the other on the pub entrance.   Mia opened the pub door releasing lively, collective banter into the frosty Chelsea evening. The pub was packed but she slipped through the crowd. Alex loved how she beamed at him as he lifted the bar's hinged door.

"Mia," said Alex warmly, restraining himself from pulling her to him and kissing her off her feet. "Condom machine in the ladies is empty; key is on my desk, would you mind."

"Got to do our bit promoting safe sex. Then I'll top up the tonic water."

Pulling a pint Alex winked. He appreciated how nicely Mia filled her trousers. She beavered away bringing up stock from the cellar and refilling the shelves, humming along to the latest tunes. She'd been a good hire. Three months in and he wondered how they'd managed without her. She worked well with Toby. He took the plated orders to the customers, cleared and cleaned the tables, arranged the menus and manned the men's toilets. Mia worked on refilling stock, food prep and cleaning. She sliced and diced like Hannibal. Each time the knife was in Mia's hand he thought he saw her smile wickedly. She was a quirky thing…interested in everything even the rat poison in the cellar.

"How'd your school disco go? Anyone sneak in alcohol or were they all pissed from pre drinks?"

Alex noted Mia's eyes stray.

"It was fine," said Mia uncommittedly.

"You didn't go, did you?" asked Alex gently.

Mia turned to Alex.

"No. I didn't go."

"Wanna talk about it?"

This was a moment, Alex felt it.

"It was nothing."

Alex felt a pang of disappointment. She barely knew him; he got it, but he wanted her to trust him. She was a hedgehog. Each time he got near to drawing out her history, she curled up into a spiky ball.

As if she felt his dismay she carried on, her tone light as if it were

82

trivial.

"Horrific wardrobe malfunction; I may never be able to talk about it," she laughed.

But Alex knew it was definitely something.

"Fairs. I didn't do the whole school disco thing myself. Being a ghoulish goth, if it wasn't The Cure or Jack White it wasn't music. I've evolved since then."

"I don't know if Taylor Swift is evolving."

"Shut up. I only like one song."

"Gorgeous?"

"Good of you to notice," smiled Alex.

****

First day of the Christmas holiday and Mia was up at six, brimming over with excitement. Eating porridge with sliced banana and chocolate drops, she felt amazing. She'd lost another three pounds. She was up to twenty lengths in the pool. At boxing the gyminals were losing interest in her: the sniggers had stopped, and the cold shoulders were down. The icing on the cake? Jay was back. But she wasn't going all obssessy over him. Out of interest she'd see if he was as hot as she remembered. She headed to Kensington; reasoning with herself, it gave her space from her mum and Kevin. Once there she covertly passed Jay's car, casting her eyes over the interior in search of clues. Like the sweatshirt on the backseat with Exeter University stitched on the front. Smiling, she walked, crisscrossing the road.

"Morning dear."

Mia looked at the elderly lady coming unsteadily out of number twenty-nine.

"Morning," replied Mia. "Ooh be careful, your frosty path looks slippery."

"Arghhhh."

Mia lunged forward, her arms wrapping around the oap underneath her armpits.

"Oh lovie," she cried shakily.

"I've got you," reassured Mia; the lady's weight burning her muscles. "Can you grab the handrail?"

"Yes lovie, I've got it," breathed out the relieved pensioner.

Mia pushed her forward toward the rail. Jesus, she was heavy.

"Thank goodness you were here dear," she said, her face mottled red, her hat too far to the left. "Would you help me inside, I'm shaken lovie."

"Sure. I'm Mia."

"Vera Hornby lovie. Nice to meet you."

With Mrs Hornby's key Mia opened the door aiding Mrs Hornby into the dark, dank hallway. Thinking this house could be the same as Jay's Mia's eyes darted around. Mothballs thought Mia…and spiders; she shivered, noting a web in every corner.

"Should I call someone for you?" volunteered Mia.

"No lovie, make us both a cuppa. Everything's there on the tray."

Indeed it was. Mrs Hornby was well prepared. Two teacups on saucers sat on a tray along with a sugar bowl and two small milk jugs.

"These are like the one's in the coffee shop," said Mia.

"Yes dear, that's where I pinched them from. It's how a pensioner lives on the edge."

Mia smiled, sitting down at the kitchen table. It was oval, covered in a once-white, lace tablecloth scarred with tea rings. Through the window Mia made out a jungle of overgrown grass, weeds and shrubs. Perfect site to bury her mum.

"Were you off to the shops?"

"Yes lovie, I need a few provisions."

"I'll go for you," Mia decided.

"Oh lovie, I can't ask that. You young ones always have places to go. Hanging out – is that what they call it dear?"

"Yes," Mia smiled. "What do you need?" asked Mia scrambling in her bag for pen and paper.

****

As Christmas approached Joslyn's drinking cranked up a notch. It was well into the early hours when Mia heard a commotion at the front door. Looking through the spy hole she saw her mum shaking Kevin off whilst firing incantations at him. Hugh, Kevin, Hugh, Kevin, her mum chopped and changed. Mia jumped back from the door as Joslyn flung it open. The gin-ch had returned. Every year she scrooged Christmas. It was never about baby Jesus!

Mia's festive vibe sunk. Closing the door brought Mia nearer to Joslyn. To her wine breath. Contaminating the aroma of the oranges, pierced with cloves, placed around the flat. Mia shrunk back as Joslyn cast a shadow over the shimmering tinsel decorating the hallway.

"Kevin stole my bracelet, the one your dad gave me for my twenty-first."

Mia bit her tongue to prevent 'liar' exploding from her mouth. The gold bracelet accusation again! How she hated that particular lie more than any other in her mum's repertoire. Mia watched Joslyn stumble downstairs before Mia slipped back under her duvet.

"Phew," Mia breathed out, then in, then out "Phew."
Relaxing was tricky when your drunken mother might set the flat alight with a cigarette left burning.

"Meeeeeeee.errrrrrrr."

"Christmas is going to be a fucking car crash."

****

Stan opened at six twenty and there she was, sitting on a crate, huddled in a coat, her large bright eyes peeping out between a scruffy bobble hat and a fur collar.

"Family had enough of you?"

"Sort of."

She had either no family or they were shit because she was a fucking chatterbox who talked about everything under the fucking sun apart from friends and family.

"Better put the kettle on," said Stan offhandedly.

"Did you see last night's episode?"

Love Island! For fuck's sake, she had him watching it. He cracked a smile. She clanked the mugs, setting them on his office table, taking the seat opposite. He knew the first time he saw Mia there'd be no getting rid. A girl didn't come to a gym like this unless she was desperate. Maybe that's why she was tolerated; abused people recognised their own.

"Can't believe I'm up so early. I did a double shift at the Bear because Toby was at the Lovebox festival. He's a huge Childish Gambino fan. Well, he likes all music but..."

"Stop moving your mouth."

"Ok."

They drank. Mia stared into her mug as half her soggy digestive plummeted into the darkness of black tea.

"Your fitness has improved," said Stan.

Mia nodded not wanting to break the spell of Stan speaking.

"It's quiet now, I'll do the circuit with you."

"Really?" Mia gushed, her tea spilling over the mug rim.

"I must be fucking mad," he said shaking his head

****

Becca put the condiments on the table. Then the placemats. Then the cutlery.

"The brown sauce," he commented lightly.

She felt herself jolt...before turning hastily to the cupboard then almost running to the table with it.

"This fork is dirty."

She froze. It couldn't be. She'd washed it so hard beforehand.

"Only joking. Come and sit down, eat the chips while they're hot."

She sat down, she had no appetite.

"Nearer."

She moved up the sofa.

"Nearer."

Her bare thigh touched his.

"Where's the vinegar?"

She tensed.

"Don't worry. I'll get it."

Immediately, fear began to smoother her. Her chest tightened, her throat constricted.

He put an empty glass in front of her before shaking vinegar over his chips smiling.

"I'll pour yours."

He removed the plastic top off the vinegar, allowing the liquid to pour into the glass. He filled it a millimetre from the top.

"Don't spill any."

Her hands shook as she placed them around the glass. Scared to lift it Becca lowered her mouth to the glass and swallowed her first mouthful. Her eyes watered from the sharpness of it. On the third mouthful its acidity caused her throat to burn. By the time she'd finished the glass, intestinal pain struck.

****

The train pulled into High Street Ken. Mia positioned herself in front of the doors, ready to jump off. She didn't register that Jay was on the platform, ready to board. The doors opened. They mirrored each other's side-stepping. Smiling, Flynn recognised the girl who had huge difficulty conquering the most basic, routine movement.

Mia looked fleetingly at Jay.

"I've made a mistake," she blurted out, stepping back to allow Jay to board.

A few times Flynn looked in the girl's direction catching the merest glimpse of her head turning. Was she looking at him? Yeah, she was, he decided. Flynn smiled to himself. Initially, she stood out for all the wrong reasons but today? She'd lost considerable weight since he'd seen her last. Good for her. She looked fashionable but her hair remained unstyled; it was thick and dull. Her lips were dry and cracked. Her nose was red and flaky. Yet he felt this ridiculous impulse to talk to her.

Mia studied Jay's reflection in the train doors. His hair looked chestnutty shiny and glorious; Mia wanted to touch it, to feel its richness between her fingers. Mia felt a gnawing in her stomach; once again they were apart but together.

Nearing the centre of town, people filled the aisles and Jay's image was distorted by movement and bodies.

Mia stood when he stood; she exited through his door.

At the ticket barrier, their bodies compressed together; it was too good an opportunity: Mia gently tugged once, twice, until the scarf came away from Jay's neck into her hands. She didn't think of it as stealing more as primary research. Quickly she pushed it into her rucksack. Up the stairs at Piccadilly the wind rushed her, she wanted to laugh, she felt elated. At Leicester Square he hesitated, looking around. Mia squatted as if doing up her lace; waiting…until she saw his Timberlands cross the square to a ferris wheel.

"Hey mate, how much?"

"£3 mate."

"I'll have a ticket…Cheers."

Jay sat in a carriage.

"Any singles? £3 a go," the operator shouted.

Mia's heart jumped. Was Jay kind? He seemed to be. Would he mind her sitting beside him; a fat, plain girl. The yearning to be physically close to Jay was subdued by doubt and minimal self-worth. Mia wanted reassuring arms around her, a tender kiss against her cheek, Jay's warm hand covering hers. What did those endearments feel like she wondered?

"Flynnnnnn."

"Kira, quick, pay up and jump in."

Mia clutched her chest; her pulse increasing till it hammered. She turned from Flynn? Not Jay. Flynn. A heart arrhythmia struck as a tall, red head, equally as beautiful as Flynn, clambered into his carriage, all legs and floaty-ness.

Mia's legs barely carried her back to Warwick Avenue. What had she been thinking? Of course he'd have a girlfriend. Flynn and Kira made Flynn and Mia sound lame. It hurt, like when Tommy Prichard booted the football in her stomach. And the time one of her mum's sleazes came onto her but Joslyn took the sleaze's side. It was then Mia realised her mother didn't have her back.

Mia was gutted. Her insides torn out by some Victoria Secrets model. All that remained was for her to climb back into her cocoon and shrivel up; another caterpillar who never made it.

Unconsciously, she found herself at the nail bar. She needed comfort; some form of human contact. Sitting on a sofa she studied the skin on her hands. It was like sand on a deserted cove; no footprints. Maybe she was one of those unreachable beaches.

She thought of Flynn on the short walk to the flat. He had a girlfriend; good! It was a reason to move on. Out of nowhere Mia thought of Alex. God he cracked her up, he was so much fun. She felt totally comfortable around him. He was a top boy. Mia wondered if he had a Victoria Secrets model too?

Mia entered the estate cautiously, her eyes scanning the landscape. Recently she'd avoided confrontation, but an attack was imminent. She must have a second sense because on opening the flat door she was met with white feathers. They might seem fluffy and cute but covering your carpet they were a message…like they were calling you out because you were weak or a coward or some other shit. She pulled them painstakingly from the carpet because they'd meshed with the rough carpet fibres. They'd completely taken the shine off her lovely Russian Blue manicured nails.

Shaken, she got down to homework. She was progressing well on her diet, mainly because she was too frightened to eat! The sound of Mia's door handle made her jump.

"Hello love. Fancy a cuppa?"

Mia swore the room temperature dipped a few degrees. Her mum hadn't knocked. There was no mutual respect. It was a shitty way to live, but after the feathers she was glad not to be alone.

"Yes please.   Mum, have you ever been on a sun bed?"

"No Love."

"There's a sunbed shop in Shirland Road. Fifty pence for one minute. I know it's dangerous long term but maybe a few sessions to get a base would be ok. It would be nice not to be so pale in my swimming costume."

"They'd have a weight restriction love. They're for slim girls. You can sit on the balcony and catch a colour with me in the summer. We can have a glass of wine."

Even when she was nice she was horrific. Mia hoped that tonight in the car with some sap they'd have a fatal accident that only harmed her mother. It was her and only her who should be catapulted through the windscreen and impaled on railings.

Hairs on Mia's neck stiffened as the malevolent force mutated from caring to critical. Mia eyed her Bear Grylls' poster. He'd seen many faces of danger but not her mum's.

"What are you doing."

"Art."

"Isn't that a waste of time."

"No," replied Mia through gritted teeth.

"You don't get a job studying art Mia."

"Architect, marketing, advertising, web design, there's loads of jobs."

Joslyn picked up Mia's hand mid-drawing.

"You painted your nails Mia."

89

"Yes."

"What? You painted them yourself?"

"Erm, no, a nail technician painted them."

"Why lie about it?"

"I wasn't lying, I thought you were making a casual comment about my nails."

"You spent money on your nails? How stupid. You haven't a boyfriend."

Be brave Mia.

"I did it for me."

Joslyn looked at Mia like she was nobody – before exiting the room and shortly the flat. Picking up her guitar, Mia strummed away, playing around with lyrics.

"My mum's a bitch,
Wish she was found dead in a ditch,
 yeah, yeah, yeah.
She causes pain,
I'll push her in front of a train,
 Yeah, yeah, yeah.
Am I bad?
No…she fucked over my dad,
Yeah, yeah, yeah."

****

Early the following morning Mia woke under the burden every child with a broken parent bears. She remembered the small triumph of standing up to her mum. Then she remembered the feathers, pushed back the quilt and got round the gym. Although it was barely eight, the gym buzzed. Some members slept rough, some members got chucked out of their hostels early.

"Morning Stan," Mia said sheepishly. "Can."

"No, you can't, you're still banned."

"Stubborn old goat."

"I heard that," said Stan.

Mia went straight for the punch bag, hammering it while thinking of her mum.

"You!"

Mia, startled, looked over to Stan who was ringside.

"Me?" she asked incredulously, even though she knew she was the only 'you' in the gym. There was Tink, Steve, Mick, Tombstone and Mia was 'You'.

"You wanna learn how to box or not?"

Tombstone was in the ring. Stan held up the ropes. Mia ducked under.

"Your aim is to not let Tombstone make contact."

Mia stood there like a gherkin.

"Arms up, protect yourself," said Stan.

Mia looked seriously at Tombstone.

"Remember I'm a girl. Make allowances; as of this minute I'm not into equality."

"Shut it," said Stan.

"Fine. I thought some ground rules…"

Tombstone landed a soft blow to Mia's abdomen.

"Ahhh, that hurt. I'm not even eighteen; I'm a child!"

Stan was pushing a mouth guard toward her mouth.

"Open."

Mia daren't think where it had last been.

Next a guard was pulled over her head squashing her ears.

Tombstone made contact again.

"Oi, no one said the word go."

Tombstone struck again.

"Ahh."

"Fists up for fucks sake!" shouted Stan bewildered how he was gonna teach this one!

"Christ," he said stepping forward, positioning her fists, demonstrating how to move for maximum protection.

The slight blows didn't hurt exactly, not at first, but repeatedly getting roughed up was hard.

"Move your arms up and down. Don't stand there. Make it difficult for him; cut and weave. Christ. Not like that. Like this. How many times have I got to show you."

Mia tried to pay attention but she was losing focus.

91

"You're going to have to get a fucking lot lighter on your feet than that…Jesus keep your eyes on Tombstone. You don't have to look at me to hear me."

Mia was stumbling all over the ring.

"Time," called Stan.

Mia attempted to high five Tombstone with her glove. Not raising his hand Mia fell forward onto the ropes.

"Christ," said Stan shaking his head.

"Stan is there a box to put my gloves in…my mum doesn't know about boxing."

"Take a locker, might as well, you've nearly moved in."

"Would that mean a lock might go on the shower door."

"Fuck off."

Mia sensed a smidgen of endearment in his tone.

"I'm off to work now," Mia shouted in the middle of the gym, no one paying the least attention. "Happy Christmas. I've left mince pies in Stan's office." No goodbyes but she wasn't jeered either. Her sense of well-being increased as she approached The White Bear.

"Morning Alex, Happy Christmas," shouted Mia walking into the empty pub.

Alex sprung up from behind the bar, loving Mia's almost lyrical tone.

"Morning. Glad you're here. I'm on my own and I have a two-person job."

"Ok," said Mia. "I'll hang up my coat..."

"No, stay," Alex said coming around the bar, approaching Mia, firmly putting his hands on each forearm.

"Back-up, good, now one step to the left, perfect," he said. They stood, eyes locked. She had an impulse to brush aside a stray hair from Alex's forehead. A thought dawned. She looked up, at the mistletoe hanging from the beam, then at Alex, who slowly lowered his mouth to hers, kissing her gently.

"It's bad luck if you hang mistletoe and the first two people to come across it don't kiss," he said authoritatively, lying through his teeth.

"Really?" asked Mia, totally surprised, unsure what to say.

"Absolutely," Alex continued to lie. "I know how professional you are. That and the fact you love Christmas made you the perfect tester. Also a kiss under mistletoe protects you from Christmas humbug."

"But I didn't kiss you back, so maybe it wasn't a proper kiss," said Mia, it dawning on her that maybe Alex wanted to kiss her…and…that she wanted to kiss him too.

"Good observation. We've got to do this thing right. Ready?"

Mia, on tip toes, reached up and found his lips with hers and gently pressing, then pulling, they kissed, for at least twenty seconds, all the while their hearts beating hard.

"Ok," said Alex looking into Mia's sparkly blue eyes, feeling like he'd conquered the skin walkers. "Second job of the day, stocking the shelves while I make you a cuppa."

Alex returned with two mugs a little scared things could be awkward.

"Mia, take it easy, you're clinking bottles dangerously down there," laughed Alex. "What's got your goat…you're usually Little Miss Happy."

"My mum…her boyfriend."

"What about him? Not perving on you is he?"

"No, his eyes don't stray where they shouldn't but this morning I found myself in an uncomfortable position squeezing past him in our narrow hallway. It's horrible; a strange man sitting at the table where your dad should be. It's bothersome having to be suitably dressed and having football and racing on our only t.v…and I hate small, aimless talk: How are you? Fine. School ok? Yes. What's worse is my mum's pretence of interest in my life." Lining up bottles of tonic water and orange juice, Mia's body stiffened thinking of her mum's sickly sweet proclamations of love. "She keeps harping on how she's dedicated her life to me and I want to scream: no mum you fucking didn't!"

"Sounds shit Mia; sorry."

Mia glanced up at Alex, craning her neck and smiling.

"It's fine; someone kissed me better."

Alex grinned like Wallace, his lips framing white teeth. His eyes were ultra-glossy and so focused on her, Mia fell into them.

"Everyone's scared to be alone these days," sighed Alex.

Mia nodded thinking Alex's nose was perfectly central.

"My dad's the same."

Alex had a dark, sharp chin-strap beard and his mouth…well…she could vouch for that.

"I thought after my mum passed he'd take up golf or bowls but no he joined online dating. He doesn't drive so I drop him off, pick him up…sometimes with an old dear in tow. I've moved back in; he's a diabetic and is clueless without Mum. Silly old sod."

Alex squatted down beside Mia. If he was reading her signals right then maybe he'd go in for kiss number two. A bitter lemon in hand, he turned. She was bright-eyed, gentle and as beautiful inside as she was outside. He leant in about to press his lips to hers…

"Hey guys," called Kelly leaning over the bar.

Alex sprung up like Zebedee, disappointed by the interruption.

"Hey Kel. Jesus is that a skirt or a girdle? You'll create a riot."

"This is my best tipping skirt Al," laughed Kelly. "You're one to talk, why is Mia on her knees in front of you?"

Mia laughed; her cheeks blushed madly.

"If you're not busy next week I'm going to see Gator," said Alex casually to Mia.

"Oh my God, definitely; I love a croc film. Have you seen Rogue?"

"Yeah and Lake Placid. Shall we grab a burger on the way home?"

"Lovely. You coming Kel?" asked Mia from behind the bar. Mia didn't see the cheeky wink between Alex and Kelly.

"No Mia…I'm on a blind date."

"Ever dated someone with sight?" joked Mia.

"Yeah, but then they looked at her and turned to stone," added Alex.

The eve of Christmas Eve began promisingly.

"Happy Christmas Ellie," said Mia handing her a carton of Celebrations.

"You too Mia. Cheers, I'll quietly work my way through the box. I'll leave Bradley the coconut," she smiled. "Remember it's half day tomorrow. We close at two."

Mia felt comfortable chatting to this slim, blond receptionist who each day had added a few words to her welcome and before Mia knew it they were chit chatting away.

"Looks like you have the pool to yourself."

"Perfect," said Mia.

Upstairs, in the mixed changing room, it was coldly quiet like a mortuary. Mia hesitated and listened. A solid, icy silence filled the air. An uneasiness quivered across her shoulders. Everything freaked her out lately. Shaking her head, she walked between two rows of empty cubicles, choosing one nearest the lockers. Pulling on her new size fourteen floral tankini, she took a moment to smile. Her thighs were no longer gargantuan. Her flesh didn't overspill the costume. She had a full figure, but she loved it; her firmness; the physical strength she had. About to leave the cubicle Mia heard footsteps. Nothing unusual in that; until the cubicle door beside her squeaked as it swung open. Really? There were a hundred free cubicles thought Mia.

She paused, her ears on red alert.

The door to her left didn't swing closed. The lock wasn't drawn. Noise of undressing was absent.

But Mia heard heavy, raspy, deep breathing.

Tension pierced Mia's calm like a splinter. Something was wrong.

Mia strained to hear stuff going in a locker. No shuffling. Nothing.

Unconsciously she retreated, her back touching the cold, tiled wall. The breathing was male. If was fast, deeply wheezy and erratic. She didn't want to hear it. About to cover her ears, its rhythm came to an abrupt end.

Mia stared at her door handle. It's not going to move. It's not g...It. Moved. Sh.i.t!

Goosebumps, the precursor to danger, collectively broke out on

Mia's skin. Her eyes shot to the top of the cubicle expecting an overhanging lunatic with crazed eyes and flailing arms.

Her bare feet iced to the tiled floor whilst her upper body lurched back. She'd watched too many horror movies not to take signs seriously.

Voices. From the stairs. Footsteps. Laughter. It was the coffin dodgers approaching: Philomena and Ethel; they swam daily.

The adjacent cubical door squeaked. Footsteps receded…whoever it was had left.

Mia emerged. She stood in front of the adjacent cubicle door. Maintaining a distance, Mia reached out, prodding the door open with her forefinger. On the bench was a collection of kitchen roll. Mia felt sick; it was totally gross. She swam five lengths preoccupied with the sicko whacking off. The following twenty lengths she thought of how Alex's kiss made her heart skip. It didn't need to pump out of your chest and make you sick with longing. With Flynn she was all fingers and thumbs and she got brain freeze. Maybe you could like a boy too much?

Tired from swimming, the last thing Mia wanted was to traipse to Oxford Street to her mum's office. Her mum needed help carrying presents and leftovers from the Christmas lunch home. Mia was awkward around fashion people and her mum came out with embarrassingly weird comments. And she did this awful, freaky thing. She'd put her hand on Mia's stomach fat and publicly wobble it; squeezing Mia affectionately. It didn't feel affectionate, it felt proper sick. She was highlighting Mia's main body flaw with a smile.

Mia needed armour. She needed to look good. Not just this afternoon but when she went to the cinema with Alex. She intended to spend her pay on fashion…but Mia's fashion sense was underdeveloped due to Joslyn's selfishness; so what if Mia bought the girl version of what Jay wore? He was bare trendy. The Beckhams did it. Everyone in Hello magazine did it. So she stood outside Flynn's until he appeared. Wearing skinny, ink blue jeans, a karki parker, a mulberry beanie. Perfect; that's all she needed from him. She turned. Walked up the path and rang the doorbell of number 28.

"Mia lovie," said Mrs Hornby. "Come in."

"I'd love to but I'm busy. I wanted to drop off this cake and say Happy Christmas."

"Lovie that's kind. I won't keep you then but don't be a stranger in the New Year."

"I won't," said Mia her mood brightening because of Mrs Hornby's warm smile.

"Happy Christmas lovie. Get away with you now. Go shop till you drop."

In Oxford Street H&M Mia purchased a karki parka, a mulberry beanie and jeans! What sort of mother tells their daughter they're too fat for jeans?

In the changing room, she pulled off the tags. About to slip into fashion she looked in the mirror; her reflection was fab; the fat rolls were gone. No obliques or ribs were visual, and her muffins were still formed but she was toned and shapely, in fact her waist was small. With a little jiggling and breathing in the fourteen jeans were on. She pulled on the silky, simply cut t-shirt; its narrow chest emphasising her boobs whilst widening around the middle so no tummy cling. Parka zipped up, mulberry bobble hat on and heeled ankle boots; Mia loved herself.

Until walking into her mum's building. Mia's self-image gained pounds. These arty designers wafted around, light enough to ride a breeze. Passing a mirrored wall Mia's confidence plummeted. She was a blubbery blob. A shapeless mass of fatty matter.

The reception was buzzing. Staff sat on both couches merrily enjoying the effect of a Christmas lunch and champagne. Looking at her mum's loose features Mia knew she was wasted. It took less than a nano second for Joslyn to start.

. "Mia don't stand there like a doorstop. Come here."

Mia knew the jeans would be the catalyst of some scathing assessment by Joslyn. She was temporarily saved by the entrance of the Head Buyer who glided in, her bright pashmina making an impressive fashion statement.

"Mia, you look wonderful."

"Thanks Katya," Mia beamed, a pound lighter.

"Yes," added Seb.

Another pound fell away.

"You've your mum's eye for fashion Mia. Khaki is this Winter's power colour," added Flo. "You look vibrant Mia."

Mia couldn't help herself.

"My boyfriend chose it."

Well he chose the one he wore; it was an obscure truth.

"She's lying, she hasn't got a boyfriend."

An uneasy quiet descended. Mia noticed Katya's, I told you so, eyes dart to Brian's.

"His name's Flynn, but everyone calls him Alex." Mia continued determined.

"She's lying."

"He's a film student at Exeter but he works in a pub during the holidays."

"Mia! I told you! You're too chunky for jeans. You're like a lesbian."

A shocked silence cut the air. Mia hated how her mum used lesbian as an insult. Mia looked around. Brian was shuffling uncomfortably. Flo, sitting beside Joslyn, altered her pose to create space between them. Colleagues were taken back by the anti-gay slight but even more with Joslyn's treatment of her daughter. A sea of sympathetic faces homed in on Mia who hated being pitied. Joslyn's mask had slipped. Alcohol was a revealing spell, a transparency trick. The real Joslyn was present.

"On the contrary," said Brian. "Mia could wear anything and look stunning."

"Mia, hurry up, get the bags," ordered Joslyn her words tight. "No not that one!"

As Mia picked up the bags they clinked. Not more sodding wine she thought.

"Mia, you're so clumsy."

Mia wanted to drop the bags and leave her mum rotting.

"The larger you get the more cloddish you are."

"The drunker you get, the more malicious you are," Mia muttered.

Eyes met eyes. Opinions were formed.

Walking toward the door, Joslyn swayed into Mia and the bottles clinked again.

"For feks sake Mia!"

Mia was determined not to feel ashamed; she was not her mother!

"Happy Christmas everyone," she said "Sorry about…" A sea of faces focused on her. She blushed but remained strong. "Sorry about my mum." There, she'd done it! Taken the first step of separating herself from her mother.

Waiting for the lift, Joslyn muttered incoherently. Mia heard the words 'boyfriend, tramp, liar, tart'. If Father Christmas was real the lift doors would open prematurely and her mum would free fall down the shaft. Maybe she needed Krampus for that?

The tube escalator was tricky. Mia couldn't stand beside her mum because of commuters running down. The bags were another obstacle; passengers butted them causing sharp, jutting corners to poke painfully into Mia's legs. And there was the awful smell? Just for a moment. That's all it was. Mia peeked in a bag; bloody, fucking pate! As the escalator steps flattened Joslyn stumbled. An arm swung up. A leg gave way. Mia automatically dropped the bags to grab her mum...but it was too late. Joslyn was a fluffy heap on a hard floor. Her newly acquired blond faux fur coat covered in pate. A stream of blood flowing from her head, red wine actually, and the sparkling of a hundred beads of broken bottle. Mia watched as mini scotch eggs rolled toward the Bakerloo line.

As station staff asked Mia questions her instinct to protect her mother kicked in.

"She's suffering from flu."

There was nothing as vicious as detained rush hour passengers.

"She's under a lot of pressure."

But the smell of whisky in the air said different. It overpowered the intensely pungent pate being walked all over the station and probably into people's homes across London.

"Yes! She's a drunk! I'm sorry but where's your fucking Christmas spirit?"

As the crew loaded Joslyn onto the ambulance Mia felt herself withdrawing.

"Let's go," said the ambulance man.

"I'm sorry, I can't."

Picking up the Christmas pudding, Mia walked away...toward the Bakerloo line. Holding it tight to her chest on the journey home.

The estate was still, like it was holding its breath. Mia had her pudding ready. One false move from anyone and she was lobbing it!

99

Safe inside and suddenly hungry Mia looked in the fridge at the invisible turkey, unique because it took up no fridge space, and the cauliflower cheese, cleverly disguised as out of date olives, lastly the potato, that was actually just a potato. There was never going to be a Christmas dinner, not at this address, not including Mia.

Waiting for the kettle to boil Mia picked up her mum's Irish, indulge your depression whilst dragging your daughter down with you CDs; snapping them in half. In went Eminem's greatest hits. Mia put Cleanin Out My Closet on repeat as she tucked into the microwaved plum pudding. It tasted perfect after the seismically rubbish day she'd had. In bed Mia wished on a star; that instead of a young mum dying of cancer, her mother would get MRSA.

****

Waking up on Christmas Eve was serenely tragic; at a time when people reached out to each other Mia was alone. Well, not completely, she smiled as she tucked her dad's presents in her rucksack and headed to Ealing.

"Hey Dad! Happy - Christmassssss."

Reggie wrapped Mia in a huge hug. That coppery smell lingered.

"Mia you're beautiful. You've lost more weight."

Mia nodded, delighted her success was acknowledged.

"Yep, a stone. I'm a size fourteen how mega is that?"

"Mia, that's great. You know I was thinking about the swimming gala in Year Six."

"Oh my God Dad, please don't go there."

"Mia subconsciously you did it. You were upset about being dropped for the relay."

"Daaad, how can you think that?" Mia laughed.

"You got out the pool, steady on your feet until you were beside her."

"I'm telling you Dad, it was a freak fit, the medic said my pulse was erratic."

"My heart was bloody erratic when my daughter pushed the headmistress in the pool."

Mia and Reggie laughed. Mia enjoying the familiar ring of it.

"Thanks Dad."

"For what?"

"For taking me swimming every Sunday, for spending time with me."

"Mia are you in trouble?"

"No.www."

Mia hated to see that deadbeat expression on her dad's face.

"I started running yesterday."

Mia decided to keep the boxing to herself.

Reggie's hand reached over the table and squeezed Mia's.

"It's great Mia. I'm proud of you. Running hey?"

"Yeah, I overdid it though, a bit sore today."

"How's your mum."

Mia had no intention of telling her dad the truth.

"Ok I suppose."

"She seeing anyone?"

Mia blinked away a pop-up of her mum snogging a junior doctor in the broom closet.

"Depends what minute of the day you ask."

"How's school?"

"Good. Actually better than good."

"Revise over the Christmas. It's an important year Mia. Passing A' Levels leads to university; you'd get a chance to live away from home. Meet new people. Try new things."

They both knew he meant escape her mum. He just couldn't say it.

"I'm applying to Exeter."

"Jeesuus Mia, that's far far."

"Dad, you can come on holiday. Maybe there's live-in pub jobs in Exeter, we could move together."

"Now that's a plan."

"Don't you hate working Christmas Day Dad?"

"It's not for long, come four I'll be sitting with my feet up."

"What will you eat?"

"I've got Marks' finest microwave Christmas dinner; no fretting honey."

This was not how her dad's life should be. This was not his dream. If only Joslyn had flown to America instead of sailing to England. Mia wouldn't be Mia, but her Dad would have averted catastrophe.

"Mia?"

"I was thinking about the Christmas you got me a wall-walker," Mia responded trying to make light of the sadness settling like dust.

"You were mesmerised. Again Dad. Again. You were easily pleased. Little things made you happy and it's a credit to you that you haven't changed love."

An ache strained in Mia's heart. Her dad was a wash-up…there wasn't the slightest hint of hope in his voice. It was gut wrenching for Mia to know that although he loved her, she wasn't enough. He couldn't look beyond Joslyn. She had ruined him.

"You cooked crispy fried bread."

"Yes…your mum was sleeping in…she'd worked the night shift. The staff had a drink in after-hours."

Great parenting thought Mia as tears stung her eyes and she swallowed the lump in her throat. She couldn't break down…it would kill her dad. She diverted their attention back to now. Mia took a few wrapped presents out of her rucksack.

"No peeking Dad. Also, some chocolate brazils."

"Thank you darling. I'll phone you tomorrow and let you know how happy I am. Mia, here's a present to unwrap and an envelope. Go sale shopping with it."

"Thanks Dad. Twenty eighteen is going to be a great year for both of us."

"Here's Rob Mia, let's go grab a fry up in the café," smiled Reggie.

******

He appreciated the way she ate. There was an order to it; he could tell by how she arranged her food on the plate. She looked pretty. He wanted to pull the band from her hair, the buttons off her blouse, he wanted to push down those lacy knickers she'd bought recently.

He'd be patient. The others would suffice but he was disinterested; they were too compliant. He needed a distraction, but not Mia…not yet…she'd be a challenge; he needed to do it right. Mia was a keeper…but yes, someone new…someone close.

****

102

Mia placed her one present beneath her one-foot, table top tree; it was only her dad who thought of her at Christmas and birthdays. She'd bought the smallest number of lights and trailed them on and around her tiny tree. A little morose, Mia turned Kiss on for company. Today she needed to dance her depression off. Years and Years floated in the air as her hips swayed, her shoulders rolled, her feet tapped. Maroon 5; Girls Like you.

"Dingdongdindong."

Mia didn't hear the bell. She was too busy swirling, her pelvis rotating.

"Dingdongdindong."

"Jesus," said Mia hearing the doorbell and persistent thuds on the door.

Gripped by panic she slowly ascended the stairs. It could only be her mother.

"Shit!"

Terrified she looked through the peephole and saw…the police? Half relieved, half freaked out she slowly opened the door, sticking her head through the gap.

"Hello," said Mia quietly.

"Mia Dent?"

Could this be the good news she'd prayed for? Her mother struck down by an air bubble in her I.V. Mia prepared to look grief stricken.

"I'm Mia."

It was surreal; the hand on her head as she manoeuvred into the back of a police car. In the panda Mia watched London pass by; groups of friends bantering, couples, hand in hand; normal people, celebrating Christmas. What did normal feel like Mia wondered?

****

Detective Sergeant Raymond looked at the primary interview info. Jesus he hated teenage girls with their dirty mouths and sluttish binge drinking. Always falling head over tits then crying wolf when they had drunken sex. Rape? Shit they wanted it. Raymond glanced at the printout: Mia Dent. Seventeen. Possible gbh. Most of these tarts were fucking dangerous. And fucking selfish. It was Christmas Eve! He'd look in on her, in say ten hours.

****

Mia jerked, woken by voices. Startled and groggy she lifted her head from the table. The man looked grim and Constable Hall looked bare sorry.

"Sit up!"

His tone was harsh. The seriousness of her situation sunk in.

"For the purpose of the tape can you please state your name and today's date."

"24 December 2017, Mia Dent."

"Present DS Raymond and Constable Hall. Ms Dent has waivered legal representation."

He coughed, clearing his throat.

"Joslyn Dent, your mother, has made an allegation against you of attempted mur…"

Mia sniggered, attempted murder, what a fantasist her mum was.

"Something funny?"

"Sorry, but my mum's an architect of drama."

"Your mother has made a claim of a…"

"She's lying," interrupted Mia.

"As I was saying, before being rudely interrupted a claim of…"

"But it's not true," interrupted Mia again.

"What's not true?"

"Everything. Whatever she says, it's a lie."

"And she's lying because?"

"Revenge."

"For pushing her down the escalator?"

"No! You're not taking her seriously are you?"

"It's our job to take assault seriously," replied Raymond stiffly.

"She was drunk. You should arrest her for wasting police time or section her."

"You think she's crazy. You can't stand her so you lashed out," Raymond interrupted.

For a moment all were silent.

"She's bare crazy, but I didn't lash out."

"Come off it. I've Constable Hall's notebook. You were here! Mouthing off about killing your mother."

104

"Yes, but she's not dead, is she? The escalator steps evened out. She fell. I can still smell the pate."

"The what?

"You had to be there."

"Why would your mother make a false allegation against her own daughter?"

"Because she's the anti-Christ."

"Do you have any one to substantiate your statement?"

"Well, I did call a priest once to discuss exorcism."

Raymond looked hard at Mia.

"That she'd been drinking!" he said, his voice raised.

"Oh. Yeah. Um. The staff at her job and the ambulance crew."

Raymond mulled it over. The mother wanted to press charges. Interviews, statements, he'd be here till next Christmas.

"Get lost," he said abruptly standing "Constable make sure she leaves."

Mia just about got up; her back ached and her feet were numb. She followed Emma through the rat runs of the station. She felt weak and off kilter and not in the mood to talk.

"Sorry Mia...I had to share the information I had."

"It's fine," Mia replied, wanting out.

"Mia, I don't want to see you here again. Keep your head down at home."

Mia's smile lacked confidence. Her mum had gone too far! Involving the police was totally premeditated; there was no excusing or forgetting. A murder charge was imminent.

****

Joslyn was searching Mia's room; enraged by Mia abandoning her in the hospital. Joslyn aggressively emptied drawers, spilling Mia's stuff onto the floor, stripping Mia's bed, carelessly casting clothes from the wardrobe into the space behind her.

"Fekking nothing!"

Joslyn's anger heightened at an accelerated rate as she guzzled whisky. Wanting to punish she knocked the glass of water with paintbrushes in over Mia's art coursework book. Then she saw the guitar...

Bitch!"

Mia's despair for her ruined art and thrashed guitar had her sinking to the floor crying. She didn't know what to do with the hate that swelled inside her. As the dusty carpet absorbed her tears she yearned for Alex; his arms, his chest, his lips. She was pig sick of dealing with drama alone. Why was life so aggressive, so packed full of hate, jealously and greed. If your mother didn't have your back then who did?

Mia pulled herself up catching a glimpse of herself in the mirror, she was the visual definition of stressed. Losing weight had thinned her face; mother venom saddened her eyes.

She surveyed her room. The creased clothes. The torn books. The carpet strewn with her things. Mia was running out of insults to describe her mother... until she thought of one beginning with c; she just couldn't say it.

The day of the cinema Mia had finally worked up the courage to go to Toni and Guy. They'd trimmed, feathered and given her a fringe. Everything her mum had said about her face was a lie! Her chin did not jut out!

At the flat Mia sat in front of the mirror, legs folded, in underwear that begged to be seductively removed. From her new makeup bag she pulled out primer and nervously applied. Did foundation go on next? Gabby would know. Working her way through her new cosmetics she finally breathed out assessing she'd done an ok job.

Alex arrived early wanting to reach the cinema first. Standing around the wind's chill was infiltrating his warm duffle coat. He couldn't believe how nervous he felt. He'd been single for over a year but dated regularly, usually he felt comfortable around women but Mia was different. He didn't just fancy her, he liked her.

Alex spotted Mia in the distance. Blue jeans, red puffa and navy bobble hat; she looked gorgeous. As the distance between them reduced she waved and her gentle warm smile added a serene richness to her face. Mia wasn't a show stopper; she was classic. Her features were symmetrical, her eyes bright, her lips full and when she smiled you took notice.

"I knew you'd beat me," Mia said warmly. "Am I late?"

"No," said Alex bending to kiss her red, cold cheek. "Christ, you're freezing," he replied pulling her into the crook of his arm. "Let's get inside, I've got the tickets."

Mia, not the quickest in the world, suddenly got it.

"Alex, is this a date?"

Alex laughed.

"Yeah Mia, it's a date...here let me take your coat," he said after slipping his off. Mia noted Alex's moss green woollen polo, skinny blue jeans with the knees missing and Timberlands. He looked casual but he'd made the effort.

"Hold the popcorn...I trust you...actually I don't."

Finding their seats, Alex was quick to start up conversation.

"Can you believe my dad's got two dates lined up for Sunday, one in the afternoon, one at night? He's turned into a player. I don't recognise him anymore."

"He must be lonely, he's probably trying to fill the space your mum left."

"Yeah, we're both trying to do that," Alex smiled sadly. Mia squeezed his hand and he wanted to lean in and kiss her. Instead, he kept hold of her hand.

"I was worried you might suggest Fifty," revealed Mia.

"I thought we'd watch that on DVD."

"Oh you did, did you?" laughed Mia punching him playfully in the arm.

Mia was surprised at how easy this thing with Alex was. During the film Mia repeatedly glanced to where Alex's fingers folded over hers. It was such a common, date thing yet Mia found it amazing how it took the edge off her loneliness.

"You know Mia," whispered Alex at the end of the film. "I like you…a lot."

While all around headed for the exit Alex's lips brushed Mia's and slowly Mia kissed Alex back. It was soft and warm and Mia's forlornness ebbed away.

"Hungry?" asked Alex.

"Starved."

"Frankie and Benny's ok?"

"Perfect."

Alex loved how excited she was, how she read every word on the menu, verbalising possibilities.

"I'll have a burger if you don't judge me for getting tomato sauce down my chin and crumbs everywhere. It's hard to talk and eat burger," said Mia.

"Let's talk business now. Mia…you've never mentioned a boyfriend but sometimes you have a wistful look in your eye…is there someone?"

"Well…it's a long shot…I like him but it's not got off the ground…it's a dream. A bit like marrying Adam Levine."

"So you're open minded to possibility?"

"God yes!"

They ate, they laughed, and for the time they were together Mia didn't think about her mum, Kevin, not even Flynn.

Trying to elongate the date Alex waited with Mia on the platform planting a series of kisses on her lips. As the train approached he cupped her face, kissing her deeply and she wrapped her arms around his neck kissing him back.

"Your train," Alex said smiling like a kid. "I'll see you Monday…but no feelin' me up at work," he laughed. "I don't want to bring a case of sexual harassment against you."

"Umm…that might be hard…you're pretty cute."

"Cute? I'll take that."

Alex swiftly kissed Mia again and pushed her gently onto the train. "See you Monday."

"Monday."

"Mia!"

"Yes?"

"Text me."

"Ok," beamed Mia.

Mia couldn't help smiling to herself. She was so backward. How had she not seen Alex liked her? Her first kiss, and under Mistletoe! She'd never forget it, it was like one of the stories she'd invented for herself. God he was adorable, funny and easy to be around. Her thing with Flynn was weird; she knew it…a psychiatrist would probably have a name for it…but Flynn was the past, Alex could be the future. Mia knew it was for the best…she had to try and love a boy who could love her back. Flynn was a dream. Alex was real.

****

On the platform, barely two meters away, he'd observed how her hand slowly moved up the material of the boy's jacket. It slipped around his neck. Maybe her fingers felt strands of his hair between her fingers? The boy's head lowered. She kissed him. Perhaps their tongues touched. There was no doubt; it was a full blown fucking kiss. His anger wasn't directed at her, if anything he was pleased for her…but it couldn't continue. The boy couldn't keep touching her. Kissing her. He watched her step on the train. He didn't follow her. He followed the boy.

****

109

They'd texted, bantering back and forth until the communication abruptly stalled. He was probably helping his dad…they were obviously close. But it was late…what could they be doing? Maybe he'd fallen asleep.

****

Alex knew he was crying; he tasted salt on his lips.

****

George Stone looked out of his bedroom window. The rain was falling hard…Alex would get soaked. It's funny how you worried regardless of your kid's age. Come to bed Miriam, he used to complain. Worrying won't bring Alex home any quicker. Now here he stood, exactly in his wife's lookout spot, where the carpet was most worn. Staring into the rain; wishing his son home safe and in his bed.

****

Alex didn't understand. He was barely conscious, his ribs broken, his nose cracked, his head bleeding. He was dying. He knew that. He thought of Mia…his dad…and then his mum. Wait for me mum…he asked the darkness…Mum…I'm scared. His heart slowed, his pulse weakened. Another tear escaped. His lids flittered down. At 11.03 pm Alex Stone was dead.

****

He watched as another's blood swirled down the plug hole. He'd made a serious error not wearing gloves. It wasn't premeditated; it was a curve ball. He had no idea he'd feel such raging anger. He thought watching someone kiss and touch her would excite him; he usually liked the role of voyeur. Perhaps it was the ease at which they fell into a physical relationship. Unfortunately, there was no perhaps about it…he'd killed a man.

****

Alex was dead. Murdered. To Mia the words didn't make sense. Following hours of questioning, Mia signed her statement and walked from the police station into startlingly bright sun, wincing as it stung her eyes. She was hollow. She never imagined it possible to feel this empty. For the first time ever she felt thin; so non-existent she might disperse in the air and be blown like a dandelion to different corners of the world.

"It's fourteen ten, stopping the tape for a comfort break. Myself and DS Raymond leaving the room."

"For fuck's sake Steve. You've prior experience of this girl. She's the girlfriend of a murdered young man and you say nothing?"

"Sir, it was one date! It's unconnected to her assaulting her mother."

"I'll decide what's unconnected. Get me the file on Alex Stone. Now!"

Webber paced the floor until his inbox pinged.

Webber clicked open the file named Stone, Alex. It was sad reading. More and more he was understanding the thinking of this near broken girl.

Standing he walked to his sergeant's desk. It was a tip. Folders piled high, papers everywhere, discarded food cartons.

"You've let me down Steve. Your decision-making and sharing of information is something we need to seriously discuss. Till then, let's get in there."

On entering the room, Webber reinstated the recording, giving names, date and time.

"I'm sorry Mia. Your friend's murder must have hit you hard."

Mia bit her lip. She couldn't speak; she could barely breathe. Everything inside her was tensing and twisting – grief was strangling her internally.

"Take a minute," said Webber.

A minute? What the fuck? In a minute Alex will still be dead.

"Mia take us back to immediately after Alex's death."

CHAPTER 15   AFTERSHOCK

Mia couldn't shift the tide of darkness dragging her under. She was on a merry-go-round trying to speed up every day, as if the passage of time would mellow the anger swirling around her stomach, desperate to rise, to tear shreds in her mum, Kevin and every deadbeat on the estate. She had no idea she had the capacity to hate this brilliantly.

Today, like many days over the past month, she walked up and down, not Flynn's road, but Alex's. She stood where decaying flowers marked the spot. She knew only what was revealed in news reports. He'd been frenziedly beaten in what they called a random attack; translation - the police were fucking clueless. He would have felt each strike. He would have known he was dying. Had he been scared? Yes. Terrified.

Mia choked on tears; her arms wrapping around a tree. Mia's imagination drove furiously in a figure eight, an infinity of dark thoughts and what-ifs. If he hadn't walked her to the station. If they'd seen an earlier film. If they'd skipped dinner.

Outside Alex's house Mia saw Mr Stone moving about inside. She wanted to knock…see if he was coping…if he needed help.

Neighbours were spooked by the tree-hugging girl.

A panda drove up.

"Are you ok there?" asked a constable leaning out the window.

Mia nodded.

"You can't hang around, it's unsettling the residents."

She walked on, toward the train station; leaving felt like her intestines were being twisted like popping bubble wrap. The panda car drove passed. Her life had become so entangled with the police she felt like the Greek gods were playing with her, creating havoc and tragedy, for entertainment.

Mia felt an unfamiliar vibration from her pocket.

It was Alex.

Mia froze; so solid she was incapable of moving.

Alex?

Mia's mouth opened, no words, instead short, heavy breaths panted into the air.

She opened the message.

"I can see you."

Her head shot up. To the heavens. Incredulous…until tension crept beneath her skin. Nervously, she looked up and down the road. No one. Incomprehension stunned her. She stared at the phone screen. I. Can. See. You.

Shaking, she hurtled toward the train station; her heart hammering so loud it blocked out traffic. She blinked away the zooming in and out of her focus. Still her eyes couldn't lock on to what was in front of them. Unsteady she held the escalator handrail. She looked down at her trainers, they were ten feet away. Walking toward the platform, travellers heading towards the exit knocked into her or did she knock them?

"Mind the gap."

Looking down, the gap between the platform and train seemed enormous.

"Mind the doors."

They almost trapped her. She sunk into a chair. She didn't see him at first. When she looked up he sat directly opposite and her first thought was he looked nothing like Alex. They were complete opposites. Mia wondered what her type on paper was. Her tall, thin, sharp, dark haired dead boyfriend or the bright, graceful, beautiful, shiny Flynn who she'd felt drawn to, even more so now, because she needed to tell someone how totally fucking broken her heart was. After a while she realised she was staring so with a sharp turn of her head she looked away, down the length of the carriage, her eyes burning with unshed tears.

"Bleep, bleep."

Mia flung her phone in shock. It hit the train floor. The back fell off. The battery out. She dropped from her chair, her knees against the roughness of the carriage. Gathering the pieces, sitting back, she reassembled the phone and clicked on the new message.

"I. Can. See. You. Still!"

****

Flynn felt uncomfortable. He recognised her. She was the same but different. Much slimmer. Sportier. Her hair styled. Her clothes fashionable. But she was behaving scarily oddly. Unnervingly so. She stood. Her chest visibly rising and falling. Looking down the carriage both ways like she was being pursued. The train doors opened and she fell out onto the platform. Somehow he knew it wasn't her stop. She'd simply flung herself off the train.

****

A plausible scenario occurred to Mia. She caught the Northbound train and double-backed to Mr Stone's house. Through the gate. Up the path. Knocking rapidly on the door.

"Mr Stone, please, it's Mia, are you texting me?"

No answer

"Mr Stone. I know you're in there. Have you Alex's phone?"

Mia continued rattling on the door. She had to know.

The gate clinked behind her.

"Shit!" said Mia frustratedly.

"This is harassment," said the same policeman from earlier.

"It's not me, it's Mr Stone, he's texting me."

"I don't think so," said the constable leading Mia by the arm to the panda.

"In you get; we'll take you home."

"No, please take me to the station, I need to log this text...Its...Well...I don't exactly know...Someone's playing a hateful game."

"It's never good to react immediately. Let's get you home and you can sleep on it."

The flat isn't a home, thought Mia staring out the panda window, seeing row after row of prettily lit houses, tidy gardens, flowery hanging baskets. The two constables looked at one another uncertain as to whether they should bring her in for an official caution. After all this was the fourth time a neighbour had reported her strange behaviour.

Not wanting to do the paperwork the police pulled over outside Mia's estate.

"Mia," said the constable. "What happened to your friend was awful, but you can't return to Orchard Road. Do you understand?"

What if her mum had bought a phone? But she wouldn't have Alex's number.

"Mia!"

"I won't go back," lied Mia looking down at her feet.

A short vibration and 'ding' alerted Mia to a third text.

115

"I'm not Stone."

She said nothing to the policeman. Walking along the road adjacent to her estate, Mia involuntarily threw up. She hung her head over the estate wall, her vomit falling at least twenty feet to the underground carpark. She wondered if anyone had been murdered down there? Wiping her mouth with the back of her hand she walked swiftly onto the estate. Inside her head Mia was screaming, clawing her way out of a mind that was sucking her into a dark abyss. She was near her block when, in the distance, she saw Forty. And. He saw her.

"Fuckkkkkkkkkk!" Mia screamed at the top of her voice, catching the attention of those walking through the estate.

Mia stood tall, tensing every muscle, prepared.

He was alone, on one of those small, stupid bikes.

"Shit!"

Forty, his back hunched, his head almost touching the handle bars, cycled furiously.

"Bitch!" he screamed as she threw herself onto the grass verge avoiding collision.

He turned, one foot on the ground, dust flying in the air, making a complete three sixty.

Mia scrambled to her feet, nearly spraining her ankle, and ran, but not fast enough.

"Cunt!" he fired, circling her before speeding off, turning and riding at her again. She couldn't run any faster. He was too quick. Peddling hard, shouting every insult for a girl at her: slag, slut, whore, his front wheel was barely an inch from her calves. Nearly ramming her, she moved tactically, left, them immediately right, to kamikazily throw herself sideways onto Forty. She heard the screech of breaks, the skid, the vile language, the threats and she bolted.

****

In the flat Kevin was coming out of the bathroom in boxers and a vest.

"You should buy a dressing gown," Mia said, her filters down.

"Have you been crying?"

"No. Hayfever," said Mia offhandedly.

116

"In February?"

"Yeah, spot on, it's February."

****

"Let me get this straight," said Webber. "You received texts from Alex Stone's mobile after his death?"

"Yes," confirmed Mia.

"And you flagged this with a member of staff at this nick?"

"Yes."

"Who?"

Mia looked at Raymond. He was turning red.

"Him," said Mia her eyes shooting between Webber and Raymond.

"For the purpose of the tape can you say the name of the person you reported your concerns to."

"I reported receiving texts from Alex's phone to Detective Raymond. And. I reported the threatening behaviour of gang members to Detective Raymond."

On the outside Webber looked unrattled; on the inside? He was fucking fuming.

"Ok Mia. Continue if you will."

Mia woke sweating, caught up in the quilt. For the merest moment recent horrors had yet to seep into today's reality. Alex was fleetingly alive. Then he wasn't. A fierce stab punctured her heart before she threw the quilt off. She remembered Forty.

"Shit," she said woefully.

She remembered it was mocks week.

"Oh fuck!"

It was hard to revise when she kept seeing Alex laying in a pool of his own blood. Taking a steady breath, she pulled off her nighty, throwing Justin Beiber in the bin. Slipping into her, now oversized, uniform she gritted her teeth as she pulled the front door behind her.

On the train she stared at her phone, *I'm not Stone*. The text frightened the shit out of her. She continually felt she was on the edge of a panic attack. Alex's death was somehow related to her and that's what she told Sergeant Rain Man. How could someone be that shit at their job and still be employed? Mia's anxiety worsened when she saw The Metro headline.

Eighteen-year-old Becca Smith; on the anniversary of her abduction the police are like lost lambs waiting for The Wolf to strike.

Instead of staying calm, knowing her first exam was only an hour away, Mia read and reread the article, nearly missing her stop, only managing to jump through the doors before they closed. Walking across the Square Mia felt agitated; almost angrily tearful. Becca should be sitting her exams. Petra should be clubbing. Was Becca dead like Petra? One day breathing, the next not.

"Breathing…not breathing, breathing…not breathing."

"Mia," called Mr Coombe through his car window.

"Breathing…not breathing."

"Mia Dent!"

Mia looked around, confused, what was she even doing on this road?

"Mia…get in," said Mr Coombe reaching over about to open the passenger door.

Mia stared at him. Mr Coombe who'd been instrumental in helping her climb out of her rut. He smiled, he looked harmless, still she wouldn't get in the car.

"Hi sir, I'm dizzy, nerves I think. I'm stretching my legs and getting some fresh air."

"Were you talking to yourself?"

"Absolutely, I've been studying zen; transcendental meditation."

"Well if you're sure you're ok?" he said unconvinced.

"Totally sure."

Mia watched as the car pulled away. The Wolf could be anyone.

****

He almost felt sorry for her. He'd sent her into a tailspin with the texts. She'd make the perfect heroine in a thriller. Her wide, scared eyes. Her lips forming the perfect scream. Her breasts rising and falling as she struggled to draw air. He bet right now, as she paced the streets, scared of everyone, she was thinking of him.

****

"The exam is over."

Mia's pen went down.

"Mia?" whispered a voice from the exam table beside her.

"Hey Ben. How was it?"

"Fucking hard...what d'ya think?"

"I don't know...what the hell was question three about?"

"Fuck knows. Fancy going Nandos? Me, Megan, Tom and Daniel are going."

"Not today, maybe next time."

"No Mia," said Ben firmly. "You're coming. You spend too much time alone."

Mia walked quietly amongst the small group simply enjoying the buzz of belonging. As they piled into Nandos Mia saw Flynn immediately. Not waiting for a waitress, Mia moved quickly between the seated customers to the table nearest Flynn.

"Shit Mia, you're hungry."

"Starved," she smiled looking at Flynn...then noticing another table...Gabby. Trying hard not to indulge her fascination with a stranger she turned her attention to her friends.

"Ben, did you drop Spanish?" Mia asked.

Fuck yes, you?"

"Music," she replied, the memory of her thrashed guitar still fresh.

In the corner of her eye Mia saw Gabby glance her way. Casey was gassing in Gabby's ear. Gabby turned to listen. Mia thought she was dismissed but Gabby quickly shone a smile Mia's way. A lump formed in the back of Mia's throat. This is why you have to choose life. People change, hearts mend, friendships rekindle. There is always hope. Not for Alex.

Ben saw Mia's face drop.

"How's boxing?" asked Ben interested.

Mia swallowed her grief.

"I'm growing on Stanley," she laughed. "I think I've worn him down. I'm there five out of seven days. I've been cast in the latest Guardians of the Universe."

"Thought any more about competing?" asked Ben.

"No way. My dad would lay an egg."

"Your dad works in a pub doesn't he Mia?"

"Yeah, he does."

"Can you get alcohol?" blurted out Megan.

"No," Mia laughed. "My dad is old school."

"My mum too," sighed Megan. "I've got a party next week and need alcohol."

"Sherry trifle," suggested Ben.

"Tiramasu," Mia added laughing.

"I was thinking more like jelly shots," laughed Megan.

Flynn was distracted from Gav's pre match analysis of the Chelsea Barcelona game by 'her'. She'd lost her advert for 'Crisis' look. For some unfathomable reason she piqued his interest. He liked her squeaky laugh. He snuck a look. She wasn't animated like the others, she was quieter, detached. She looked fantastic. Her eyes, her skin - they had a luminosity about them. Her hair was shiny.

Mia snuck a look at Flynn. She felt warm. Not hat and scarf warm, but warm like a fire was spreading outward from a central place within. Raising her drink, Mia's eyes met Flynn's. It was fleeting; probably imagined. Isn't that what she did? Imagine their eyes meeting across a crowded room. She was such a dope; obviously it was imagined.

Everything good in her life was. Mia immediately felt guilty. Here she was with friends, school was ok, she was being tolerated at boxing…and Flynn? Well they were in the same room, eating, breathing the same air. Her eyes sprang to his again…she nearly fell off her stool…he was staring directly at her.

After Nando's instead of heading home she went to the library; a place she remained till seven; a place that wasn't the flat. In the silent study room, on her laptop, Mia hit every link on the Exeter website, looking at courses, uni accommodation, bursaries and grants. She studied google maps – street view, imagining her and Flynn hiring bikes and riding all over the countryside.

On the way home Mia replayed that Nando second when their eyes met. It was like he'd struck a match and ignited her goofball gene – she'd dropped her fork, knocked over her cola, choked on a spicy chip; it was horrific.

Reaching Warwick Avenue Mia prepared for trouble. She nervously hovered before the stairs leading out of the station…listening. She didn't hear them. She knew exactly how they sounded…like killers.

Her uniform was in her bag. She wore all black, second hand Gym Shark sportswear. Tying her hair up she tucked it under a black beanie. Mia sprinted up the station stairs, along the canal, slipping into the estate unseen.

Inside the flat she holed up in her room. She had zero tolerance for her mother. And Kevin? He was a leech. She took her art book out. It was her safe space. It shone a light on her life, she was naked, pouring out her sorrow and insecurities until she hardly had the energy to clamber under the quilt. She dreamt about her mum; it wasn't a nightmare, it was a happy dream. Her mum had gone on holiday. Mia imagined airport security finding planted drugs in her mum's luggage…The accusations…the body search…being detained on foreign soil…the language barrier…the crack down on drug trafficking…the squalid foreign prisons…perfect.

Mia woke refreshed. Putting her ear to the door she listened. Confident her mum and Kevin weren't up she scooted to the bathroom, locked the door and weighed in.

"Jesus."

The scales read nine eight. She'd hardly eaten since Alex. She'd gladly pile on every pound to get him back. He'd liked her from day one, muffins and all. Now here she was only months later chasing a boy who had probably never seen a naked muffin in his life.

Mia pulled on her black underwear, jeans and t-shirt. Mia hadn't expected to return to the Bear…ever. It must have been two weeks after Alex's funeral that Kel had begged her to come in and it seemed wrong not to at least try if Kel needed her. It was nothing like she expected. She didn't hate seeing Alex's ghost behind the bar, she felt comforted like she connected with him there; it's where she'd had her perfect, first kiss. It was the cinema complex that made her involuntarily spew, the burger bar that made her feint. Those memories were like pulling a plaster off…they ripped raw emotions to the surface and it was hard to deal with them. Flynn was her deflector. Like today. Watching his house was calming.

"Mia dear."

Shit, thought Mia.

"Vera."

Mia felt awkward. How long had Mrs Hornby been at her gate?

"So glad to catch you lovie. I have a chocolate fudge cake and the kettle is on."

Mia felt a wave of longing; she hadn't eaten cake in months, but she was on a mission and this was side-tracking…though being a pleaser Mia had to accept the invitation.

"You pour the tea. Here's a generous size; you're shrinking in front of my very eyes."

"Thank you," said Mia realising this near-stranger was kinder to her than her mum.

Mia savoured the cake. Eating it in small mouthfuls.

"Got a lovely letter from my niece in Australia. Surfboarding she was. I keep telling her about the great whites, but you young ones never see the dangers under your nose."

Mia nodded, swallowing a little sponge with a little chocolate butter cream.

"Watch Jaws, I said but she laughed; then there's alligators, spiders; ooh, I do worry."

"It's probably more dangerous living in London," replied Mia reassuringly.

"Lovie you're right, no woman is safe with The Wolf."

"Vera I've gotta go but I'll pop in tomorrow with shopping."

"Lovie two pastries; you choose and milk for porridge; if you forget I'll use water."

"Don't get up, I'll pull the front door firmly after me, you finish your tea."

"Lovie, that sounds like a grand idea."

****

The sky was grey and the temperature bitterly cold. He was behind the girl as she boarded the bus; near enough to inhale her scent. She in turn was behind the Mason boy. He liked her commitment to the cause. She was running because the boy ran, drinking Earl Grey, wearing his coat even giving blood. He and her were not dissimilar; she understood indulging a fantasy took time and effort.

Walking past, he ever so slightly touched her hand. He felt tense in her presence, on edge, the taste of the hunt fresh on his tongue.

He sat. She remained standing, holding the rail. He'd looked at her wrists; they were small. He saw himself tightening electrical ties around them.

****

The mobile donation unit was not what Mia expected. In the back of her mind she'd seen herself in a waiting room amongst other donors blending in.

Flynn would be lying if he didn't admit to feeling uncomfortable. She was like the FBI; she was everywhere. He sat on a chair, she was two chairs up. Coincidence? Was he seeing her because he looked for her. Perhaps she was always in his air space and he'd never noticed…which was reasonable because she wasn't his type on paper.

"All done," said the nurse. Flynn nodded one eye on the girl; how she moved when he did. He was standing, as was she albeit it a little unbalanced.

"There's squash and a biscuit as you leave," said the nurse.

Putting on his parka it struck him she had an identical coat, she caught its zipper. He pulled his beanie on…as did she. Popular colours, they were the fashion, decided Flynn.   Mia felt woozy. It was hot in the portacabin and seeing her blood leaving her body made her queasy. Putting a step forward she wobbled precariously and instead of falling left against a wall she fell right, against the water butt.

Flynn was surprised how quickly those butts emptied. She was like freak weather; there was no warning. Christ, her boyfriend would need to be well insured. Flynn noticed how calm she remained. The nurses, the donors, screeched and blamed. She didn't go on the defensive or crack; standing in an inch of water she absorbed criticism like she was porous.

****

"Where?" asked Flynn, standing in the Mason building, by the window, with Security.

"There! Sitting at the bus stop. Khaki jacket," the guard pointed out.

"You've seen her before?"

"Flynn she's your shadow."

"Yeah, she's been on my radar. I thought it was coincidence."

"No, trust me, she's got footage."

"You think she's taking photos of me?"

"I can sort it."

"No…I'll sort it - but thanks."

****

In Costa Mia queued behind Flynn. She knew what she was doing was freaky but she needed solace from someone. Her mum, Kevin, even her dad weren't comforters, in truth they barely knew her.

"An Earl Grey please," ordered Flynn.

"Any sandwiches or pastries with that?"

"Not today thanks."

Mia liked how well-mannered he was. There was something sexy about it. Taking a seat behind Flynn Mia pulled out her art book. She had multiple drawings of him. None were full faced; creating a genuine feel of unrequited love which of course it was because Flynn didn't know who the bloody hell she was.

Who is this girl? Flynn didn't know what the fuck to think.

"Excuse me," he said attempting to confront her.

Nothing prepared Mia for the thrill of Flynn's words directed at her. Or for the panic.

Flynn watched her turn every shade of red. Her eyes sprang around like a rabbit on speed before snapping her book shut quicker than an alligator seizes a gazelle…But not before Flynn saw multiple interpretations of himself.

Joslyn's words rang in Mia's ears – stop squinting, your eyes are too sharp. So Mia stretched her eyelids wide.

Jesus thought Flynn she's morphing into a bullfrog.

When Mia needed Flynn to feel real, in shops, using a tester, she'd spray his aftershave on. Mia was inhaling it now; he smelt delicious.

Shit, thought Flynn, this girl's weird, she's doing a breathing exercise.

"Paper?" he said because his brain was addled by her strange responses but he noted the newspaper on her table.

Romantic gravity pulled her toward him; her bottom was off the stool as she leant over the table. Flynn worried she was going to scramble onto his lap. Mia thought of snogging; Flynn thought of a restraining order.

Her hand, holding the newspaper, reached toward his. They touched. He lingered long enough for Mia to feel flustered and heated and shivery altogether. Long enough for his body to respond unexpectedly.

"Thank you," said Flynn flatly, annoyed this whacko girl stirred up a heated response.

"Thank you," Mia repeated, simply prolonging.

"I didn't help in any way?"

"I was thanking you for your thank you," she gently responded.

Flynn couldn't help but smile at this radiant, sparkly eyed, slightly mad girl who he saw had a massive crush on him. He relaxed.

Hope of extending their conversation dipped as his phone rung. She listened as he answered the call. He talked with the confidence of someone who never tripped over their words...who'd never been hung out to dry because he'd said a 'no' instead of a 'yes', a 'won't' instead of a 'will'.

Walking towards the office Flynn's mind was occupied by her. Flynn, usually assured with women, felt ruffled by a five-foot-four teenager. In his defence she could be a psycho stalker. Intermittently, Flynn sharply turned; to catch a glimpse. But she wasn't there.

Stood in a doorway, looking opposite, Mia saw Flynn's reflection. He knew.

****

It was entertaining watching her trail after the boy. She was very good at surveillance. She appeared different when she looked at him; her body straightened, her chin rose, her eyes shone. Swimming, running, boxing were altering her body. How he yearned to touch her. To feel her new structure. To feel the changes. Her confidence was increasing. She was no longer the easy target he'd selected, but no matter. He'd rise to the

127

challenge. He looked down at his trousers, to where his cock pressed against his pants. He laughed.

****

Speaking to Flynn, seeing him up close, had sent Mia off the rails. She'd been watching his house for over an hour now. The lights were off. There was no internal movement. She noted security lights above the front door and down the side ally where the shiny, aluminium bins sat. A nervous giggle escaped, followed by another. Who was she? Spying, hiding beneath a baseball cap, creeping about in a black gym kit; in the dead of night – well nine fifteen. Mia laughed again. It was fun; didn't everyone deserve fun in their life?

Like electricity was sizzling inside her, Mia scuttled down the side ally to the bins. It felt good to be dangerous. She imagined Flynn catching her in the act. She didn't think of how she'd smell of rubbish or that she might have carrot peel in her hair…she thought only of him, touching her. Reality didn't go down as well as fiction.

"What the fuck are you doing?"

Flynn didn't want this weirdo to think he was a push-over. Better to go in hard and see how she responds.

Mia was in shock.

Flynn stood, in striped pyjama bottoms and a penguin t-shirt at the head of the alley.

He must be frozen, thought Mia.

"I'm…I'm."

Mia couldn't think of a reasonable explanation…she bolted. Away from Flynn, further down the side alley, throwing herself at the ornate garden gate, flinging it open, then speeding across the perfect grass, exertion burning her throat…towards the back fence which was way too tall.

Flynn was breathing down her neck…he nearly had her.

"Fuck that!"

He wasn't following her onto the log cabin roof.

"Shit," said Mia. Flynn's house backed onto a garden thick with trees. The only way down was the way up. Suddenly the ground appeared a lot further away and Flynn looked cold and exceedingly pissed off…but still totally gorgeous.

128

"Come down, otherwise I'm calling the police."

Yep, Flynn was undeniably cross but his voice was bloody sexy.

"It's Mia...isn't it?" Flynn asked more gently.

The girl on the roof nodded.

"Mia, I don't want to call the police, but I will if you don't come down. It's dark and I'm fucking freezing here."

"I...I...I'm scared."

"I've no intention of harming you."

"I know...it's such a long way down."

"Jesus, you got up there!"

"Sorry Flynn."

"Do not say my name...you don't know me."

Flynn took a deep breath...he was going to have to help her...it was bloody ludicrous.

"Come to the front edge, lower yourself down and I'll get you."

Physical contact! Oh. My. God. Mia couldn't move in anticipation.

"Don't be scared."

Far from it, thought Mia, taking too big a step and wobbling wildly.

"Fuck! Be careful."

He cared.

She probably wants to sue thought Flynn.

Turning her back to Flynn; Mia slowly shuffled off the edge of the roof. She was semi-on, dangling, when she felt Flynn clutching around her ankles.

"Keep coming."

Flynn was touching her.

"Mia."

God he said her name so warmly. It was like hot chocolate custard.

"Hurry the fuck up."

"You won't let me fall?"

"No...I've got you."

"Sure?"

"Yes."

Flynn was talking to her...touching her...it got confusing...Mia let go.

"Urgh!"

Flynn lay flat out on the frosted grass, the cold dew penetrating his thin t-shirt. A bundle of a girl lay on top of him.

"Get off," he spurted out as fur from her hood got stuck in his mouth.

Mia scrambled away, her knees damp as she knelt on the grass over him.

"Flynn, are you ok?"

"Don't fucking use my name," he said, pulling himself up.

Flynn was standing in front of her…tussled and beautiful. Mia panicked again and swiftly turned to run.

In a second Mia was up against the log cabin. Flynn's outstretched arm keeping a distance between them, his hand gripping her shoulder.

Flynn felt her longing and it startled him; the fierceness of it. Desire hypnotically danced in her eyes; Flynn knew how to shut that down.

"What the fuck are you up to?"

Mia didn't respond. His lips were a distraction. His tone was rich and smooth; Mia thought of honey - no it was deeper, like melted Nutella. She reached out to him.

"Don't fucking touch me!"

Mia's plan to touch him into wanting her wasn't working.

"Alright?" he added sternly.

"Alright," Mia agreed – but not really.

"Whatever you're up to, it has to stop."

"Stop."

"Yes, you're everywhere."

"Everywhere."

"Yes on the train, at the bus stop outside my work, pacing up and down my road."

"Road."

"Stop fucking repeating me."

"You're making me nervous."

"Yeah, vice versa... I don't want to involve the police, but I will if you don't desist."

"I'll try...to desist that is."

Mia reached out; she couldn't help herself - she wanted to feel him.

"Do. Not. Touch. Me."

She raised her other hand to assure him that...

"Jesus! What did I just fucking say."

"Do. Not. Touch. Me," Mia enunciated with massive emphasis.

He hadn't expected her to repeat it. It came across as ridiculously paranoid like she carried some contagion.

"Flynn...I mean...Well, sorry then."

He stared at her for a while. She was bloody odd, yet crazily endearing.

"You smell of cabbage?" he noted.

"Did you have it for dinner? It's one of my favourite vegetables. It contains sinigrin."

"What's sinigrin?"

She knew he'd ask...he had an inquisitive face.

"It helps prevent cancer."

He stared at the flecks in her eyes.

"What did you take from my rubbish?"

Mia blushed, saying nothing.

"Don't make this more difficult than it needs be. Give me my stuff."

Mia took a spray can of deodorant from her pocket.

Mia thought Flynn looked frightened.

"What else?"

She pulled a collection of loose paper from her other pocket.

"My lecture notes. Really?" he questioned.

"You've lovely cursive writing."

He snatched the pages.

"Anything else," he asked grimly.

Mia bit her lip and repeatedly swung her head from side to side. She was lying.

"Ok. Fine. Whatever fantasy you have going on upstairs...or downstairs, forget it, it's never going to happen."

"I know...I don't expect anything from you."

"Good, so you won't be disappointed. This is a friendly warning. I don't want to see you again."

He dropped his arm.

"Now get lost before I call the police."

That came out harsher than he'd meant. It was too dark to see her expression, but he guessed it would be sad. He spoke gentler in case she needed to be sectioned.

"You need to go Mia."

She turned, her shoulders down, her walk heavy, in the direction she'd come.

"And stop dressing like me...it's weird."

She wanted to run back to Flynn. Tell him everything. That her mother was slowly squeezing hope from her and estate life filled her with trepidation. Worse; she'd kissed the loveliest boy and he was cold-bloodedly murdered. Instead she tried to impress on her memory every moment of Flynn: his husky tone, his glinting hazelnut eyes and his touch, especially his touch, on her skin, on the length of her neck running to her coat collar. In two weeks her bare skin, gripped by Flynn, would be dusty particles floating in the atmosphere. In its place a new layer of skin; untouched by Flynn. Sometimes being educated stunk.   Mia thought about each word Flynn spoke. She ran them back and forwards, up and down. She stored her favourites in her Flynnary. She liked 'desist' the most. She wished her mum would desist breathing - immediately. Yes this 'desist' word worked well for Mia.

Walking toward the station Mia assessed the situation. Getting caught raiding rubbish was embarrassing but worth it. Mia pulled out the phone card from her pocket; the sim was in a phone. What if it belonged to Flynn – she'd have his number. In her pocket was a second treasure, a t-shirt, his unwashed t-shirt! She rushed home excited to put it on.

Mia found Joslyn slumped over the kitchen table, her forehead on its surface, her mouth open, squashed against the wood, a pool of saliva forming at one corner.

With no sign of Kevin, Mia made a cuppa and some jammy toast. Upstairs Mia pulled Flynn's shirt from her bag. She dropped her face into its softness and breathed in Flynn. Tonight they'd had dialogue. So what if it included calling the police. They'd laugh about it when they were grandparents.   She wanted to dream about Flynn all night. Lying in bed a love scene from The Night Manager was on repeat in her saucy mind, she was Jed and Flynn was Jonathan Pine. Oh, God, she liked Flynn so much. Like was the wrong word. She wanted him. With her. Naked. Against the wall. Mia exhaled the deepest, shakiest breath. Thinking about Flynn gave her a severe case of butterflies, so severe butterflies became bats swooping around her tummy, flapping madly. Her hand slipped between her legs and she fell asleep on the wings of desire.

****

Flynn lay staring up at the cosmos printed on his ceiling. He'd had another flare-up with his dad. It was hard being an only child, having parents all to yourself, no sharing the burden with siblings. Did Mia have sisters or brothers? He thought not. She struck him as insular. Where did she live? What were her parents like? Why the fuck did he care? He didn't he decided, it was natural to wonder about the stalker who fixated on you. Was she dangerous? Should he tell his parents in case she hung around? He'd sleep on it.

****

Mia walked into Sullivan's like she belonged. She appreciated the nods of recognition. She wouldn't say she felt at ease; these were men that had committed serious crime: armed robbery, mugging, maybe even sexual assault? The last one she didn't believe because Stanley seemed honourable...like there were limits on what was acceptable...but Mia had no idea what these men were capable of. Boxing was a combat sport...she was there because she might need to pound an enemy into the ground till he or she couldn't see; till they couldn't stand.

After ten minutes in the ring with Tombstone, who remained mute in her company, she was spent. Each minute had been a lifetime. She was heaving, trying to get her breath back. She hugged her stomach, hurting from the shots she'd not anticipated.

"You've got to turn your whole body into the punch," said Stan. "Your jabs should be long, and your hooks short; how many fucking times do I have to tell you?"

"Maybe once more, probably a lot more, but I'm getting better."

"In a manner of speaking," agreed Stan.

"So you'll help me again tomorrow?"

Silence...for a moment.

"We'll work on defence, pivoting in particular. You waste a fucking lot of energy running away from Tombstone."

"I know…but I imagine most people that come across him feel like running."

****

He walked behind her, so near he could reach out and tap her shoulder. At the cemetery gates he lengthened the space between them. She sat at Alex Stone's grave. He sat opposite, only the headstone of Harriet Ruddy between them. He strained his ears keen to hear what her thinking was but she was silent. Perhaps she couldn't share how her mum led her around like a dog on a lead or how she trotted after a stranger, panting each time he glanced her way.

****

"Thank God," said Mia throwing herself on her bed. Visiting Alex wasn't easy. At the graveside her throat felt so tight she couldn't swallow and her heart pumped so violently she imagined it rupturing. She looked over at her drawers; each one pulled out a different length: an inch, a centimetre; her mum had been rooting again. It hurt…it shouldn't because Mia knew what her mum was…but still…the person who should love her wholeheartedly didn't. Mia closed her eyes tightly and succumbed to the feeling of her heart being kicked to death. She reached for her phone and the stolen sim card adding the number to her phonebook. For a while she cradled the phone. Flynn told her to 'desist' so ringing him was a bad idea…but she felt so despondent…but hadn't he rejected her too?

She pressed the call button.

"Sorry, I don't recognise your number, who is this?" asked Flynn

"I'm…nobody."

"A woman with an air of mystery," Flynn said.

"Erm…no…I..I."

"Mia! Is this you?"

Mia disconnected. Turning her head into the pillow, she cried until she fell asleep.

****

Flynn woke. Mia was the first person he thought of. Her eyes were pure blue, and they darted around him like the twinkle of fairy lights. His deodorant? Jesus that's serious stalking. It's what you read about before an acid attack. She frightened him, like a mermaid would if he saw one swimming. There was something completely unique about her…yeah, she was a fucking head case?

He got out of bed. In boxers he peered out the window. There was no sign of her; maybe she'd got the message. But the phone call? It was her. Passing his antique full-length mirror he looked at his ruffled hair, his unshaven jaw, trying to see what Mia saw when she looked at him.

"Christ!" he said, his hand rubbing his jawline.

At least today was his last at Masons. Tomorrow he'd be back at uni.

****

Mia had slept so deeply she was nearly late for work. Bursting through the pub doors she smiled brightly at Kel who was about to say hello when her mobile rang.

"Mia, looks like you're on tables today – Toby's thrown a sickie."

"Kel, I'm so slow."

"You're brilliant. Hands to the deck bitch – it's time to get this party started."

Between nine and twelve Mia hadn't even taken a breath. She found working with food decreased her appetite. In the mornings she smelt of bacon but Fried Fish Friday was worse. Whilst Mia breaded cod, Flynn was arranging payday lunch; he intended to sink a few bevs to get him through his last afternoon at Masons until after his exams.

"Mia, table nine."

He was unmissable. The familiar thrill of Flynn coursed through her body. He sat in a group tightly clustered around a table, immersed in conversation.

"Tuna baked potato and medium steak?"

All heads rose. Flynn looked aghast…but broodingly so. It was like he'd hotwired her heart. The spark burnt until she scarpered back to the kitchen.

"Oh. My. God," cried Mia. "The timing is shit! How do I go back?"

Flynn was no longer deep in conversation; his eyes were on the kitchen swing door. She reappeared. Her long hair was tied back. She wore all black…she was curvy and dangerous. As she advanced, Flynn noticed a bald bloke appraising her appreciatively. Flynn felt a twinge. Of something. The bald bloke put a hand on her arm and Flynn felt a deeper

135

twinge. She smiled, giving him cutlery. Flynn's eyes remained put. Mia moved tentatively toward him, her hips subtly swaying, her eyes screaming I want you. Here. Now.

"Ham, egg and chips and a chicken korma."

She put one shaky plate in front of a woman which only left Flynn. She placed the korma on the table at an angle. Flynn's onion bhaji rolled off. Mia panicked. She picked it up between her thumb and forefinger, returned it to his plate and gave it two slight pats.

Back in the kitchen Mia worried. She'd crossed a line she couldn't uncross. Flynn would call the police. Kel would sack her. Her world would once again shrink to the estate.

"Mia!"

Mia dropped the dirty plate she was holding, it shattered on the ground.

"Jesus, Mia!"

"Sorry Kel."

"There's a customer out here who wants to thank you. A fucking hot customer!"

Mia had no idea what she could say to Flynn to prevent him from calling the police. But when she saw him leaning against a wooden column; the police were far from her saucy thoughts. She walked towards him; whatever way he looked her up and down she felt naked. She blushed. She wondered how transparent she was? Could he see she wanted him more than she wanted her mum to stop drinking?

Flynn didn't understand why he wasn't phoning CID or Interpol. Her face was flushed from heat. She stared at him like she wanted to lick ice cream off his chest.

"You smell of tuna," he noticed.

"I dropped a baked potato on my trainer."

Flynn nodded.

"You work here?"

Her turn to nod.

"Toby's off sick. I'm kitchen staff. We will probably never meet again."

Flynn moved closer. Mia held her breath. He touched her hair.

"Sweetcorn?"

"It was a marrowfat pea yesterday."

"Are you spying on me?"

"No!"

"You sure about that?"

"Positive. I'm truly sorry about before. I got carried away. It was a silly crush."

"From my angle that doesn't seem to be the case."

"This is a coincidence, a random meeting. I don't work out front usually. When you caught me in your rubbish, which I know was very, very wrong, I promised to desist and I keep my promises. I'll resign if that reassures you."

Flynn said nothing; she was so engaging. He could watch her deliberate and gesticulate all day. Her mouth was soft and hypnotic. She'd obviously invested in lip balm. He'd like to taste it.

"You phoned me," Flynn accused, rejecting the feelings she stirred in him.

"Only the once."

"And I flirted."

"You didn't mean to," she said glumly. "I'm sorry Flynn, I mean Mr Mason."

"I won't call the police, but keep your distance. Don't follow me or call me...Ok?"

"Ok."

She looked sad; her shoulders slumped.

"Goodbye Mia."

She couldn't say goodbye, it wasn't in her Flynnary.

****

It was interesting, he thought, watching the relationship between them. The boy appeared to be as drawn to her as she was to him. He was fighting it but the boy was smitten, no doubt about that. An unexpected animosity toward the boy was emerging. His confidence was irritating. He'd rattle the boy's cage a bit. Give him something to think about.

Walking into the estate Mia found Kevin waiting at the lift. She wanted to bypass him via the stairs but it would be an obvious slight.

"Evening Mia," he said; his tone bland, his face unattractively sweating.

"Hey," was the only greeting Mia could muster for this creepy bloke who bit his nails and reeked of a hot, stuffy smell Mia couldn't label. Mia thought he had a smirk to his mouth. His thin upper lip slightly lifted in the centre…or was she simply looking to find fault? Him dating her mum didn't automatically make him the enemy…maybe he too was taken in by her flirtatious innuendo and playful smile…boy was he in for a surprise.

"How's life treating you?"

"Fine."

What else could she say? The truth? I went on a first date and my boyfriend was battered to death…oh, and his murderer's texting me?

"What are your friends like?"

"Easy going and fun."

Mia thought of Alex. Dead.

Come on lift. Come on lift. Mia repeated steadily in her head.

"Boyfriends?"

The lift door opened. Mia pretended not to hear the question. Mia thought how annoyingly raspy his breathing was. Mia had this urge to dart from the lift, flee down the stairs, catch a train to the nearest port and jump on a ship. Instead, she rummaged for her key.

"It's ok Mia I've got mine."

His! Was her mum crazy? She'd known this loser a couple of months and had him a key cut. Mia's back was well and truly up when she entered the flat.

As Kevin hung his coat up, Joslyn appeared from her bedroom, her lips so compressed they disappeared; it was like looking at a skull.

"Kevin, pour me a glass of scotch, we're out of wine."

"I'll stroll to the offy and pick up a few bottles."

"No. Mia can go."

Never had her name been said with such malice. Mia hovered

between nervous and not fucking caring.

"Why were you so long coming up in the lift?"

The wine breath, the lipstick clotting at the corner of Joslyn's lips and the large pores visible beneath the partly worn-off foundation fixated Mia.

"Think I don't see the way you look at him?"

Mia was speechless…her mum was fucking insane.

"Go get a bottle of wine. I think it's the least you can do."

Unease transfused with the blood pumping around Mia's body. She'd knocked Forty off his bike and she'd pay for that…but her mum wouldn't care, and Mia had no intention of arguing with someone off their trolley. Mia wondered if she had a death wish.

****

Flynn was shocked. What had Mia done! The jagged line scored into the metal of his car was angry…was Mia angry? He'd rejected her and in her crazy head that hurt? Flynn touched the compressed, raised paintwork, drawing his hand back instantly at the sharp pain. He looked at his fingers; blood eased between the sliced skin.

****

Mia entered the off-licence; her stance straight, her head held high. Yes! A new cashier; young, that was good. Mia perused the white wine, lifting bottles, checking the volume. Joslyn liked fourteen percent.

"Don't fucking move."

Mia turned around.

"What the fuck did I say?"

"I didn't know who you were speaking to. I turned around to find out."

"Shut the fuck up."

"Ok. Yes. Good idea."

The sales assistant was crying hysterically; she hadn't worked up to it, it was instant and full-on. Maybe it was the gun pointing at her.

"Hurry up."

Robber one was short and stocky. Robber two was tall and brutally strong.

The cashier couldn't open the till; fear muddled her brain.

"Fucking open it."

It was like being in a film. It didn't feel real. Mia moved.

"What the fuck are you doing?"

"I'm helping. I'll get the money."

Mia suddenly found herself staring into the barrel of a shotgun. She didn't feel scared, not like she did of Forty Pence and Scar Tissue.

"Do it, open the till!"

The till was the same as the Bear's.

"Bing."

"In here," said the robber pushing a rucksack at her. Mia looked up and into his eyes. The only facial feature uncovered by the balaclava. Mia swallowed hard.

Both robbers filled rucksacks with champagne. Sirens wailed and although they moved fast they were calm.

"Time," one said to the other like he knew how long it took the police to respond.

Within minutes of the getaway the shop quickly filled with people videoing on phones. Pulling up her hood, Mia snuck a bottle of wine under her coat. She darted across the road and bowled into the entrance...

"Youz up late princess."

There were seven: five male, two females. Two blocked the east exit door, another blocked the stairwell, two by the lift, one sat on the floor and the last - Forty Pence - he was behind her. She tasted their anticipation. In their heads they'd played this out. It was an attack they'd done numerous times; like a magician turning a flower into a rabbit, except they turned girls into victims. She was above watching; isn't that what everybody says? A birds-eye view of violence.

Forty grabbed her hair; viciously yanking her back. His hand was up under her coat, between her tracky legs, pulling at the elasticated waist. From the front savage hands pulled her coat apart. Tearing at her blouse. Touching her roughly. She wasn't above; this was happening now! To her!

The bottle in her hand was cold to the touch. A glancing blow to Scar's head and wine, sharp and pungent, poured down Mia's pyjamas between her barely covered breasts.

She jerked free screaming!

"Don't fucking touch me!"

She didn't recognise her voice; ferocity distorted it. Holding the

140

half-broken wine bottle by the neck, she brandished it wildly. Her body was stiff with fury as her mind calculated her chances.

"Fuckkkkkkkkk!" she screamed, so loud the syllables reverberated in her brain.

"Calm down sister."

"I'm not your fucking sister."

On the floor Mia's keys lay between her and them. This was bad. Through the door, in the distance, outside the off-licence Mia saw the glaring, lurid lights of police cars. Help was so fucking near!

"Youz dead bitch," screamed Scar. Blood poured from his temple, it ran down his pasty, acned face, into his mouth. His teeth were red, spit flew from his mouth. It was his eyes that glared "kill". That crude realisation fired strength into her limbs. She ran at the one who'd called her sister, wielding the broken glass. He moved only at the last minute and her weight rammed into the door swinging it outward, propelling her headlong onto concrete. Hitting the ground, the bottle smashed, embedding in her hand, but she felt only stark terror; sharp like a flare bleaching the darkness. Her reflexes were quick; she sprung up, her fists ready, her mind focused. She'd faced taller, broader, hencher…but they'd been kind…this was estate life…nothing kind about it. She felt dead already. The tighter she curled her fists the deeper the shards of glass went. Scar lunged; drugs made him sloppy, Mia's powerful uppercut spun him off balance. Her eyes leapt from him to the others. Scar straightened; his smile pure evil. He advanced, expecting Mia to retreat but she flew at him landing blow after blow until they came en masse for her. The girls were quick, but Mia's hook left one sprawling, the other holding her stomach in agony. Mia was breathing hard, energy exhausted, focus lost. The knock to the ground was damaging; her face cracked. Blood rushed to her head filling her mouth as hot pain burned in her cheek. Snatching at her hair she was dragged along the hard ground screaming and struggling, away from the entrance, away from the police, into the darkness of the carpark. A gag was stuffed in her mouth.

"I'm fucking the bitch first," declared Scar Tissue.

****

He nearly interceded. His dick stopped him. It was solid. The weight of it between his legs was simply too good. She'd come running

141

out, her blouse torn, her breasts bouncing and her fists up. She was magnificent.

****

The hospital had called the police. Her statement was taken. She'd had to summon her wits to talk through the ordeal. Her cheekbone was fractured. She had a pre-assessment appointment with the surgeon in ten days. The swelling and bruising needed to settle before surgery. The nurse brought her Tramadol. The swallow was so painful it took four attempts to get them down. Then she was discharged. Just like that. Standing at the bus stop she was simultaneously shattered yet wide awake. Phone in hand she stared longingly at the name on the screen...until she pressed the ring button.

He answered.

"Hi, who's this?" Flynn was friendly and unguarded.

"Hi, it's me."

She couldn't believe he'd picked up a second time.

"Good evening, you with the sexy voice, did Aaron give you this number?"

A few moments passed.

"Mia?"

Mia disconnected. His voice was enough to hook her. She couldn't remember the train journey, or the walk from the station to Flynn's home. His light was on. She took her phone from her pocket and stared at his name. She could ring ...if things got unbearable he'd help...she was certain. Mia looked at his porch with its large flat step. Mia sunk onto it pulling up her parka hood. She couldn't go to her Dad's; not like this. She closed her eyes.

****

He was tired; getting older. He needed a release. He chose the most compliant one; the most broken.

"Remove your clothes."

She stood in a dress that hung off her shoulders. Her fingers no longer trembled as she undid the buttons, her body no longer shrunk back in fear. Nothing scared her now.

"Slower."

She eased the dress down. Her bones were prominent from

142

malnourishment.

She was sitting at the breakfast table with mum, dad and Kieron who couldn't wait to tell his friends he was going to be a big brother.

"Tia does having a celery hurt," he asked.

"It's a caesarean, knobhead, celery's what we dip into humous."

"Come here."

There was a stack of pancakes on the table. She cut up a banana for Kieron.

"Don't tell mum I called you knobhead, knobhead."

She smiled, he was cute. She watched him pile on blueberries.

"You'll turn blue you will," she laughed

"Really?" asked Kieron looking scared.

"No silly."

"Nearer."

She liked hers with warm pear and chocolate spread. Umm.

"Kneel."

She intended to live.

****

"Mia! Jesus! Are you fucking insane?"

"Wh…wh…what's happening?" Mia was disorientated.

"Christ!" he said appalled by her physical state. "What the fuck happened?" Flynn demanded, taking in the facial swelling, bruising and torn clothes. "Jesus Mia, who did this?"

"I was attacked," she said so low it was barely audible. She hurt all over. Her body was painfully rigid from the cold night air. She struggled onto all fours when strong arms underneath her armpits pulled her up. She stumbled; her legs weak. She knocked into Flynn.

"Are you on drugs?"

"I fucking wish," said Mia her tone totally defeatist.

Mia brushed herself down trying to give herself a minute to think but her blouse, held together with safety pins provided by the police, was stiff and her fingers red raw.

Flynn had difficulty dealing with this situation. It was totally out of his comfort zone. Her jaw was swollen double its size, her lip split and bruised. She looked blue; like a smurf, and small and bewildered, like she'd lost the plot.

"Come in."

Christ! Did he actually say that?

Mia looked past Flynn, down the hallway. Like it was a trap.

"I don't think so…I need to go…"

"Mia! Come in! Now!"

She was scaring him…she seemed vacant. Jesus how did this happen to her?

"Are you sure?" asked Mia meekly.

"I'm not sure of anything around you."

He motioned for her to come in.

Mia walked passed Flynn. She'd practiced this entrance often in her mind. Reality really fucked your dreams up!

Flynn disappeared and returned with a throw wrapping it around her. Mia couldn't speak, she was filling up with emotion that threatened to overspill. The warmth he emanated, the deep, spicy smell of him, it might tip her over the edge. More than winning the lottery, she wanted to disappear in Flynn's embrace. But not more than the wretched, gnawing desperation of wanting Alex back. She didn't realise her tears were falling freely from eyes so desolate Flynn wrapped his arms around her.

Mia cried with such anguish it scared Flynn. Her arms wound around his waist; small fists twisted his t-shirt as her body racked with sobs.

She'd do anything, live with her mum forever, if that's what it took to rewind time and bring Alex back.

Tightening his hold; stroking her hair, Flynn's imagination ran wild. She looked pulverised. A sharp twinge of outrage jabbed between his ribs. Who the fuck did this?

All cried out, her arms dropped to her side and her floppy body felt all done in.

"Sit."

In the wide, square hallway, with Mia on the chaise longue, Flynn slipped off her trainers. Without thinking he rubbed her frozen feet. If he put them together her socks formed a pug's head. He smiled. He looked up. Her eyes were dark and sullen and in that minute he felt protective and strangely attracted – Jesus she was baffling.

"Follow me…keep your hands to yourself." His tone was brusque

144

but there was no telling what would happen next with this girl…she was predictably unpredictable.

Mia walked in socks to the kitchen. All the while taking in the décor, the family photos, the fridge bigger than her room, the eight-seater long glass table in a huge kitchen with an island. Wow thought Mia…not in response to the kitchen, but she couldn't keep her eyes off Flynn's backside.

"Stop looking like you're casing the joint. If we get robbed I'm giving you up."

"I'm not a thief," said Mia.

Flynn turned and raised a questioning eyebrow.

"Rubbish doesn't count," said Mia defiantly.

"Follow me."

Off the kitchen was a utility room and off that a wet room.

"Take a shower. I'll leave some clothes and a towel on the rail. Here, I'll get it going for you…temperature is nice and warm."

Mia stood in the shower looking at herself, specifically the amount of bruising on her body from being kicked and dragged; no wonder she was in pain. She washed her hair gently, keeping her face away from the spray. After, she dressed in grey skinny jeans, a white t-shirt and a yellow zip hoodie. Underneath was a new white bra and panties, not skimpy, more practical – Flynn's mum's she presumed. The bra was a bit small in the cup. She put the towel in the laundry, her clothes in the bin and wandered into the kitchen.

"Take a seat."

"Ok, but I'll bring it back," smiled Mia weakly because facial movement hurt like hell. She noted Flynn smile as he filled the kettle. She made Flynn Mason smile, it was a foundation to build on. She watched him crack eggs into a pan. He was a domestic God thought Mia…but grounded enough to be considerate.

It was impossible for Flynn not to feel her. He'd become accustomed to her eyes on him. It was weird but at uni he missed that sensation, he missed their close encounters…he missed her. Flynn thought that was pretty fucked up.

"Here, drink this."

Flynn put a coffee in her hand.

Mia felt the heat from her mug warming her chilled fingers, she smelt the eggs scrambling with butter and the bacon and her stomach rumbled with hunger. When had she last eaten? She couldn't remember. When had anyone cooked for her?

"Flynn...I..."

"Don't Mia." Flynn stopped her before she'd begun. "I barely know you, but I feel gutted someone hurt you. I can't see any circumstance in which you deserve what's happened, but I don't want to know. This must stop, here, today...after breakfast."

He swung his head around to meet her gaze. Jesus, he was callous. She looked tough yet fragile...she had a physical strength that she'd not had when their paths first crossed...but darkness circled her eyes and her features looked drawn. Fuck why had he asked her in...she was a mess. She needed professional help.

"You need help...go to a doctor, social worker, someone, but don't come back here Mia...my parents will hit the roof. Since the note, then the car, they've been hounding me to report you to the police."

He searched her face for recognition, guilt, embarrassment and got confusion.

"The note?"

She looked genuinely puzzled. He hesitated then pulled the folded up piece of paper from his pocket handing it to her.

I hate you.
You make me sick.
Watch your back.

Reading it, her eyes widened; she jumped up, she seemed petrified. "The car?" she asked.

Flynn scrolled through his photos, while Mia, behind him, leant over his shoulder. Tapping the screen, an image of his car, he zoomed in at its defaced side panel. Passing it to Mia he watched as her expression widened with alarm.

"Flynn, the police need to see this. Something weird is going on with me."

"You don't say?"

"Flynn, this is serious. Some sicko who knows where you live is

146

out to get you. He could be following you. Waiting for the right time to strike. There are people out there Flynn, that…that do awful things to lovely people. Promise me you'll take it to the police."

Her eyes implored him and unless she had split personality, she did not send the note.

"Please Flynn, promise me."

Flynn nodded placing two breakfasts down. She seemed genuinely scared for him.   "Do you need money?" he asked knowing it was an unwise question…she could start turning up uninvited looking for cash.

"No thanks…food is good."

Mia's face throbbed. Chewing was insanely painful. She chopped her bacon up into small pieces and mixed it into gooey eggs. She wished she wasn't starved so she could eat slowly and draw out her experience but swallowing the last soggy square of toast she had no reason to remain…she still had a centimetre of tea…she sipped it.

Flynn felt at ease…which made him uncomfortable. He should be running to the hills; deadlocking her out.

"You need to go Mia."

She stood. Pulled on her coat and trainers.

"Flynn."

Reaching, she took his hand placing it on her good cheek, holding it there. Flynn didn't pull away. It was only his hand, her cheek…then why did it feel intimate. She closed her eyes and he wanted to kiss her so badly it angered him. He jerked away.

Mia felt a lump in her throat and quickly turned away. She struggled with the lock. Flynn leaned over her and Mia wanted to reverse into him, pull his arms around her and die there. Or live there – that would be ideal.

The wind blew in through the gap in the door. It was like a cool noose loosely blowing Mia's hair back and encircling her neck. The gap widened and Mia stepped out. Flynn looked down at the step where Mia had slept. Christ how bad must her life be. To sleep out in the cold. On a slab of hard concrete.

"You won't do anything stupid…will you Mia?"

Mia grinned up at him.

"Like attach myself to a stranger on the train?"

147

Flynn smiled unreservedly.

"Like raid his rubbish."

Mia's smile drooped.

"You'll go to the police won't you Flynn?"

He nodded finding it hard to form words.

"If you could avoid mentioning my name," she added stepping from sanctuary into reality.

Walking down the road, Mia couldn't bear to turn around and see his shut door. If she'd looked she'd have seen Flynn, leaning against the door frame, watching.

Flynn didn't recognise himself when he was with her. It was unsettling. Maybe he'd return to uni today.

Upstairs he threw stuff into a sports bag: his Mac, his boxers, his fucking senses.

"Oh fuck!"

Flynn sunk onto the bed, aghast by the state she was in. He was at a crossroads. Did he believe her? Or did he tell his parents? Jesus, she was fucking up his life. God, he was a total shit. She'd been battered! But he felt conflicted. She was in jeopardy; real or imagined and he was being threatened; maybe by Mia herself? What if he said nothing and things went sour? If he talked and made her crap life crappier could he live with that? It was mental! His life had been jogging along nicely until this crazy girl, who'd morphed from a dumpling to a breezy, curvaceous, streetwise stormtrooper, wreaks havoc on his life. He shook his head; it just so happened Star Wars was his favourite movie.

****

Mia looked at the address the social worker at the hospital had given her. Hayes. She'd never heard of the place; it wasn't even in her borough; it had no tube; she had to get three buses! It took fucking ages! Getting off the final bus Mia found herself at an enormous Sainsbury's. It was one with a trolley escalator. She was full, from breakfast, but decided on snacks for her room – she knew it was a shared kitchen; did she need her own saucepan? Plates? Utensils? She didn't have a fucking clue. She bought a biscuit tin along with Oreo's and chocolate digestives as well as a cheap kettle and cappuccino sachets; that way she didn't need milk or sugar. She added t-shirts, underwear, pjs and trainer socks.

From the supermarket Mia had no clue where to go; unwise in Hayes – a place where fresh meat stood out a mile. Like Paddington it was multi-cultural but poorer and clickier. Mia swallowed; her throat dry, like ground coriander. Jittery and pessimistic she pulled out the address again dropping it. Bending down headrush knocked her balance. Unsteadily she rose. Her strength sapped, she felt on the edge of melting. Her attack; still so raw, impending surgery and now this. Jesus, life was one fucking pothole after another!

"Stop being chickenshit!" she berated herself, blinking tears away and focusing on the hand-drawn map.

"Walk past Sainsburys, cross three roads, turn left at Bishop Road, turn left again onto Branker Road, number twenty-one."

Mia walked purposefully; quietly shitting herself. She should have come earlier because the night was dark, the road was darker and the house was grim. It was a large terraced property. Like its neighbours the front garden was overgrown and littered with rubbish. The doorbell had been vandalised, so Mia knocked. No one answered. She knocked harder, maybe too hard. What was she supposed to do? She looked at the bay windows. One was cracked right in the corner with fractures branching through the pane like a spider's web. Inside, curtains were thrown up like a shot-putter had aimed at the rail. Crap. She couldn't do emergency accommodation. She. Really. Could. Not. Do. This. She'd have to go to her dad's, even though she didn't want to burden him. About to turn away a reality check had her walking down the side of the building. A tall wooden gate hung off hinges; as Mia tentatively pushed it, the door swung back into her. Knocking it away harshly it banged loudly against bins, piled high with rubbish. There were too many broken bottles and crushed lager cans to pretend this wasn't a halfway house; for Mia to pretend she wasn't halfway through her life, yet she'd already fucked it up.

"Who. Fuck. There?"

The accent reminded Mia of Boris. Walking further into the garden she saw outlines of two bulky men sitting on a trampoline drinking.

"Social Services sent me."

Mia had no idea what else to say.

"Ub-stairs," said one bluntly before dipping into his own language punctuated with shit and bastard. The way in was visible by candles flickering within. Mia walked through a galley kitchen into a dark hallway and up wooden stairs to a dark landing. Standing outside four closed doors, unsure which room was hers, she knocked on door one. It opened, barely an inch, and an uplit face scared the life out of Mia. It was a kid, three or four with a torch beneath their chin.

"What. Fuck. You. Want?"

Mia was relieved the angry voice behind the kid remained out of sight.

"Social sent me?"

"Nedzzz doorrr."

In a square room without carpet, mould on the walls and a window that didn't close, Mia stood unsure of…everything. Hearing a creak in the hallway she turned the key in the lock. She flicked the light switch – nothing.

"Typical!"

In the dark, she lay, in a bed she worried was covered in the dead skin of multiple people. Her bed was probably the living world, David Attenborough could make a film – Poor People's Planet. She stared up at the ceiling. She thought about the Leavers' Year Book. Cleo Hammond got voted most likely to marry a footballer, Steven Potter got voted most likely to become a millionaire and her, Mia Dent, beneath her photo it said Most Likely To Live in A Caravan. Right now Mia had no argument, her lifestyle was of a transient nature but it hurt to be voted most likely to be a fuck-up.

Her room smelt of sick. Tomorrow she'd get some bleach. Right now she had the energy of a squashed grape. She simply laid there listening to the soundtrack of homelessness. A baby wailing. Repeated flushing of the toilet. Arguing. What disturbed her most was her mobile. She saw it, on the quilt on her estate bed. Jesus. The person who most hated her had access to Flynn. She prayed to hit the numb stage, when the brain processes a matter is out of your control so flicks emotion off. But Mia's switch didn't flick.

At first light she was in Sainsburys buying a new phone and texting Flynn.

My evil mum has my phone. This is my new number in case you need it. Please believe me. I'd hate you to think badly of me. Go to the police!

That was quick! Because returning from the library to the Hayes house she was met by two police officers and promptly put in the back of a squad car...again!

****

"Mia Dent, contrary to the Protection from Harassment Act of 1977, you made menacing communications to Mr Flynn Mason between 6th April and 7th April. Mia Dent contrary to the Section 2A, offence stalking, you did stalk Mr Flynn Mason from 4th September 2018."

Mia fighting the urge to cry said nothing. She'd never imagined it would come to this.   "Not going to give me any trouble are you?"

"No...I...I just."

Mia's words trailed off. What was there to say? She was a stalker. A weirdo.

"Take a seat there."

Mia sat on a plastic chair below a notice board with the number of the Samaritans.

"Too late," she concluded.

"Keep your chin up and look directly at the cross."

"FLASH."

"Up you get. Let's get you fingerprinted," said the custody sergeant. Mia expected an ink pad, but instead she was taken to what looked like a cash dispenser where her hand was scanned. From the corner of her eye she saw Constable Hall and felt ashamed.

Constable Hall looked at the arrest sheet raised by DS Raymond.

"Prick!"

In holding cell three Mia slept like the dead; she'd been drained of everything good.

Lunch woke her, not hunger pangs, but the noise of chains, keys, locks and heavy booted feet on tiled floor. Mia looked at the tuna cucumber sandwich and ate it because her stomach was barren. Eventually, she was taken from her cell for questioning.

"In the room: myself DS Raymond, Mia Dent and her appropriate adult Mr Coombe of St Thomas More School. Miss Dent has wavered legal representation."

"Do you realise the offences you are being accused of are serious?"

Mia nodded.

"And you refuse legal support?"

"Yes. I haven't done anything wrong. Well, I have, but not the notes, car or texting, hardly anything really."

"What exactly do you think you've done wrong?"

"I did a little stalking, ages ago. I promised Flynn I'd stop and I did."

"So you admit stalking?"

"Yes, but it was gentle stalking. It was more staring."

"But you followed Mr Mason home one day."

"Yes."

"You loitered around his house and kept him under observation."

"I didn't loiter. Umm, maybe it was loitering at first?"

Mia was thoughtful, trying to relay an honest account of her history with Flynn.

"But once I saw Mrs Hornby struggling I had a purpose at Hamilton Road."

"Mrs Hornby?"

"An old lady at number 28. I do chores for her."

"You followed Mr Mason to work and you spied on him."

"Yes, that's true up until the rubbish."

"So you admit you went through Mr Mason's garbage."

"Yes. But I did apologise."

"But you kept the empty sim card with his number on didn't you."

"I did."

"How did you feel when Mr Mason asked you to stay away from him?"

"Sad."

"So you thought you'd punish him. Tell him you hated him, that you hoped he died."

"No! I did not send horrible messages to Flynn. I'd cut off my hand first. Anyway, I would never think badly of Flynn. Ever. It was my mum. She's...she's not right...she's vindictive and manipulative. I left my phone in the flat...she had access to it."

"Did you report it to the police."

"It's a £4 phone I knew my mum had. You wouldn't investigate that. You didn't even investigate the text from Alex's attacker; you fobbed me off."

"You're the girl who cried wolf. It's hard to take you seriously. Right now I need to talk to Mr Mason before we proceed. Interview suspended at eleven fifteen."

Raymond left Mia sweating for twenty hours before calling Flynn Mason.

"It's DS Raymond. We have Mia Dent in custody. She admits harassment, but denies the other charges; claims it's her mother. How do you want to proceed?"

Raymond listened, his irritation growing. Someone needed to teach this girl a lesson.

"I understand, yes she's young."

She's a fucking liability, thought Raymond, prosecute you dick.

"You don't want to ruin her career prospects with a criminal record."

Wanker.

"Mr Mason these things turn nasty quickly. Mia Dent is well known here at the nick. She's a very needy, unstable girl with a propensity for lying."

Fucking time waster.

"Ok," said Raymond smiling. "We'll charge her."

****

Disconnecting the call, Flynn's uneasy heart nosedived to his toes. He'd damaged her future. Worse he'd hurt her. She'd feel flattened. She cared what he thought. She wanted him to want her back. He'd felt it. The powerful longing.

****

This was a day she'd dreaded. Two weeks after being charged, here she was, standing outside Uxbridge County Court, wondering would Flynn come. Now a dull pain, he was like bottled champagne waiting to be uncorked or a snow globe waiting to be shaken. Mia was scared seeing him might lead to an emotional crisis. In turmoil, she entered and headed for the loo. She breathed out shakily; this was a hard thing to face alone. Her dad offered to come, but he seemed so weak lately; a virus he said; no need to bother a doctor.

"Mason vs Dent, court room 2."

Mia wished she could swop the versus bit to Mason for Dent forever, that's what should be carved on wood somewhere on this planet. Instead, she entered the small court room to listen to Flynn's solicitor tell the judge she was a voyeur, a stalker, a vandal, a danger to Flynn. It was a nightmare.

"There is no evidence to support the accusation that Mia Dent is responsible for vandalism. Miss Dent denies threatening behaviour, but freely admits she has unrequited feelings for Mr Mason and has acted against The Protection of Freedoms Act 2012. As her compulsion to seek out Mr Mason is still strong, I hereby grant a restraining order of twelve months. Miss Dent you are free to leave the court. Refrain from seeking out Mr Mason. To do so would be a criminal act incurring a jail sentence. Do you understand the seriousness of the situation?"

"Yes sir."

She understood Flynn was in danger. Who was behind this nasty business? She wanted to discuss it with Flynn. Lord, she was her own worst enemy.

****

He'd watched her waiting. In her smart, long-sleeved floral dress. Her hands tightly wringing her cardigan, her foot anxiously tapping. Her face was faintly bruised yellow, a reminder of the attack. He thought of last night; how he'd pushed Lizzie against the cold kitchen wall...all the while seeing Mia. Sweet, sweet Mia.

****

Mia dropped her bag on the bed. She opened the rickety, rotting window; fresh air gently breezed in replacing the staleness. Frustratedly, she pulled off her dress, dropping it in the laundry basket. Pulling a chicken sandwich and cola from her bag, she flopped onto her creaking bed; finding solace in estrangement from her mum - in central Hayes, in one hundred and forty-two square feet, Mia could finally live. From charity shops across Hillingdon, Mia had a fresh, floral bed with crazy cushions, a clean rug, a bright voile and a desk lamp that illuminated when you touched the base. On the desk her things were neatly arranged. More than her address had changed: The White Bear was history and Stan and Tombstone a far-off memory. Here, nobody knew her history, nobody bothered her. The attack had changed her. She had a greater understanding of violence and so she enrolled in a local mixed martial arts club. All she needed was to put Flynn Mason behind her.

****

Becca was making sandwiches for lunch. He leant over her and planted a kiss on her bare shoulder. Over the years she'd learnt to suppress negative reactions. He was totally revolting; he made her skin crawl, but her response was always pleasant. She had adapted; it's what survivors did. It's what Petra found impossible. Petra fought him tooth and nail and died for it.

In the window Becca saw his reflection; he sat watching. He was constantly on his guard. Upstairs they wore only underwear. No clothes meant no concealment; of themselves or a weapon. She'd got used to low temperatures; she no longer shivered uncontrollably, not even when he touched her.

The newspaper was on the kitchen table. The terror she felt seeing Petra's headline was like the life being vacuumed from her. Her chest was so tight she thought her ribs would snap, puncture her lungs and she would internally drown in her own blood. The papers speculated whether they were dead or alive. If alive, where were they? Did he keep them restrained? Yes! But more for pleasure than necessity.

It had been a month since she'd displayed her art in the sixth form exhibition and sat the art exam. A week ago she'd sat Spanish and tomorrow was English. Her last exam. Her very last day of secondary school education.

Mia took the lid off a flowery A4 storage box containing important paperwork; her GCSE certificates, birth certificate, passport, her restraining order! At the top was an offer letter from Exeter University for a place on their Fine Art undergraduate degree. She had no idea what the judge at the county court would think. She shouldn't be within a mile radius of Flynn...yet she'd attended a portfolio interview, walked around the campus, checked out the accommodation, seen Flynn at a distance and turned away.

From beneath the letter she pulled out an A4 laminated number - one hundred and six. With safety pins Mia attached it to her t-shirt. She glanced around her tidy room, shut the window and patted her pockets for bank card and key. Running down two flights of stairs, Mia passed Remi in the kitchen. The eight-year-old was pouring cornflakes in bowls for her and her three-year-old brother.

"Zegnaj," Mia said smiling.

"Pa," said Remi smiling back.

Stepping outside, a hot blanket of air engulfed Mia. Three bloody buses in this heat!   It was barely ten when Mia got to Kensington Gardens and already she was sweating between her shoulder blades. It was the hottest June in twenty one years. Mia could blame the temperature for this moment of madness. No way should she be taking part in The Royal Parks half-marathon...alongside Flynn Mason.

Stretching and warming up, her reservations piled high like unstable Jenga bricks. For months she'd been caught in a vortex of grief. She'd struggled with recurrent flashbacks of her attack. They'd found a footing in her memory; attaching themselves to her history alongside Alex. These traumas mutated becoming one long nightmare that increasingly disturbed her sleep. She ran, at every opportunity, attempting to shift her mounting depression. More than ever she needed sight of Flynn; even if fleeting.

There were nearly two hundred participants, which was good for Mia. They camouflaged her as she weaved through them, her eyes darting from one to the next to the next until her heart lurched painfully.

There he was. The man she risked everything for. God he was edible. He had long satin shorts on like boxers and a gym t-shirt. She wanted to bound over to him, talk to him, touch him. She remembered the way he'd held her. How he'd stroked her hair. How he'd tightened his hold on her like he cared.

At the sound of the klaxon the mass of runners diffused. There were a hundred runners in front of Flynn. Mia was twenty people behind him. The first ten k she ran comfortably with Flynn in her sights. When he picked up the pace some runners between them petered out and some fore runners fell back. Determined, Mia kept her position. A kilometre later her body hurt, she was soaked in sweat, blisters raised on her heals and her neck ached from keeping Flynn in sight. Another 7k, Flynn picked up speed; suddenly it felt like a competition, was she sure, yeah, her nipples were on fire! One by one runners between her and Flynn dropped back whilst Mia drove forward running unstably right behind him. Pushing herself a fraction too much Mia's body began crashing. Her legs wobbled from exertion which she failed to notice because she was staring at Flynn's beautifully shaped bottom. She was thinking how firm it was when, one misplaced jelly foot dropped too near the other and she was faaaaa-lllllling. Unconciously her body stretched out, her arms reached for Flynn and he was faaaa-lllllling too.

Flynn took the impact of hitting the ground as Mia landed on him. Trapped beneath her, flat on his stomach, Mia's hoarse breaths dampened his neck as she pinned him to the ground; a lioness with a captured gazelle.

Flynn scrambled to his knees; Mia's slid to the side, onto the hard ground.

"Urhhh."

Like Flynn Mia scrambled into a sitting position. Flynn's face, covered in red clay dust, looked dazed. Mia stretched her hand to wipe it but he scuttled backward, scared, terrified in fact.

"Hi Flynn."

Jumping to his feet, Flynn took a karate stance.

"I didn't know you knew karate," smiled Mia weakly, rising.

Flynn couldn't speak. His lips moved but no words emerged.

Mia reached out, but he stumbled back.

"Did I wind you? Shit! I haven't broken your ribs…have I? Flynn?"

"Don't talk to me. You're twisted. You need help. NO! Don't touch me."

"Flynn I…"

"Jesus, you're fucking insane. You're still at it…following me…watching me. You were in Exeter weren't you?"

Mia blushed and cringed.

"Fuck!"

He looked so disappointed in her she felt tears welling.

"I'm going to the police, you seriously need help. You're not right upstairs."

He started backing away.

Mia wiped her sweat covered face. Her stomach was pitching and rising; she felt totally sick with herself.

"Flynn please don't. I'm sorry about this…about everything. My head's been all over the place with…"

"I don't care where you head's at Mia, explain it to the police."

Tears freely ran down her cheeks. Flynn hated himself.

"Thinking of you made my life tolerable. You were my mirror…I didn't see a fat loser when I looked at you…I don't mean that you…It's complicated."

"Let me know when it gets simple."

He was being a total bastard but he couldn't help it. She'd backed him into a corner unearthing emotions he didn't know what to do with. So he cut her off.

"If you care about me Mia you'll stay the fuck away."

She was nodding repetitively, still silently crying.

"I'm utterly, completely sorry Flynn. Please don't involve the police. Go to my school; St Thomas More. There's an exhibition of my work."

"Mia I'm not fucking listening – alright. I don't want to hear you. Or think about you. Jesus Mia you're a paradox or full of shit. I can't gauge how dangerous you are or how vulnerable, but I can't be your rock, your hero; I'm just a bloke Mia, like any other. I've broken hearts, slept with too many women, I'm selfish, I do shots and spew, I fart, my uni room's a dump, I tell girls I'll call but never do. No! Do not come fucking nearer."

"At St Thomas More School, in the hall, you're my muse Flynn, please go."

"Goodbye Mia."

"Please go look Flynn. I swear I'll never ask anything ever again…Please Flynn."

A rush of desire, of pure wanting left her unable to continue.

Her eyes were mesmerizingly beseeching. Why the fuck was she doing this to him? Flynn watched as she walked away. Her shapely legs were firm, but white, like they'd never seen the sun. Her shorts were girly, an aqua blue with a blinding white vest. She was different, but the same. He felt a knot in his gut as she walked off.

****

The park was busy. Runners and spectators everywhere. Many looking and pointing at the girl who'd made a spectacle of herself. She'd been publicly humiliated.

He conceded there was something about…Mia. He didn't usually refer to them by name so soon, but he liked the way hers rolled off his tongue. He smiled creepily. He wondered if he'd roll off her tongue as easy. Feeling the pressure of arousal, he enjoyed the torment of being near…of wanting to touch. Pain was so much a part of pleasure. She would come to embrace that concept. He would lead, and she would follow – it's what she did.

****

In The Admiral, pulling a Guinness, Mia worried about her dad. He'd slowed down considerably; he was forgetting stuff. She'd found bloodied handkerchiefs in the wash; his Father's Day ones. He blamed nose bleeds; hay fever, sinusitis. He claimed the doc said it was nothing, but Mia knew her dad hadn't seen a GP. So, she worked shifts when he was ill and shouldered the burden of admin; cashing up, banking, ordering stock as well as his laundry and meals. Her dad knew she'd moved out. They never discussed Joslyn.

Wiping down the bar Mia looked up and smiled.

159

"Hi Pete, the usual?"

"Yes Mia love."

Pete put £1.49 on the bar.

"Take a seat; I'll bring your cappuccino over."

Pete wobbled to an alcove. He was a regular; friendly enough. As Mia poured milk into the jug for steaming, she wondered what Flynn was up to. Maybe he was with that bit of fluff from the Ferris wheel. Mia shook the chocolate powder.

"Today's paper," said Mia putting the hot mug down in front of Pete.

"Mia you're a sweetie."

"A sherbet lemon?"

"I would have gone with a strawberry bon bon."

"Hey Mia,"

Mia looked up to see Rob.

"Hey Rob."

"I'll make a brew; your dad not around?"

"Upstairs…a bit poorly."

"Needs to get himself to a doctor Mia, we both know that."

Mia nodded. She didn't know why her dad was so stubborn. He had a constant cough, his movement was laboured and his patience with customers was waning. Mia knew a time would come when Reggie wouldn't be able to continue; she just didn't realise how soon.

****

Flynn stood outside the school gates. He hadn't intended to come; but this slip of a girl madder than Keith Lemon, was hard to shake off. It had been two weeks since the race. Time for him to get over the shock of being taken down. Walking into the school, he acknowledged Mia would be an outsider. In a school where labels meant everything, teenagers judged on branding, and Chelsea was affluent.

Flynn noted the glances toward him. He knew he was attractive, but the attention was significant. He followed the signs to the Art Exhibition. It flowed from the reception, into the hall and upwards to the atrium, where the A level work was displayed. When he reached Mia's work, he understood the enquiring, surprised looks.

"Fuck."

160

Those around him tutted.

"I apologise."

"It's you," a man said.

"Yes."

Flynn was lost for words. An A1 image of him was centre piece. It was like looking in a mirror except it was so fresh and engaging. Around it was sketch after sketch; from each one a sewn, meandering path led to other pieces. They were all related to Mia; telling a very intimate story. The honesty of the work made it exceptional: waist measurements, her mother bent over a table, a charge sheet, boxing gloves, a hooded man. Everything positive, Mia trailed back to Flynn's image; all the negative energy pointed to a painting of a women, Mia's mother, Flynn presumed. It was dark and witchcraft scary. Her skill was astonishing. Mia was fucking spectacular. Flynn had never felt so out of his depth...yet so connected to someone.

"Mia's muse."

A tall man, balding, offered his hand.

Flynn took it.

"I'm Mr Coombe, Mia's form teacher and appropriate adult when she's arrested...which seems to be surprisingly regular of late."

The words weren't delivered accusingly, simply matter of fact.

"Hi, I'm..."

"Flynn." Coombe finished.

"Yes."

Flynn's fingers ran through his hair. It's what he did on the rare occasion he was uncomfortable.

"Her work's good, don't you think?" he asked Flynn

"It's brilliant, but a shock. Seeing myself through Mia's eyes. How shit her life is."

"Mia's a straightforward girl. She didn't mean for her attraction to impact on you negatively. It doesn't excuse her unwanted intrusion into your life but her intentions were not malicious. Anyway, stay, take your time or come again even."

And Flynn did come again, two hours later, with Kira.

"Oh my God Flynn," Kira gushed.

"Exactly!"

"Wow she's lost so much weight. Oh my God yeah, look at this heart Flynn, it's made up of weighing scale print-outs. If you start at the bottom, she was eleven stone, eight pounds, then follow the trail to the centre of the heart and she's nine stone, six."

"Flynn, is that yours?"

"Shit! She lied about the rubbish."

Flynn's t-shirt was PVA glued to a board creating a torso. Behind it was an outline of a female, a breast semi-revealed. It was Mia. She was his shadow. A heart with its chambers and blood vessels was sewn onto the t-shirt.

"Well, she's on the pill, her Microgynon strip is the left ventricle, along with a condom."

"Fuck." Flynn felt winded.

"Flynn, we're in a school for fucks sake!"

Flynn raised an eyebrow.

"Wouldn't it be cool to help her?"

"Kira, I've a restraining order against her…which she's violated!"

"I know, but now you've seen this you can't go to the police."

It was crazy, but her crush was romantic - even he saw that. On the other hand, she was probably schizophrenic: scared Mia one moment, scary Mia the next.

"I don't know Kira."

"Oh Flynn, that would be a big mistake. She's not a stalker, she's in love with you."

"You know what's messed up Kira?"

She shook her head.

"I love her back."

****

He knew this was it, there would be none after her.

There was a 'but'.

The exhibition rankled him; its subject matter, its intimacy. There was no reference to him and why should there be? So far his activities hadn't impacted greatly on her life…he intended to change that…to bring her into his world.

Waking up with KISS FM was startling. Mia hit the snooze button, snuggling back down, trying to figure out today's riddle. Eight am, the news. Missing, seventeen-year-old Gabby Preston.

"What?"

Mia pushed off the quilt and sat on the edge of the bed staring at the radio, willing it to rewind, replay, rename the missing girl.

"Gabby Preston? There must be loads of Gabby Prestons."

Mia scrambled into her clothes, pulled her rucksack on and left.

Flynn boarded the train. Jesus there she was. He hadn't expected to see her. He quickly moved seat; to get a better view. She looked beautiful...but anxious. She was fidgeting, and her eyes darted to the train map like it was an unfamiliar journey? Usually her eyes would run the length of the carriage searching him out. She probably thought he'd returned to Exeter or because he'd been so wretched to her she'd let him go.

"Shit!"

The woman next to Flynn jumped. Normally he'd apologise, but his head was filled with feelings for Mia and regret about binning her off.

"Shit!"

The woman stood, walked up the carriage and sat; next to Mia! Five minutes later the woman moved again, convinced Flynn had dangerous intentions towards her...but it was Mia Flynn focused on...how ironic.

The nearer school, the more stricken she was. It had to be a horrible reporting mix-up. Maybe she'd misheard simply because she'd bumped into Gabby and her name was at the forefront of Mia's consciousness. Maybe Aleen had said Abby...Abby? Weston. As the train pulled into Sloane Square, Mia was out the doors and up the escalator; Flynn hot on her heels. The weight of apprehension slowed her down; like in a nightmare when you can't run. She crossed the square, bumping into those heading determinedly to the station. She didn't apologise...she couldn't...she felt sick.

Turning into Cadogen Gardens, her heart stopped...or was it time...or did sheer panic make her lose all sense of reality. There were panda cars outside the school gate. Students crowded around uniformed police, ignoring the deputy head blowing her whistle. Mia flung herself back around the corner, against a wall. This had to be a nightmare. It couldn't possibly be real. Mia pinched herself.

"Wake up, wake up."

Flynn was at the end of the adjacent pavement. Observing. What the hell was she doing? He watched her repeatedly sneak a look around the corner. Her body language was all wrong. She was agitated - walking away - turning - running back to glimpse the activity in Cadogen Street? At one point she crouched, dropping her head in her hands. Crying? He needed to see what she saw. He walked around the block, approaching Cadogen Street from the other end to Mia.

"Fuck!"

Police cars, officers, the press.

"Mia what have you been up to?"

He watched teachers round up students, ferrying them into the playground away from flashing cameras and reporters. Quickly Flynn googled the street. Without reading the article the words 'wolf, abduction, Chelsea,' explained everything. Flynn walked passed the school, along the road, towards the corner where Mia was on surveillance. He was preparing in his head what he was going to say. Taking a deep breath, he turned her corner.

"Shit!" He searched the length of the road. "Mia, where the fuck are you?"

Mia was in Peter Jones. In the toilets. Shaking. She felt weak like her blood had been siphoned from her veins.

"Gabby, oh my God, oh my God, oh my God."

It was true. The Wolf had Gabby. Her Gabby. Sitting on the loo Mia's arms wrapped around herself as her stomach ached from tension. It was like someone was pulling on her intestines; unravelling them so they no longer resembled a grand prix course.

"Excuse me are you alright in there?"

Startled, Mia said nothing.

"Is it Mia?"

Was this woman psychic?

"Yes. I'm Mia."

"Your carer is worried. He asked me to check on you?"

Mia opened the door. The woman didn't look crazy.

"I'm fine thank you."

"I'll let him know."

Mia gripped the edge of the sink as head-rush momentarily struck. She steadied herself before washing her hands, simultaneously shaking her head. It couldn't be him.

It was.

Opposite the ladies' restroom Flynn relaxed against a wall like a GQ model. A wave of heat travelled at breakneck speed from her face to between her thighs. She felt appalled. Gabby had been abducted and still her body yearned for Flynn. She looked at him and for once had nothing to say. He most probably hated her.

Flynn saw she was crushed and the desire to fix her led to...

"Let's have tea."

Had Mia imagined it?

"Sorry?"

"I want to buy you tea...maybe even a bacon roll."

Mia looked left and right. She did a three eighty.

"Is this entrapment? Is your floaty girlfriend videoing this?"

"Floaty girlfriend?"

"Kira."

"My cousin and there is no restraining order Mia."

"No restraining order?"

"I've filed an Order to Terminate with the court."

"Order to te

"Mia...stop repeating me...ok?"

"Ok."

Flynn smiled taking her hand.

Mia's heart span like a weather vein. The pressure and warmth of Flynn's hand scared her; it was false hope wrapped in silky comfort at a time she needed it. Already she dreaded the loss. No Flynn. No Gabby.

They sat in a café. Mia studied the small laminated menu scared to look at Flynn in case he wasn't real...in case Gabby's abduction had lead to a psychotic breakdown.

"They want HOW much for a bacon roll?" Mia said, astounded.

"Ok, this might be Location, Location, Location but this is the Chelsea version of getting mugged. There is a lovely Polish café next to my launderette, phenomenal bacon rolls, three slices with the rind on, a wedge of grilled tomato and a crusty roll with real oozing butter."

Flynn thought she sounded tired.

Two teas and toasted sausage sandwiches arrived. Flynn watched as Mia spread ketchup evenly over her toast.

A quiet pause. They ate.

"My carer? Very funny."

Flynn smiled.

Mia reached to the next table for the paper. Unfolding it, she put it between them.

Chelsea Schoolgirl Missing.

Flynn took his time. Sipping tea. Eating. Reading the article.

"Were you friends?"

"Gabby's important to me."

Flynn nodded.

"Do you think it's him Flynn?"

"The Wolf?"

Mia nodded, her mouth too full of bread and sausage to answer.

Flynn shrugged, not wanting to be the one who confirmed it.

"I'm bad luck," declared Mia.

"I should move to another table."

"It's wrong how a killer camouflages himself by being ordinary and can walk unnoticed among us. Bad people should have scars and missing teeth."

"Sounds like my Great Uncle Archibald."

Mia smiled. She appreciated Flynn's endeavours to calm her mounting dread.

"Mia did you send me a note?"

"We've been through this!"

"Not that note Mia."

Flynn pulled it from his pocket.

"This note."

Ask her what happened to Alex?

166

"What happened to Alex Mia?" Flynn asked.

"He um. He. Alex died." A heavy silence hinted at more. "He…He was…beaten.. And he died Flynn." Mia swallowed her tears. "We…we…I liked him Flynn…a lot and."

Mia was breathing hard, her eyes ached painfully with restrained tears and her throat narrowed so tightly she couldn't get enough air.

"Mia, it's ok, breathe," said Flynn.

She was visibly distressed.

"It wasn't like you and me. Alex liked me back. You told me to forget you and I tried and Alex was lovely." Her words tumbled out at warp speed. "We kissed and he put me on a train and then some brute hit him again and again until he died and that monster has his phone and he's texting me…and he's latched on to you…which puts you in grave danger."

It was almost too disturbing to believe. An uneasy silence fell between them.

"Mia…it can't be the same person. Whoever killed Alex might have access to his phone book but they wouldn't know anything about you, certainly not me."

"It's him Flynn – I'm certain. In my gut, I feel it."

"I don't know," said Flynn totally perplexed. "I need to mull this over…Have you reported it to the police?"

"Yes! To a complete dick-head who hates me."

"Detective Sergeant Raymond?"

Mia nodded.

The man who convinced Flynn of a restraining order.

"Did he trace the texts?" asked Flynn.

"He laughed when I asked, said I'd been watching too much American tv."

A heavy silence prevailed.

Mia didn't want Flynn to be the first to call time on their uneasiness.

"I'd better be going."

"Me too. Late for work," said Flynn quietly.

Flynn paid.

"Thank you," said Mia as they stood outside the café.

"You're welcome. Where are you headed?"

"Ealing, I guess. I don't know why I came here; I could have googled the news; maybe I had to see it to believe it," she said shaking her head. "I think I'll go to school quickly, see if there is any news.

"I'll walk with you."

Flynn's head was under siege. Alex, Gabby, him and Mia.

"Mia, we can't do this."

"I know Flynn, but why are you here…now…with me?"

"You're hard to ignore."

"Am I? I feel I've gone unnoticed for seventeen years."

Flynn found himself kicking one foot with the other. He disliked feeling like an emotional teen. A cowardly emotional teen.

"Flynn, do you hate me?"

Mia searched Flynn's face expecting to see at least a shadow of hate.

"No hate isn't what I feel."

Flynn pushed a stray hair off her face and around her ear. Instead of withdrawing, his fingers brushed her smooth cheek, its complexion milky; no concealer or primer, one hundred percent Mia. Mia saw an opportunity. Clumsily, she pressed her lips to Flynn's. His arm snaked around her waist as his lips more than brushed against hers. This unconscious display of affection was unexpected. For them both. Mia closed her eyes as a yearning sigh escaped. Flynn knew he was perpetuating her fantasy but he couldn't help himself. For a moment they hovered between casual and deep kissing. About to tumble into an irreversible position, Flynn pulled away…immediately missing her rich taste.

"Ok. Fine. Right."

He stared into her sea-blue eyes that swept him away and left him adrift. He pulled her to him, hugging her tightly, before pushing her away and holding her at arm's length, like a dangerous substance. Mia's head was almost spinning.

"Look after yourself Mia. You've got my number."

****

Mia put the float in the tills and helped her dad change over the Guinness barrel. What did Flynn mean by, 'you've got my number'? Was it an invitation?

"Mia love, did you phone up about this remote payment machine?"

168

"Yeah Dad, that's the replacement in your hand. I told you, remember?"

Concern registered but the bar was understaffed, and her dad wasn't cutting queues like he used to. Mia didn't have time to freak out about her dad or Gabby or rewind every word and gesture of Flynn's. She worked flat out till nine, finishing while it was still daylight. so she could cross London in relative safety.

The following morning Mia was awake by six, which was a bummer because now her day would be even longer. What she hated most about today was she couldn't remember Flynn's kiss as vividly as yesterday and she knew that tomorrow the memory would be less clear until eventually it wouldn't be a memory, just a title of a memory – The Time Flynn Mason Kissed Me At The School Gates.

Mia popped her fresh pyjamas on – she was squeaky clean from her shower at the swimming baths. No way would she shower here; in this communal living, where each week released criminals checked in. She wasn't judging, the others were ok, they didn't bother her, they kept to themselves; but this wasn't anyone's home, it was a holding area, cleanliness wasn't a priority to those that came and went.

Sitting on the end of her bed, facing The Wolf board, she conversed with herself.

"Gabby, I know you'll be praying to be found and I'm working on it, but I've stared endlessly at this wall and can't make a connection between you and the others. I know his choices aren't random. He selects you but how? And why you Gabby? The girls are all Londoners, they attended different schools, had no shared interests, had never met one another, have different physical attributes. Some had boyfriends. You must share some similarity?" said Mia. "Or…the connection isn't with the girls but the parents? The police would have considered this…"

Mia jumped up.

"Oh. My. God! They are all single parent families. What if the mums used dating sites? What if a date was the abductor? No! What am I going on about? Gabby's parents are together. Her mum isn't dating. Shit!" said Mia exasperatedly.

Mia slid into bed pulling the quilt over her head.

"What if Gabby is the exception? What if she was abducted to hurt me? Don't be such a fucking idiot – go to sleep!"

Mia burrowed further under the quilt.

"G'night Mia. G'night self."

But Mia couldn't sleep. She thought about her window with its drawn curtains. Was there a man out there watching? She thought she was being followed…that for some reason Alex's killer was after her, but it was as Constable Hall had explained – a sick person had found Alex's phone and was playing a game they would tire of…but how did they know about Flynn? Possibilities and conclusions rattled around Mia's brain for more than an hour before she fell asleep. She had spooked herself, and so her dreams were disturbing. If she had crept to the window, peeped through the curtains, she would have seen his outline and had good reason to be disturbed.

****

Mia woke exhausted. Alex's death wasn't the first thing to hit her today because her head was filled with missing girls. Sitting up she pulled the quilt around her because, although it was late June, this large, rambling house was damp and cold. She turned her attention to her Wolf board; to the collection of images and articles cut from papers. Mia focused on a photograph of a young man; Sean Flynn, Petra's boyfriend. According to the paper, he worked in Kwik Fit, Kilburn. She knew what he looked like from Facebook. It had to be worth a try. She pulled on Flynn's jeans, locked her room and travelled across London. Approaching the garage, she spotted him.

"Sean. Sean Flynn?" called Mia. Someone wolf-whistled. The garage was pure testosterone and Mia felt out of place; she didn't even have a car.

"Who wants to know?" asked a hench, short bloke suspiciously.

"My name is Mia. You don't know me but I need to speak to you about Petra."

His features hardened and he looked resolute.

"I told the police everything. I've nothing to add."

"Sean, please. My friend Gabby is missing and the DS is shit and time is ticking."

Sean looked at his mates and nodded for them to go ahead without him.

"Lunch break is only forty-five minutes. What do you want to know?"

"Everything you can tell me," said Mia following him to the café. They sat. They ordered. Mia opened Sean up.

"We hadn't been going out long."

"But you were in the same year at school, so you'd known each other for ages," Mia pointed out.

"True. We were mates then we dated. It was ok until she started with her paranoia."

"What do you mean?"

"She'd fallen out with a girl, said she was stealing her stuff. She

171

was narky about it."

"Was Petra right?"

"I don't know. At first the police were all over it, convinced The Wolf had stalked her and nicked her stuff...like he'd got off on it or something. "

"What went missing?"

"A perfume one week, a vest the next."

Mia nodded for him to continue.

"We argued about it...the day she was taken."

"By the sounds of it Petra, wouldn't have gone without a fight?"

"She was quiet. I liked that about her, but she wouldn't take shit."

They sat for a few moments in silence.

"I've gotta split," he said suddenly, pushing his seat back and standing. He put his hand on Mia's arm; his skin was clammy. He looked uncomfortable.

"If we hadn't argued, she might still be alive."

"Or the Wolf would have found another opportunity to take her."

Sean nodded unconvinced.

"Sean, Petra's death was not your fault; it's The Wolf's."

Mia didn't know if she was talking about Sean and Petra or her and Alex.

"Give me your number...if I remember anything else I'll text," assured Sean.

Mia caught a bus en route to St Michael's Secondary School, seeking out the friends of Olivia Weston; second to last girl abducted. An after-school netball match was published on the school website; Olivia had been wing-attack.

Mia waited for the teacher to put the reserves on then followed the two substituted players to the girls' changing room.

"Excuse me. Are you friends of Olivia?"

"Who wants to know?" asked one cautiously.

"I'm Mia Dent, a friend of Gabby Preston, the last girl abducted."

The girls looked at one another.

"I don't want to cause trouble, I'm trying to speak to people connected to victims."

"Why?"

172

This was the bit where Mia felt like an idiot.

"Police miss clues…they're not as conscientious as people think."

"How can we help?" the taller one asked dropping down to a bench. Mia pulled out her notebook turning to the page allocated to Olivia.

"Did Olivia have a boyfriend?"

"No."

"Did she think she was being followed?"

"No."

"Would she have fought back?"

"No."

"Was she ever in trouble?"

Reagan said no, Sarah yes.

"Not in school," clarified Reagan. "At home her mum's boyfriend Carl was too strict. He was on her case all the time. For years it had been Olivia and her mum then Carl comes on the scene and he drives a wedge between them. She was miserable over it."

"I didn't read anything about a boyfriend in the news reports. Was he questioned?"

"Don't know. We heard he scarpered soon after Olivia went missing."

"Did she ever think any of her things had gone missing?"

"What about her brush?" Reagan said to Sarah.

"Oh yeah. She had this brush. It looked Victorian. It was heavy and decorated. It belonged to her great grandma…there was no way she'd lose it – she had a hissy fit about it."

"Is any of this helping?" asked Reagan.

"I don't know yet…but this is my number and email. Please let me know of anything strange or different even if it's silly. I'm not giving up on my friend Gabby."

The girls hugged Mia like she was Olivia's saviour and Mia suddenly realised she may be spreading false hope. That her, playing detective, could hurt people. A girl had been buried: a sister, daughter, niece. But if she didn't snoop, she was giving up on Gabby.

Mia slept with a heavy heart; twisting and turning she woke entwined in the sheets clammy, still tired. The fact that it was results day dawned.

"Shit!"

Mia stood quietly in the queue marked A-D. Those around her were hollering, wailing, fist-pumping, hugging. Mia was nervous, she wanted to go to Exeter a success, instead of ten steps behind everyone else. She wanted to tell Flynn she'd got three A's.

It so happened Mr Coombe was releasing the results for A-D.

"Good luck Mia," he said smiling, putting the brown envelope in her hand.

"Thank you Sir…for everything."

She'd intended to head to the art room with her envelope.

"Mia!"

"Ben!"

They hugged quickly and Mia could tell by Ben's face that he was bursting to tell her.

"Go on then," she smiled.

"Two A's and a B," he grinned.

"You are such a jammy dodger," laughed Mia hugging him again.

"Open yours," encouraged Ben. "Do it quick like ripping off a plaster."

Mia unfolded the paper.

"Oh my God. A*, A, B."

Ben whisked her off the floor swinging her round.

"Megan, over hear."

"Sorry guys," said Mia. "I'll be back in a sec, gotta take this call."

"Morning Dad."

"Is this my daughter's number?"

"Dad it's me," Mia laughed.

"Mia?"

"Yes, it's Mia. Is it a bad line dad?"

No response.

"Dad it's me are you still there?"

"Yes, I'm waiting for Mia."

"I'm not coming today Dad, it's results day remember?"

"Does Mia know?"

"Dad, you're scaring me. What's wrong?"

"No…tell Mia not to come…I've a pain in my chest."

174

Mia panicked. Her brain jolted from one line of action to another. Should she go to him? Should she phone an ambulance? Should she do both?

"Dad, I'm coming. I'm putting the phone down now."

"Mia, is everything ok?" asked Megan.

Mia didn't want to spoil the day for them.

"Fine, my dad's got in a tizwaz over the float, I'll catch you guys later."

Mia ran from school choking on fear. She phoned Flynn.

"Mia?"

"It's my dad Flynn...something is wrong."

"Where are you?"

"The square."

The line went dead but a minute later an incoming text from Flynn. He was coming for her in a silver zafira.

Flynn saw her in the middle of Sloane Square, her hair blowing in all directions. She looked frantic.

"Mia!"

She jumped in the cab.

"Where to?" said the driver.

"The Admiral, Ealing, off the Greenford Road."

She was shaking. Flynn pulled her under his arm.

"He's got cancer or liver disease or he's having a heart attack; he said his chest hurt."

Flynn phoned 999.

"How much further?" Flynn asked the driver.

"Five minutes tops."

He felt her quivering in his arms and a rush of protectiveness came over him.

"He didn't know who I was Flynn. He was confused...like he had concussion."

"We're here gov."

Mia was out the moving car, Flynn hot on her heals. The pub door was unlocked. It shouldn't have been. The bar and tables were swamped with last night's glasses. Mia bolted up the steep staircase, petrified.

Reggie was dressed. Flat on the bed. Barely breathing. He was gold.

"Dad, it's Mia."

He wasn't lucid. He called for Mia but didn't recognise her.

"Dad, I'm here, its Mia, I'm with you."

Flynn couldn't bear the hoarseness, the near cracking of her voice. Hearing the ambulance nearing, Flynn reluctantly left Mia, running straight into Rob.

"What the fuck's going on? Who the fuck are you?"

"I'm Mia's friend; she's upstairs with her dad; he's seriously ill."

"Christ, I told that fucker to get to the doctor. Jesus. How's Mia?"

"Shaken."

"He's all she's got."

"What about her mum?"

"The woman would have you running in circles whilst emptying your pockets and frying your brain."

With Reggie on a stretcher, the crew struggled down the steep, narrow stairs. Mia knew he'd die of humiliation if he was conscious.

"Can I ride in the ambulance?"

"No love, your dad's too poorly. Meet us at Ealing hospital."

The A&E receptionist confirmed Reggie's arrival. She released the door lock and they walked through to the assessment area. Mia's dad was in the corridor on a stretcher and an initial examination was being made. Flynn, who had private health care, was shocked. He looked at Reggie; with an oxygen mask over his nose and mouth, he literally was gold – not the shining, bright gold but the dirty yellow, dull gold. Mia was on her knees, holding her dad's hand to her heart. Flynn removed his light jacket and folded it.

"Mia...Mia." He shook her slightly until she looked up.

"Kneel on this."

Flynn slipped the garment beneath her knees. His presence was the one thing holding Mia together. Mia's eyes hadn't moved from Reggie's chest, she was monitoring its rise and fall. She was suspended in time, too frightened to speak or move in case it speeded up her dad's demise. But Flynn knew there were things you never came back from – this was Reggie's 'thing'.

"Flynn!" Mia's tone was bound in dread.

"Flynn, he's not breathing, he's not breathing," she screamed.

It was crazy, shambolic, scary. Flynn pulled Mia away from her father as hospital staff seized the trolley and rushed to the crash unit.

"No Mia, stay."

Flynn, gently restrained her against him, preventing her running past the '*strictly no visitors sign*'. Flynn was breathing hard into her hair, himself unnerved by the sudden onset of activity. He knew one thing for sure...he never wanted to be poor.

Loosening his hold on Mia he noticed what a little thing she was; curvy and cuddly – yes – but a good head and a half beneath him. Her shoulders were narrow, her waist small, her hips wide. She'd transformed herself in the last year. Whilst thinking this, Flynn was rubbing Mia's back and kissing her head. He wanted to neutralise her pain. He couldn't imagine watching a loved one die such a painful death. For them to be so bewildered you were unrecognisable, yet they called your name. It was doubly cruel.

"Flynn?"

"Mia?"

"Thank you Flynn, I...I...couldn't do this on my own but it was selfish of me letting you drop everything for my drama."

He held her away from him.

"I've been thinking about you...rather a lot...and...and..."

The doors flew open. Flynn felt Mia's body stiffen.

"Mia Dent?"

"Yes!"

"Your dad's been taken to intensive care. It has a waiting room. You'd be more comfortable there. We've got his records online, his next of kin is Mrs Joslyn Dent. We've contacted her. She's on her way."

"He won't want her here. She's not a good person to be around."

"We're legally obliged to act on the information we have."

Mia nodded.

"Mia let's go?"

Flynn wasn't running away or calling the police or blaming her. He was holding her hand whilst walking through the maze of corridors following the signs for Intensive Care. Flynn worried he loved a girl with a thing for emergency services. First the police, now the hospital, all she needed was a fire. In love? It was crazy but true.

"I think it's called a waiting room because it's where you wait for someone to die?"

Mia didn't look at Flynn for an answer. She sat on a plastic chair beside him. She imagined he was sad for her; that's why their fingers were interlocked.

"If only x-men were real. I'd choose the power to extract illness. But there are no miracles, no quick fixes."

Silence followed for a while.

"How's uni going?"

"Extremely well; I've been binge drinking, but after today I've got that under control."

"Do you smoke?"

"No."

"Drugs?"

"No."

"Me neither." She looked up at him and smiled. "You're my only vice."

God, she was beautiful, thought Flynn right at this moment, hauntingly so. Like Ophelia. He wanted to fix everything for her; but there was no mending her father. It made him realise how sheltered his childhood had been and how protective his parents were.

"I'll need to get him pyjamas, underwear, wash stuff. Oh my God she's here."

Flynn felt Mia shrink behind him.

A tall, probably once very attractive women, semi stumbled in. A man held her arm. The nearer she came, the more obvious the smell of alcohol. It was like she sweated it.

"Mia, love, you look awful...who's this?" her tone was sickly seductive.

"I'm Mia's friend, Flynn."

Joslyn's resentment was glaringly obvious.

"Mia, is this the man you threw yourself at who didn't want you?"

Internal hate burned quicker than Mia's mum's cigarette. She wanted to scream at Joslyn, why isn't it you dying?

"It's illegal, you being near him. Mia you're pathetic, he doesn't want you."

Humiliation burned through Mia, the fire lit by a vindictive mother.

"You're wrong Mrs Dent. I want to be with Mia."

Flynn pulled Mia against his solid chest. Thank, God – she felt emotionally battered.

"I'll tell you no word of a lie Mia; you drove your poor dad to this. He's ashamed of you Mia. Flaunting yourself at this boy. It's degrading. He'd never be attracted to you."   Flynn was lost for words. She wasn't a mother she was a rat who fed off her own.   "Let's go to the drinks machine, get a coffee, we can see the ward doors from there."

Mia nodded.

"Is she like that constantly or is today one of her good days?"

"That's her warm-up routine."

"How do you stand it?"

"I don't, I sit."

A deep longing stretched between them. Flynn wasn't a romantic but words like destiny and chemistry buzzed around his brain. He'd fought it tooth and nail; even the legal system was no obstacle to her.

"I want to kiss you," said Flynn huskily, his eyes burning like embers as their attraction stoked the coals.

Mia closed the space between them; his lips met hers halfway. They moved slowly at first: tentative, nervous, knowing this kiss altered their relationship. Until Flynn's desire kicked in hard and he pulled Mia closer, holding her tighter. As their mouths opened Mia felt weightless, like she was in space. Her fingers clenched Flynn's top and their kiss deepened until neither knew where they were.

"Slut!"

Joslyn's teeth cut words that tore.

"You've no shame. You make me sick. Spreading your legs everywhere."

This woman's fucking terrifying thought Flynn.

"Shut. The Fuck. Up,"

Mia's tone wasn't raised. She wasn't making a scene.

"You're poison: you're incapable of caring, of loving, of being a decent person. You're totally wrapped up in yourself. Why the fuck did you get married? Why the fuck did you have a child? I'm sorry but I can't find one good thing about you so I don't want you to be my mother. You're fired. Don't say one more fucking word."

"Mia Dent?"

Joslyn flew between Mia and the doctor. She brushed her hair from her face in an unsubtle effort to look attractive.

"I'm Reggie's widow."

Mia gasped, but Joslyn was on a roll.

"My husband and I were great friends, even after the divorce. It was the drink. He was mad for it."

"Excuse me," said the doctor dismissing Joslyn and directing his words at Mia.

"Your dad is seriously ill. His liver is badly damaged."

"But livers repair don't they?" Or had Mia made that up.

"Not when the damage is significant. Mr Dent's diseased liver is irreparable. He also has a severely ulcerated leg. It's eaten away most of his calf. Walking would have been excruciating; he most probably used alcohol for pain relief."

An ugly wail erupted from Joslyn who slumped into Kevin's arms.

"But he will get better. Now he's here. He could have a liver transplant."

"That's not an option. Prepare yourself that your dad's not going to make it."

Flynn felt gutted for Mia who was stricken with grief she wasn't ready for.

"He wants to see you Mia."

With that Joslyn uncrumpled. She positioned herself an inch from the doctor's face.

"Only Mia and her companion, Mrs Dent."

"But I'm his widow," she snarled, her whiskey breath infiltrating the starchy atmosphere. "He's got no right to be here," she screeched pointing at Flynn before aiming her gel nail at Mia. "And she's a criminal. I'm calling the police. Mia, do you hear me, I'm calling the police on you?"

The doctor swiped his ID against the reader and Mia and Flynn walked through the doors. Reggie was hooked up to various IVs and monitors.

180

"Is he in much pain?" Mia asked the doctor.

"Some. He's on a morphine drip and he's sedated, but he was lucid enough to say he didn't want to see Mrs Dent."

Mia nodded, pulling up a seat and holding his cannulated hand. They sat there quietly, observers of the thin thread of life Reggie clung to.

"He's dying Flynn, right now, right here and I can't stop it. I can't fix him." Her voice was unnaturally high, her emotions taut. What could Flynn say? The situation went way beyond reassurance. Her dad was undoubtedly dying.

"From what you've seen of my mum, this is probably hard to believe, but he loves her, he's never stopped...he's never gotten over her. You know what Flynn my dad saw his future and he didn't want to live it. He gave up. That's why he wouldn't see a doctor. Maybe I'm like them both. Repeatedly you've asked me to stop my pursuit of you and I haven't. Like my dad, I can't jump from the plane and pull the parachute."

Flynn crouched down, pulling her to him. Her tears slowly rolled down his neck; her pain soaking into his t-shirt. For what seemed an age, they remained. Mia barely breathing; her chest tightly knotted.

"Mia, he's gone."

Mia couldn't speak; grief had wrapped itself around her memories. She was lost in the past, tracking way back, to a time her dad was happy. She couldn't find it. Mia deduced love was torture, and her dad broke early.

Mia dressed in the same cheap, black dress she'd worn to Alex's funeral; after today she intended to shred it. Arranging the burial had been hopelessly grim. Among her dad's things she'd found an insurance policy with a note attached.

Sorry love, you deserved better. This will cover the necessary with some to spare. Go on holiday. Somewhere sunny. Love Dad.

Mia read and re-read the note like it was encrypted. As if, surely, these couldn't be her dad's final words. They didn't comfort or enlighten; they were crap. Meanwhile Mia was struggling with the brewing bitterness that her mum was responsible for her dad's death. She'd asked herself a series of 'what-ifs'. Like, what if, Joslyn's flirtatious nature was the cause of Reggie's drinking. Mia's train of thought was interrupted by Flynn's call.

"Ready?"

"As I'll ever be. See you in a sec."

Flynn was resting against the cab looking beautifully fresh.

"Lets do this," he said gently kissing Mia's forehead before she slipped her arms round his waist and he embraced her. He wanted to keep her wrapped in his arms for a lifetime but she eased away. In the car she sat silently, her hands in her lap. She looked serene, but he felt the turmoil within. She wasn't distant just contained.

There was no church service but there was a performance. Joslyn arrived at the cemetery…in a Daimler. She wore a tight fitting black number, sheer black tights and black stilettos. She placed herself between Mia and the mourners, welcoming them with a hint of heartbreak and tears on the horizon – yet her makeup remained perfect – not a tear fell.

When the coffin arrived, Mia couldn't look. Her dad was in a box, lifeless; he was going under the cold, dark ground and there would be six feet between them. It should be pouring rain, there should be thunder and lightning, not this glorious, good-to-be alive August sunshine. Every muscle in her face strained to keep the despair in. Think about Flynn, her heartache implored. Was it wrong to think of him naked? No, not under these testing conditions she ruled.

"Mia. Your mum."

Mia looked across to where her mum was attempting to pull the coffin from the hearse.

"Oh my, God," Mia whispered appalled by her mum's behaviour but unable to look away. The pallbearers were in a state of confusion. Mia looked at the faces among the crowd; there was a grimace, a raised eye, a ducked head. Followed by all-round astonishment, as Joslyn attempted to jostle a bearer aside and take the weight of the coffin on her shoulder. No one could look away; it was ghoulishly entertaining. Unable to shift the bearer, Joslyn went in front of the coffin, raising one arm in the air whilst placing a hand on the wooden coffin end. Like Moses parting the sea she walked to the graveside. Mia saw people glancing from Joslyn to herself wondering, was the daughter as mad as the mother? With all eyes on Joslyn, Mia looked to Flynn, who lightly kissed her like it was the most natural thing to do. They watched Mia's mum; her performance in full swing. She was on the edge of the grave, wailing, her body perilously positioned. Flynn and Mia couldn't look at each other; she felt him convulsing with trapped laughter.

"Fuck," whispered Flynn.

"Oh. My. God!" moaned Mia.

Earth gave way and Joslyn joined Reggie.

After the burial mourners reassembled in The Admiral. Her mum, still grubby from her graveyard stumble, got horrendously drunk and made a public display of damning Mia. It was meant to be her dad's day; it should have been all about him. Now his burial would be remembered for all the wrong reasons. In the cold evening air Flynn and Mia walked to the car, he pulled her tightly to him kissing her mouth gently. It was the only part of the day Mia wanted to remember.

"So you blamed your mother for your dad's death," Raymond almost shouted.

"Yes, totally," replied Mia calmly. "Alcoholic poisoning said the death certificate, but it was suicide. He didn't want to live. Often I found the certificate in my hands, minutes, hours passing. I couldn't cope with how horrendous his death was. Wouldn't the pain have been excruciating? How had he bore it? How scared had he been coughing up blood?"

Mia breathed in deeply and blew out. It was hard to say the words aloud.

"I'd think of my father dead and my mother alive and I felt cheated. I wanted to travel back in time and warn my single, twenty year old father about an evil spirit in human form. Tell him she'd turn his head but he had to fight it."

Mia's face momentarily sunk into her hands but then she straightened.

"What if there's no heaven and he's in the ground forever...alone. I put him there."

"Mia," said Webber, "Did you interact with your mum following the funeral?"

"No."

"And Flynn?"

"Yes, we interacted."

In her room, which she appreciated for its solitude and peace, Mia googled each abduction again. Reading article after article, she came across a photo of Julie, Olivia Weston's mum, with her boyfriend…and Mia faltered as an icy shiver quivered the length of her. His face was out of focus and side on, yet Mia had an inclination she knew him. She was racking her brain when her phone vibrated and she jumped out of her skin.

"Hey Ben."

"Remember, get in my queue but don't make it obvious. Keep your passport at the ready. There's CCTV on the doors."

"It's in my clutch," said Mia excited for tonight. Ben was working as a bouncer over the long summer holiday and would turn a blind eye to Mia's age when their group came along to go clubbing.

"Cool, I'll stretch my break to an hour. Gotta go."

Mia couldn't remember when she last did something for herself…if ever. Flynn sprung to mind. Each day she'd hoped he'd ring, text, send a naked photo. She stared at his name till the letters blurred…till she heard the ring tone. It just happened.

He picked up after one ring.

"Mia!"

"Hi Flynn."

"You called."

"I did."

A charged silence clung to their lips.

"You did warn me that you promised to ring girls then didn't."

"You're not one of those girls Mia."

"Is that good or bad? I'd rather be a one-night stand than left sitting…I get if me being the date of a murdered boy put you off, or was it being the friend of an abducted girl? It's me being a stalker, isn't it?"

"Maybe it's because I'm a dick…or that I'm scared."

"Of the person sending you notes?"

"No…well yes…but I meant of you."

"Admittedly, I'm a nuisance but not dangerous."

"You took me down at the race."

"That was an accident!"

"Mia…I'm trying to tell you that I like you."

"Oh…erm…would you like to go on a date?"

"I'd love to."

"A short notice date?"

"For you I'd clear my diary."

"Tonight, ten, Nightjar in Shoreditch."

"Eager…I like it."

Silence. Mia's heart was sending blood round her body at warp speed.

"What are you doing?" asked Flynn, not wanting to disconnect.

"Research."

"Is that code for secret?"

"I'm withholding information that might disturb you."

"I was disturbed the moment I heard your voice…what are you really doing?"

"Investigating a link between the missing girls."

"Jesus Mia."

"I warned you Posh Boy."

Silence.

"Listen, Council Girl, get your head out of crime solving and leave it to Morse."

"Flynn you're dominant this afternoon," teased Mia trying to find lighter ground.

"Ah, Council Girl is flirting."

"Are you smiling or frowning?"

"I'm something rhyming with card."

Mia gasped and then fell about laughing.

"Flynn," Mia whispered.

"Why are we whispering?" asked Flynn.

"I don't know," Mia's voice lowered further. "I don't want to say goodbye."

"Then say, see you in the club."

"How will I find you?"

Mia heard Flynn laughing down the phone.

"You're like a heat seeking missile. At uni, you'll be covertly signed by the Ministry of Defence. Mia, I've got to go…work beckons."

186

****

So many times he'd held his finger over the call button. Her voice was this mix between gravelly and upbeat. Not only did he hear longing in her voice he recognised it in his own. But where she was going with this abduction thing, was any mad person's guess. He'd argued himself in and out of reasonable explanations for the threatening calls to Mia from a dead boy. The nasty notes, his car, and today Bert: poisoned, the vet said? Who was it, and how far did they intend to go? The idea that, some fuckhead randomly found Alex's phone and sent Mia malicious texts, was no longer credible. Did Alex's killer take the phone and torment all Alex's contacts? Or did he pick Mia casually and obsess over her? Or worse - was he already obsessed and that's why Alex was murdered?

****

"Mia?"

She turned too quickly; his tone sending hormones bounding around her body.

"Steady," he said, his hands light on her forearms helping her regain balance.

"Flynn!"

"You're in a club!"

"Yes, this is a club," Mia smiled, glad it wasn't just her who'd felt blown away.

Flynn was gobsmacked. Here she was, looking chic in a short shift dress with its bright bold pattern and five inch strappy heals.

"You're wearing a dress."

"I am."

He knew he was staring, but her short, wavy bob framed her fine features perfectly.

"And your hair!"

"I had it cut."

"It's perfect...Are you here alone?"

"No." Mia turned to see her friends gawping.

 "I'm with this lot, school's out."

"Right. Hi everybody...I'm Flynn."

Eyes widened. Flynn continued to stare at Mia. Maybe he should buy her a drink. Flynn broke the uncertainty taking her hand.

"Let's dance."

"I..I...Flynn, I've only ever danced in the kitchen."

"Look, over there, a coffee machine."

"Lol," Mia smiled.

Flynn pulled Mia into his arms. They were so close Mia felt herself flushing.

"We'll slow dance till you get your swag going."

"It's Cardi B."

"So?" Flynn's grasp on Mia tightened drawing her closer. There was nothing else to do but relax and wind her arms around Flynn's neck. He smelt glorious, like a rain forest, like the Sahara, like a thousand roses. He was an adventure, yet at the same time he was home. A home Mia wanted to move into.

Flynn's night had just got better. Mia in his arms. It felt right. It felt fucking amazing. He wanted her so bad, but Mia was an assault course and a sudoku rolled into one. If she were any other woman, he would be giving her the late-night message, but not Mia. Mia was a relationship girl. Now. Holding her. The contours of her body against his. He could see himself a relationship boy. Imagining got him turned on so he pulled free, still holding her hand, raising it up in an arch for her to twirl under. She laughed and her eyes twinkled whilst her mouth looked totally wanton.

"You're ready to go solo," said Flynn reluctantly, wanting to be her significant other, to not let her slip through his fingers again. Her friends joined in, and, while they danced like Drake, Flynn's eyes rarely left Mia. They danced all night. Mia hadn't imagined Flynn dancing. A slow dance, yes, but not fast dancing; yet here he was playfully grinding his hips, doing air press-ups and teaching Mia Latin! A few shots later, Mia was back in Flynn's arms. She was a little drunk. As her energy depleted, she rested her head on his chest, her arms falling loosely and low around his waist.

"I love dancing with you Flynn. And touching you and you touching me...Flynn I've missed you."

"Mia?"

"Ummm?" she replied looking up and randomly rubbing her nose against Flynn's, Eskimo style, before burying her head deep into his neck.

"It's home time," said Flynn.

"I think you mean bed time." Mia pressed her warm lips against his neck. "We should go to a hotel so I can feel you up."

"Really?" he asked gently smiling.

"Ummm. I want a memory of us to carry around with me always. I want a piece of you to be mine."

Flynn pulled Mia nearer; his breath blowing gently through strands of her hair. His hands were on her back. They glided across the silkiness of her dress; their only obstacle her bra. Thinking of her bra led to him picturing her breasts which snowballed into his hands on them. Once more he released her until his body deflated.

"Guys, I'm gonna take Mia home."

"How safe is she with you?" asked Ben protectively.

"Safe," replied Flynn pleased, Mia had friends that cared about her.

****

He'd followed her into the club. She was tipsy. Happy tipsy. Giggly tipsy. She had no idea how glam she looked, how she moved gracefully, how when she sat her dress rode up to reveal even more of her slender legs. He sipped away at his sparkling water. He didn't drink alcohol during the chase; it loosened him up and he wanted to be alert, sensitive to every touch and sensation. Like right now. Watching her sexy dress fall over her breasts, the material moving against her thighs as she walked in those elegant heels. His hairs were on end; stirred by her presence. His left eye was twitching, a sign he was getting aroused. He wanted to lift her dress up. He wanted his hand to creep up the inside of her thigh…and what he wanted, he was sure to get.

****

She'd dozed in the cab, her head resting against Flynn's shoulder.

Arms around one another, Flynn paid for a room in a pricy hotel. In the mirrored lift Mia giggled.

"Look Posh Boy it's you with me," she smiled stating the obvious. He looked at their reflection. "Or am I with you?" she asked confused but not needing an answer. "We're together Flynn...Have you ever thought of us together with no clothes on? I have," she said, giggling along the corridor.

"Mia, shush."

He rested her against the wall while he scanned the key card and she very slowly slid down until her bottom met the floor with a small thud. Flynn took his shoes off and put them against the door to hold it open.

"Flynn carry me."

He tried picking Mia up in his arms. But she was giggling and wriggling and singing.

"Mia - shhhhush."

Putting his hands underneath her armpits, he dragged her in.

Flynn rested Mia against the bed, retrieved his shoes only to find Mia trying to pull her dress off without undoing the neck button.

"Mia, hold up."

Her hands flopped by her sides whilst her dress remained scrunched round her head, completely covering her face like a snood. It took all of Flynn's restraint not to notice Mia's lacy underwear. Or that her body was curvaceously toned and her legs were silky smooth. Unhooking the catch at the neck of her dress, Flynn tried to think pure thoughts.

"Let's get you under the sheets my beautiful tulip."

Flynn pulled his black jeans off and laid them over a chair. He rang housekeeping. They knocked quietly, and Flynn passed them Mia's dress and his shirt. Gently he lifted the quilt, climbing in and settling on his side…watching her.

"Flynn?"

"I'm here."

"Flynn's here, he's here. I love you Posh Boy. I love you so, so, so, so, so, so much."

Flynn whispered.

"I love you back, Council Girl."

****

Mia's eyes sprang open. She half expected to see Flynn beside her. She sat up and saw a note written on hotel paper on her bedside cabinet.

Morning Mia, got to work this afternoon, bill's paid,
includes breakfast, pick from menu,
have room till 12,
F

Mia reread. Was it curt? Maybe. Could he have been friendlier? Yes. Was it a brush off? Possibly. She threw the sheets off. Too hungover

190

to dwell. Instead, Mia let the power shower rapidly stream over her. The unused toiletries she put in her clutch along with coffee and sugar sachets. Wrapped in a fluffy towel, she sat on the sofa by the heated radiator.

"Had Flynn wanted to make love?"

Mia couldn't tell, she'd drunk too much and had a headache as proof.

"Maybe he still sees you as a hopeless case?"

But when they were dancing she felt him responding to her.

She pulled her clean dress from the laundry wrap slipping it on. It seemed Flynn knew all about hotel assignations.

Downstairs in the dining room, Mia relaxed, enjoying a full English while analysing Flynn's note. As if sensing Mia's consternation, he rang.

"Flynn."

"Sorry I left Mia."

"No worries, I'm tucking into breakfast. So this is how the other half lives then?"

"Something like that. Can I come round later. I think we need to see where are heads are at and…are you laughing?"

"You've been watching Love Island. Where are heads are at?"

Flynn laughed. "It's addictive isn't it?"

"I'd say watch it at mine but I haven't a telly."

"I'm still coming…with wine…and a curry."

"I was thinking of painting us."

"Are we naked in this painting."

"You're flirting with me again Flynn."

"Yeah but this time it's intentional."

They fell quiet simultaneously. It was a heavy quiet. A quiet so filled with the future Mia and Flynn felt nervous. Too much depended on what was said next.

"What's our painting going to be called?"

"Posh Boy and Council Girl."

"That'll sell it."

"It's not for sale."

****

He thought of them together, naked and sweating. He wondered if she would think of Flynn when he fucked her. He didn't think so. What

191

he enjoyed was unorthodox. He suspected the boy and he would have very different styles.

He followed her onto a train. Sat beside her. His arm pressed against her shoulder as strands of her hair static-ed to his coat sleeve. She carried the burden of the Preston girl around like a drowning man weighted to the seabed. Poor Mia. Constantly doubting herself. Never sure of anything. How much fun he would have with her.

****

Mia woke to a persistent ring tone. She searched under the covers. Flynn! She accidently pressed the reject button.

"Shit."

It rang again.

"Flynn? I disconnected by accident."

"You're sleepy."

"Yes. What dwarf are you?"

"Ahh, Council Girl's back. Come down and let me in…quick. There's a bloke hanging out a window, saying something in Polish, which I think is fuck off."

"Coming!"

Mia straightened the quilt, puffed up the cushions, looked in the mirror; big mistake. Running downstairs Mia opened the door to a demi god.

"Flynn, I'm such a mess, don't look."

"Arghhh!"

"Flynn!"

"I fell up the stairs because I wasn't looking," joked Flynn.

"This is me," she said, Flynn right behind her.

He wanted to cross the room, push her against a wall and…except not these walls. The nicotine-stained wallpaper, ripped off in parts, was a passion killer.

"It's bleak, I know, it's temporary, I'll be in uni in September."

In broad daylight, Mia's reality looked way too real to Flynn despite Mia's efforts: a flowery bed, pink stacking boxes in the corner, a clothes rail with only a handful of garments, a reed diffuser, the notice on the wall.

"I framed it," she said referring to the official letter from the court

192

quashing the restraining order. "I enjoy seeing proof that I can legally be near you."

Beside it a framed sketch. The fine detail, the care taken; undoubtedly a labour of love.

"Alex?" asked Flynn gently.

Mia could only nod, it hurt so fucking much.

Flynn peeped under a pink sheet pinned to the wall. His face dropped.

"Sorry...mood killer...that's why I keep it covered."

Mia removed the sheet and together they stared at the collection of photos and news articles whilst eating bad curry.

"I think we need to go to the police Mia...together."

"But I haven't the phone with the texts! Flynn I've been going out of my mind trying to figure this thing out and I never thought you'd believe me because it's farfetched and I've been insane around you."

"Mia, if you told me squirrels could dance, I'd believe you."

"You mean you didn't know that?" replied Mia. "University education and you don't know that!"

Flynn laughed and kissed her nose. In that moment the tension changed; the emphasis no more on imminent danger but on desire. It swelled between them, a charged look, a touch; it pulled them in. Flynn's lips were hard on Mia's. His weight toppled them backward onto the bed. Mia's hands were messy; in his hair, round his neck, pulling his t-shirt up.

"Dring, dring, dring," the incessant ringing, ignored, until a hammering on the door.

"Answer da fucking phone...pleased."

Breaking apart, breathing hard, Mia scrambled onto the floor to her dropped phone.

"Hello?"

Too late.

"Unknown number," said Mia. "Should I return the call?"

"No!"

Flynn looked genuinely scared.

Mia tackled the uncomfortable silence.

"I've an offer from Exeter."

"That's brilliant Mia. Exeter?" he said raising his eyebrow.

"Are you cross with me?" she said almost remorsefully.

He leaned over kissing her tikka lips.

"Show me where to put my toothbrush," said Flynn standing. "That's code for I ain't goin anywhere on my own in this building."

"It's not so bad…apart from the transport links."

"Your optimism is off the charts."

In the bathroom, the running water failed to drown out rap music from another room.

"Dance with me," Flynn whispered in Mia's ear before pulling her to him.

"I'll get your shirt wet," she laughed as he tightened his hold.

"So? I'll be taking it off shortly."

Flynn had this magic about him that, though she was scared witless one minute, he had her crazy turned on the next.

"Let's get naked," Flynn said, his voice uneven and deep.

Mia nearly tripped over herself turning toward the door.

"Your exuberance is commendable."

"English please."

"You're desperate."

"Come on silly," she giggled pulling him back into her room, her nimble fingers quickly unfastening his shirt buttons.

"Breathe Mia," laughed Flynn.

Ignoring him Mia pressed her lips against his chest as she pushed the shirt from his shoulders. His skin was cool. It heated as she kissed it. Flynn gently separated them. Their eyes met and emotion swirled, lighting their pupils like Monet's Starry Night. They smiled, sexily, on the edge of intimacy. Reaching for the hem of Mia's summer dress, Flynn pulled it over her head. She wasn't shy; she stood cheekily in red lacy Brazilians and a matching bralette, her nipples pushing hard against the lace. Flynn unzipped his jean shorts, nearly falling over trying to get his legs out.

Flynn looked accusingly at a laughing Mia.

"Mia, try not to laugh at your lover."

"What if he's a fool?" she giggled.

Mia felt insane that Flynn was in front of her, his shirt off, about to touch her without a gun to his head. When his fingers fluttered onto her wrists she breathed out pure, uncut ecstasy. Locking her eyes on Flynn the dynamic altered from frivolity to serious sexual tension. Mia was drowning in it, pulled into a tidal current of desire and sensation. The headless horseman could be on her tail but, in this moment, all she felt was Flynn's touch.

Flynn inhaled her breath, its depth rich with yearning. He really did not want to fuck this up. His hands gently roamed up her arms, their velvet touch making Mia feel like a giant marshmallow or a fairy; all giddy. She felt Flynn's fingers on her bra strap. Push it down she willed and he did. She'd been right, they were telepathically linked. Was it bad if she orgasmed now, she wondered?

They jumped in unison - clutching each other as if a pistol had fired…but it was a phone; Mia's, reverberating and buzzing. Flynn moved first. He reached for the phone, passing it to Mia.

"Hi Sean, hold on a sec I'm putting you on loud speaker my…"

'Boyfriend' mouthed Flynn, marking his territory.

"Boyfriend is helping me. Ok, go for it."

"I got to thinking; there was something weird. Petra was getting dirty texts."

"Did you read any?"

"Yeah. I love your smile, you look cute in your underwear; stuff like that. Then they got dirtier; I want to touch you, you make me come. We argued over one – your breast fits my hand – I mean, what the fuck?"

Sean fell quiet. Mia looked at Flynn.

'Crying' Flynn mouthed silently. They waited.

"It was like he knew…like he'd done it…I lost my rag…it was stupid coz she wasn't a girl to piss you about."

"It's ok Sean."

Mia waited patiently. 'Rubbing his eyes,' Flynn motioned.

"Then out of nowhere, one that really freaked her out – I can see you."

Mia's eyes darted frenziedly to Flynn's, whose eyeballs looked like they were about to fall from their sockets and roll across the floor.

"And then she was taken."

The grief that followed was cut off as Sean disconnected.

"I can see you. Flynn! I. Can. See. You?"

Flynn looked scared.

"Alex's murderer can't be the Wolf – it's preposterous, no fucking way."

"I think he might be," said Mia shakily.

"Fuck. I've got to fill my dad in, he might have some sway with the police. Don't give me the raised eyebrow, you've been my girlfriend less than twenty four hours."

"Girlfriend? I was one of those before, for about an hour, it didn't end well. Flynn. You're in danger because of me."

"No Mia, I'm in danger because of him. If you hadn't crushed on me, I wouldn't have met you and that would be my loss."

"Give it time Flynn; I think you'll find living preferable to loss."

****

He considered ruses to get her alone. There would be little opportunity with the boy in tow. He felt his heart racing; surely this excitement couldn't be doing his angina any favours. He was near to having her. He needed a distraction. Someone to pass the time with.

He pulled her from the basement, dragging her kicking and screaming. He bent her over the table. Thinking of Mia, he came in a matter of minutes, but for Gabby it was a life time.

****

They'd had an unsettled night; scared and sexually frustrated, they'd spooned until daylight. While Flynn showered Mia committed everything to memory: his keys on her desk, his shorts hung over her chair, his mobile by the bed. She felt completely terrified of losing Flynn. She looked up as he came through the door wearing her pink robe and unicorn slippers and her frown upturned into a wide smile. He covered the room and she melted into his arms, their zip seal lips locking. Mia felt weightless when he kissed her; a freefalling spirit, no edges, no density.

Flynn reluctantly pulled his lips away.

"It's going to be ok Mia, we will get through this…together."

Flynn, body confident, talked casually as he dressed. Mia's artist's eye travelled along the naked length of him. His body was lean and toned with tight muscles, no bulk; he was like a tennis player, like Novac Djokovic.

"Right, kiss me quick," said Flynn.

196

Mia saw him to the door then rushed to the window to see him disappear inside a cab.

****

Mason senior was in his home office. He looked up to see Flynn walk in; Flynn hadn't been in his office since he was a kid. Gareth had a flashback of shouting at his seven year old son. He knew he'd been a bad father. It was a fact; like he was a brilliant financier.

"Dad I need your help."

"Please tell me some girl's not pregnant."

"Some girl's not pregnant," repeated Flynn deadpan. "Dad, you know the girl that has a thing for me?"

"The nut job?"

"She's not a nut job…it was a misunderstanding."

"Scavenging through rubbish, poisonous texts!"

"Dad, for once, please fucking listen."

Gareth let the expletive pass.

"She's in danger, as am I."

Somehow this girl had gotten to Flynn.

"Flynn, this girl,"

"Dad you are not listening, you are not asking the right questions. When I'm cold in the morgue don't tell Mum you never saw it coming. I am being deadly serious, I'm shitting myself."

"Grow up Flynn!"

"That's rich coming from you."

Flynn turned his back on a man that was just a name on a birth certificate.

Flynn walked towards High Street Ken. He needed to blow off some steam. At Nero's he popped in, sitting for a moment, wondering where his head was at.

****

He followed the boy to the coffee shop. Even holding the door for him as he left.

"Cheers mate," said Flynn.

The boy was on the edge of the pavement looking for his cab.

It took one push.

****

197

Mia was restless. Music from the radio filled the long silence. Where the hell was Flynn? She repeatedly checked her phone, staring at the screen. When it eventually buzzed she hated her mum more in that minute than usual, simply because she wasn't Flynn.

'I'm going to jump'

"For fuck's sake, do it!"

But already Mia was pulling on trainers.

****

Flynn heard screeching of brakes and screaming. He felt pain. Then nothing.

****

The estate was worse than Mia remembered. She noticed every piece of discarded rubbish, the bird shit burned into the concrete, the chewing gum spat out and hardened on the ground, the zigzag blunt expletives sprayed onto surfaces by gangs claiming rights on the landscape. Striding across the bridge, she looked downward at the dark semi open car park and shivered. Turning the corner she saw the play equipment comprising of tyres grotesquely burned; melted in so many places the structures were unsafe. The council wouldn't care until some kid's back was broken. Mia walked warily into the building. In front of the lift, spewed vomit of carrots, sweetcorn and vodka shots splattered up the wall. What equally disturbed Mia was the used condoms; sex in the stairwell – was that any girl's fantasy?

Mia tightly held her personal alarm.

She pulled open the heavy fire door leading to the flat's corridor.

Stale air infused with dread as Mia put an unsteady foot forward.

Outside 175 Mia stopped breathing…long enough for her chest to tighten.

The door was ajar.

Not entirely unusual; drunk, her mum left the door open, sometimes left the keys in the lock…but this felt wrong…it screamed run.

Looking up and down the corridor, Mia expected a ghost from her attack to materialise, but she was alone with her foreboding.

She pushed the door, jumping back like she was about to be seized. It swung open revealing the small square landing.

"Mum," she called from the safety of the corridor.

No response.

Drawn in by silence, she stared, shocked at the bundle at the foot of the stairs. Her mother, with her legs and arms in unnatural positions, lifeless.

She heard him.

Behind her.

A smell.

Her airways covered.

Panic.

A dark vacuum.

It happened too quickly to experience fear. The real terror would come later.

****

"Excuse me Nurse. Nurse!"

"Mr Mason, you need to be patient, we're very busy."

"I understand, but have the police been contacted?"

"All in good time."

"Jesus, someone tried to kill me. I want the police here, now!"

The nurse remained tight-lipped disappearing between the curtains.

"Fuck!"

Flynn lifted his bum up, pulling his phone out; the pain was unreal.

"Fuck!"

Four missed calls from Mia. He went to voice mail.

"Fuck! Gone to your mum's? You are fucking joking, pleeeese," begged Flynn.

Flynn pressed the buzzer that beeped persistently at the empty nurses' station.

"Fuck this," said Flynn panic swirling in his stomach. He looked at his wrist at the cannula inserted there, he pulled gently on the needle end.

"Fuuuck," he screamed, still pulling until the needle was out. He stared at it and felt woozy. Shit! His Great Aunt Gertrude could knit with it. He looked at his leg; it was swollen from ankle to knee. He put his good foot on the floor; his bad one followed.

"Arghhh."

Pain shot from toe to arse!

"Hoo, hoo, hoo."

199

He blew out the pain. Pulling the curtain, he looked around until he saw one beside a sleeping pensioner slumped in a chair. It wasn't stealing it was an emergency. He continued searching until ten minutes later, on two crutches, he swung into a taxi.

****

Mia fell in and out of consciousness; her mind leaping from one bad memory to another. In the background a disturbing certainty that she was…she was…she…darkness.

****

Flynn was worried he might pass out. Sweat ran down his face. He had no idea where he was. When he saw the flats, he nearly shit himself. There would be any number of people on this estate that would want to kill him.

"Twenty-four quid mate. You sure this is where you want to get out?"

"I don't want to…I must."

"Good luck with that one mate. Lotta police around, probably another shooting."

Flynn's pain was numbed with the most effective anaesthetic – fear.

"But that probably makes the estate safer today gov."

"Nice try. Thanks…ahh."

Flynn pulled himself out of the car by leaning on the door. He bent in grabbing the crutches and the pain in his leg was crucifying.

"Ferrrrrrrrr.Uck!"

Standing, on a strange road, with no idea how to find Mia and the taxi driving off in the distance, he'd never felt more alone in his life. It was the increasing police presence that determined his direction. He had the most awful, sick notion that while he'd been unconscious in the fucking hospital the fucking Wolf had abducted Mia.

Flynn dropped the crutches and ran…badly…painfully.

"Sir, you have to stop there."

"No…my girlfriend's in danger."

"Inside there?"

"I…I don't know…I've got an address written down…Here!"

The constable looked.

200

"What's your name?"

"Flynn Mason."

The constable walked a short way off; he was on his radio. Flynn knew the constable recognising the address was bad. This opened the floodgates of pain. His vision zoomed in and out, in and out. He bent over and threw up.

"Mr Mason? Flynn? What's happened to you?"

He lifted his body upright with such effort he staggered.

"Gerry, we need another ambulance…pronto," DC Hall radioed.

"Mia's in danger."

"Do you know where she is Flynn?"

"Here…she's here."

"No she's not here."

"She must be…there on the stretcher."

"That's Mia's mum. Joslyn Dent was attacked; Mia is wanted in connection with her assault...Mr Mason?...Flynn was no longer receiving, he was falling…into darkness.

****

He drove, his foot light on the accelerator, his arm catching the sun as it leant out the window. He was smiling. Knowing who was in the back of the van. She was the beginning of the end. The one. The game changer. They'd live together or die together.

****

Her thoughts were cloudy with confusion and a flat fear made her reluctant to push through the haze, but her gut was screaming wake up! She tried. Her heavy eyelids clung together and she had a bitter taste in her mouth like she'd swallowed air freshener. Through the thin parting of her eyelids everything was blurry. She stretched them open and her eyes strained to see but her head wouldn't process; the pain was too acute. Taking a deep breath, her mouth filled with rough cloth. Realising her head was covered, she panicked; each breath sucking in more material until her airway blocked. She could die, here, now, within minutes. The fear of dying levelled her. Breathe gently she begged, slow down. She thought about her mum lying at the foot of the stairs, lifeless? You're dead too Mia, Joslyn told her scornfully. No mum I'm alive. Her breathing slowed but panic gave way to pain. Her hands were tied tightly behind her back…with electrical ties. Her shoulders were red hot with strain, she didn't move them fearing dislocation. Each new realisation made her want to scream with terror; like her feet were bound at the ankles. How would she escape this…that's what she was planning…there was no other choice…rape then death would not be the epilogue of this story. Think! Mia ordered herself. She felt motion: bumps, swerves, traffic. She was in a van, getting shaken up, rolling, toing and froing. She gave herself a shaky pep talk; Mia the van is gonna stop. You're gonna be filled with utter dread but don't let it paralyse you. Mia, listen! He's slowing, stopping, he's coming…Don't be scared…but I am. I know. Pretend it's a movie and you're an actress…the script says play dead Mia. Play dead? That might not be difficult.

****

CHAPTER 26 THE INTERROGATION

"That's your story?" asked DS Raymond sceptically.

"The word 'story' implies fiction; this is fact."

"Maybe you haven't been missing. Maybe you ran away and holed up somewhere," accused Raymond.

"No," denied Mia categorically.

"Come on Mia," DS Raymond interjected. "I've got kids your age and I wouldn't swallow that bullshit for one minute."

"Please give my commiserations to your children."

The detective was about to continue.

"You're a very suspicious person."

He opened his mouth to speak.

"You looks for flaws...you're a very small-minded, sceptical man."

"Mia, this is serious," warned DI Webber.

"Yes, I know. My mum's in hospital, Flynn was run over and I'm a miscarriage of justice, so why aren't you out there gathering clues?"

"It's lie after lie," accused Raymond

Mia's eyes bored into him.

"This is typical of you...like Alex's texts...totally dismissive."

It was apparent to Webber that Raymond's processing of evidence was questionable. He needed a time out to clarify the points raised in Mia's recount of her and Flynn Mason's interaction with his sergeant.

"But you're right. Everything is my fault. I attracted the killer and I led him to Gabby, Alex and Flynn. If I wasn't a pathetic, lonely loser I wouldn't have endangered them."

"Mia, no one is responsible for a crime other than the person that commits it," said DI Webber firmly. Mia's expression was doubtful, and Raymond wasn't letting her off the hook.

"Alex dead. Gabby abducted. Flynn attacked. Your mum in hospital. You're the common denominator."

"That's speculation Sergeant," said Jim Pascoe

"Let's refocus please. Tell me about your mum's boyfriends," asked Webber.

"She bought a string of men into our home. It was horrible having adult men in my flat that weren't my dad. What did my mum know about these men? Only the lies they spun her."

Mia took another sip of water.

"Most of them were married. She loved the idea of taking a husband from his wife. "

"Did she have sex with these men?" asked Raymond.

"What do you think?"

"Answer the question," ordered Raymond his tone bordering on aggressive.

"Yes, probably, it's not like I was in the room with them. Apparently nothing happened...she concocted condition after condition. Ok perhaps Matthew couldn't get an erection. And Bruce might have been kicked in the balls by a horse so there was no action down below. But then Dennis had prostate cancer. Robin had a bungled vasectomy and Donal was suffering PTSD from childhood sex abuse; yet he had four sons. According to Mum she'd only ever slept with my Dad...and it was so painful...it took three nights to consummate the marriage. Who tells their daughter that?"

Mia breathed out frustratedly.

"Sex was a topic my mum periodically addressed. She said it was a duty. Really? It was a duty with all those men?"

Mia's cheeks billowed like a blow fish before releasing a defeated sigh.

"I was dying. She was like cholesterol, her constant put downs amassing and slowly clogging my heart. She's a woman who purposely chooses contention, who thrives on drama. Her bad choices affected my life...her emotions affected mine. She was killing me."

"Mia, are you ok," asked Joe Pascoe noting a decline in his client.

"I feel a little vacant."

"I understand," said Raymond sarcastically. "Lying is exhausting."

"I'm not lying," Mia said cuttingly her eyes boring into Raymond.

"Why can't you do your job? Have you spoken to Petra's boyfriend Sean? Have you contacted our phone providers and compared texts? What about Kevin? Where is he?"

Mia attempted to sit up straight, her eyes struggling to focus. She touched the side of her head and winced and once again Raymond's eye rolled upwards as he discharged a heavy, inpatient sigh.

"What?" Mia demanded angrily.

"Nothing," replied Raymond.

"No, go on, say it because you're boring me now."

They glared at each other; him thinking she's a waster, her thinking he's a dick.

"Look. I didn't intentionally set out to waste police time or be a nuisance to Flynn...events snowballed."

Mia looked down at her hands, at the remains of Cherry Red on her broken fingernails. Mia looked at Sergeant Raymond.

"I feel queasy."

She stood unsteadily.

"I need fresh air."

The sergeant pushed his chair back as Mia approached.

"Stay there!" ordered Raymond. He knew she was coming for him. Mia's back was to Flynn, but the spewing was unmistakeable.

"DC Hall take Mia to Medical and send the doc my way after her exam. Mr Mason, Mr Pascoe, maybe go grab a coffee or lunch."

"Stupid bitch," said Raymond pissed off.

"You had it coming Steve...get yourself and this room sorted."

Webber walked up two flights of stairs to MIT. He closed his office door.

"Shit. Fuck. Bollocks."

He breathed in and out a few times before buzzing his PA.

"Fred, would you pick me up a sarnie, danish and cappo."

"That bad?" said Fred sympathetically.

"Gorier than an episode of Holby."

On his white board he wrote Mia dead centre. Alex, Gabby, Joslyn he wrote around her. From Gabby he branched out with the abducted girls.

"Sir," said Fred putting his boss's meal down.

"Fred, get uniform to bring in Mr Coombe, teacher at St Thomas More, Chelsea. And I need CCTV retrieved from the leisure centre by Latimer Road station."

Constable Hall knocked on D.I. Webber's open office door.

"Sir, the doctor has finished her exam."

"Send the doc in please constable, give Steve the nod."

Webber noted Steve looked shifty, as well as aggrieved at having been vomited on.

"Steve, did you chase those toxicology results up?"

"Not yet boss, but it's on the list."

"Steve, let's get a few things straight. One - innocent until proven guilty. Two - let the evidence talk and listen. Three - procedure first, gut second. We've a top of his class legal on our backs demanding an account of the chain of custody…and the case involves the son of a high-profile banker. Oh, and did I mention The Wolf? The spotlight is fucking on us Steve. Now, as you dealt with Mia's transfer, where the hell is her medical report?"

"Denham nick picked her up, they should have dealt with the medical but didn't. Now she did see a nurse and bloods were taken at Denham so I presumed she'd had a medical."

"Fucking hell Steve, she's under eighteen, in our care, claiming The Wolf abducted her. Investigating that is priority."

"Boss, her abduction story is an attention seeking stunt. I didn't want to waste time."

"Jesus Steve, it's not wasting time it's called doing your fucking job. And Steve? Think about this phone business because I will contact internal affairs if you've screwed up."

"Sir, there was no texts. She's a liar."

"Flynn Mason's lying too? You're not thinking Steve."

Before Raymond responded, they were interrupted.

"Hi Frank, nice to see you as always."

"Hi Doc, this is Steve Raymond my sergeant. What have you got for us?"

"Is she fit to be interviewed?" Steve bulldozered in.

"Certainly not," the doctor firmly declared glaring at Raymond like he was a jackass.

The DI threw Steve a withering look. He sympathised with Mia, yeah, you could want to kill someone.

"I've taken a full set of bloods. If tox comes back positive, any case against her is compromised."

"Shit!" Raymond began pacing.

"Does she show signs of being drugged."

"Yes. The symptoms have worn off but her lethargy, poor coordination, dizziness, brain fog and nausea are signs of being drugged. Possibly chloroform. I spoke to the hospital; she's being admitted as we speak."

"That's bullshit. She's playing you," spat Raymond aggressively.

"Steve. You'd better rein yourself in. I don't think you want a case of insolence on top of negligence brought against you."

"That girl has injuries consistent with being forcibly held; restraint marks on both wrists and ankles and bruises running the length of her consistent with being dragged on a rough surface. She's a head injury which needs an x-ray then stitching. Her BP's low. She's dehydrated. She could have internal bleeding. Shall I continue?" asked Dr Kirby her tone purposely condescending.

Fred hovered at the door.

"Fred, what have you got for me?"

"Denham police called. There seems to be some confusion. They have Mia Dent's tox results, but the contact number you gave them was wrong Steve. They've spent best part of the morning chasing you up – they wanted to ensure you personally got them as you were convinced Mia Dent was fabricating her abduction."

Webber looked across at Steve Raymond who was shuffling uncomfortably.

"Sir, the number I provided was correct; it must be an admin error on their side."

Webber shook his head disbelievingly. It was as if Raymond was sabotaging the case.

"What's the tox summary Fred?"

"There was significant chloroform in her system."

"Shit!"

Webber leant back in his chair; a tension headache nipping his temples.

"Fred, update Mr Mason and his legal that Mia is no longer a suspect."

"Yes boss."

Raymond and Hall looked uncomfortable.

"Sorry boss, I cocked up," admitted Raymond suddenly weary.

"One thing worries me more than you blatantly ignoring

procedure...your instinct. You have history with this girl, you know her, and you want to throw away the key. I rely on my sergeant for a heads-up. Your head, unfortunately, is up your arse. Then there's your interviewing technique. She's a young, vulnerable woman with a history of obsessive behaviour and you ploughed in like she's Norman Bates. There's also the issue of threatening texts not being followed up?"

Webber shook his head.

"I'm losing patience quickly Steve…Go chase up CSI," Webber instructed Raymond. "Emma, stay. Steve close the door behind you. Emma did you record your first encounter with Mia?"

"Yes."

"Good, tell me everything from the beginning."

****

Mia's eyes opened. Startled she jerked upright.

"Mia, it's ok," said the nurse placing a reassuring hand on Mia's arm. "I'm Sarah, your nurse. I'm taking your blood pressure and temperature."

Mia nodded and a sharp, fizzing pain pierced her head.

"My head hurts," complained Mia sick with pain.

"Here, take these with some water," said the nurse passing the tiny, paper cup with multicoloured tablets to Mia. "A couple will kick in immediately, the other two are slow release. How bout I remove your cannula?"

Mia blinked a yes.

"You'll have a nasty headache for a few days but we'll manage your pain. Your boyfriend left a bag for you. It's there on the seat. He said he'd be back for tea time. If you'd like to shower you're ensuite. There's an emergency cord if you need help. Ok?"

Slightly raising her arm Mia gave a little wave of confirmation. Once alone she pushed away the bed cover. The room was pleasant; shiny clean, bright, with a flat screen tv. Mia moved to the sofa. Opening the holdall, she pulled out chic pyjamas. They were 'the' pyjamas! The ones to wear when an emergency struck and a hero rescued you. A tear rolled down Mia's cheek. The relentless questions, the hours of being asked: where, when, who, how left her raw and exposed. She gently pulled out a matching dressing gown. She could have buried her head in it and wept.

She was on Flynn's mind, a place she'd longed to be…and he was kind and thoughtful and gentle. There was more: a soft tracksuit, trainers, socks and underwear. The lingerie wasn't tame or sexy; it was delicate and beautiful. He hadn't tried to guess her bra size, instead there were matching cami vests with support.

In the bathroom, Flynn had made showering uncomplicated. Everything was in arms reach. In the shower, under the pulse of hot, comforting water Mia let her fears and anxieties swirl down the drain. She exfoliated her tender skin, washing away the horrible sergeant's criticisms along with the dirt. Her head hurt considerably, yet Mia washed and conditioned her hair because it was a gruesome mass of calamity and the products were fab. She looked down at her purple feet with their horribly raw toes; thank goodness for slippers. She picked up the nail brush; Flynn had thought this showering thing through.

The natural warmth of the room dried her. She pulled on her new pale blue underwear, rolled deodorant under her arms and went to retrieve the body lotion from the bag. On the bed, she sat in her underwear, gently rubbing in the lotion that matched the perfume she'd sprayed on. She breathed in a fresh, floral aroma smelling of hope. Showering, moisturising…was it always this exhausting. She yawned. She'd close her eyes for five minutes...ten at the most.

****

"Mia…wake up," said Flynn sitting beside Mia on the edge of the bed.

"Mum?" Mia mumbled.

"Mia, it's Flynn."

Mia's eyes, heavy from pain and medication, struggled to open; groggily she threw herself at Flynn who wrapped her in reassurance.

"Honey you're safe."

Mia didn't respond. Reality was on pause whilst she tightened her grip on Flynn and breathed him in and put her ear to his steady, calming heart.

"Excellent impression of a boa constrictor," smiled Flynn feeling the loss of her warm body as she withdrew. Needing to be useful he propped up her pillows averting his eyes from her softly covered breasts.

Her physical state shocked him…the restraint bruising was particularly hard to ignore. He wanted to break fucking Raymond's face...but only after The Wolf's.

"Good news! You're no longer Britain's most wanted. I say we crack open the prosecco."

"Flynn?"

"Umm?"

"What time is it?"

"Twenty past sex…I mean six…tea time," he smiled.

God, he looked epic, thought Mia.

"I believe we are having soup and sarnies," he continued

"I forgot to put my pyjamas on."

Smiling, Flynn reached over to the sofa and retrieved them.

Mia let Flynn take charge, happy to relinquish any task requiring effort.

"Raise arms," he asked with a smile. She complied – for the first time ever, compliancy had its rewards. He slipped her arms in and then the top over her head.

"Bottoms next."

Mia wobbled off the bed. Flynn's hand was on her waist, his fingers on the bare skin between her top and knickers. She caught her breath. His hand was warm...Mia imagined it on her breast. For a moment her troubled heart slowed and she was lost in a tender touch. She looked into Flynn's eyes; she was an astronaut floating in space.

"Lean on me," said Flynn bending over.

Flynn wanted to say, fall into me. Make me come.

Mia's hand was on his shoulder. She felt muscle; the solidness of him.

"Lift."

Raising a foot, she felt Flynn's sweet breath against her thigh.

"Lift again."

Words fluttered across her skin and Mia wobbled from the ecstasy of it. Was it wrong wanting someone so much you momentarily forgot girls were missing?

Flynn was careful, not wanting to put pressure on her bruises. There's not enough of you on me, Mia thought. Flynn was mesmerised by her knickers. Standing, Flynn wondered how wrong it was? Thinking about getting a girl naked after she'd been abducted? Without thinking, his fingers loosely ran around the waistband, stopping at her hips. Momentarily he rested his hands there, while he planted a kiss on her forehead. The kiss was all too fleeting; Mia needed his soft lips to touch her skin and remain there till she counted to a hundred.

"There we go."

Unable to relinquish their connection, Flynn gently straightened the hem of her pyjama top. He glanced at Mia; her eyes were hungry. Shit! He was relying on Mia to be strong for them both. Sod it, his eyes moved to Mia's lips and his heartbeat trebled its normal rate.

"All done," said Flynn, platonically rubbing Mia's arms, whilst an image of her straddling him played havoc with his senses.

"Thanks Flynn," Mia said throatily…leaning into him as he slowly lowered his mouth…almost…When an orderly entered with food. Flynn's arms dropped and Mia excitedly surveyed the tray. The smell of fresh soup had Mia nearly cartwheeling. Mia's hands were shaky, so she ate carefully. She didn't want soup running down her chin in front of Flynn or her sandwich getting stuck in her throat and her coughing up a fit.

"Am I a private patient Flynn?"

"Yes."

"How's that?"

"Don't sweat it; the Met will be meeting the costs since your deterioration was a direct result of their incompetence…What the hell was up with that sergeant?"

"Raymond hates me."

"He's a fucking dick."

"I'm taking that dick down!"

"Council Girl's on the mend."

Mia nodded, swallowing a spoonful of soup and taking a small bite of her sandwich.

"I love everything in the bag Flynn. Thank you."

"You're welcome."

"You're very good at picking out women's stuff."

"Are you implying I'm a bit of a girl."

"Well, you are very pretty."

211

"Maybe I'll have to provide hard evidence to back up my masculinity."

"Oh my God Flynn," Mia blurted out through giggles.

"What did I say?" Flynn asked innocently.

"Hard evidence?" Mia laughed into Flynn's chest.

"Council Girl, you're filthy!" Flynn teased before saying "Jesus Mia, it's good to hear you laugh."

"Yeah, it feels good to laugh."

She raised her hand to run through her hair, unconsciously bringing attention to her breasts.

"Oh Flynn, it's all messed up."

"Your hair? Yeah," he said gently pulling two crumbs of bread from her fringe.

"My mum's in this hospital Flynn. In intensive care. Like my dad."

Flynn took Mia's hands in his.

"You've been through a harrowing ordeal Mia. Tonight rest. Tomorrow the chloroform cloud may lift and you can visit your mum."

Mia nodded. She still cared; it was the burden of every daughter with a flawed mother. But Mia was battered physically and emotionally she simply wanted to sink deep into kisses…Her mum could wait.

"Are you spending the night with me."

"That's very forward of you Council Girl...but yes...the last time I left you alone you managed to get yourself abducted and arrested."

"It's nice here," smiled Mia.

No wonder, thought Flynn who was gaining a clearer picture of Mia's shit home life.

"Move over fatty," Flynn grinned. Mia shuffled over, smiling at his endearment – fatty was cute. They were shoulder to shoulder. Flynn picked up the tv remote.

"The News?"

"Too depressing," answered Mia.

"Antiques Roadshow?"

"Too stuffy," she said.

"Pointless?"

"Now that's rude," Mia smiled. "I've got an inkling you're more pointless than me," she laughed poking him in his side.

"Ow," cried Flynn. "You're deep!"

"You are not allowed to say 'deep', you're Made in Chelsea not Waterloo Road!"

"Shush now, let's play," smiled Flynn like he was a part of something real and precious. He'd lost his virginity to a friend of his mums in about four minutes in her utility room. He'd felt nothing for her; it just happened…and a pattern formed…sex without love. Although he and Mia hadn't made love, their relationship had depth but also a humour that brought them intimately together. His feelings for her felt…real.

"Meds," said the nurse cheerfully, her entrance interrupting Mia's naughty thoughts. Flynn too, pulled out strips of painkillers and downed them. He was in considerable physical pain but not the mental anguish that added to him keeling over at the estate.

"And two hot chocolates and biscuits," said the nurse leaving them to it.

"Don't even think about dunking that digestive in your drink," ordered Flynn.

"Listen here, Posh Boy, dunking is a great British tradition. I know you lost half your biscuit once but you've got to man up."

"Mia, if you keep wriggling against me like that my man will be up."

Mia looked sideways at Flynn. He winked and Mia felt all gooey like the chocolate in the middle of a fondant.

"Billy Idol songs; easy," said Mia, her eyes on Pointless.

"Sweet Sixteen."

"Yes!" agreed Mia. "Umm, Dancing with Myself."

"Good one. Jesus everyone knows Hot in the City."

Mia eyes soaked-in every minute of being with Flynn. He was everything: enigmatic, charming, playful. He casually kissed the side of her head when Sweet Sixteen went to zero.

"Mia? You ok?"

"The thought of tomorrow…the questions…the revisiting every disaster in my life…it's..."

"Embarrassing?"

"Excruciatingly," replied Mia.

"Revealing?"

"Undoubtedly."

"Shameful?"

Mia elbowed him.

"Mia, inside your head are clues. You are the key to finding him."

"I know…I just…" Mia stared deeply into Flynn's eyes. "Want this time with you to last forever."

This was a moment. Flynn knew it. He could have her now and fantasy would become reality. The Flynn before Mia wouldn't have thought twice. He'd been too casual in the past, too blasé with women's emotions.

"Flynn?"

Shit, her eyes were real. Idiot! Obviously they're real, they're in her head.

"Your eyes are stars; they'd light up an abyss."

"I want to sleep with you," she said.

"You are sleeping with me."

"You know what I mean."

With his hands around her waist, Flynn pulled her over him.

"Arrhhh."

"How bad did that hurt?" asked Flynn concerned.

"Your touch made it bearable."

"Perhaps I've healing hands."

"Perhaps you touch me and we find out?" Mia invited. They were head to head, her over him; her knees either side of his waist.

"Don't put any weight on my leg because us Chelsea lot don't do pain as well as you Council lot."

They didn't speak; momentarily neither moved…until Flynn reached for Mia's hair, floating wildly around her face. With each hand he gathered a few strands and gently felt them between his fingers.

"Your hair's bouncy today," Flynn said his tone low.

"I used shampoo with bounce technology."

His finger gently ran along Mia's jaw line, stopping when he felt a slight scar.

"Ice skating; four stitches…"

"Did the other person need CPR?" he said before kissing the scar.

"You've got a sprinkling of freckles under your eyes," Mia noted.

"Yeah, I'm the white Morgan Freeman."

"Can I touch you?" Mia asked.

"Tentativeness from the girl who'd rummaged through my rubbish? Go for it."

Her hand gently brushed his jaw, she felt a slight stubble, it was a texture that was completely new to her. It was such a male thing.

"Did you shave today?"

"No."

"How often do you shave?"

"Two or three times a week."

She reached behind his neck pulling the tie and releasing his hair. Running a strand between her fingers, she straightened it watching the hair spring back to curly when released.

"Your hair was the second thing I noticed about you."

"What was the first?"

"Your confidence. It's like you have kinetic energy or Jason's technicolour dream coat."

She ran her finger slowly across his lips as if assessing them: length, width, depth.

"I improvised your mouth in my art. It was frustrating rarely seeing you face on."

"How about you improvise right now?"

Mia licked her lips. Good start thought Flynn.

"Ready?" she asked.

"No," he said truthfully. "But kiss me anyway."

Mia put her hands on Flynn's chest for balance...and...because she wanted her hands on Flynn's chest!

"I'm not touching your sore ribs am I?"

"No."

Her eyes were on his mouth; wishing her lips could kiss an indelible stamp of ownership. Instead, she placed tiny kisses across his mouth, slowly working in gentle pulls; she'd bathe in this slow, sensual love for eternity.

Flynn's hand moved from her waist, ever so slightly up the swell of her breast, lingering there, before feeling the curve of her shoulder. Gently he pulled her in, prompting her lips to cross his, until satisfied they'd tasted the length and breadth of one another. Somewhere in their hazy, gentle teasing, passion spiked and lips pulled and pushed until breathlessly parting. She got that she needed to breathe, but every part of her needed to be against every part of him. Now…ish.

He'd swear her eyes were darker. Her lips were definitely darker. She looked wild and it sort of scared him because, for the first time, kissing meant something. He lifted his arm; a cue for Mia to reverse into him. Grease had started but the audio was muted.

"Is kissing always like that for you?" she asked.

He heard the tremor in her voice; the desire and the feeling of being overwhelmed.

"No…never." He took a moment for rational thought. "That was deep."

"You're using the word 'deep' again Posh Boy."

"That's because I'm trying to use words you recognise, Council Girl."

"Oh yeah, I forgot us council lot only understand one syllable words!" Mia responded playfully, "Like hug, kiss…sex."

"I think we should watch Geese," said Flynn. "I mean Grease."

"I think what you think."

Grease was perfect. They didn't think of sex again until the outdoor cinema scene; Danny moving his hand toward Sandy's breast. Flynn moved his hand, clumsily like Danny, exaggerating the movement, gently slapping the side of Mia's face, covering her eyes with his fingers. Mia flopped over him giggling and snorting. Her words muffled.

"Smooth? You are outed Flynn; you're a bumbler."

"I am not," retorted Flynn in mock insult.

Mia sat up, her eyes dancing while Flynn's clouded with a desire that rose regardless of how matey he worked at being.

"Ok, a fumbler then," she said. "Here," she said picking up his hand. "Let me help."

Mia held Flynn's hand to her breast and he responded cupping it. She dropped her hand and a breathlessness fluttered in her throat as Flynn's hand moved over her breast, gently caressing. As his finger found her nipple, she blew hot air and buried her head in Flynn's neck, pressing hot, long kisses onto his skin. It would be easy for desire to escalate, but Flynn gently pulled back.

"I think having mad sex is against hospital rules."

"They'll never know," replied Mia.

"I think you'll be a screamer Council Girl."

"What?"

"Oh Flynn, oh Flynn, OH Flynn, OH FLYNN," cried Flynn, his volume increasing. "Why are you laughing?"

"You. You make me laugh. You'd better be good at it Flynn because after all this biggin yourself up my expectations are high."

"I'll give it my best shot," laughed Flynn. "Come on, let's snuggle."

Mia lay wrapped in Flynn's arms; her hand beneath his t-shirt; his love topping up her pain killers. Her eyes were closed, but she was scared to sleep, thinking the nightmare of the abduction would hauntingly return…but wasn't that was she wanted? To remember every detail, to bring Gabby home.

"You'll be here when I wake up, won't you Flynn?" said Mia sleepily.

"Always Mia, always."

Mia fell asleep and awoke eight hours later in Flynn's tight embrace. It was complete reassurance. Her head was resting on Flynn's stomach; one arm stuck beneath her, the other laying across Flynn's face. She moved her hand over his chest; it felt firm and cushy.

"Are you conducting a quality control test?" smiled Flynn.

"You passed," Mia responded throatily, her breasts pressed against Flynn's chest; her leg between his, feeling a presence that was all male. A thick silence fell. Mia's flat hand moved slowly down Flynn's chest to the waist of his boxers. She felt where he strained against the fabric. She was on the tipping point of trust and intimacy. Awkward at first, her hand moved over Flynn. Part of him considered was this too much, too soon after her ordeal. But he knew how hard it would have been for Mia to initiate and so he relaxed…and came.

"Flynn?"

"Don't ask me to move, I can't, I'm in my happy place."

"Oh good…I wasn't rubbish at it then," concluded Mia.

"Well it's like playing an instrument, you can never practice too much."

"I thought you could go blind," Mia teased.

"Sign me up for a guide dog now…take these," said Flynn passing Mia some tissues as he went to the toilet.

"I'm relieved I got a handle on it," said Mia as he returned.

"Yep, you definitely got your hand on it," laughed Flynn, spooning Mia so snuggly they fell back to sleep.

****

He hovered outside the door. Through the porthole window he saw the outline of two bodies beneath the covers. On hearing the clanking and bustle of breakfast he moved on. Further down, to a single room, was a pensioner. He entered the bay. Pulled the blinds down. Looked into the pale, watery eyes of an old man before blocking his airways with a pillow. The old man was too weak to make even the frailest attempt to save himself.

****

"Good morning my loves. What can I get you for breakfast today?"

In an instant they invented a new Olympic sport; synchronised response.

"Porridge," they responded together

"With sugar?"

"Yes please," they synched.

"Toast?"

"Yes please," they synched again!

"White or brown?"

"Brown."

They were smiling at each other, enjoying a moment of normal crazy.

"Marmalade or jam?"

"Jam," shouted Flynn

"No marmalade," Mia laughed.

"Come on Mia, jam always does marmalade.

"Not if you live in Paddington."

"Good point."

"Tea or coffee?"

"Mia?" prompted Flynn

"Two teas please, one with one sugar."

"It scares me what you know about me," laughed Flynn.

Mia sat upright in bed, with its clean, stiff sheets.

"I'm weird, aren't I Posh Boy?" Mia said seriously, her voice hollow.

"Maybe, maybe not; you're the only council girl I know."

She swallowed a mouthful of porridge; she saw her mum at the bottom of the stairs. She bit into her sticky toast; a heap of brittle bones unmoving. It was ok, her mum was here, being cared for. Malt scotch in her blood cushioning her frame. She'd bounce back. Mia needed to think about herself. Breakfast in bed; it had taken an abduction to make it happen.

"Mia…it must seem like your life is a road crash…"

"It does," interrupted Mia.

"We're together in this; the good, the bad, the deranged, got it?"

"You haven't been my boyfriend for long, but you're bloody good at it Flynn."

"I'm bloody good at something else," Flynn boasted, his mouth moving in on Mia's."

"Morning."

Startled Mia and Flynn found themselves surrounded by a medical team.

"Your MRI is normal. Your staples need removing in ten days. You sustained bruising to your ribs but they're not cracked. Your bloods are good. Happy to go home?"

Private hospital was nice. Clean environment. Food on a tray. Fresh bed. Sleepovers allowed. Mia suddenly felt winded, like life had punched all breath from her lungs. She wasn't sure if she could leave the hospital.

"Miss Dent?"

Mia realised all eyes were on her.

"Do you feel up to going home today?"

"Sure…yes…home today…fine."

****

DS Raymond shuffled in, his legal rep beside him. He took a seat.
It was fucking scandalous he was this side of the table.

"Morning Steve, you know the drill."

DI Webber pressed the tape's record button.

"25 August 2018. Present: DI Webber, Chief Inspector Adams,
Internal Affairs, interviewing DS Raymond, accompanied by his brief
Malcom Smyth."

"DS Raymond I'm interested in processes and procedures: failing
to log evidence, tampering of evidence, failure to investigate the
authenticity of evidence," stated Chief Inspector Adams.

"Steve, out of professional curtesy, I'll cut to the chase," said
Webber. "Do you have an alibi for April 6 2015, late afternoon onwards."

"Are you fucking kidding me?"

"Sergeant, must I remind you you're a serving police officer and DI
Webber outranks you, so respond accordingly," ordered Chief Inspector
Adams.

Raymond shifted uncomfortably in his chair.

"What relevance has that day?" asked the brief.

"It was the day Petra Smith was abducted.

"Are you having a laugh?"

"Do you hear me laughing?" asked the Chief Inspector.

"I was here."

"I've cross referenced hours worked and your Met system login
periods against the abduction windows of all girls. You were neither on
site or logged on at those times."

"I was at home with Shirley and the kids."

"We spoke to Shirley Steve," Webber interjected. "She chucked
you out thirteen months ago citing a drink problem and anger management
issues."

"She's frightened of you," continued the Chief Inspector.

"That's bullshit. She's exaggerating. You know what the job's like
boss. She's struggling understanding it's not nine to five."

"Funny you should say that Steve. Your weekly hours don't clock
up to the minimum expected of a sergeant.   If you're not at work and
you're not with Shirley, where are you?"

Two knocks gently rattled on the interview room door.

"Sir, a minute please?" asked DC Hall looking toward Webber.

In the hallway DC Hall filled her DI in.

"Joslyn Dent died twenty minutes ago sir."

"Fuck! This is getting more complex than the plot of Lost."

"Gov, that's not all, Kelly from forensics wants an urgent word."

The DI nodded, stepping across the hall to the control room to use the phone.

"Kelly, it's Frank from MIT, you have something for me?"

Webber listened.

"That is a break-through. Great work."

DI Webber exhaled deeply into the air as he ran both hands through his hair. Investigating your own was always gruelling but Steve Raymond was either a total fuck-up, a bent copper or a serial killer.

"It's eleven thirteen and DI Webber has re-entered the room."

"Joslyn Dent died from her injuries. Her body's headed to the Herbert Centre for a pm," informed Webber, addressing the group. Webber turned to his sergeant. Webber's expression was semi-weary, semi-accusatory.

"Forensics came back with a positive match…Mia's clothes were covered in Gabby Preston's DNA, also Olivia Weston's and Tia Patel's…and yours Steve. We've spent twenty one hours questioning an innocent person and now someone has to tell Mia her mum's dead. Christ Steve, you really know how to fuck up a case."

"Perhaps that was your intention Raymond?" asked Chief Inspector Adams.

"No. I made some errors is all."

"I agree. You got sloppy. Mia escaped your clutches. You worried your DNA was on her so you purposely didn't get her suited. You knew any evidence on her clothes would be deemed corrupt. You collected her from Denham therefore it made sense your DNA was on her."

"No…I'd lose my fucking job."

"Get real Raymond, you don't care about losing your job, you're barely here, when you are you're drunk or hungover. It's a prison stretch that frightens you. We all know what happens to cops inside."

"I'm being stitched up. Honest to God, I had nothing to do with those missing girls."

"Let's talk about Miss Dent. When did Mia first come to your attention?"

"Christ Sir, I don't know, she's a yoyo she's been back and forth so often."

"Think."

"Erm." Raymond scratched his head.

This was going to be a very long day, thought Webber.

****

Two hours later Mia was discharged and, in a cab, driving to Golders Green.

"I'm talked out. My tongue is exhausted."

"You're tongue tired," said Flynn trying to lighten the mood. Mia raised her eyes before resting her head on Flynn's shoulder. "You're reliving the last year on speed dial; it must be gruelling."

"Is something wrong with me Flynn?"

"Without question, undoubtedly, absolutely."

"You're not on the fence then...is it Fatal Attraction weird?"

"No. It's good weird...beautiful weird...sexy weird."

They stared at one another. Openly. Wantonly.

"Can we be together tonight?" Mia asked.

"Fuck yeah! I've no intention of being on my own. I've been having nightmares since your abduction. I nearly got into my parent's bed when you were missing."

Mia loved how he didn't pretend to be macho.

He rubbed her hands feeling very slightly raised skin here and there. He thought about the fading scar on her cheekbone. He gently touched it."

"Glass in your hand and a shattered cheekbone." Mia felt Flynn's muscles tense. "Jesus, I shouldn't be bringing it up," said Flynn bitterly

"No...it's fine...it's just..."

Mia took a breath.

"Umm...you know."

She took another moment.

"It could have been worse."

"You turned up at my house looking broken and I blanked you.

222

What a dick."

"You're not responsible for me." She squeezed his hand. "I'm over it now Flynn."

"Mia…it's me…you don't have to pretend."

"Ok…I'm not over it…I have horrible nightmares…sometimes I wake up screaming…I'm a mess Flynn. Jesus, I don't know how you put up with me."

Flynn felt winded by yesterday's revelation. How the fuck did Mia cope. The worst experience of his life was having his tonsils removed.

Flynn leant in and slid his lips against Mia's. As the kiss deepened, he cupped her face and she pressed her lips firmly to his. A few minutes later, breathless, the taxi pulled up at a terraced town house. The houses were all tall, with long rectangular windows and large steps leading to large doors. Mia followed Flynn, through the small iron gate, down an iron, spiral staircase, leading to a small patio with potted plants and the front door of a basement flat. Flynn unlocked the door. He flicked a switch and a long hallway was lit with small lights embedded in the ceiling. The walls were white and the carpet fawn. She copied Flynn taking her shoes off and dropping them in a basket.

"What a lovely smell," commented Mia. Flynn pointed at the fragrant plug-ins. Mia stood, her eyes locked on the air freshener.

"The smell of wine is potent; it was my mum's version of a diffuser."

"Was she ever happy?" asked Flynn. Mia shrugged.

"I see fragments of happiness. When I was little, I thought she was a real princess with her beautiful hair and her long dresses."

Flynn reached for Mia's hand and squeezed before gently tugging her onward. Passing doors either side of her, Mia saw her reflection in a long mirror, on the end wall, between the lounge and kitchen. Crap! She looked like a battered vagrant.

Flynn led her into a large, square front room, with tall bay windows, a high ceiling, and paint matching the hallway. She collapsed onto a large, soft, oatmeal sofa with extensions on both ends. She shuffled right back against the cushions and smiled weakly.

"This is heaven. Is this a friend's place Flynn?"

"My grandmother owned this house. She bequeathed a floor to each of her three grandchildren. I rented the place out," explained Flynn. "Conveniently the lease came to an end and so here we are."

Pulling a throw from an ottoman, Flynn laid it over Mia; a minute later she was spark out. Flynn sat opposite doing a Tesco shop on his laptop. He smiled; her body had sunk slightly into his velvety chenille. He thought of Thumbelina and grinned. His phone vibrated.

"Flynn Mason," said Flynn authoritatively.

"It's DI Webber. Is Mia with you?"

"Yes but she's asleep."

"Joslyn Dent died."

"Fuck."

"Exactly. It was my intention to come around personally and inform Mia."

"It would be best for Mia coming from me."

"It's our responsibility."

"I realise that, but Mia needs a break from the police."

"Fair enough. There's a car out front and back. Purely precautionary."

"Thanks, that's reassuring. What time do you need Mia tomorrow?"

"Early. The car out front will bring you."

Webber disconnected.

Jesus, didn't she have enough to deal with without Joslyn's death. He looked toward her, she'd woken, their eyes locked. They stared at one another. What they wanted was out there on a giant billboard! WE WANT SEX. But there was this whole complicated backdrop.

Mia felt awkward. She'd dragged Flynn back into her turmoil and now she felt selfish. Maybe she was becoming her mother?

Flynn felt pure dread having to tell Mia her mum was dead.

"Hey you're up," said Flynn stating the obvious. "How'd you sleep?"

"Like this," said Mia closing her eyes, resting her head to the side on prayer hands."

"Funny girl…You look rested."

"Yeah, I feel tons better."

"Good. I'll make dinner. Come and watch me fuck it up."

224

Sitting at Flynn's table, music played in the background. She followed Flynn's graceful movement around his square kitchen. Mashing potatoes, he looked over his shoulder.

"What?" asked Flynn.

"You've occupied so much of my mind, now here we actually are."

"I'd like to occupy another part of your body in the near future."

"Ooh, Posh Boy talking dirty," Mia teased. "Are you sticking it on me?"

"With my Prick Stick? Maybe."

Mia laughed at Flynn, he was funny and gorgeous and playful. She hated tainting what they had.

"Flynn, I don't know if it's a good idea you sitting in tomorrow."

"Mia, you are not shutting me out because you think I can't handle what I'll hear."

"It's not that you can't handle it Flynn; you seem nervous around me...like I'm glass."

Flynn looked stricken.

"Flynn, what's the matter?"

"Shit Mia, there's no good way to say this..."

"Say it Flynn," she responded terrified he'd changed his mind about them.

"Your mum died Mia."

He may as well have thrown ice water over her. She stood, shaking her head.

"No Flynn...that's not true."

He took a step toward her.

"It's true Mia."

"Did you see her?"

"No."

She stepped back, as if space between them protected her from reality.

"Then it's not true. She'd never die. It's not something she'd do Flynn. You've met her. She's unkillable."

Flynn reached for her, but she slapped his hands away.

"Think about it Flynn. She was in the hospital, wasn't she?"

"Yes."

"Then they've put the wrong name around her wrist; they make these mistakes all the time. She'll be in another bay, the men's probably. She's jammy Flynn. Honestly, that woman's Lazarus. One minute you think she's dead, then she springs up like Michael Myers."

Her raw voice croaked denial after denial until she slumped to the floor like a shot pheasant. Flynn dropped down pulling her onto his lap.

The silence that followed was the loudest statement of grief imaginable. It was eerie; how she nearly wasn't breathing, how her body was so still so suddenly.

Mia watched her finger weave a figure eight over Flynn's joggers like it belonged to another Mia. She felt like her insides had been gouged out.

"Flynn?"

"I'm here."

"I think she died on purpose. For the attention."

Mia continued to trace the pattern.

"I refuse to cry. She wasn't a mother. For years she guilted me into playing along with her craziness. Now it's over."

Mia turned over; her head on Flynn's lap. She looked up at him.

"I probably won't notice; she was never home and when she was I didn't want her there...Thinking about it, I was motherless...she never read me stories or helped with my multiplication. It's very stressful in school when a teacher fires seven nines at you and you don't know. She never remembered the cake sale or the harvest festival or the Christmas fair...She was an utterly awful parent...she stank at it...I should be compensated."

Mia sat up resting her back against a kitchen unit. She swallowed; her throat felt tight and tart.

"You know what Flynn?"

"What's that Mia?"

"If I wished my bad memories away, I'd have no life."

Unconsciously, she took Flynn's hand tracing the lines in his palm...she pressed her palm to his palm, her fingers against his fingers.

"You've very long fingers Flynn. Can you play the piano?"

"Badly."

"That's funny, I play the guitar badly."

A loud silence rang in the space between them.

"I wasn't there Flynn. She hated me not being with her. She shouldn't have died without me Flynn." Mia bit her lip to stop herself crying. "Do you think she knew I wasn't there?"

"I don't know Mia," Flynn responded totally gutted for her.

"She might have called for me...and I didn't come."

The tears were so weighty they were unstoppable. He pulled her to his chest. He held her whilst her body shook with grief. Both her parents had turbulent deaths, leaving Mia pulling on the remnants of her dysfunctional life. It was total shit!

"Flynn?"

"Mia?"

"I want to see her."

"We'll talk to Webber."

"Thank you. I'll tidy myself up."

He took Mia's hand in his. Rising, he pulled her up with him. She looked wasted; the strain of the last few weeks...months...correction, years, was taking a toll.

"Let me give you the tour," said Flynn kissing her hand. "Ok. This is the bathroom.

"Wow, it's big for a flat...ooh, your bath has feet. I see myself...candles flickering, bubbles to my ears."

"Your breasts dipping then breaking the surface."

"Umm," said Mia an explicit image forming in her mind.

"This is the loo."

Mia felt the loo paper.

"Do you regularly feel toilet paper?"

"I'm excited. I've not seen Andrex up close."

Flynn wrapped his arms around her waist, bent over and kissed her nose.

"No need to get shirty, Council Girl."

"Don't you mean shitty," Mia laughed, turning in his arms. She was bouncing back already.

"You're amazing," he stated.

"Are you making a pass at me in your toilet? In front of an innocent bidet."

He dipped his head; in anticipation she raised her mouth to

227

his…glad to be lost again in a swirl of emotion that knocked her off her feet. She wanted to tell him how much she needed this…his touch…his lips…satisfying the hunger tightly coiled in her stomach. He was the key to everything wild and beautiful sweeping through her body. She loved him…but saying it felt like entrapment.

"Ok then. You sleep here," he stated pointing at the bed. "You have an ensuite shower and loo. I sleep next door. There's clean towels in the bathroom cupboard. Everything else you've got in your bag or is in the bathroom."

"Thanks for everything even the tampons." Had she said tampons?

Flynn smiled shaking his head. He went to slip his hand from Mia's.

I don't want to let you go Flynn. Mia refrained from speaking as it translated as needy, but if you couldn't be needy when your mum was murdered when could you?

Mia sunk on the bed. It was bong-y. She looked around her. The room was spacious and modern. It was a page in the NEXT catalogue. Modern furniture, wooden floors, cool blue furnishings. Immediately she thought about Flynn's room…and how she'd prefer to be in there…with him. He was giving her space…she got that…but space didn't reassuringly squeeze you. She turned on the bedside light; it wasn't too bright; she could leave it on overnight.

As Flynn heated the chocolate fudge cake Mia returned in her pjs.

"Knew the chocolate would bring you around," said Flynn gently. "Vanilla or chocolate ice cream."

"Vanilla, please," she said, watching Flynn scope ice cream on top of warm apple pie. Then following him next door to watch TV. Flynn loved how she shuffled right beside him, he hardly had elbow room to move his spoon from bowl to mouth…but she did make her pyjamas look like Vogue's star buy of the month, so he'd get used to it.

"The thought of arranging another funeral is crap. Obviously I know how it all works, but I wish the funeral parlour was more all-inclusive and did the annihilation there."

"You mean cremation," corrected Flynn.

"No, I don't."

Flynn smiled.

"There is a plot beside Dad, but maybe I should burn her to ashes to ensure she's definitely dead. Don't want her doing a Buffy and clawing her way out of the ground. Oh, I know what my mum would enjoy; a Viking burial. I could douse her in brandy, set her alight and say bon voyage as she floats down Little Venice."

"I second that," said Flynn. "How about we watch Beauty and the Breast?" asked Flynn.

"Is that a porn version?"

"What do you mean?"

"You said Beauty and the Breast," Mia laughed.

"Did I? Umm talking about breasts," he smiled boldly.

"Oh no you don't. I want to see that movie."

"You haven't seen Beauty and the Beast?"

"Don't get deep with me, Posh Boy, we don't all have a car up one sleeve and a flat up the other."

"You're sexy when you're pissed. Let me get the sweetie jar, then we can snuggle."

The night was a battle between good and evil; one minute Mia was soaking up the Disney magic, the next she was remembering the flashes of light as he snapped multiple images of her shaking and naked. She'd hate telling Webber; maybe because she'd simply stood there allowing it instead of trying to beat the shit out of him. Sometimes doing nothing was the hardest thing to do.

The film moved the night along nicely. Towards the end they were both yawning.

"Right then," said Flynn totally shattered. "Umm, bed. Yep...definitely bed...early start tomorrow."

Flynn noticed Mia blushing and realised that on top of abduction, parental death and regular arrest she was young and inexperienced, but she wasn't the only one feeling awkward. Flynn, typically a smooth operator felt fifteen again.

"I'll get you a bottle of water. Never know might get thirsty."

Flynn disappeared then reappeared with water.

"Here you go."

"Thank you."

The air was thick with yearning and hesitation.

Flynn suddenly pulled his t-shirt off and Mia quietly gasped in shock at his bruising.

"I know...I'm brave and strong. You can reward me very soon," he said offering the top to a quizzical Mia. "In case you get lonely...I know how you like a man's laundry."

"Not a man's...a Flynn's."

Mia closed the gap between them, not so close they could kiss, but close enough for her hand to brush his abdomen.

"So this is a sore pack."

Flynn gave Mia a lopsided smirk, he was body confident but not into definition.

"Six packs are so last year...You can keep the t-shirt...no need to steal it. Sleep well Council Girl."

"Posh Boy?"

"Yeah?"

"Stay."

"Fuck, I thought you'd never ask," he smiled clambering over the bed and disappearing under the duvet. "Come on...don't dilly dally."

Wrapped in Flynn's arms Mia lay thinking. Not about her mum, but about the robbery and attempted rape. In the interview room she'd nearly said too much. She'd nearly mentioned the tattoo which was foolish, luckily Emma had left the interview room at that stage. Wouldn't want her digging around. She'd played it down to Flynn but right now it was a film reel projecting onto the big screen of her memory...The Near Rape of Council Girl, 18 rating.

Blood tickled down Mia's chin. She knew they were going to rape her, maybe kill her. Her dream of Flynn being her first was over.

She'd heard a scuffle?

"What tha fuck! Ahhh, what tha fuck."

It was dark. Mia couldn't see for shit; she didn't know what was happening.

"Do you like your finger?"

A deep, curt voice, alien to all, put the rape on hold.

"What tha fu...Don't cut it...don't fucking cut it."

"Do you like your finger?" the interloper repeated.

"Yeah, yeah, I likes it. Cool bruv..."

"I know everything about you. I know you live at 219 Whitstable Close. I know all of you. If you talk to this girl I cut off your finger, if you threaten this girl I cut off your balls, if you touch this girl I kill you. Then I'm finding your mother, your sister and I'm going to do to them what I know you want to do to this girl. I do not make idle threats. I take pleasure from pain. It's my job to hurt people. To be clear. If anything happens to this girl, if she scrapes her knee I'm coming for you."

Mia wanted to collapse and run simultaneously.

"Take your shirt off," he ordered Forty Pence. "Put it on the ground. All of you put your phones, keys, money on the shirt."

They hesitated.

"Do it fucking now or I machete his fucking hand off."

"Fuckin' do it," cried Forty.

"You! Pick em up," said the interloper addressing Mia. Mia could barely walk. Holding her stomach, painful from the kicking, she bent over gathering the bundle up, wondering if her stomach was ruptured.

"Let your anger go. Forget this girl. She's nothing. Think about me. I'll think of you, your families, your friends. I have your keys. Your contacts. Now fuck off."

Mia stood covering her breasts with the goods.

"Let's go."

Mia wasn't scared. If he'd wanted her hurt he'd have left them to it. She wanted to thank him but her facial pain was unbearable.

"BEEP."

"Drop the stuff in the boot. There - t-shirt - put it on."

In the car, her fingers stiff from shock, she couldn't belt up. He leaned over clicking in the belt. He turned the heater up. He drove barely five minutes before parking.

"Stay."

She watched him climb the stairs, knock hard on the door, then, as lights came on, he returned, opened Mia's door, reached in, picking her up like she was a feather.

"Christ, the state of you," said Stan.

The floodgates opened. She sobbed into Tombstone's chest. Sitting down with her in his arms, Mia clung to him; the magnitude of what happened overwhelming her.

"Mia, let me look at you."

Mia winced. Already the facial swelling was substantial.

"Fractured cheekbone." He examined her hands. "The glass is too small for me to extract. She needs the hospital."

"No…she's traumatised…that makes her unreliable."

"Tombstone; the girl needs surgery."

"She'll talk."

"I won't," said Mia resolutely.

"You think you won't but you will."

"My fingernails could be prised out and I wouldn't talk…not after…after…I won't fucking talk ok…not about…anything…ever, to anyone." She touched his hand, specifically the tattoo she'd seen as he passed the rucksacks. She looked at a face that had been concealed by a balaclava. "I owe you…you can trust me…there is nothing anyone could do to turn me against you…if you hadn't…" Mia couldn't continue.

"She won't talk and she'll never step foot in here again. I'll take her to the hospital, drop her off at A&E," said Stan.

"Look at me," said Tombstone. "It was dark, there was a gang, they attacked you, you grabbed a bottle, it broke in your hand, they saw police, they ran. Repeat," demanded Tombstone.

"It was dark, there was a gang, they attacked, I grabbed a bottle, it broke in my hand. They saw the police and ran," repeated Mia.

"Did you recognise them?"

"No, it was too dark."

"What happened in the off-licence?"

"There was a robbery. I helped because I was scared."

"What were their voices like?"

"Scary."

"Low? High? What?"

"Scary."

"Any distinguishing marks?"

"No."

"Tombstone, enough, she needs to get her face looked at pronto. She's safe."

"I'm safe," muttered Mia.

Flynn pulled her nearer.
"You're safe Mia."

****

Waking up, the first thing Mia thought about wasn't The Wolf, it was Flynn; his touch, his lips, his...She thought she'd combust from longing. Turning to him, she studied his face. He looked restful. He'd been pushed in front of an oncoming car, yet he'd battled through it. Now here they were, pillow pals.

Mia pressed her body against his. She slipped her hand inside his t-shirt travelling across the smooth surface of his back, lingering at an inch scar.

"I fell off my bike doing a wheelie," Flynn murmured groggy from sleep.

Gently she ran her tongue along his lips till semi-asleep, he responded, moving his lips across hers. He pulled gently on them until arousal flipped a switch and his kiss hardened along with another body part.

Mia's leg slipped over Flynn's who needed no prompt; his hand covered her breast. Mia kissed Flynn hungrily, her fingers running through the length of his silky hair. He's mine, she thought, pushing the quilt off with her foot as her temperature soared.

Flynn loved the way she kissed him; ravenous with a hint of desperation. Every kiss before hers was staged and over rehearsed. Mia deserved romance, to be seduced...his habit of a quick fuck and run was out the window. He didn't want to spook her, not after her ordeal. So his hand moved slowly from her breast to her waistband; giving Mia the chance to intervene. Instead, the anticipation was driving her crazy, but Flynn needed for her to be sure. He caressed her hip, stroked her firm rounded bottom and ran the flat of his hand low against her slightly rounded abdomen, then lower and lower until she gasped.

****

Tia was weak. She'd been coughing for days. She knew she had pneumonia. She'd covered it at uni, studying to be a pharmacist. That was another life. Emptying the cell toilets into the collection bucket, she wondered, had it been real?

Sian lay on her damp mattress, facing the wall. Tia gently shook her. God, she was cold.

234

"Sian, wake up, you're on porridge duty."

Shaking her again, Sian fell onto her back.

Tia didn't scream. He hated hysterics, so she choked it back. But the still, glassy eyes, in a face turned blue, had Tia's insides trembling. Was this it. Living like an animal then dying in captivity. No...this would not be her life. That girl. The escapee. She made a promise and Tia believed in her. That girl would save them.

****

Flynn took the bathroom. Mia took her time. Showering. Moisturising. Styling her hair. She'd laid fresh underwear on the bed and a new t-shirt. She felt...how did she feel? Sparkly and desirable and wanted.

Flynn knocked before entering; he put a breakfast tray on the drawers. He noted underwear on the bed. The underwear he'd picked for her. And then she walked in. Naked! No uncomfortable silence. No grabbing a towel. Mia walked to him, he to her, and the minute his lips crushed hers it turned manic. Flynn held her, kissing her hungrily, his fingers caught in her wet hair. Her lips pulled his till she caught his lower lip between her teeth and held it...till...till...the sensation of Flynn massaging her nipple had her gaaaasping. Pulling his t-shirt roughly free from his jeans, her splayed hands roamed his back, god his skin was velvety smooth! His tongue in her mouth darted in and out, the rhythm of it coursing through her. She pressed her body tightly into Flynn's, needing the pressure of his arousal against her. Desperately, she pulled at Flynn's clothes, getting nowhere, because undressing a man with finesse took practice Mia didn't have. And his kissing, his continual searching for her mouth as she pulled at his jeans button, was crazy. She was melting; her every edge, bone, muscle soft and malleable to Flynn's touch. She didn't recognise herself, she was this needy stranger, determined and driven to get Flynn naked.

Flynn felt it too; a kind of insanity. He wanted to rip the clothes from his body and plunge into her. He'd never felt so fucking desperate and basic...till it scared him...that he might hurt her.   "Mia, slow down."

"I don't know how to."

"Let's each take a step back...Good."

235

"I don't want to stop Flynn."

"We're not stopping."

Flynn pulled the hem of his sweatshirt, together with his t-shirt, and pulled them off in one motion. He was pulling at the button of his jeans. His hands were shaking.

"Shit."

A minute later his jeans with the boxers still inside were tossed on the floor. Naked, they reached for each other. The sensation of skin on skin was so new to Mia, she wanted to touch Flynn everywhere. She pressed her breasts into Flynn's chest, feeling his downy body hair…it was so male…so different…it had her reaching down to the pressure of his arousal against her. There was so much urgency, the air was a whirlwind of desire. Flynn had her mouth; she was breathing in his carbon dioxide whilst her heart beat giddily; literally hopping in her chest. Like Flynn the strength of her desperation scared her.

"Flynn, remember I'm a virgin."

Flynn slowly pulled back. They stood still. Mia's breasts were rising and falling against Flynn's chest. He held her loosely; his hands remained on her body, one on her bottom and one on her back. He was breathing heavily into her hair.

"Ok. Don't touch me below the waist until I say go."

Mia laughed.

"What are we? Five?"

"I mean it Mia."

She looked into his almost scared, huge eyes.

"I'll touch this head instead," she giggled reaching up, pulling the lace from his hair.

"You're such a head teaser, Council Girl."

"You're so fucking gorgeous, Posh Boy."

Mia shakily loosened the strands…then began laughing even more.

"Simba," she snorted, her shoulders rising and falling with laughter. What surprised Flynn was that, in this moment, laughing and making out, he'd never felt so intimately close. As a grand gesture he scooped her up, carrying her to his bed, cradling her onto the mattress. Laying over her, his hair falling, framing her face, he kissed her properly, no rushed capturing of lips. Her hands ran down his body, resting on his hips.

"I want you inside me Flynn."

"I want what you want."

Mia laughed against Flynn's smile.

"Shit! Condom. Don't move."

Flynn rolled off, darting to the bathroom, coming back with the packet between his teeth, tearing the cellophane so vigorously the packet flew across the room.

"Fuck."

Mia was laughing.

"You have done this before, haven't you Posh Boy?" Mia teased leaning back on her elbows.

He winked. Pulled a condom out and Mia watched as he put it on.

"Yes! Don't worry Miss, you're in capable hands," he grinned as he resumed love making. "Right, where were we?"

"That was here," Mia said as she took one of his hands and placed it on her breast.

"Oh yeah," Flynn smiled as he took her other hand and placed it on something stiff.

He looked lovingly into her eyes.

"Ready?"

"Affirmative, Posh Boy."

"Hold on tight, Council Girl."

Flynn held back, moving slowly, not taking his eyes from Mia's, determined to prove the first time could be good because he wanted Mia to remember this always.

Mia's hold on Flynn tightened as he gently entered and she stretched around him. They tenderly kissed until the burning peaked and he held still. Mia had no idea what she was doing, only that her limbs were entangled with Flynn's and she never wanted to unravel. Never Ever.

Flynn moved slowly, tenderly, as Mia gripped him, waiting for her to relax. She let out the longest, deepest breath. Her grip loosened and she kissed him between smiles. Reaching for her hand he put it between them and they moved together.

After, they lay on top of the covers, naked and sweaty. Flynn's head was buried in the side of Mia's neck; one hand on one breast like he didn't want to remove it in case another made a claim.

"So that's what it's all about."

"Uh huh, did it live up to the hype?"

She loved the slight vulnerability in his voice. She turned and kissed him deeply, reassuringly, adoringly.

"You lived up to the hype."

Gentle kiss.

"You exceeded it."

Slow kiss.

"You had me hyper-ventilating."

Deep kiss.

"Your enthusiasm is commendable, but I think I can up my game."

Mia's eyes wandered down Flynn's body.

"I think your game is already up."

They made love again. Caught up in each other it was easy to block out the horror of the last few days. No abduction. No dead mother. Just body locked to body.

****

In his chair, Webber rolled back from his desk and stretched out. He'd done an all nighter and felt every gruelling minute of it. There was so much to cover because it was a series of interlinking crimes.

"Sir."

He looked up at Constable Hall who was now his right hand.

"Mia's arrived.

****

"If at any stage you need a break, say so."

Mia nodded. She felt slightly on the edge of hysteria. After their love making, her emotions were racing around her body like spooked horses. The interview room was the last place she wanted to be.

"You were in a vehicle," prompted Webber.

"Yes."

"The vehicle stops. Your head is covered with a hessian sack, your hands and feet tied. What happened next?" asked Webber.

Mia swallowed hard. She didn't want to remember what came next.

"Mia?"

She felt under immense pressure to say something crucial.

238

"Tell me about the van. Could you hear traffic through it?"

She focused on the table. On a bottle of water. It looked cold. She put her hand around it and a memory unfolded.

"I couldn't hear anything. I was lying on cold metal; freezing, shivering, scared I was in a refrigerator like in restaurants…but from the motion, I knew it was a cold storage van. I wondered how much oxygen there was."

As Mia talked, Webber scribbled notes to Constable Hall.

"What happened when the vehicle came to a halt."

"Bolts were pulled. The cold rushed in. I wanted to scream but my mouth was coated in dust and fibres, and with every breath, I drew the sack further into my mouth."

Mia gasped, her hands rising to frame her jawline.

"You've remembered something," whispered Webber his eyes darting to the others; messaging them to stay still.

"What is it Mia?"

"I…I heard metal crushing like when the bin lorries come round…And…A sort of dumping noise. I thought of Petra. How her body had been dumped. The papers indicated she'd been raped. I wondered was it once, was it multiple times? Did it happen on the first day he abducted her?" Mia breathed out. She addressed Webber.

"You have those answers…don't you?"

Webber said nothing.

"From the autopsy. That's how you know what a sick bastard he is. I thought about my body on a slab. Incision scars. Stitches from my chin to my pelvic bone. I couldn't imagine anything worse for a girl…her first time…being violated…sorry…it's just…I was alone and…you can't possibly understand that fear."

"Go on," pushed Webber.

"His hands pulled my ankles. My shirt rode up; my skin caught on the latch, then my legs were hanging out of the van. I thought – lucky I wore jeans...silly really," added Mia almost to herself. "I was terrified he'd drag me out and I'd bang my head on concrete and die. It was strange…the passage of time…as if fear slowed it down so I could imagine so many horrendous outcomes…Anyway, he picked me up; he was strong but dipped on his left leg like it might give way. Maybe he had an Achilles heel? Maybe if I got a weapon, slashing his achilles would take him down? He put me on the ground; it was rough like asphalt, except..."

"Except what Mia?" demanded Webber refusing to let the memory slide.

"I inhaled a strong smell of rubbish, a real pong, but it masked another odour...um...um...it was like sour milk."

"Sir," interrupted Constable Hall. "I live in Harefield and there's a waste and recycling centre that is next to a dairy farm."

"Hall, I want the detection dogs there now. Mia, I need a piece of clothing," Webber asked looking her over. "Your socks."

Mia slipped the trainer socks off passing them to Webber.

"I want every employee interviewed. I want alibis and witness statements."

Webber turned his attention back to Mia.

"What followed?"

"I heard a car bleep. He stuffed me in a boot, like I shove my swimsuit in a rucksack; he was rough and that scared me. Maybe I was in the car five minutes or fifty; it simply seemed a lifetime. I was coughing, literally choking; my mouth, nose, ears filled with dust. I thought about Flynn; I knew he'd be frantic. He'd look at my murder board and know what was instore for me and that would torment him. The car stopped. I shuddered as the boot opened. By now my muscles cramped and my neck, wedged on my chest, felt like it would snap. I was pulled out, dragged across wet, stony ground, to somewhere without light and then dumped. I lay unmoving. He didn't leave. He crouched beside me; his catch of the day. I heard his wheezy breathing whilst my breathing was so harsh my lungs nearly collapsed. I tried to shift my body away from him, but the tension of the plastic ties around my wrists dug too deeply. His hands moved over my jeans, checking my pockets. I thought he'd undo the zip. I saw my knickers coming down as he dragged my jeans off and I thought I'd choke on my own vomit. Laying rigidly, his wheezy, erratic breathing filled my head and I heard this weird repetitive, dull slap - then I realised - he was getting off on looking at me and I wanted to badly fuck him over; to prise his nails from his fingers with pliers. I heard a snip and my ankles were released. He rolled me over and snipped the tie at my wrists. He spoke. *Play nicely and we can be friends. Don't make me punish you Mia.*

You know what happens when I get bored Mia. Think about how you're going to keep me interested. Living depends on you."

"Was his voice familiar?" asked Webber.

"Yeah but the answer flushes, I mean flashes past me at warp speed."

"What followed?"

"I pulled the mask off. I tried to stand, but the ground kept rushing up to me. On all fours, I scrapped around, scratching the walls, the floor, looking for a sharp object, trying to find a weakness in my cell. There was nothing. Absolutely fucking nothing. I lay flat out for a while, my hope plummeting along with the temperature. Not only did I feel like I'd been hit by a bus I was shaking uncontrollably, all the while thinking, no one knows I'm here. I dragged myself to the door, rattling the lock, digging around the hinges with my nails. I whispered. *My name is Mia, are you there?* I repeated it a thousand times. The hours passed, my eyelids drooped and I slept until my head rolled violently to the side waking me. I'd start again. *I'm Mia. Please answer.* My throat was burnt dry from whispering. Then she spoke – '*Shut. Up*'. The words were so quiet I thought I'd imagined them. *Please,* I begged. *He'll come if you make a noise. Be quiet! We'll be punished.* The fear in her voice was the realest emotion I've ever heard…but I had to know. *Is Gabby alive? Yes, now shut the fuck up. He's coming. Oh, my God. Do as he says. The better you please him the easier it is, for us all.*

I stayed near the door listening for noises: his limp, his cough, opening of doors until his footsteps stopped outside my cell…then I scuttled into the corner. He opened the door, blinding me with a high powered torch. He told me to take off my shirt, which I obviously didn't. He relocked my door and unlocked another jail. A shriek of pain communicated violence. He said he'd break her nose if I didn't co-operate. I had no choice. He came into my cell. I removed my blouse. *Your bra* he demanded. At that moment I felt only violent anger. I wanted to wrap the fucking bra around his neck and tighten it till his eyes burst from their sockets. Instead, my shaking fingers unclasped my bra. I don't know how long I stood there whilst he shone the torch on me; it seemed like forever. He took photos. He got off. He went. I redressed."

Mia took a drink from her water bottle.

241

"And so a pattern emerged over the next couple of days. The stripping was humiliating; I was petrified what it might lead to. It was a HBO series – but it was real and brutal - a programme where the tv station warns viewers some scenes may be upsetting. Redressing was shit. My clothes were dirty and damp; they clung to me. All the while he laughed. I was bitterly cold with anger and I couldn't get my legs into my fucking knickers. My mind was running in all directions but each conclusion was the same; there would be no cavalry. It was down to me…And I had to escape because I was going to be abused."

Mia fell quiet. A single tear rolled down her cheek. She brushed it away.

"It's mad I'm crying now…It dawned on me I wasn't sobbing; I wasn't a quivering, hysterical wreck. Despite abduction, pain and humiliation, I was coping."

Mia took another sip of water, her throat still hoarse from the chloroform.

"I can't believe it was only three days; it seemed a lifetime. My mind ran in a hundred directions; all dead ends. I had to catch him off guard; he was too strong to overpower. But once free, where did I run to? What about the girls? It was desertion. He'd punish them because of me; undoubtedly."

Mia paused before speaking.

"Yet I still ran."

"If you hadn't, those girls wouldn't have a hope and you'd be with them. Now what's the point in that?" asked Webber.

Mia felt unconvinced but continued.

"Panic welled inside like a twister moving upward until, in the corner of my cell, I was so sick I thought I'd drown in my stomach contents. I didn't wee until my bladder was fit to burst. It was degrading, squatting in the other corner. What did I smell? Vomit, piss and bleach. I had to get out. I just had to, but how? What happened in films? The victim runs too slowly. The victim looks behind her and catches her foot. She attacks him half-heartedly. She runs in the wrong direction."

Mia paused letting the resurrected fear and hopelessness pass.

"Resting my forehead against the door, a breeze blew from my left. Not strong, more like through a slightly open door or window. My thoughts were processing this when I heard him. I wanted to turn to dust, to float away on the wind and rematerialize beside Flynn, preferably in his bed."

"What did you surmise about The Wolf?" asked Webber.

"That he's a dirty, seedy, sick fuck. That his sexual needs would escalate…that right then he was coming for me and he'd need more than a naked body to whack off to."

Mia's chest was rising and falling; it felt constricted. She breathed in and out and took a few moments to calm herself.

"He coughed up a fit; all chokey and phlegmy. Being ill might adversely affect his reflexes, his thinking. He wouldn't anticipate trouble. The girls he'd taken all shared one trait – compliancy. Good girls. Frightened girls. That was his taste. I think Petra was too much trouble – that's why he killed her. Anyway, he swung the door open. He had a hose in his hand. Aiming the nozzle at me, he opened the valve. I remember screaming. It hurt so fucking much; freezing, hard water powerfully striking my body; it was a physical assault. Move at your peril, he warned, blasting me again. He sprayed water over the floor and walls; there was a drain in the centre of the cell and I saw my life swirling down it. Every second or so he darted the spray back to me. With my eyes trained on his shoes, I saw his left foot, the least stable, swivel away indicating his back was to me. My movement was drowned out by the pulsing spray. His stature was more intimidating up close. He was about to turn. I struck out; an upper cut to the back of his head. He folded, and I kicked hard into the crook of his bad knee flooring him before wrenching his head back to fucking bash it off the floor. I had this animal urge to kick him until his guts spilled, instead, I ran; so hard, so fast. My breathing was ragged, my lungs exhausted, but I didn't stop, I didn't look behind, I ran until the passageway became so narrow, I had to squeeze forward; one limb at a time, bruising muscles, banging bones. I prayed with every grain of will I had the walls wouldn't compress me like garlic in a crusher. On my belly, I dragged myself forward, following a dull light. As I approached an exit, not much bigger than a laptop screen, I was petrified he'd be at the other end. But I had no choice, so head against floor, I put my arms out, I twisted, tightly, dislodging stone and rubble, squeezing my shoulders together, right up to my ears, to fit through."

243

All eyes were on Mia.

"Then I was out. Sort of. Fighting through privet into daylight. My eyes watered from strain, like they'd been dunked in raw onion; they'd had no opportunity to acclimatise to bright light."

Mia sat back blowing out into her prayer hands. She was on the edge of the memory, the fear of it, the illusion of safety.

"I looked around. How would I remember the exit? When it was bush after bush? So, I tied my belt to a tree."

"What colour was it?" asked Webber. "Would it stand out?"

"Maybe, it was pink."

Webber was aware of Mia's rapid physical deterioration.

"Good. You did well Mia. Let's break for lunch."

Mia stood, glad to be able to stretch. Flynn reached for her hand and gently pulled her towards the door. Even under stress Mia's skin fired up under Flynn's touch.

"You're doing great Mia," said Joe, as they walked through the traffic of police, in the direction of the canteen. Mia nodded, distracted by the smell of food, and the rumblings in her tummy. It was a large food court. It felt comforting to be surrounded by police – safe.

"Mmm, what to choose. Mac and cheese please, and rhubarb crumble and custard?"

"Likewise," added Flynn before finding a table far from police officers.

"Umm, this mac and cheese is good. My mum used to make a tasty cottage pie. When we lived in the pub I had great dinners: chicken supreme, beef stroganoff, curry. She never cooked after we got evicted."

Mia ate a little. It was hot. She blew on it. She had no idea how sexy she looked. Flynn ate, watched and got turned on.

Joe glanced toward them. They were eye-catching. He'd known Flynn all his life, so was no stranger to Flynn's magnetism; he was undoubtedly a good looking boy…but Mia…she was not his type…yet she looked more beautiful by his side than any woman he'd seen on Flynn's arm. She was so still and understated that she shone. If Flynn was gold, she was pearl…that's how he saw them.   It was good to see his mate with a real girl…ok…she was a little unorthodox…

"My dad had a criminal record," said Mia out of nowhere. "He stole money from the bar takings and gambled it away. He kept thinking the next win would cover what he'd taken. With each loss the amount stolen increased. When I think about the word gambler I think loser...isn't that what gamblers are there for...to lose? If they weren't, they'd walk away once they'd won and they'd be winners and not gamblers. Does that make sense?"

Flynn nodded. Mia ate a little more.

"My dad cheats on my mum," said Flynn. "She knows; she pretends it's not happening but then she blows up over the smallest thing he does wrong, like not cleaning Bert's paws. Last month, she went into one because he left his golf tees on the book shelf. The three of us know it's where he leaves his dick, that's the problem."

"Glad we didn't choose sausages," added Mia, shining a smile at Flynn.

Reluctantly, they returned to the interview room. Webber joined them. He gave Mia a reassuring squeeze on her shoulder. Before sitting, Mia swung a glance towards Flynn. She couldn't believe that she could touch him. That he welcomed it. That he desired it.

"Tell me about Kevin," Webber asked.

"Once he'd moved in, I didn't belong there. He walked around in trunks; it was horrific. Picking his teeth with cocktail sticks. Oh and when he blew his nose he inspected the tissue...and he'd leave his toe nail cuttings in the bathroom sink...Urhh."

"Did he work?"

"Not that he mentioned, but we barely spoke, especially after my mum accused me of being into him."

"Describe him."

"Five-eleven-ish, not fat but not trim, muscular arms, ginger hair; bowled shape; its texture odd; very dry yet he has a real greasy look to him."

"And you don't know his surname? Or where he lives?" asked Webber.

"No. Do you think he's involved? I mean, is it possible that he, and not the Wolf, attacked my mum?"

"It's a line of enquiry we are considering," Webber said. "Let's get back to the Wolf. Did you see any part of his face Mia?"

"I don't know. He had a woolly hat on, one with a peak and long sideburns. Who has sideburns these days? He was hairy too; it was strange because men aren't hairy anymore. Well, not men on the telly. Or Flynn."

Heads turned to Flynn who momentarily felt a flicker of the scrutiny Mia was under.

"It's not enough is it?" asked Mia weary and dejected. "I know shit about The Wolf. Shit about Kevin…Shit about…Hang on…the Wolf smelt; a strong aroma that I've smelt before…I don't know what it is or where I've smelt it."

Mia shook her head, agitated, desperate to help.

"This is mental," decided Mia angrily. "Do something police-y or with forensics, because if finding them depends on me those girls are going to die!"

Webber gave Mia a moment to compose herself.

"Sorry," apologised Mia.

"Be assured we are doing everything we can."

Mia nodded.

"Where do you shop?" asked Webber.

"Mostly Primark, Hammersmith; obviously I've hung around High Street Ken. a lot."

"You're looking for him following me, aren't you?"

Webber nodded.

"We've got you on CCTV at the leisure centre; behind you this man? Do you recognise him?"

Mia cast her eyes over the image. The man had a beard, wore a beanie and a puffa jacket. Like a trillion men!

"No…I don't know any bearded men."

"Our image analyst tells us the beard is false. Either he's disguising himself because he's CCTV aware or because you'd recognise him."

The room suddenly felt smaller and muggier; Mia felt claustrophobic.

"Mia…are you ok?" asked Webber sensing Mia was onto something.

"Can you enlarge it a bit more?"

Mia watched, as the beanie on the man's head enlarged. A shiver as cold as an Icelandic glacier rolled through her body, so slowly, chilling her heart.

"Mia?" prompted Webber.

"Kilkenny football. Alex's dad is from Kilkenny. Alex loved that hat."

The room stilled. Mia wondered, could they hear the crack in her heart and feel the weight of guilt she bore, knowing Alex was murdered because of her?

"If I hadn't chased Flynn I wouldn't have gone into the Bear - Alex would be alive."

"You are not responsible for the echo of crime that ensues," said Webber.

Wasn't she?

"What do you think Flynn's neighbours thought about you?" asked Webber moving on.

"You think if they saw me, they might have seen him?"

"It's possible." Webber looked at Emma. "Co-ordinate a door-to-door."

"Mrs Hornby at number twenty-eight's a good person to ask. She's nosy and she'll tell you everything; no filter. Bugger, she'll wonder why I haven't knocked."

"Tomorrow we begin the search. The dogs managed to follow your scent from the refuse centre to dense woodland in Harefield. We'll need you Mia, if you're up to it. So rest…have dinner because tomorrow will be physically tough."

They nodded.

"Inspector Webber?"

"Yes Mia?"

"Can I see my mum?"

It was a reasonable enough request.

"I'll send a car for you at seven a.m. Once you've identified your mum the car will bring you to the search location. Your ride home is ready. Remember, lock up securely.

In the panda car, seated side by side, their eyes straight ahead, Mia's hand rested on Flynn's denim thigh, slowly it moved to his inner thigh until it settled on his crotch. She snuck a sideways look at Flynn.

247

Who caught her in the corner of his eye and smiled. Mia moved her hand, pressing down, gently squeezing, loving that he was hard. The panda pulled over. Flynn used his rucksack to cover his bulge. The constable walked them to the door.

"I'll be in the car."

"Sure," said Mia.

"Absolutely," added Flynn.

The key was barely out of the lock when they fell through the door and chaotically came together. Flynn was kissing Mia's neck, sucking on the skin by her clavicle whilst pushing her joggers down around her thighs. Mia was pulling Flynn's t-shirt up from the back until it bunched around his armpits, so he bent forward for Mia to pull it off. Tugging too hard, her joggers around her knees, she toppled back, but Flynn's arms quickly encircled her. He unbuttoned her shirt, pushing it off her shoulders and pushing her bra up above her breasts to find a hard nipple with his mouth. Up against the wall, they made love, until exhausted, they collapsed where they stood.

"I can't get up, you'll have to drag me to the bathroom," demanded Mia.

"No…you drag me…you started it."

"I'm a victim…where is your compassion?"

"Next to my boxers."

"I'll let you have a bath with me?" bribed Mia.

"Umm."

"I'll wash your hair."

"Umm."

"It can be a real girls night in."

"Lovely," said Flynn doing the chivalrous thing by standing.

Mia, lying on Flynn's wool runner, looking up at the ceiling, found herself being drawn along the hallway by a naked Flynn wearing only socks.

"Your stop, madam. I'll run the bath."

Mia watched Flynn. Never in her wildest imagination had she devised this scene, Flynn, so comfortable in his skin, pouring pomegranate and honey in her bath.

"Come on, Council Girl, stop sleeping rough," he scolded pulling her up.

Mia's body fell flush against his. Flynn raised an eyebrow.

"I semi-fainted," she said.

"In you get," he said holding her hand before pulling his socks off and climbing in behind her, placing his legs outside hers. Mia laid back against his chest.

"Bliss," sighed Mia.

They lay back, relaxed; the steam from the hot bath dampening their hair and opening their pores. The world outside forgotten for a short time.

"What are we doing for dinner?" asked Flynn. "Chinese?" he suggested.

"Umm…sweet and sour chicken balls…lovely. Shall we watch Shallow Water?"

No answer.

"Flynn?"

"I was thinking about us, but I don't want you to think I'm weird. Not that you can judge! But, I want you to take your time and consider my proposal."

"Ok, what is it?"

"You should move in here."

"Flynn, you barely know me. And what you do know, is fucking mad!"

"We've known each other for nearly a year."

"You're using the definition of 'know' loosely. Flynn, I don't want you to feel responsible for me because we're in a relationship. Time out! Oh. My. God! I want to say that last bit again…we're in a relationship. Ok, carry on."

"Mia, I don't see you as a victim or me a hero. Trust me…I am never doing anything heroic again…not even giving my tube seat up to a frail old lady, because who is she really? Shit, everyone scares me."

"But Flynn, you hit the nail on the head, we haven't even dated…you may not like me…we could have nothing in common…I might snore."

"You do snore."

Mia looked aghast.

"Mia, I'm joking; you don't snore. We'll be at uni most of the time…we need a home to come back to. Here would be a safe space for you; a real home."

"Flynn…what if you fall out of lust with me?"

"What if I don't…ever."

Mia had no answer. She felt half elated, half terrified, happiness was so fragile.

Eating Chinese in front of Shallow Water, it was fun to be scared of a force of nature instead of dwelling on recent events. At bedtime, Flynn double checked the doors front and back, the windows, then after turning out the lights he peeped through the curtains to check the surveillance out. He couldn't see it; but then again wasn't that the point of surveillance?

Flynn found Mia under the quilt in his room.

"Is it ok…me sleeping in here with you?"

Flynn laughed.

"I love how we pretend I have a choice."

"Flynn…what you said about me moving in, have you thought it through?"

"Yes…I can't have you standing outside casing the joint and scaring the neighbours."

Mia threw a pillow at Flynn.

"Your boobs wiggled beautifully then."

Mia gave Flynn a pretend look of scorn.

"I'm serious Mia…your breast wiggling is turning me on."

"Flynn…focus!"

"Sorry, ok, I'm focusing…on your jiggling breasts."

Mia launched herself at Flynn. After a short scuffle, Flynn pinned Mia to the bed. Her hair fanned out, eyes dark with promise and her lips full and shimmering. He realised he was totally in love with a little scruff gooseberry who had catapulted herself into his life and conquered all resistance.

"Mia, I'm positively certain."

"Is this house insured?"

"Yes," laughed Flynn. "What do you say?"

"I say you should make love to me to seal the deal."

"No. Absolutely not."

"Come on Flynn, one more time, I'm getting good at it."

"Trust me Mia, you had it from the word go."

"I think someone's body is ahead of their mind."

"Mia, I'm sore," laughed Flynn.

"Liar."

"Who ever thought you'd be such a bad girl…Is that your phone?" asked Flynn responding to a repetitive tinkle.

"Can't be? Everyone I know is dead."

Flynn passed the phone.

"It's Mrs Hornby asking if I can pop in; she's poorly."

"Yeah, no problem. Tomorrow your mum, then Denham. Thursday my mum and your old dear."

****

He sat in a car twenty-five metres behind the unmarked police car. He looked towards the window at the front of the house where the curtains were drawn. People always felt protected behind windows; he'd never understood it himself; it was only a thin pane of glass. Even if it were double glazed it took a matter of minutes to remove a window. With practice and the right tools it could be a quiet operation, particularly a small toilet or hallway window. He looked down in the passenger footwell where his tool bag was. Unzipping it, he pulled out the polaroids. They were numbered in thick, black marker pen on the back. He shuffled directly to number ten. He knew she'd be trouble, but what the heart wants, the heart wants.

****

Mia, with Flynn at her side, walked tentatively through the modern, pristine, clinical building. A forensic assistant took them to a small viewing room where a window divided the viewer from the body.

"Can I see her up close please."

It was a personal preference as to how close the relation wanted to be.

"Sure."

Mia and Flynn were taken to the second room. The body was on a metal slab, a blue sheet covering it.

"This end please," guided the assistant. He stood at one side and Mia and Flynn stood at the other.

"Ready?" asked the assistant.

Silence.

"Mia," asked Flynn. "Ready?"

"Yes...Ready."

The sheet was pulled down to Joslyn's shoulders.

The stillness is what struck Mia first. For as long as she could remember, her mother's body was uncorking, gulping, inhaling, blubbering, shoulder shaking. Even when she'd slept she'd drunkenly mumble and throw her limbs around. Mia looked down at Joslyn's ice-blue face; it was as if she'd been photographed through a blue filter. Her brassy blond hair was now a subdued, grey blond, swept back from her face. Her features no longer appeared loose; the low temperature her mum dwelled in had kindly firmed her face. She didn't look like a witch or an evil spirit; simply a woman with a strong attachment to whisky.

Mia swallowed.

"Can I touch her?"

"Yes."

Mia gently touched her cold cheek. It was true. She was dead. Mia was free from cruel criticism disguised as caring because it began and ended with an endearment. It was as if half of Mia's history was wiped out, obliterated, because her memories of her mother were ones that could not comfortably be shared around the fire-place or over a glass of wine. She would have to bury them with Joslyn in the hope they did not haunt her mum in the afterlife.

A heavy tear rolled slowly down Mia's cheek.

"Death would have scared her Flynn...because it's nothingness, and she wanted to be special...she won't cope with darkness and quiet...she wanted the stage, the lights."

Mia wiped her tears away.

"One day I want children. Do you Flynn?"

"Yeah, I can see me being a dad."

"I'll never be casual or offhand with them because carelessness is like ivy, it spreads quickly and it smothers. I keep wondering what she felt when she first held me in her arms. She must have loved me that day at least. What makes me saddest is that this is it. When people are dead you can never fix things. Not ever. You need to tell your dad this Flynn. Yeah, he may be a crap dad and a terrible husband, but when he's gone…it hurts a lot Flynn."

He kissed the top of her head, at a loss what to say.

Like the drawing of the curtains at the end of the play, the assistant pulled the sheet over Joslyn. There would be no encore for her or Mia…their relationship was now dissolved.

"I have her personal effects. This way please."

In an office Mia signed for her mum's watch, bracelet and rings. She looked at the solid gold wedding band.

"I want to melt it down because it signifies a wasted life. My dad went into a jeweller, excitedly picked out this ring and when he slipped it on the finger of the woman he loved he must have seen a bright future. He was cheated Flynn, and this ring kept him shackled to a sinking ship."

A heavy silence hung in the sterile air.

"We'd better join the search," said Flynn.

"Yeah. Let's go find Gabby."

****

"Sir, it's been four hours and nothing," said Webber over his mobile to his Chief. "Sir, if I may interrupt, we need that chopper. I don't think you are hearing me sir. The dogs are ineffective; Mia zig-zagged around, she double backed, her scent is everywhere…Sir please I understand budgets…think how this will look in the national news if these girls turn up dead because you didn't ok heat-seeking technology. This landscape has no variation; one bit looks the same as every other blasted bit…Think about the MP's daughter. Thank you, sir." Webber disconnected the call.

"Wanker! If it were street kids we'd be in the shit."

Hall looked up at the greying sky.

"Sir, we've only a couple of hours tops, before rain.

"How's Mia?"

"Visibly in pain, sir, but she won't give up."

"And Flynn."

"He's right by her side ready to whisk her into his arms should she feel faint."

"Young love, hey?"

"Wouldn't know sir."

Mia's eyes were sore from strain. Exhaustion made her uncoordinated; she was tripping herself up. Alongside the police her and Flynn worked methodically and slowly, left to right, returning like a typewriter for the next line of ground to survey. Despite excessive tiredness causing her feet to drag, Mia refused to let up. Half-an-hour passed and then another. At first she thought she saw pink because she'd willed it so fiercely. Was fatigue making her see things? She pulled back, bringing Flynn with her. She looked. Nothing. She stepped back further.

"I see it too!" The words shot from Flynn's mouth. "Here! Over here!" he screamed. Police stopped in their tracks, too exhausted to leave their position until it was confirmed.

"Emma! Over here," cried Flynn again.

Seeing the belt, a wave of fear dragged Mia under; she turned away and threw up. Whilst Flynn comforted her, the team stared incredulously at Mia's sparkly pink belt. They had total respect for this kidnap victim who'd made a brazen escape then had the ingenuity and commitment to the girls to take off her belt and tie it to a branch.

"Keep the line, each person clears the two metres in front of them," shouted Webber. The opening is hereabouts."

"Jesus Mia," said Flynn as she sank into his arms. "How the fuck did you do it?"

"Mia, Flynn, go grab a coffee from the mobile cafe," said Emma. "You look like you've died and been exhumed."

Mia was about to argue.

"You were drugged Mia; your spacial awareness and concept of time would have been impinged, your belt may not be as near the opening as you remember."

"Mia," said Flynn nodding in the direction of the mobile café. "We'll see everything from there."

"If I sit I won't get up."

"Don't worry, it'll be like a Greek wedding, I'll hoist the chair up with you in it."

"Govvvvv," shouted one of the sweepers. "Here! Quick!"

Mia and Flynn watched officers converge in a flurry of activity. Flynn stood firm; his chin resting gently on Mia's head as she leaned back into his chest.

"Are you ok?" asked Flynn; himself a wreck with apprehension and foreboding.

"I've got the heebie-jeebies."

"I think that's contagious," Flynn responded.

"Oh my God, Flynn I can't look."

Mia turned in his arms burying her fear in the solid warmth of his chest.

"I'll look for you."

But his eyes were closed. Flynn felt her frame literally shaking out of her skin.

"You're thin, we need to feed you up."

"I'm going to be so into cake if the girls are safe. What do you think?"

"I think what you think," he said kissing the top of her head and snuggling her in.

"Do you remember when I started dressing like you?"

Flynn laughed.

"Yeah, it scared me, but I found it endearing...why did you do it?"

"When I lost weight I needed clothes but I didn't know how to put garments together, what went well with what. You were cool so I copied your wardrobe."

"We've got something," shouted one of the uniforms.

Flynn felt Mia's body stiffen...or was it his own. Together, stiffly, they moved forward but couldn't see anything; their view blocked by numerous police officers. Webber's voice boomed over the team.

"Everyone take a few steps to the side. Let Mia see."

As they did, an opening about four foot by two foot was revealed. Dead or alive these girls were no longer lost. Their friends and family would have closure. Mia would not be tormented for decades and decades wondering about the lost girls.

As the hole was tripled in size, Mia and Flynn waited on the peripheral for news of Gabby and her fellow victims. The momentum changed from a fast, almost frenzied need to gain access to a deathly quiet lull whilst word from the initial entry team awaited. Fireman, medical teams, forensics were on standby, knowing the strategies they adopted depended on whether there were signs of life.

"Flynn!"

Movement near the opening caught Mia's eye. It was Constable Hall. She was crying. Mia buried her head in Flynn's chest. Unable to hear the words. If she didn't hear them, they couldn't be true. Flynn was pulling away from Mia but she gripped him tightly.

"Mia, Mia."

His hands were on her upper arms, he was shaking her.

"Mia look at me."

She didn't want to but she did.

"Gabby's alive Mia. Alive."

Huddled together, Mia, Flynn and Constable Hall, with tears running down their cheeks, watched as medical teams swiftly entered. It was over.

"Over, over, over, over," Mia repeated.

"Mia? Are you ok?"

Flynn caught her as she fainted.

"Turn the alarm off," Mia mumbled groggily shuffling back into Flynn's embrace.

The alarm continued beeping annoyingly.

"Flynn...pleeeeese...honey," she added.

"I thought you were an early bird swimmer."

"That was before I had a reason to stay in bed."

"Umm," he replied distractedly as he kissed her. "Thought any more about us?"

"I Mia, no middle name because my mother couldn't be arsed, Dent do solemnly swear to sleep in Flynn's bed from this night forward."

"I need to rubber stamp this."

Mia laughed as Flynn settled over her. For a moment they were quiet, their eyes reassuring one another that today was the start of normality.

Flynn's kiss soothed her like a tranquiliser; she simply laid there as Flynn kissed her mouth; his tongue pressing against hers, seeking out all the velvet places of her mouth. One physical surge followed another, as their breaths filled each other's mouth. Her arms drifted above her head, Flynn's hands cupped her breasts; immediately she wanted Flynn between her legs.

"It's weird how I think about my life before you and I don't feel bitter. Despite everything, I'm the luckiest person in the world because of you Flynn."

"I love you Mia."

"I'm scared I made you love me," she said quietly.

"If you had that power, you'd be married to Adam Levine."

"Adam who?"

They kissed. The pressure they each applied was firm and sure, and lingered. Flynn eased inside Mia enjoying the tight pressure around him before slowly moving, then finding a rhythm that had Mia biting on his shoulder before reaching that perfect moment.

Laying naked, Mia felt sublimely relaxed. Flynn smiled...she looked bright-eyed and exhilarated. Being loved suited her...she glowed.

"You're beautiful Mia. The very first time I saw you on the train with your weapon."

"You mean my guitar."

"Yes, that lethal bludgeon! I thought how beautiful you were; very Kill Bill."

"While I, saw you, wanted you and being selfish, I turned your life upside down to get you. My mother would be proud."

"You're nothing like her. You're tenacious, brave and selfless Mia. I'm fucking punching."

Mia kissed Flynn's chest.

"Note to self about Flynn; gorgeous but low IQ."

He playfully pulled a few strands of Mia's hair.

"Another note to self re. Flynn; vindictive. Ahhhh. No, Flynn, no," shrieked Mia as he poked her gently in her ribs and tickled her. She was breathless and laughing and totally captivating.

"Right, we seriously have to get up. After visiting your old dear, how 'bout we go for a Wimpy, come home and watch The Haunting of Hill House?"

"Umm," agreed Mia before moaning with pleasure as Flynn wriggled down the bed, his mouth covering her nipple.

"Oh my God Flynn. If you want me to get up, stop teasing."

"I can't help it, you're so enthusiastic. Your nipples just reminded me to get goodies for the sweetie jar. I remember when we first met; you didn't look like a sharer!"

"That is mean, Flynn Mason," laughed Mia trying to pinch him, but he had no fat. "For that I'm using up all the hot water," she smiled running naked to the shower.

An hour later they were in a Panda headed to Flynn's parents. Flynn sprung from the car to Mia's door opening it.

"Shit, I miss you already. If I didn't think my manhood was at risk, I'd make love to you right here."

"Exhibitionist."

"We can't keep how good we are together a secret from the world."

Flynn lowered his head capturing Mia's lips. Her mouth tasted of cola cubes. Within seconds the heat he permanently felt in her company was rising and rising.

"Shit, you've given me a boner again. I might have found your

Xmen power."

Mia giggled. She felt about ten; it was impossible not to laugh when Flynn used words like boner.

"If I'm out before you, I'll sit in the car. Ok honey?"

"Yes honey," laughed Mia.

"Miss you honey."

"Miss you more honey."

"Hey!"

They both turned to the constable leaning his head out the window.

"I'm going to fill up on petrol while you're in there; I'll be back before either of you honeys is out…but, if not, stay put…got that?"

"Got it," replied Mia before brushing her lips against Flynn's. "Any time I want I can put my lips on yours and not be arrested."

"True, but no riffling through bins, it unnerves my mother."

"You're never going to let me forget that are you?"

"No. Go on then, your old dear's opened the door."

******

"Come in my lovely, I've missed you. The kettle's on."

****

Flynn shouted hello on entering his parents' house. He wouldn't say home because it wasn't homely; it was a show house. Maybe that's what boarding school does for you, makes you a nomad. Although now, with Mia, his flat was home.

The house was spotless. Betty, his mum's cleaner, came in three times weekly. The decor and furniture were contemporary and minimalistic. When he'd visit friends' houses, photographs lined their walls; football trophies and music awards filled their shelves; clutter his mum said. One time, bouncing with pride, he couldn't wait to show his dad a football medal; his team came second. His dad's cruel response - second means you're the last to lose. That's the day Flynn realised his dad was an total dick.

Picking a biscuit from the jar; he left a trail of crumbs as he climbed the stairs. Note to self – fill Mia's biscuit tin with Oreos and Happy Faces.

He found his mother, sitting on the edge of the bed, holding a lipstick, crying.

"Mum?"

Seeing Flynn, she quickly wiped her eyes dry and smiled lamely. "Flynn, this is unexpected."

"Mum, let's not pretend. Dad's cheating on you and you're suffering in silence."

"Oh Flynn, this lipstick was in your dad's car. The valet put it through the letterbox. I don't know what to do. Twenty six years of marriage. Does he look unhappy Flynn?"

"I'm not the best person to ask. You're unhappy Mum; start with that. Tell dad how you feel. He might tell you how he feels?"

"What if I don't like what he tells me Flynn?"

"It'll be tough but you're stronger than you think Mum. You'll figure it out."

"I never wanted you to attend boarding school Flynn. Your dad was insistent and I was young and wanted to please him. I should never have let him send you away. It's my biggest regret. Each time you came home you felt a little less mine and more your dad's."

"Mum...I'm your son ok? Please don't liken me to dad or I might throw a wobbly."

They embraced tightly. Flynn's mum comforted by a son who always seemed calm and reasonable. Flynn took the lipstick, cinnamon swirl, Steph's lipstick.

"Flynn, is that a bruise on your temple? And you're limping?"

"I was in an accident."

"What sort of accident?" his mum asked concerned.

"One you'll need a strong cup of tea for."

****

Sitting in Mrs Hornby's kitchen Mia felt edgy; maybe because she was apart from Flynn? She looked up at the once white ceiling, now a dirty cream, to the menacing shadows cast by the garden trees; claw like branches and witches' brittle fingers. On the table was a fruit bowl with fruit that looked way past it's best before date. From the bowl Mia picked up a pack of matches; their Exeter landscape catching her eye. Opening the pack Mia found toothpicks, not matches. Mia shifted uncomfortably in the seat. She looked over to Mrs Hornby. Exeter?

****

"I love her Mum."

Flynn's mum nearly spat out her tea.

"Flynn, are you completely mad! She was trouble before but now – pushed in front of a car – you could have been killed, and who's to say she was abducted – they could be in it together. Flynn this is serious."

"Mum...this isn't the movies...there isn't going to be some obscure twist. I agree we are in danger, but we have police protection...And...I love her mum."

"No Flynn. This has gone far enough."

Mum it's real...she's here."

His hand went to his heart.

"She's brainwashed you. Good sex shouldn't be mistaken for love."

"Mum – I love her – get used to it – she's in my life."

"She's too young for you Flynn."

"She's eighteen next week...I'm nineteen; it's nothing."

"It's awkward Flynn. What would I tell people? The girl stalked you. You took out a restraining order against her."

"Yeah, I was a dick, but Mum she gets me and I don't want any other woman but her...forever...for eternity...she's perfect...perfect for me."

"Oh Flynn, she'll let you down. Eternal love doesn't exist, only compromise, turned blind eyes and hidden resentment; that's what long relationships are based on.

"You're wrong Mum. That's your marriage; it won't be mine."

Mrs Mason smiled. Always optimistic and full of promise; if anyone could conquer love it would be Flynn. But this girl, Mia? Council estate, alcoholic parents, arrested, infatuated with her son – that was some leap of faith.

****

"Why don't I do that for you?" asked Mia getting up and taking the heavy milk from Mrs Hornby. Jesus, her hands had quite a span.

"You are shuffling very slowly today. You seem much worse than usual?"

"I am, lovie. My legs have swelled with the old arthritis and I've been low with a chest infection but no point complaining, only the birds listening."

"Well, here's lemon drizzle cake, it'll put hairs on your chest, as my dad use to say."

"Has he passed love?"

"Yes, a few months back and my mother a few days ago."

"Oh no Mia love. How awful. You're an orphan."

"It's ok, we weren't close. It's odd though. It hasn't sunk in. I didn't think I'd miss her, but I do. Life's messed up. Has your life been complicated?"

"Indeed, lovie. Had a father that was too fond of us children, if you get my meaning."

"Oh my God. That's terrible."

"Hush, it was a long time ago, lovie."

"Umm. You remind me of lovely man who comes in for a pint at the pub - Pete. He has a limp. Maybe that's arthritis."

"If he's dishy, arrange a blind date for us. Have you heard of online dating lovie?"

"Yeah, it's very popular."

"There's websites for people in uniform, for dog owners, do you think there might be one for people with arthritis?"

Mia laughed.

"You could be on to something. Vera, could I use your loo? Suddenly I'm bursting."

Mrs Hornby hesitated.

"I can hold it."

"No lovie. Just don't go in any of the rooms. I struggle to keep things as tidy as I used to. I was very house proud in my younger days."

"Promise to keep my eyes shut. Be back in a tick."

A stillness filled the dark, windowless hallway; the musty smell of it following Mia up the stairs. The carpet was the brown, patterned stuff oldies liked, but it was threadbare.

"Erh. Sticky banister," said Mia quietly.

Upstairs the long landing was darker. Its window covered in layer upon layer of dust. The first door happened to be the loo.

"Yikes," Mia whispered. No wonder Vera wasn't keen on her using it. The toilet basin was stained brown; it couldn't have been bleached in a year. The toilet seat was up; Mia gingerly lowered it. No loo paper. She had tissues up her sleeve.

Next door was the bathroom. Mia pulled on the light cord…nothing. Vera was either financially challenged or a member of the Green Party. Thinking about it, despite her arthritis she seemed a strong lady, like a swimmer. Mia could imagine her petitioning Downing Street about cuts to disabled people's budgets.

"Jesus," whispered Mia looking around. It was filthy. How did Vera cope. Downstairs was cute and country cottage, this seemed almost out of character. Not that she knew Vera well. Washing her hands Mia felt shivery. Something was wrong. The toilet with no toilet paper, the seat up? Points she'd generally not notice but at Flynn's she had to let it down. Why would the seat be up in an old lady's toilet? Unless she'd had a male visitor before Mia? Washing her hands her eyes darted around. No jars of cream. No talc. No bathrobe. Was she stereotyping? Looking for soap she quietly opened the bathroom cabinet.

Lurching backward, clutching herself tightly, she almost toppled into the bath.

"Fuck!"

Her hand covered her mouth; her eyes darted to the unlocked bathroom door.

"Oh my God," she laughed in relief; her face muscles momentarily relaxing. "Honestly, what am I like, they're only false teeth."

The smile died on her lips. False teeth that should be in Vera's mouth? Spares? They must be. It was the item on the top shelf that sent Mia into panic mode; the hairbrush; the ornate, Victorian esque brush belonging to Olivia. Drilling home the point, Mia picked up a red tube of cream; she unscrewed the cap. She didn't need to breathe in the muscle rub, it's smell was potent. It's what they used: Vera, Kevin, Pete…and him…The Wolf.

******

DI Webber was signing off paperwork when his boss strode in.

"Chief," said Webber in salute.

"What's the S.P?"

"We start interviewing the girls today. I don't expect a quick result; it will take time. Some of the girls aren't fit for questioning. We need to have a psychologist in with us."

263

"How helpful will the girls be?"

"They'll know more than they think, we need to prise it out."

"What's the situation with Becca Smith?"

"She found keeping track of time hard; she's unclear as to when she fell pregnant so we don't know how old the child is. Social are supporting her with getting a birth certificate. She and her daughter are in the parental home. She's currently coping."

"And the pregnant one?"

"Melissa Canning. She's in a state of denial. She'll need time."

"Anything on Ashley Tate?"

"Psychologist told us to hold off on that one, but Hall is easing into it."

"Has Sian Hickey's body been formally identified?"

"Yes, father came in straightaway."

Webber blew out frustration mixed with regret.

"She was near to making it; if we'd gotten to her twenty four hours earlier she'd have been with her family. That's gonna hurt for some time to come."

"You did everything you could. We've another headache with silly bollocks Raymond. Could he be The Wolf?"

"No. The Weasel? Yes. I hear he's suspended."

The Chief Inspector nodded.

A knock on Webber's office door had both men looking up at a perplexed Emma.

"Sir, perhaps Mia got confused. A Mrs Hornby did live at number twenty-eight, but she passed away over a year ago. There's no council tax being paid on the property and I checked the Voters' Register, no names for that address. So I chased up the utility providers and one supplier confirmed an active account at that property; the bills are paid in cash.

"Christ!"

"Sir…Edwards said Mia was visiting Mrs Hornby."

"Patch me through to Armed Response then get every available car there! Alert Edwards. He's not to approach the property. He's to go directly to the Mason residence and remain there until further notice."

****

264

Flynn threw his ipad charger in a bag, along with uni text books. Tomorrow he intended to speak to his dad. He didn't know what he'd say. Perhaps...you are going to lose everything if you can't stop dicking around. A little vulgar? Dad, stop fucking mum about – be faithful or cut mum loose. It was tricky and his dad would be pissed but he couldn't sit back and watch his dad hurt his mum.

"What's that Mum?" Flynn realised he wasn't listening.

"Must be quiet and lonely all by yourself in the flat after living here, not that me and your dad make much noise."

"I've company."

"Flynn, tell me it's not that girl?"

"Her name's Mia and you said never tell lies."

"Oh, Lord. Flynn you know how fickle you are with girls. What happens when you dump her? How will you get her out of the flat? It'll be stalker hell all over again."

Flynn's mum stared at him like he'd lost the plot. His phone vibrated in his pocket.

"DI Webber, hi, what's up?"

The phone flew from Flynn's hand as he crashed toward the house opposite.

******

Mia couldn't control the speed her brain drew conclusions. Vera was schizophrenic; she had multiple identities; some sweet, some sick.

"Fuck!"

Mia felt acid rise up her throat. She was back in the cell, cowering one minute, running the next. The horror of that memory hit her full on. She clutched at her chest struggling to breathe. Staggering around, her chest painful and tight, she fell out of the bathroom and into a bedroom.

"Fuck."

She stood unsteadily; her eyes disconnecting from her brain because she couldn't cope with visual confirmation! Four mannequins. A greyish, short haired wig on one, with a checked shirt and a man's cardigan and trouser – Pete. Jeans, a stained polo shirt and a ginger wig - Kevin. A black, hairy wig with sideburns and workman's boiler suit on the other – The Wolf...And a nude mannequin. Vera. Mia's stomach contents rose, but she swallowed it down. Straightening...she saw...Vera's reflection in

265

the mirror. Mia winced as he removed his old lady wig. He was bald, not a hair on his head.

"Oh, dearie, has the penny dropped for slow Mia?"

He ran at her. His hefty weight knocking her on the bed before a scream formed.

He was on top. His stale breath damping her skin. He spoke with a Mrs Doubtfire voice, how had she missed that! It was amateurish.

"You know dear, let me tell you why Kevin was my favourite. Oooh, Mia's turning red. He got to watch you sleep. Watch your breasts moving up and down under a thin, cheap, white nightie. He loved touching your underwear. The underwear of an on the edge virgin. Oh, I see from your blush the horse has already bolted. Lucky Flynn. Yet he fought so hard to keep you at a distance. I toyed with killing him first, but I had a falling out with mummy dearest; her wailing was incessant. We were at the top of the stairs and I told her what a weeping whore she was and that it was you I wanted. It killed her Mia. Her jealousy of you was the end of her. Poor wee thing was grabbing and begging and whaling and wining and she grasped my wig and as she pulled it from my head she toppled backwards. Right to the bottom of the stairs, dearie. It didn't kill her, but she got there in the end. While she was conscious and all broken, I looked into her fucking terrified eyes and said, Mia, it was only ever Mia. Then my grip tightened until her lips deflated and hung open; I thought she was dead. I did it for you, Mia. You wanted her out of your life. I understood. Jesus. She hated you. Whereas I'm not even fucked off about your escape. This one's got balls, I thought. This one's a keeper. I'll take Flynn's leftovers. In fact, he's probably taught you a thing or to…you'll have to show me."

She wanted to be angry. To be aggressive. But she felt petrified.

"What about Ashley?"

"Your voice, so sweet when it's scared but, Mia, let go; she's dead."

His voice in her head, taunting her, made Mia want to stuff toilet rolls down The Wolf's fucking throat.

"Get the fuck off me." screamed Mia struggling and twisting.

His heavy body pinned her to the bed, squashing her lungs preventing the slightest movement. Mia, shit-scared, pushed herself into the mattress and channelling her energy head butted The Wolf so hard pain shot through her temple.

He staggered up.

Mia struggled off the bed, disorientated, falling against a set of drawers. The door seemed miles away.

"Ahhh," she screamed as her arm was viciously yanked dislocating it from her shoulder. Shooting pain pulled her back to him. For one moment their eyes connected. They both heard it; someone coming through the front door. His eyes darkened; he hit her hard with the flat of his hand, striking her down. On her knees, crawling toward the door she saw footsteps; pink converse...oh my God things just got worse.

Flynn was not a fighter; Mia grasped that fact immediately. His torso was bent painfully back, over a set of drawers, as The Wolf squeezed Flynn's throat. Flynn's hands frenziedly rooted behind him, across the surface of the drawers. The Wolf's squeezed harder. Flynn, struggling to breathe, terrified, with about four in his hand, stuffed cotton buds up The Wolf's left nostril. As The Wolf's grip loosened, Flynn clumsily swung at him, ramming the buds right up his nose, before Flynn jumped back. A thick stream of blood ran from his nostril onto his lips. He looked fucking terrifying. Using a commode on wheels, Flynn charged with all his might, pinning The Wolf to the window, before clipping him hard on the forehead with a potpourri dish. The Wolf squinted, his eye watering as blood rapidly oozed from a deep gash. Flynn, frenziedly searching for the next weapon, lunged for a spray, rammed The Wolf again, then atomised him. Flynn, manically, threw everything in arms' reach: books, ornamental sheep, picture frames. This happened in seconds. Snapshots of violence. Intervals of sheer panic. The Wolf's arms flailing, his fists clenching, his eyes popping viciously, his teeth bared at Flynn. It's true, he wasn't a man.

Flynn glared frenziedly at Mia.

"He won't fucking go down Mia."

The Wolf had Flynn grasped tightly by the shoulder and his large closed fist was in motion and heading toward Flynn's beautiful face. Mia launched herself, her feet leaving the ground, clamping onto The Wolf's back. His weak leg buckled and his grasp on Flynn loosened. Mia haphazardly clung to him with one arm whilst her other hand blindly clawed at eyes, mouth, cheeks.

"Arh!" Mia grunted as The Wolf rammed himself against the wall, leaving Mia sandwiched between it and him.

Meeeeyaaaaa could-n't breeeeath. She was losing consciousness as she dropped to the floor.

"Flick!"

They both heard. The blade clicking into a rigid position. An action evoking further horror. The Wolf advanced. The light was dull; it was hard to distinguish the position of the knife. Momentarily Flynn was paralysed; only his eyes rolled, searching for the small steel knife that could puncture three inches deep.

"Flynn!" Mia screamed at him.

Desperately Flynn snatched at the talcum powder, pulling the puffer out and tossing the box high. Lily of the Valley clouded the space between the two men. Backing from the room, Flynn violently tugged the lamp with its wire out of the socket before finding himself in the hallway. The adrenalin that had fired Flynn into attack was spent. Only Mia kept him from screaming like a kid and running for home.

It seemed an age before whoever this motherfucker was stepped into the hall. When he did Flynn swore, he looked taller and broader, or was it that Flynn felt smaller and weaker. He couldn't see Mia. Was she still on the floor struggling to breathe? Or had he killed her? That pain drove a boy still scared of spiders to rush a man who couldn't spell the word fear.

Mia crawled to the doorway. She saw it all:

Flynn striking The Wolf ferociously.

The knife dropping to the ground.

Flynn losing his balance.

The Wolf wrapping the lamp wire around and around Flynn's neck And tightening and tightening.

Mia lurched for the knife. Flynn's face reddened and bulged as his fingers desperately tried to get between his throat and the wire. Mia, with a speed and force she never knew she had, flew at The Wolf, puncturing his gut and knocking him off Flynn. The momentum taking them both over the edge and down the stairs.

The blow of bodies impacting with the hard stairs and slamming into the wall jarred Flynn's eardrums. Please don't let that be Mia's body.

Please let it have been that bastard that bore the impact.

Flynn couldn't speak nor could he pull the flex from his neck. He was disorientated and weak and unable to swallow. He managed to get on his hands and knees and crawl to the top of the stairs, the lamp bumping behind.

"M. EEEEE. ERRRR," he barely croaked.

She was at the foot of the stairs.

Next to The Wolf.

Utterly still.

A bone sticking out of her arm.

Flynn started crying. Oh my God Mia, what has he done to you? Fuck. The bastard was moving. Pushing Mia off. Grunting. His hand holding his side where blood ran freely...until it followed the other hand reaching for Mia's neck. For her windpipe. Pressing.

"WHALLOP!"

CHAPTER 29   THE UNLIKELY HERO

All involved agreed that today was unlike any other they'd had or were likely to have. Flynn was sitting on the bottom step of the staircase; red impression marks around his neck, encircled in his mum's arms.

"So, Mrs Mason, I'll read this back and if you agree you can sign your statement."

Mrs Mason nodded. She was pale and tearful and wouldn't let go of Flynn.

"Your son received a phone call. He dropped the phone and ran from your house number twenty-seven Hamilton Road. An instinct had you pulling a heavy based frying pan from the cupboard. Outside you couldn't see Flynn, but you saw number twenty-eight's door smashed open. You entered the property believing your son was in danger from a girl who'd been stalking him – Mia Dent."

Mrs Mason nodded.

"You saw a man, unknown to you, choking Mia Dent. You believed it was this man's intention to strangle Miss Dent. Approaching, you saw your son at the top of the stairs, a wire flex around his neck. It was then, the attacker looked up and you struck him with force."

Flynn waved his hand, then scribbled on his white board before holding it up.

"With reasonable force," read the constable."

"Yes, that's exactly how it happened."

"You knocked him unconscious and were thinking of restraining him when Constable Edwards entered."

"Yes."

"I need your signature here please."

As the constable walked away Flynn looked at his mum.

"Oh Flynn, you could have died! Look at your neck."

Flynn's throat was too painful to respond.

"Mr Mason, we're ready to leave now," informed one of the ambulance crew.

"It's ok Flynn, you go, I've called your father home. Mia needs you son."

An image of his father stuck across Steph added to Flynn's torture.

"Look," she said pointing out the door. "Here's your father now."

Flynn climbed in the back of the ambulance, staring at the woman he loved, who'd saved his life.

Mia was wheeled straight through to surgery while Flynn's neck was x-rayed and MRI'd. Afterwards, he went to the canteen even though his throat was too swollen to swallow. He wanted to cry. He thought about Mia nearly dying and his heart literally galloped in his chest. His head dropped to his hands...he'd take a few minutes to gather himself.

"Flynn?"

"Ur huh," croaked Flynn suddenly awake.

"Sorry, I didn't realise you were asleep."

Flynn straightened up as his dad sat opposite.

"I'd ask how you're holding up, but I think I know the answer."

Flynn leaned back in his chair. His throat was too painful to talk so he texted.

"I'm in pieces...it was unreal. Fucking mental. Then Mia...lying there...her arm."

Flynn's fingers stopped, he took a sip of water and continued.

"I love her Dad...and he had his fucking fingers around her neck."

Flynn stopped again. He was shaking.

Gareth's hand took Flynn's.

"Flynn, she's going to be fine. She'll be out of theatre shortly and in recovery."

Flynn, shaking his head, returned to his phone.

"Dad she's so fucking unlucky she'll probably die under anaesthetic."

Gareth looked at this man in front of him who had tears of frustration and fear welling in his eyes and realised he knew nothing about his son...Not how he loved this girl...Not how he found the courage to fight for her...Nor how much he needed Gareth to be a dad.

A silence descended.

"Fleetwood regained consciousness, his wound was patched up and he's been declared sufficiently fit to be moved to the station. Interviewing commences tomorrow."

"Fleetwood? Crazy motherfucker more like. I hope he's shanked," texted Flynn.

"Do you want to come home tonight?"

Flynn shook his head.

"I'm staying with Mia…be there when she wakes; she'll be confused," he texted.

"Flynn…It was not my intention to turn into my own father, yet I did. It doesn't come natural to me to nurture. I'm sorry."

Flynn had an incoming text which he forwarded to his dad.

"Mia's surgery went well, no complications, she should be out of recovery and in her room in an hour. Imaging of neck; no broken bones or permanent damage to vocal cords."

Flynn felt close to tears; holding it together was hard. He'd probably bawl like a baby once he saw Mia; with Mia he could always be himself. She loved him. Jesus, he was fucking lucky. He stood. As did his father. Together they walked to the lifts. Flynn could have stayed cool. Walked away. His dad was a cheat. He was a cold bastard but he was the only dad he had. He knew what it would mean to Mia to have her dad so Flynn closed the distance between them and the two awkwardly hugged. Flynn's fingers flew over his phone keys again.

"Dad, Mum knows about the affair. You need to stop."

Gareth Mason took a long look at Flynn wondering how he'd missed his son mature into a man. Gareth put his hand out. Flynn took it.

"I love you Flynn. I'm proud of who you are. If you need me, call, I'll make time."

The lift dinged, the doors opened and Gareth Mason walked in. Christ thought Flynn, walking toward Mia's room, that was deep.

Mia lay motionless; so pale her skin looked paper thin. He wanted to wake her, to hear her voice, to hold her. He watched her intently for some time. Growing tired, but wanting to be awake when she woke, Flynn put on the telly as a distraction, only to find their story headlining BBC News. Interest in their relationship was gaining momentum. Random snippets of info. were forthcoming: Threshers, her dad's death, her art exhibition. How long before they dug up his dad's affairs. He could see the headline; father and son share employee perk. Jesus it was going to get rough…especially on his mum. Soon the vultures would dig up the restraining order. He turned the volume up. Someone from Joslyn's work was revealing how toxic Joslyn's relationship with Mia was. The media were all over Fleetwood, talking to work colleagues, neighbours, teachers and those he went to school with. He'd been weird from the beginning: a loner, a history of hurting animals, bullying children. He'd creeped women out and played sick tricks on people he disliked. There were warning signs; only no one could be arsed. Fucking typical.

Mia woke confused, in pain and in plaster.

"Flynn!"

"M.i.a," he choked out squeezing her hand. Shit, his throat was on fire. So he held up what he'd scribbled on his board.

The Wolf is alive and in custody

"How long have I been here."

Flynn held up eight fingers.

"Eight days!"

Flynn smiled and shook his head.

"H.ou.rs," he croaked.

"When can we leave?"

Flynn shrugged again.

"I don't want to stay here Flynn. I know you are going to think this is silly, but have you seen the Halloween films."

Flynn nodded.

"He comes hunting her in the hospital."

"He's."

Swallow of water.

"In custody."

"I know...but..."

Flynn nodded and stood

"Wait, I'm coming with you. It's always when the boyfriend goes for help that he's murdered."

Two hours later, they were at home, that's already how Mia saw Flynn's flat. They checked the windows, double locked the door, made tea and took it to bed.

"We're Mr and Mrs Bump," said Mia.

"Mr...and...Mrs...Smith," squawked Flynn.

Mia started laughing.

Flynn raised his hands in question.

"You," Mia said laughing harder. "A box of tissues...talcum

powder...Mr Smith?"

Flynn pointed to himself.

"In...geni...ous," he wheezed.

"It was scary wasn't it, Flynn? I think I'm going to cry again."

Flynn held up his phone then texted.

"Don't hold back on my account. I've been blubbing all night. Seriously I've cried at least ten times whilst you slept. I've never been so shit scared in my entire life. I've turned off the news. Each time his photo appears I fall to pieces. We might have to go to couple's counselling for PTSD."

"The knife, Flynn."

"I was fucking petrified. I thought I'd piss myself. He is one scary dude."

"What happened?"

"What's the last thing you remember?" texted Flynn.

"Running at a bald man in a woman's dress."

"You were like the human cannonball. He was going to kill me, Mia."

"I know Flynn but you were ridiculously brave."

Flynn's fingers flew around the touch screen keyboard.

"Then you were downstairs, your bone protruding from your arm and he was on top of you his hands around your neck, squeezing."

"What stopped him?"

"My mum with her frying pan. She nearly took his fucking head off. A bit more oomph and she'd be doing time," texted Flynn looking up and smiling.

"I feel tired, but I don't think I can sleep," said Mia.

"I...Know...A...Game," voiced Flynn painfully, like he'd swallowed glass.

Reclined on pillows, she rested whilst Flynn spelt words on her midriff.

"Flynn! Kiss, sex and wank aren't challenging! Move me up to level two I'm ready."

"Ok?"

"Go for it."

Mia was thoroughly enjoying the sensation of Flynn's touch on her

274

tummy.

"Urm relay?"

"No."

"Frapay?"

"Nearly. Keep going."

A few seconds elapsed. Mia started laughing.

"Foreplay. Flynn. Stop torturing us."

He blew a raspberry on her belly before turning on his back and resting his head on her lap. Mia stroked his forehead and marvelled at how he managed to stir the greatest longing in her even though she was beat up, bruised and fading quickly.

"Flynn."

His eyes sprung open. She spoke and Flynn responded...all those years of no one listening and now she was the centre of someone's world. Flynn was in love with her. She saw it deep in his velvet chocolate eyes and she felt drunk on it.

"It's nice, isn't it?"

Flynn smiled back knowingly and nodded before pulling the quilt over them.

Laying awkwardly because of her cast Mia thought she wouldn't sleep but she and Flynn, knocked out, slept late into the morning despite mobiles ringing. One caller left a message.

****

DI Webber had a serious dilemma. They'd had Fleetwood in custody for over twenty four hours and he'd not spoken. His body was present but his mind was elsewhere. He was a fiend who wouldn't have stopped. Forensics found his DNA all over 175 Whitstable Close, the leisure centre, The White Bear and The Admiral. Although Webber had yet to find evidence, Fleetwood was undoubtedly the murderer of Alex Stone. Webber had used every interview technique he knew to prise words from Fleetwood. He'd threatened him with tales of what happened to child killers behind bars. He'd brought in a female DI from a neighbouring patch to see how Fleetwood responded to a female. Nothing.

Webber's mobile rang.

"Flynn?"

"What the fuck is going on there? Mia's completely freaked out."

"You've lost me."

"How did Fleetwood leave a message on Mia's phone when he's in custody?"

There was no point doubting it.

"What did he say?"

"Come visit."

"I'm sorry. He's entitled to a phone call. It should have been monitored."

Flynn shook his head; he was fucking angry. With Webber and Mia!

"She wants to see him. I think it's unwise, but she needs it for closure."

"I'd be lying if I said I didn't welcome this opportunity. Maybe he'll open up to Mia."

Two hours later, Flynn was behind a one-way mirror with Constable Hall watching.

****

"Mia Dent has entered the room."

Fleetwood sat up. His hand ran across his unshaven jaw. He immediately looked different; younger, sharper. In Mia's mind she had morphed all his personas together and created a monster. Now, sitting opposite her was a man she didn't recognise. He wasn't Kevin. He wasn't Mrs Hornby; she didn't know who the hell he was.

"You look different," she started with.

"Do I? It's only been a couple of days."

"Seems like longer."

He nodded.

"Where did you get all that stuff from? The wigs, the clothes?"

"Fancy dress shops, charity shops."

"Were you related to Mrs Hornby?"

"She was my godmother…She was the first."

"The first?"

"Person I killed."

"Why?"

"The house, the bank account."

"Why do you kidnap young girls?"

"They're easier to break. Particularly strays like you, no one to miss you, no parents canvassing the neighbourhood or hounding the police…Your mum was a case. Wasn't she?"

Mia nodded.

"You sound almost sorry for me," said Mia.

"Maybe I was."

"If I hadn't escaped what would have happened to me?"

"I'd have left you in that cell, living as though you were nothing, hosing you down, starving you, kicking you around a bit. Then I'd upgrade you. Give you a cell with a mattress and a toilet. I'd take you upstairs, help you shower and give you clean clothes. You'd sit at my table and I'd feed you. You'd be so grateful you'd want to please me."

"Are the girls your family?"

"No Mia, they're no one. You, on the other hand, were someone."

"Tell me about Petra."

Fleetwood looked at his hands then held them up.

"I strangled Petra to death with these hands, choked her till she turned blue because she pushed and pushed…every fucking opportunity. She was never going to break…but I didn't think I could kill her…not Petra…but my hands were around her throat, my thumbs so hard on her epiglottis and trachea. I kept squeezing. Harder and harder wanting to feel something; disgust, guilt but I felt nothing. And then snap!"

"Why Alex?"

"I battered him to death in a frenzy. Anger management issues is what my social worker called my outbursts at school. I would have killed you too if the boy's mother hadn't interrupted. I'm grateful to her. I want you to live."

"Why take me?"

"You needed me. Your life was a mess. Alcoholic parents. You were failing school. Comfort eating. I would have made you happy and, in turn, you would've made me happy. I'd have given you children. A real family."

"Like you did with Becca?"

"I held her when she gave birth. There were no complications."

"Other than abduction and rape," said Mia.

"Mia, I have no conscience. I wish I had. I never asked for this."

277

"But you didn't fight your urges. You could have got help."

"You were my help. You would be the last. In a twisted way you have helped."

"How was I selected?"

He leaned over the desk, his eyes dark like coal.

"Randomly. I kicked your guitar and you kicked my shin. Remember Mia? I see you do."

Fleetwood rubbed his unshaven jaw.

"Interest led to wanting, wanting led to having."

"You are a sick fuck, you know that."

He smiled.

"Yeah…I know that. People will speculate what made me who I am, but nothing turned my head…I was born this way. I scared myself at first. Nobody wants to be different…you of all people get that. Didn't you want to be slim, didn't you want nice clothes, painted nails, didn't you want to be like other girls Mia?"

She nodded in partial agreement.

"Tell me about Ashley."

"When I realised I was a repeater, it scared me. I didn't want to get caught but I didn't want to stop either. Ashley was frail and emotionally unstable. One minute cowering, the next clawing. I crushed up amitriptyline into her food; it calmed her for a period so I left her unrestrained when I could. One day she went ballistic. I wrestled her hard to the floor; my hand flattening her head into the dirt."

Fleetwood raised his hand, staring at it.

"Her head was small. It nearly fitted in my hand. I don't know how long I kept her restrained like that, with my knee pressed hard into her back; my weight restricting movement…either I was too heavy or too forceful. If her neck snapped, I didn't hear it. When I stood…her body was limp…lifeless."

Mia shivered; the terror of the truth being hard to hear, but for Ashley's parents she had to continue.

"What did you do with her body?"

"I wanted her near. There was a dead apple tree at the end of the garden. I dug it up; it was a day's work. The neighbour, two doors down had a dog. It was fucking irritating; barking all times of the night and day, jumping the garden fences. I enticed it over; gave it a slice of ham before I bashed its head in. I put Ashley deep down and covered her with four foot of soil, then the dog, then I planted a rose bush and filled in the hole with the rest of the soil."

"You're going to rot in jail for the things you've done."

"Not rot, I'll be enjoying a picture show up here." Fleetwood pointed to his brain. "There's a naked girl in it, standing in a cell, shivering, full breasts and a Brazilian."

"In prison there'll be criminals stronger and nastier than you and they'll make you their bitch. That's a movie I'd go to the premiere of."

"Still feisty Mia. I like it."

It came from nowhere. Her hand made a fist. Fleetwood was on the floor handcuffed to the chair, his nose gushing with blood, he was laughing.

****

"Mia. Are you sure you're female?"

"I hope you're not comparing me to stereotypes."

"Would I dare. But you do travel light."

"Picked up that knack in my stalking days."

It was good that Mia could laugh about it now. She had struggled for a while with the concept of stalking. It was as if a bad trick had been played on her. But what hit Mia hardest was that by some cruel twist of fate she'd felt responsible for her mother's death. She'd wished it again and again and couldn't unwish it. Her mum was dead; murdered by a boyfriend that had used Joslyn to get close to Mia. It had taken Flynn's support and months of counselling to understand she was a victim. That if Fleetwood hadn't threatened Flynn, Flynn would never have involved the police and Mia could have enjoyed crushing on Flynn innocently. As for Joslyn, she'd invited a man, she knew nothing about, into her bed without considering his motives or Mia's safety.

Mia took a gap year; tutoring GCSE art students and waitressing whilst making Flynn's flat her home. They'd had a rocky year; their relationship truly tested; Joslyn's funeral, the gruelling court case, Flynn in Exeter, but nothing made either of them want a life without the other. What cemented their relationship was Interrailing through Europe during the long summer; sleeping in hostels, walking till their legs turned to rubber, laying naked on beaches, making love in the sea, drinking too many shots, holding back each other's hair as they vomited from food poisoning. They did it all...together.

A year later, Mia was finally putting the past firmly behind her and moving on. She looked across at Flynn; no less enticingly gorgeous today than when she'd first spotted him.

"You're staring, Mia."

"I can't help myself."

She poked him in the ribs.

"Owh, what?"

"Nothing," she smiled standing on tip toes to kiss him. "Just checking you're real."

"I'll take the last of our stuff. Try not to set the smoke alarm off while I'm gone."

She gave him the finger. He bent down and kissed its tip. Mia gave the flat one last glance before joining Flynn. Slamming the boot shut, Flynn walked toward his girlfriend who looked casually beautiful. Her once long, brown hair was now auburn, short and sharp. She wore a black mode dress covered in watermelons and black vans. Her confidence had roller-coastered to a high. She'd exhibited her work in a couple of wine bars in Camden and Shoreditch even selling a few pieces. Kira appointed herself Mia's agent which worked well as she only had one other on her books – Flynn. He too was working, along with a couple of other film undergrads, earning money filming events. Today was another step forward with their life. They'd pooled their money together; Flynn's trust, Mia's compensation, the money her dad left and paid the deposit on a small two bed studio; a beach shack really, in Exeter with staggeringly great sea views. After graduating Flynn would work from home and they would live off Mia's student finance as well as funds from exhibitions and the rent on Flynn's London flat. It put them on a more even footing...now neither of them had money. They acknowledged they were young, Mia nineteen and Flynn twenty-one. Maybe it was by not pressurising themselves to make it last that they found themselves even more in love.

"I've thought of something," said Flynn as they sat in the car about to leave.

"It's naughty isn't it? You've got a mischievous look in your eyes."

"We have never made love in the car."

"I love the way you articulate; it is so hot, Posh Boy."

"You want me, don't you, Council Girl?"

"I want what you want..."

ABOUT THE AUTHOR

10 Things I Love
Kiss FM
Vampire Diaries
Maroon 5
Banoffee Tart
Pyjamas
Swimming
Ireland
Shazam
Christmas
Flowers

Check out Random Attachment on Spotify for full list

Sickly sweat – iiola
Bemyself - Parcels
Amazing – Madonna
Growing Up - Daniel Bedingfield
My Lady – RECCO
You're Gorgeous - Babybird
Human - Dodie
Hollow Days – Twin Shadow
Mad World – Lily Allen
Like I'm Gonna Lose you – Jasmine Thompson
Wildest Ones – Eves Karydas
Let Me Down Slowly – Alec Benjamin
Fickle Game – Amber Run
Suncity (ft Empress Of) – Khalid
Cry Alone – Lil Peep

https://wordpress.com/view/gertrudetkitty.wordpress.com
https://twitter.com/gertrudetkitty
https://wordpress.com/view/cervicalmyelopathy.me
www.instagram.com/gertrudet.kitty

45318458R00171

Printed in Poland
by Amazon Fulfillment
Poland Sp. z o.o., Wrocław